Critical praise for

RUTH AXTELL MORREN
and her novels

THE MAKING OF A GENTLEMAN
"Engaging characters and a smooth, fast-paced
story line make this a historical to be savored."
—*Publishers Weekly*

THE ROGUE'S REDEMPTION
"A beautifully written Regency-era love story."
—*Romantic Times BOOKreviews*

DAWN IN MY HEART
"Morren turns in a superior romantic historical."
—*Booklist*

LILAC SPRING
"*Lilac Spring* blooms with heartfelt yearning and genuine
conflict as Cherish and Silas seek God's will for their lives.
Fascinating details about 19th-century shipbuilding…
bring a historical feel to this faith-filled romance."
— Bestselling author Liz Curtis Higgs

WILD ROSE
Selected as a *Booklist* Top 10
Christian Novel for 2005

"The charm of the story lies in Morren's ability to portray
real passion between her characters. *Wild Rose* is not so
much a romance as an old-fashioned love story."
—*Booklist*

A Bride of Honor

RUTH AXTELL MORREN

Steeple
Hill®

Published by Steeple Hill Books™

STEEPLE HILL BOOKS

Steeple
Hill®

ISBN-13: 978-0-373-78650-3
ISBN-10:   0-373-78650-6

A BRIDE OF HONOR

Copyright © 2009 by Ruth Axtell

www.SteepleHill.com

Printed in U.S.A.

For Pastor Rafael Grey,
a man after God's heart.

Chapter One

London, April 1812

"'I have found David, the son of Jesse, a man after mine own heart'." Damien paused in the reading of the scripture and looked from the pulpit to the congregation below him.

St. George's Chapel was filled to overflowing. Not due solely to his preaching, unfortunately, although his flock had been growing steadily in the last few years since he'd been curate there.

No, it was not the service or his preaching that brought most people out this Sunday to morning prayer, but scandal.

Damien's glance strayed to the chancel where his sister sat beside her intended. Jonah Quinn, a man who'd escaped the gallows and been a fugitive from the law, had only last week received a royal pardon from the prince regent himself.

Overnight, Jonah, Damien and his sister had become objects of notoriety. The fashionable world from nearby Mayfair flocked to catch a glimpse of the man who'd escaped detection from the magistrates by hiding out in Damien's own parsonage.

A rustle of someone's prayer book pulled Damien's thoughts back to the sermon at hand. His business was not what had brought people into the house of God that morning, but what they would take with them when they left.

"How is your heart with God today?" As he asked the question, his gaze roamed over the congregation once again, stopping here and there to make eye contact with a parishioner. Most quickly averted their eyes.

His attention was caught by a young lady in the front pew. For a few seconds, he lost his train of thought. She was looking at him as if drinking in each word.

Clearing his throat, he looked back down at his notes, wishing all his parishioners listened so attentively.

"Is your heart condemning you when you come before the Lord in prayer?"

Damien's voice grew soft and there was little sound coming from the congregation. He continued to ask the probing questions, questions he himself had dealt with in his earlier life when he'd felt inadequate to fill the shoes of a preacher.

"God's word tells us that there is *no* condemnation to them which are in Christ Jesus." He grasped the sides of the pulpit, his voice rising. He no longer needed to look down at his notes as his words tumbled forth.

His attention returned time and again to the young lady. Her look never wavered. What had brought her this morning? She certainly didn't behave like those interested in the latest scandal. Not once had her glance drifted toward Jonah, unlike so many of the congregation.

The young lady was sitting beside an older woman. Damien recognized neither. Both were fashionably dressed. Were they part of the Mayfair crowd squeezed into the pews that morning?

As soon as the service was over, Damien went into the vestry to remove his stole and surplice, then made his way to the church's entry in his black cassock to greet the parishioners. Thinking of the moment he would face the young lady, he felt a brief qualm as he listened to the tap of his wooden leg against the hard floor. Would a flicker of distaste mar her pretty features? The worry was quickly gone. What did it matter what she thought? Chastising himself briefly for his vanity, he joined his sister and Jonah who were already at the door.

"Good morning, Reverend Hathaway. Wonderful sermon." He returned handshakes and greetings, thanking those who commended him on the sermon.

Many of those who were strangers hardly gave him a nod before turning an eager eye to Florence and Jonah. Damien glanced their way but saw at once that his future brother-in-law didn't need help from him. Jonah shook hands and smiled broadly at one and all, answering those who were bold enough to ask him about his pardon.

He chuckled, rubbing his muscular neck. "Aye, the

noose was already nipping at me throat 'ere I was rescued. No, I never did ken who they were." His listeners' eyes popped open wide, their mouths hanging slack in wonder.

"Good morning, Reverend Hathaway."

Damien turned to greet an elderly parishioner. "Good morning, Mrs. Oliver. How nice to see you out again. How are you feeling this fine April morning?"

The white-haired lady smiled beneath the deep rim of her straw bonnet. "Praise be to God, I am feeling quite myself again. After you prayed for me, the rheumatism in my joints subsided." She patted his hand. "You were so kind to visit me while I was housebound."

"I am thankful to have you back among us."

With a last pat to his hand, she indicated the ladies behind her in the line—and Damien was caught by the large brown eyes of the beautiful young lady of the front pew.

With an effort, he pulled his focus from her and turned to the older lady, intensely aware of his deformity.

"I'd like to present you to my dear friend, Miss Yates," Mrs. Oliver went on in her friendly tone, oblivious to his inner turmoil. "And this is her young cousin, Miss Phillips, just returned to London from school."

He bowed to the older lady. "How do you do?" Everything about her indicated a lady of rank and distinction. Her dark cloak was edged in fur, her manner dignified.

Miss Yates inclined her head slightly, a genial look in her blue eyes. "Very well, thank you. I found your sermon most edifying. I look forward to visiting again."

Unable to resist the sincerity in her tone, he smiled. "You are always welcome. Please come any Sunday."

Damien tried to appear calm and untroubled as he prepared to bring his attention to Miss Phillips. It had been merely a trick of the light that had made her appear so ethereally lovely from his vantage of the pulpit, he told himself.

Nevertheless, a flush crept from the edges of his white clerical collar to his hairline as he turned to her.

The impact of her honey-brown eyes almost knocked him over. They were framed by lashes a shade darker. Tawny eyebrows created an arresting contrast to her golden hair.

She was even lovelier up close than she'd appeared in the pew. Blond curls framed a heart-shaped face. A finely chiseled nose curved up the tiniest bit at the end.

"How do you do?" he finally managed.

She murmured something indistinct and looked down.

He cleared his throat, searching frantically for something to say—anything to prolong the moment. But his mind had suddenly emptied of all lofty thoughts. He might never have preached an edifying sermon moments ago. "I'm honored you joined our humble congregation today." As soon as the words were out, his face grew warm. He sounded as if he were toadying for a compliment.

She looked up immediately. Her smile lit up the rich brown depths of her eyes and brought radiance to the delicate pink of her cheeks. "Oh, no, sir—it is we who are honored. I mean—that is to say…"

Her evident confusion eased his own agitation. "I hope you enjoyed the service."

"Oh, yes, sir—Reverend—" She stopped.

A kindred feeling stirred inside him as he realized how shy she was. She was very young, perhaps no more than seventeen or eighteen.

He forgot his own fears in his wish to put her at ease. "Hathaway."

"I beg your pardon, Reverend Hathaway."

He was unaccustomed to reacting so to a young lady, but then he'd never been so close to one so lovely, and so obviously of rank.

Before he could think of anything else to say—and conscious of the line of people waiting behind her—she said, "I…I enjoyed your sermon, Reverend Hathaway. Very much. I mean, I'm not certain if 'enjoyed' is the correct word…."

His mouth turned up at the corner in rueful understanding. "I hope you found it thought provoking at the least."

"Oh, indeed, yes! That is a much better way to put it. I…I've never heard preaching such as yours before. It…it wasn't comfortable, and yet—" she drew her dark eyebrows together "—it filled me with something I've never felt before."

The words were what every preacher wanted to hear. He tried to dismiss the thought that the pleasure he felt from the compliment was heightened by the fact that it had come from such a lovely young creature. To hide his confusion, he turned to his sister. "May I present my sister, Florence Hathaway, and her fiancé, Jonah Quinn."

She greeted both.

"Enjoyed the preaching, did you?" Jonah asked with a smile.

Again, she blushed, but did not lower her gaze as she had with Damien. "Yes, very much."

"Our Damien always preaches a good one. Warms the insides when it doesn't feel like a punch in the gut."

Her laughter joined Jonah's. "Oh, yes! That's it exactly."

Jonah winked at both ladies. "Why don't you come 'round for tea this afternoon for more of Reverend Hathaway's wit and wisdom?"

Damien was preparing to greet the next parishioner in line when Jonah's words stopped him. His eyes sought his sister's. Florence was rarely at a loss in any situation—she would know what to say. But Florence was looking at Jonah, stunned.

An awkward silence followed when Florence did not speak up immediately to second the invitation. Damien, who knew his sister so well, realized she must be feeling nervous about entertaining ladies of such distinction. As the silence stretched out, he knew he must say something. Except for the rector and his mother, they rarely entertained members of the ton in their modest parsonage.

Damien bowed his head toward Miss Yates. "We would be honored if you would visit us this afternoon."

"We should be delighted," the older lady replied immediately. "What time would you expect us?"

Florence seemed finally to remember her obligations as hostess. "Would four o'clock suit you?"

"Four o'clock would be perfect." Miss Yates touched her young companion on the elbow. "We must be going." She bowed to the three of them. "Until this afternoon."

Damien watched them continue down the church steps and across the lawn toward a fine-looking carriage, his mind in a daze. A liveried servant sprang down and opened the carriage door for them, confirming his supposition that they were members of the upper class. When the servant slammed the door shut, Damien noted that it was decorated with a blue-and-gold crest.

"Reverend Hathaway." The peremptory tones of another female parishioner yanked his attention back to the receiving line.

"Yes, Mrs. Cooper, how lovely to see you this morning…."

Lindsay sat in their coach as it carried them down St. George's Row along the northern edge of Hyde Park. Reverend Hathaway's sermon still echoed in her ears.

His words had seemed directed at her, exhorting her in a quiet, earnest way to become a true disciple of Christ. Church sermons had never been like this before. Sermons were usually dry, delivered in the elevated tones of a minister who seemed more concerned with his elocution than the text.

Never had she heard the scriptures in such a personal way, a way that demanded something of her even though she'd always lived according to the church's laws.

"What did you think of the Hathaways, my dear?" Beatrice asked.

Lindsay turned to the older lady, a distant cousin on her mother's side who had recently come to live with her father to oversee Lindsay's coming out. "Oh, most genial," she agreed wholeheartedly, although thinking about it now, she had to admit she'd hardly noticed the reverend's sister or her betrothed in her admiration for the reverend.

"Mr. Quinn certainly seemed genial, not at all what I expected."

Lindsay remembered the large, dark-haired man's friendly manner. "Oh?"

"I meant from all I'd heard about him."

"What do you mean?"

Beatrice's eyes widened. "Don't you know? He's a former convict."

Lindsay turned on the seat and stared at her cousin. "A convict?"

"Haven't you read the papers? He was awaiting his execution at Newgate when he was rescued by a gang of ruffians. For months he escaped the eyes of the law." Beatrice shook her head with a chuckle. "It turns out all along he'd been hiding away in a parsonage right here. The magistrates were in an uproar."

"You can't mean he was here…at St. George's?"

Her cousin nodded. "The very same."

Lindsay looked away from her cousin, her thoughts in a whirl, unable to reconcile the godly man who had delivered such a quietly convicting sermon with a man who would harbor a criminal.

"He could not have stayed hidden for so long if the

reverend and his sister hadn't helped him," Beatrice confirmed for her. "And to think, in the course of aiding and abetting him, Miss Hathaway fell in love with him. It is to her he owes the royal pardon he received."

"Oh, my," she breathed, hardly able to grasp it.

"It was in all the tabloids," Beatrice continued. "Of course, I'm forgetting you've been away at school and have missed the goings-on here in London."

"Tell me all the particulars. It sounds wonderfully romantic!"

By the time Beatrice had finished a story that sounded more incredible than anything in her novels, they'd arrived at Lindsay's home on Grosvenor Square in the heart of Mayfair.

Despite the happy ending to the tale, Lindsay found it almost impossible to imagine breaking the law and hiding out from the authorities. "You know, I believe it's no coincidence Mr. Quinn gave himself up to the authorities. If I had been residing under the Reverend Hathaway's roof all that time, I, too, would have been convicted of any wrongdoing and made a clean breast of things."

"Yes, I imagine the Hathaways must have influenced Mr. Quinn greatly. Reverend Hathaway appears to have a true shepherd's heart."

After the last parishioner left, Damien, his sister and Jonah used the footpath behind the church to cut across the cemetery and apple orchard to the parsonage.

Damien glanced at his sister, wondering if she would

say anything about Jonah's unexpected invitation for this afternoon.

But Florence remained silent during the short walk home. He would just have to wait for her to speak. He took a deep breath, inhaling the sweet-scented air, trying to reconcile himself to the coming afternoon.

When they entered the kitchen, Mrs. Nichols, their cook and housekeeper, turned from the roast she was basting on a spit over the fire. "What a crowd this morning. I haven't seen the like since I heard Wesley preach just beyond on Harper's Field nigh on five-and-twenty years ago."

"I don't believe it was to hear my preaching that so many turned out," Damien said with a chuckle, approaching the range. "My, but that roast smells succulent."

"Oh, they might come to eye Jonah, but they stay to hear your words, my boy." Jacob Nichols, their man-of-all-work at the parsonage who'd known Damien since he was a lad, clapped him on the back.

Jonah shut the door behind them with a bang. "I don't want to claim any credit, but people do seem a curious lot. I don't think I've had so many pairs of eyes on me since I stood on the gallows."

Florence shuddered. "Don't even joke about that awful day."

He draped his arm around her slim shoulders and pulled her to him. "Easy there, lass. If it hadn't been for that day, I'd never have met you."

She looked up at him a second, her hand cupping his cheek. Damien marveled afresh at the love that had blossomed in so unlikely a pair—a rough laborer and a godly woman who had long since accepted her spinsterhood. A rush of something like envy shot through him. He rapidly dismissed the unworthy feeling.

Florence began untying the ribbons of her bonnet. "Enough of that. Let me help Elizabeth or we'll never get dinner on the table—and we have company coming this afternoon." She bit her lip, frowning up at her fiancé. "Whatever were you thinking to invite those two ladies to the parsonage?"

Jonah raised his eyebrows, a puzzled look in his green eyes. "What do you mean? I was being hospitable. Now that I'm a free man, it seems you're always inviting someone from the parish over on Sunday."

"Yes, I know, but these ladies are complete strangers. They don't even belong to our parish."

"What's that to the point? Are we supposed to only hold out the hand of friendship to those within our borders?" His grin took the sting from his words.

Damien could see his sister was at a loss yet again.

She removed her apron from the hook and began to tie it behind her. Jonah immediately took over the task. "Thank you," she murmured. "What I mean is, these women are ladies, undoubtedly from Mayfair. They probably only came to our chapel to ogle the 'pardoned felon' this morning."

With a final tug on the bow, Jonah straightened. His heavy black eyebrows knit thoughtfully. "Did you think so? I confess I didn't get any such impression. The older lady seemed quite amiable and the younger—" he looked across at Damien and winked "—why, she only had eyes for our good parson here."

They turned to look at Damien, and he felt himself flush. He glanced down, closely examining the narrow brim of his low-crowned clergyman's hat which he held in his hands.

"Nonsense," Florence said, smoothing the front of her apron. "I admit, they were ladylike enough, but to have them here the first time you lay eyes on them?"

Jonah scrubbed his hands clean at the pump, took up a linen towel and leaned against the soapstone sink, eyeing Florence. "Don't you think you're good enough for the likes o' them?"

Florence took his place at the pump. "That's beside the point. They are obviously ladies of rank who accepted your unexpected invitation out of a sense of obligation. They would have found it impolite to do otherwise."

Jonah crossed his burly arms across his wide chest. "Oh, I wouldn't say that. The young one was eating up the parson's words, eh, Damien?" Jonah's green eyes danced with mirth.

Damien hung up his hat. "I didn't notice."

Jonah chuckled. "No, I suppose you wouldn't, being the godly man you are."

Damien crossed the kitchen to the door opposite, hoping to escape everyone's attention.

Florence sniffed. "Most of the congregation is usually held captive by Damien's sermons, so that is nothing unusual. Besides, why should you be so interested in distracting Damien with some foolishness about a young lady's attention?"

Once again, Jonah put his arm around his future wife. "I suppose, dear heart, since you've made me such a happy man, I only wish the same for the preacher." He looked at Damien over Florence's head. "The good book says it's not good for man to be alone. Since I'll be stealing his only kin from him, I feel an obligation of sorts to make up for his loss."

Damien was touched by the sincerity of Jonah's words beneath the lighthearted tone, even if the man's concern was misplaced. Before he could think how to change the subject, Florence turned around, disengaging herself from Jonah's hold.

"In any case, you really should think twice before inviting someone to tea." She'd softened her tone, and Damien realized she was truly worried about the coming afternoon. "You tell him," she said to Damien.

Damien put his hand on the doorknob. "I would never presume to curtail Jonah's hospitable inclinations. That is what we are here for, whether those invited belong to our parish or not." He smiled to ease his sister's concern. "Don't distress yourself about this afternoon. I'm sure everything will be fine if you behave with your usual amiability. Our guests will most likely be bored by our limited conversation and make their visit short. They'll feel under no obligation to return the invitation, and we'll not see them again." He nodded at Jonah's frown. "You did right in issuing the invitation."

Before anyone could comment further on their impending guests, Damien exited the kitchen and headed to his study.

Once he'd entered the quiet of his private sanctuary, he could put aside his mask of serenity and contemplate the coming afternoon.

He hadn't felt so nervous since the first time he'd had to stand in the pulpit and preach. He glanced down at his black cassock. That presented another problem. Would he wear it during the ladies' visit, or remove it and appear in his dark jacket and knee breeches, the way he usually did for such social calls, the only sign of his office the two white, rectangular preaching bands hanging from his collar?

He removed the cassock now, unbuttoning the long row of buttons down the front, as his mind struggled with this new dilemma. Normally, he wouldn't think twice about the matter. But now, dread of removing the ankle-length gown rose up in him.

In the church this morning, under the cassock and surplice, his wooden leg had not been so apparent. In his knee breeches, however, the dark peg strapped to his left leg called attention to itself like a lightning-scarred tree in a healthy forest.

He hung up the cassock, trying to ignore the thump of the wooden leg as he walked back to his desk. He sat down heavily, his fingers rubbing his left knee absently as he stared out the window to the garden beyond. Why did it matter now? He'd accepted the loss of his leg so many years ago that he hardly gave it any thought anymore. But on the brink of the impending visit by a lovely young lady who'd eyed him—if not the way Jonah described, at least with some measure of admiration—his peg leg loomed like a great, hulking deformity.

Today was no different than any other, he reasoned with himself. His congregation—the entire parish, even the prisoners at Newgate, where he frequently ministered, and the inmates of the Marylebone workhouse and orphanage—had grown accustomed to his disability.

It was only when his leg hindered him in his activities, or when he was meeting people for the first time, that he was at all aware of it. But that awareness usually passed quickly.

"Stop it, Damien," he chided himself in a harsh whisper. "You're overreacting! It's nothing but a simple tea with some parishioners. Nothing you haven't done a hundred times before."

Taking up his feather quill and twirling it between his fingers, he reminded himself that he was the curate of a small parish. He was the Lord's servant, not a gentleman to worry about his appearance. He was here to meet the needs of his flock.

But the young lady's heart-shaped face and large brown eyes flashed across his memory, and he recoiled from the moment she'd meet him without the long cassock. He steeled himself for the disgust that would cloud her pretty features as soon as her gaze dropped downward.

Damien swiped a hand across his eyes to dispel the image and pulled toward him the large, worn Bible that lay open on the desk. The best antidote to such foolishness was God's word. It was balm to his spirit, solace to his tortured thoughts.

The young lady had clearly been hungry for God's word. Damien bowed his head and closed his eyes, praying for something to give her when she came this afternoon. She was a precious lamb, and perhaps the Lord had sent her to St. George's that morning to receive something from Him. He prayed for guidance in ascertaining what that something might be.

Chapter Two

Lindsay's heartbeat quickened as soon as the curate appeared in the doorway. She'd had to hide her dismay when she'd first entered and not seen him in the drawing room. For a moment, she'd feared he would be absent for tea. Now, an enormous relief overtook her at the sight of his tall frame.

"Good afternoon," he said. The curate had such a warm smile, she couldn't help smiling back. "Good afternoon," she replied with a curtsy.

He began walking toward them. She sucked in her breath. He was lame! Just below his left knee was a wooden peg where his leg should have been. Her gaze flew back up to his face and their glances met. A glimmer of pain flashed in his eyes.

Oh, dear! Why had she looked down like that?

But in the next instant he extended his hand to Beatrice. "Good afternoon, Miss Yates, how nice of you to visit us here at the parsonage." He had a low, well-modulated voice that immediately put a person at ease.

Her cousin smiled. "The gratitude is all ours for your gracious invitation."

Lindsay bit her lip, waiting quietly as he exchanged pleasantries with her cousin. She hadn't even noticed the wooden leg during the service, but he'd been gowned and standing behind the pulpit. Many young men had lost limbs in the war, but this man was a clergyman. How had the injury come about? At least it was only below the knee. The loss was all the more poignant because he had such an athletic build, his shoulders broad, his waist narrow, his good leg well shaped and muscular beneath the stocking.

And then he turned to her. "I'm so glad you could join us."

"Thank you." To her chagrin her voice came out as little more than a whisper. She couldn't help responding to the kindly look in his blue eyes. They were such a beautiful shade, like a cloudless sky on a summer's day. His light brown hair, though cut short, had a slight curl to it.

Before she could think of anything more to say, his sister spoke. "Why don't we sit down and I'll ring for some tea?"

Lindsay followed her cousin to the settee Miss Hathaway indicated. Trying not to look too anxious, she watched the curate to see where he would sit. Alas, he waited until all the others were seated. Mr. Quinn took one of the armchairs opposite and Miss Hathaway the other. There were no other chairs within range of the settee. The curate went to an alcove facing the street and took a seat.

Miss Hathaway cleared her throat. "We were very gratified to have you in the chapel today."

Thankfully, Beatrice was not at all nervous. "Oh, we were delighted to be there." Unmindful of the distance between them, she turned to Reverend Hathaway with her customary warm smile. "We so enjoyed your sermon. Did we not, my dear?"

"Oh, yes." She tried to inject all the feeling possible into her words, wishing she could ask the curate more about the scriptures. She'd even brought her small New Testament, given to her by her mother, along with a notebook and pencil in her reticule.

Miss Hathaway smoothed down her skirt. "Where do you usually attend services?"

Once again, Beatrice took the initiative to reply. "At your mother church, St. George's Hanover. We live close by on Grosvenor Square."

"Oh, yes, the rector's church." Miss Hathaway fiddled with the white fichu at her throat. "How is Reverend Doyle?"

"He's very well, thank you. He is the one who first told us of your services here at the chapel."

A brief look clouded Miss Hathaway's features, and Lindsay wondered at it. She glanced at the curate and caught him looking at her. Before she could smile, his gaze flickered away.

"I see," was all Miss Hathaway said.

Beatrice folded her hands on her lap. "We decided

at last to come hear for ourselves. And we were not disappointed."

As the stilted conversation progressed between Miss Hathaway and Beatrice, Lindsay fretted, wishing she knew how to draw the curate in. Would this be the last time she ever spoke to him? Would he think them awfully tiresome visitors?

He remained silent, and she wondered what he was thinking. She stole another look at him, but he appeared as serene as he had in church, giving nothing away.

Mr. Quinn was also quiet, and Lindsay glanced at him, amazed afresh at his story. She caught his gaze as well, but instead of looking away as the curate had, Mr. Quinn grinned at her, and she found herself smiling back. There was something engaging in his countenance.

The tea tray arrived at that moment and Miss Hathaway busied herself with pouring. Mr. Quinn didn't wait for his cup to be brought to him but rose and wandered over to Miss Hathaway. He took the cup offered him, then approached Lindsay. "See here, since you've probably visited the good parson to discuss this morning's sermon, why don't you sit here in his corner and ask him whatever you like. The reverend knows more about scripture than I'll ever know in two lifetimes."

It was as if he'd read her mind. Before she could think what to say, Mr. Quinn turned to Beatrice. "In the meanwhile, I'd be glad to regale Miss Yates with tales from Newgate if you'd care to hear them." He smiled and winked at her cousin.

To her credit, Beatrice took it in stride. She replied

with enthusiasm, "I would love to hear about Newgate." She looked across at Miss Hathaway. "Reverend Doyle has told me something of your work among the inmates. I would dearly like to know more of it."

Mr. Quinn quirked an eyebrow at Lindsay and held out his arm as if he were escorting her to an assembly at the exclusive Almack's. "Shall I take you to Hathaway?"

She stood at once, her heartbeat quickening. Two armchairs and a small round table formed a cozy nook before the bow window. Reverend Hathaway stood as she approached and waited until she was seated before he resumed his seat opposite.

"Well, Reverend, are you ready for a catechism lesson?" Mr. Quinn asked in a jocular tone.

Instead of replying, he glanced toward his sister, but she was already engaged in an animated conversation with Beatrice. Lindsay heard her saying, "The inmates are kept in atrocious conditions…." Then, almost as if reluctant, the curate turned back to Lindsay. "Of course. What is it you wish to know?"

After Mr. Quinn went to rejoin the women, Lindsay cast about for how to begin. Reverend Hathaway was so much younger than Reverend Doyle, yet so unlike the young gentlemen of the ton she'd met during her coming out.

"I—you—" he began, then brought a clenched hand to his mouth and cleared his throat. "You had some questions?"

"Yes." Lindsay pulled open the drawstring of her reticule, relieved to have something else to focus on besides the awful moment he'd caught her looking at his peg leg. She removed the small Bible and laid it atop the tapestry covering the table. "That is, if you don't mind."

"No, of course not. Were you reading a particular passage?" he asked.

"I was trying to find the scriptures you spoke of this morning, but I must confess, I did not write them down." To her chagrin, she felt herself stammering. "I—I shall be more diligent next Sunday."

"I can help you there," he said, taking the Bible from her and opening it, easing her nerves somewhat. "I began with a verse in the Book of Acts, in chapter thirteen." He ruffled the thin pages. He had beautiful hands, his fingers long and slim, the nails cut short and straight across. When he came to the passage, he handed the book to her. "Here." He pointed with his forefinger. "Verse twenty-two."

She tore her attention from his hand and bent her head over the scripture, trying to concentrate on the words.

When she'd finished, she lifted her face and caught her breath when she found him looking at her. This close, he looked even more handsome. His face was slim, the lines firm and well proportioned. She was reminded of the sculpted busts and statues of the Renaissance she'd had to study at Miss Pinkard's Academy. So different from the Mayfair dandies who surrounded her at each dance.

She turned her mind back to the Bible verse. "How beautiful it sounds, 'a man after mine own heart.'" She drew her eyebrows together in a frown. "Do you think

God would regard a woman's heart the same way? Could a woman also have a heart like David's?"

"I believe God doesn't look at the externals—the gender of a person, or her status in society, or level of education—but at the heart."

The gentle look in his eyes, and the confidence of his words reassured her. She found herself smiling, and the two remained looking at each other a moment.

Then he blinked and looked back down at the Bible between them.

Her thoughts returned to his sermon. "You also read something this morning about 'being born again.'" She repeated the last words slowly, puzzling over them.

He nodded. "Yes. Jesus first uses the term in the Book of John, but I was quoting from the Epistle of Peter this morning. If you'll permit me…" He reached for her Bible again, and she quickly turned it around for him. Their fingers grazed. "Pardon me—"

"It's quite all right—" Their words collided just like their hands, and she fell silent, still feeling the tingle of the contact. Would he think her an utter schoolgirl, ignorant of every social grace?

He flipped through the pages once more until finding the verse he'd used. "'Being born again, not of corruptible seed, but of incorruptible, by the word of God, which liveth and abideth forever.'" He turned the book back toward her, his forefinger once again marking the place.

She bent over the fine print of the Bible. When she looked up this time, he asked her, "Have you never heard that scripture before?"

"I confess, I don't recall it." Her glance left his and she looked out the window at the view of Hyde Park, across the road. "I haven't been very diligent with the reading of scripture in the past few years, not since going away to school."

"That is understandable in one so young."

She bit her lip, her fears confirmed. He did think her a mere schoolgirl. "I wasn't trying to excuse myself. Your preaching this morning made me want to begin reading again. I have read the prayer book every Sunday," she added hopefully.

His fine lips curved up and she felt even more childish. "That's admirable. However," his tone sobered, "if you truly would wish to hear the Lord speak to you, I would encourage a daily habit of reading the scriptures."

"Does God really speak to a person—I mean, besides a clergyman?"

"Of course." He said it as if it were the most natural thing.

She shook her head slowly. "Papa would disagree with such a notion."

"What does your father say?"

She tried to formulate the principles her father had taught her over the years. "He does not believe that God interferes with man."

"Ah, a deist."

She tilted her head. "I'm not sure what the term means. He has brought me up to understand that God created all things but that He has left it up to humans to behave according to the reason He has given us."

"Yes." Reverend Hathaway tapped his long fingers lightly on the tabletop, as if considering. She wondered if she had said something displeasing to him, but he quickly dismissed the impression. "There is much to be commended in rationality. Unfortunately, it ignores much of who Christ is and why He came to live among men."

Her eyes widened at the direct yet gentle way he was saying her father was wrong. Up to now, the concept had never entered her head. Her father had always been the wisest person she knew. She looked down at her hands, her thoughts in a quandary. "When my mother was alive, she would read me the scriptures each evening before bed, but somehow I never continued after she passed away."

"Has she been gone long?" he asked softly.

She shifted her glance back to the view beyond the window, the sympathy in his tone bringing a prick of tears to her eyes. "Three years."

"Yours is still a fresh loss."

Slowly, she brought her gaze back to his. "Most people expect me to be over it by now."

"I would imagine you must miss her very much. She left you at a time when a girl is becoming a woman and needs her mother."

How intuitive he was. "How...do you know?" she whispered.

"You forget, I'm a clergyman. I see and listen to many people's situations and have come to experience much loss through what I hear from my parishioners."

He'd had his own loss to deal with, she thought, remembering his leg. How could she let him know without embarrassing him? She dug into her reticule for her handkerchief and touched the corners of her eyes. "I'm sorry. I've never…spoken to a man of the church the way I have with you. They seem so dignified and far removed." She folded her hands. "I mean no disrespect to any clergyman," she added suddenly, afraid she might have insulted him.

"I'm sure you didn't."

They were interrupted by Mr. Quinn, who approached the small table. "I see you've managed to answer some of the young lady's questions." He glanced at her with a smile. "I mean, I hope he has, and not raised new ones."

She laughed with a sense of relief, as if she'd kept things bottled up inside too long and now felt carefree. "Oh, a little of both, I believe."

"That's what he always does to me, lass, so you needn't fear you're alone."

Beatrice rose. "We really should be going, although I've had a delightful time. I am most interested in hearing more about your work at Newgate," she said to Miss Hathaway. "I would so like to organize a group of women at the church to help you." She walked toward the alcove. "I hear you, too, are a frequent visitor to Newgate," she said to Reverend Hathaway.

The curate stood as she approached.

Mr. Quinn beamed at him. "He's even begun helping teach a group of criminal boys there to read. The new chaplain isn't a bad chap and he thinks many of these boys are redeemable."

Beatrice looked at the curate with heightened interest. "I find that admirable."

A flush crept over his smooth cheeks. "I fear our efforts are minuscule compared to what needs to be done," he said.

Beatrice nodded. "But everything must start somewhere." She turned to Lindsay. "Well, my dear, have you had any of your questions answered?"

Lindsay closed her New Testament. "A few." She gave Reverend Hathaway a shy smile. "Thank you, Reverend, for your time."

Mr. Quinn rocked back on his heels. "If you've only had a few questions answered, and more raised, I suggest you begin coming 'round for the reverend's study group."

Before the reverend had a chance to reply, Mr. Quinn continued. "The curate has a group of us each Thursday evening right here, reading the good book and asking any questions we'd like. Miss Hathaway is present as well, so everything would be proper if Miss Phillips, and yourself o' course, would be interested in attending."

Lindsay felt hope rise within her. Perhaps she would not only have the opportunity of seeing the reverend again, but to study the scriptures under his tutelage! She looked at Beatrice.

Her cousin smiled at the curate. "Why, we shall certainly consider it. Of course, I must talk to Miss Phillips's father. As you know, Miss Phillips is in the middle of her coming out. Her engagement calendar is quite full."

"Of course," he said immediately. "Mr. Quinn only meant to suggest a possible—er—"

Mr. Quinn interrupted, addressing Lindsay directly. "Well, whenever you get bored with all the dances and parties, you're welcome in our midst."

She brought her hands together. "I should love to come. I have ever so many more questions." She turned once again to Reverend Hathaway. "That is…if you don't mind having someone so ignorant of scripture in your group."

"Remember, God looks at the heart," Reverend Hathaway replied. "You—both of you—" he turned to include her cousin "—are most welcome any evening you are not otherwise engaged."

Beatrice smiled and held out her hand. "We thank you most graciously. Now, we really must be going." She made her farewells to Miss Hathaway and Mr. Quinn.

Reverend Hathaway smiled at Lindsay and she couldn't help but notice his deep blue eyes again. "Thank you for coming to visit us," he said.

"Thank you for having us. I…I hope we can join you at your Bible study." How she wished she could say more—how full her heart felt after having conversed with him.

He gave a small nod, his eyes never leaving hers. "I look forward to seeing you some evening."

After they'd left, Damien sat back in a daze, only half listening to his sister commenting on the visit. His attention was caught by Jonah's reply. "Beautiful child, she is. She certainly seemed riveted by our Damien's conversation, but I always say he's the wisest man I know."

Florence looked up from her needlework. "She is a pretty child, indeed, but I'm sure this is the last we shall see of her. She belongs to an entirely different world from ours. You heard her cousin—her life at present is full of balls and concerts. A girl's coming out has a sole purpose to it, and that is to make a good match."

Damien said nothing though his sister's words brought about a sense of desolation in him. Jonah's regard came to rest on Damien as he replied to Florence. "And what better husband for a young girl such as she than our good curate?"

"Jonah! What foolishness will you say next?" Florence exclaimed. "Goodness, don't even think such nonsense."

Jonah's eyes twinkled in response. "No more foolish than the notion of a lady falling in love with a Newgate prisoner."

Florence turned a bright red and she busied herself with her square of linen. "Hush. You'll only distress Damien."

Jonah quirked an eyebrow at him, and he did his best to appear unruffled. "Why should Damien be distressed by the thought of a pretty young thing like Miss Phillips giving him a second look?"

"Jonah!" Florence's countenance bespoke genuine distress.

Damien stood and straightened his waistcoat. "That's all right, Florence. Jonah was just having sport. No harm done. If you'll excuse me, I shall be in my workshop."

As he shut the door behind him, he heard Florence's sharp whisper. "Now see what you've done? Your teasing was cruel."

"I didn't mean to be cruel. I told you, I just want to see my future brother-in-law all set up with a good woman of his own."

Damien didn't hear any more. He walked rapidly away from the door and headed downstairs for the small room off the kitchen, which served as his workshop. His father had been a clockmaker and brought his son up to follow in his profession. Instead, Damien had felt the call of the church. But since returning to London from Oxford to take up the curacy at St. George's, he'd continued repairing clocks as a hobby. Working on the precise inner workings of a timepiece helped settle his mind. Often an answer to a perplexing question in scripture or a difficult problem with a parishioner would come to him as he sat pondering the clockworks.

He entered the small room and was immediately soothed by the steady ticking of the various clocks sitting on shelves and mantels in the room. He bent over the fire and stirred up the smoldering embers in the grate, adding some fresh lumps of coal. His hand stilled on the tongs as he stared at the sizzling coals, unseeing or—more precisely—seeing a radiant young face. When the fire burned brightly once again, he went to the battered old table that served as his work surface. It overlooked the kitchen garden and orchards beyond, providing ample light in the afternoon.

He moved the lantern clock in the brass case closer. He had to convert it into a fusee clock, which would only have to be wound once a week instead of daily. He turned it around so its back was facing him and picked up a screwdriver. The shiny brass back was etched with fancy scrollwork.

He stared at the inner workings of the clock. What should have been a simple procedure turned into a chore. Snatches from the conversation he'd just had with Miss Phillips kept shifting his focus.

Had the Lord brought this young lady for him to disciple in some fashion? Her questions about the scriptures seemed genuine.

How would he be able to disregard the yearnings this young lady stirred in his heart and focus solely on her spiritual well-being? He pondered the brass cone-shaped gear in his hand.

Likely his sister was right. Miss Phillips would have no time for an evening Bible study. A girl's coming out was a major event in her life. How could an evening studying scriptures at a modest parsonage compete with a ball at one of the great houses of Mayfair?

Yet the shimmer of tears that had glistened in her eyes had been genuine. How he'd longed in that moment to offer comfort.

His fingers tightened on the gear. He was a simple clergyman. This young lady was as far removed from his sphere as a French gilded clock was from the parsonage. He must banish such foolish thoughts of her immediately, before they caused him any trouble.

Crowded between the other young ladies, Lindsay could hardly breathe. Her fan did little but move the stifling air in front of her.

Had she only been at the Middletons' ball three-quarters of an hour? The wall she stood against was jammed with similarly dressed young ladies, all in white or pale-colored high-waisted gowns, tiny reticules and silk fans clutched in their gloved hands. Hair was curled around faces shiny from the heat of the room. Wall sconces only added to the pressing warmth.

The music from the orchestra on the balcony above them reverberated through the long ballroom. Squares of four couples each along the center length of the ballroom carried out the steps of the quadrille. Lindsay had begged to be excused from this set. Her father had gone to get her some refreshment in the meantime.

"My, what a turnout." Beatrice waved her own fan in front of her, her eyes on the guests promenading about the crowded room.

With a sigh of relief, Lindsay spotted her father making his way toward them with cups of punch in his hands. She watched him proudly, noting how handsome he was. In his mid-forties, his dark blond hair had hardly any gray in it and was only just beginning to recede a little at the edges of his forehead. His carriage was erect and he was slim compared to most gentlemen of his age.

She marveled that he had accompanied them this evening. Normally, he was content to let her attend every social engagement with only Beatrice.

This evening, however, her father had not only made the effort to don his black evening tailcoat and white satin waistcoat, but he'd inspected her gown as well, making her change from pink tulle to white organdy lace over a blue satin underskirt.

As he came closer now, Lindsay noticed a tall, young gentleman following closely behind him. She waited, intrigued. Her father had acted mysteriously all through dinner, alluding to the wonderful time that awaited her at the Middletons' ball.

"Here you go, my dear." Her father handed her a glass of ratafia. He passed the other one to Beatrice.

He turned to the gentleman at his side. "Lindsay, I'd like you to meet Jerome Stokes. Jerry, this is my daughter, Lindsay Phillips, and her mother's cousin, Miss Yates."

Lindsay studied the man before her. His hair was dark brown, almost ebony, and arranged in a thick wave away from his brow. His eyes, heavy lidded, were a pale green. They met hers head-on, causing her to feel appraised. To her further dismay, his gaze roamed slowly over her face before descending. He paused at her bosom, causing a flush to cover her exposed skin. She felt like a specimen at the Royal Society.

Before she could think of a proper setdown, he took her hand in his, bringing it up to his lips. His hair let off a scent of cologne as he bowed. *"Enchanté,"* he murmured.

The French word sounded affected on his fleshy lips.

He was quite tall and she had to crane her neck to look into his face once he straightened. He stood a few inches too close, and she felt hemmed in, with no escape. His evening clothes fit impeccably, a navy coat with matching knee breeches and white silk stockings.

A white satin waistcoat hugged a powerful torso, and a high white cravat enfolded his neck completely, falling in beautiful folds. He reminded her of pictures she had seen of the famous dandy, Beau Brummell. Yet, his appearance left her cold.

She half curtsied, wishing he'd let her hand go. At last he did so to greet her cousin. Then he addressed her once again. "May I have the pleasure of this dance?"

Her father smiled with unaccustomed warmth. "By all means. Show Mr. Stokes what an accomplished dancer you are."

Hiding her disinclination to step onto the dance floor with this stranger, she gave Mr. Stokes her hand again. "Yes, Papa."

"Go on and enjoy yourselves. Get acquainted."

It would soon be over, she told herself. She was used to dancing with all sorts of gentlemen and didn't know why this particular one caused such an immediate antipathy in her.

They followed the intricate steps of the country dance at first, briefly touching hands and circling around other pairs of dancers for the first few moments. Then, as they stood and watched the lead couple execute a turn, he said, "Your father did not exaggerate your beauty. I thought surely he had overstated it, as parents are wont to do when conversing of their offspring."

She frowned at his dispassionate, almost scientific tone. Was this why her father admired him so? Was he a fellow amateur scientist?

Suddenly she thought of Reverend Hathaway's warm

yet almost shy speech. How different he was from this man. "If you know my father at all, you know he is a man of precise words."

He chuckled. "I flatter myself that I know your father better than most people, and what you say is true. He is a man given to accurate observation."

Her dislike grew at the familiar way he spoke of her father. Her father had never mentioned Mr. Stokes to her.

She was relieved when they began to dance again and had a brief respite from talking. But when they came together to execute a turn, he said, "When your father spoke of your beauty, I thought, he has lost his objectivity when it comes to his only offspring. His judgment cannot be trusted."

She pressed her lips together, unwilling to offend her father's acquaintance, although her annoyance was deepening.

"He has spoken much about you." His warm breath grazed her ear, and she stiffened. "You are like an exquisite Dresden vase, Miss Phillips." He was standing inches from her, his hand holding hers and guiding it over her head, to turn her about. She couldn't help looking up at him as he said these words.

A shiver went through her. Not of pleasure, but almost of fear at the predatory look in his eyes. She felt like one of the reptiles her father kept in jars along the shelves of his library, their spotted and scaled bodies curled inside the apothecary jars, helpless to escape, preserved for all time.

She pushed aside the image as she moved away from

Mr. Stokes in time to the music. Her father could not possibly be considering this man as a suitor for her!

When the dance ended, Mr. Stokes took her by the elbow and led her back to her father.

As they approached him, her father rubbed his hands together and smiled. "There now, how did you two get on?" Without giving her a chance to reply, he turned to Stokes. "Didn't I tell you the two of you would suit?"

"You did indeed."

"And did I not tell you she was beautiful?"

"A diamond of the first water," he murmured, and she could feel his gaze on her.

"She has had every advantage. She will make an admirable wife. Any gentleman here tonight would consider himself fortunate if she accepted his suit."

"Papa!" Her cheeks grew hot in embarrassment.

"May I call on you tomorrow?"

She stared at Mr. Stokes, thinking how to refuse. Before she could open her mouth, her father smiled. "Of course you may."

"I shall take her for a ride in the Park in my phaeton. It's the envy of my set."

He spoke to her father as if she weren't even present. Her heart sank. A phaeton. That would only seat the two of them. She swallowed, dreading having to sit so close to this man.

As the evening wore on and Mr. Stokes stuck by her side, Lindsay's thoughts veered to Reverend Hathaway as to a beacon. Was he sitting in his cozy drawing room with his sister and Mr. Quinn, sharing the scriptures? Or out visiting the poor of the parish? Her cousin had told her of all the good works he did. She could well understand now how he had offered an escaped convict refuge.

She'd read compassion in the curate's blue eyes. For a second, she wished she had a suitor like him. Warmth suffused her cheeks at the audacious thought. Immediately, her heart sank as her gaze rested on her father. He would never countenance such a match.

Chapter Three

Damien eyed the young men seated around the parsonage drawing room. The room was filled to capacity, every chair brought from the dining room and study—even from the bedrooms upstairs—to accommodate the visitors. And still, they kept coming. A few were forced to stand along the wall or perch on a chair arm. Another instance where something besides the thirst for scripture brought the crowd.

Damien's gaze went to Miss Phillips. Although he'd tried to avoid looking at her during his scripture lessons, he couldn't help being aware of her each time she came to the parsonage. In the fortnight since she'd begun attending the weekly studies with Miss Yates, turnout had gone from half a dozen earnest young men to over two dozen.

He closed his Bible as Jacob and his daughter brought in the tea things and the assembly started to break up.

"Reverend Hathaway, there is a passage in Hebrews I was pondering this week which I wanted to ask you about."

He dragged his attention to the young man who'd approached his chair. "Of course."

As soon as he could, Damien made his way toward the tea table, although he was waylaid once or twice more by young men eager to discuss a point he'd made earlier in the evening. He tried to answer as briefly as he could, promising to take up the questions once their lesson resumed after the tea break.

Even though he endeavored to maintain a professional distance from Miss Phillips, he always felt drawn to her. Berating himself for his weakness, he told himself he was no better than all the young pups who flocked around her chair.

She never seemed to encourage any familiarity, however. If anything, she all but ignored the young men who were clearly there because of her and stuck to her cousin's side. Of course, he was relieved to discover she was not a flirt, nor a flighty young rattlebrain. Her questions to him during their studies indicated she grasped the scriptures and was sincere in learning.

He knew the gentlemen present were all vying for her attention, and yet he didn't think any would ever cross the bounds of propriety. Had any of them said anything to offend Miss Phillips? Is that why she acted so timidly?

She looked too pale and serious for a young woman enjoying her introduction to society. He knew little of such things. Perhaps she was exhausted from all the dances and social engagements.

By the time he reached the tea table, he was relieved that everyone had been served. Miss Phillips had found a place on the settee between Florence and Miss Yates, as if she needed guarding from the young men.

He took the cup and saucer Florence handed him. "Thank you," he said to his sister before turning to Miss Phillips. Her face broke into a smile as soon as his eyes met hers.

His heart never failed to be jolted by the radiance of her smile and he couldn't help but respond. "Good evening, Miss Phillips. How have you enjoyed the discussion thus far?"

"Oh, very much. You always manage to bring out things in the scriptures which I have failed to see."

"Don't give me the credit. I've spent years studying them under very learned teachers."

She tilted her head a fraction as she continued looking at him. "I believe God has also given you insight into them besides what you have gleaned from others."

He bowed his head, saying nothing. "God's grace is beyond measure."

He read agreement in her eyes. As he scanned her face, he discerned the faint shadows under her eyes. "Are you feeling quite well?"

Her smile faded and the light in her eyes dimmed.

When she said nothing, he added, "I know you must be very busy. I appreciate all the more your attendance at the Bible study."

"I wish I could come to services at the chapel, too, but, alas." Her voice dropped. "My Papa…doesn't approve. I—" She stopped as if hesitating to say more.

"I don't wish you to incur his disapproval."

"My cousin has asked him to allow me to accompany her, and he has reluctantly agreed…but I don't know for how much longer." Her voice dwindled away, and he felt alarmed at the thought of never seeing her again.

"I do hope I can attend for a while more. Miss Yates and I so enjoy your evenings." Her voice regained some animation.

Miss Yates turned to them with a chuckle and glance about the room. "I notice your attendance has increased dramatically. I hope you'll still have room for us."

"Of course." He couldn't help the concern that they might stay away on account of overcrowding. "I'm afraid if you ceased coming, attendance here would also fall as dramatically."

The two smiled in understanding at each other, before Miss Yates glanced sidelong at her young cousin. "Lindsay has been garnering attention wherever she goes this season. Her papa is most proud of her."

Damien strove to keep his expression neutral. "I'm sure he must be." His glance strayed to Miss Phillips, expecting some coy expression. Instead she looked almost distressed. He sought about for another topic. "How is Reverend Doyle?"

Miss Yates blinked. "Quite well. He was by for a visit just yesterday. Haven't you seen him yourself?"

Damien hesitated. "Not recently. He is a very busy man." He didn't add that he'd never gone so long without a visit from his superior. Florence was already fretting that it did not bode well. Ever since the rector had discovered Damien's role in Jonah's escape, he had been notably cold toward Damien. With a nod to each lady, Damien excised himself.

He had no more reason to linger beside Miss Phillips although his brief talk with her had only increased his misgivings. Something appeared to be wrong.

He made his way back to his seat and conversed with the small core of students that were truly eager to learn more of God's word, but his mind and attention remained fixed on Miss Phillips.

When the group dismissed for the evening, Damien stood at the front door to bid his guests goodbye. Most of the gentlemen had departed, but Miss Yates remained speaking with Florence about the prison ministry.

As he turned from bidding farewell to a couple of gentlemen, Miss Phillips approached him. She had already donned her bonnet and pelisse.

"Miss Phillips."

"Might I…" She bit her lip.

"Yes?" He strove for a tone of reassurance, eager to know what she wanted to say.

She began again. "Might it be possible to ask you something?"

"Certainly." When she said nothing, he said more gently, "You may ask me anything. Is something the matter?"

"No." She wet her lips and looked away from him. "Yes."

He reached out a hand but dropped it before it touched her sleeve. "What is it, Miss Phillips? What is wrong?"

"I...that is...I just needed to ask you something. Is there...somewhere we can meet?"

His heart began to pound unnaturally loudly. "Yes. Could you come by tomorrow with Miss Yates?"

She shook her head immediately. "Not here." Her cheeks grew red.

His mind cast about for a suitable reply. "Would you like me to...er...come to your house?"

"No."

He recoiled at the immediacy of her reply. Would she be embarrassed by a visit from him? Of course. He didn't blame her, even as the pain shot through him. He stepped back.

Almost as if reading his thoughts, she said more softly, "I mean...I'd rather it not be at my house."

He considered. She wasn't his parishioner and even if she were, it would be unseemly to meet her alone anywhere. "Is there somewhere we could—ahem—meet, then?"

"I have a music lesson tomorrow afternoon in Marylebone—that's not so far from here." The words came out in a rush.

He blinked, not expecting that. At a loss, he blurted out, "Do you sing?"

"A bit, and play the pianoforte."

How little he knew of her. "How nice."

"I finish at three o'clock. Could…could you perhaps meet me there afterward? It's at number four, Portman Square."

He thought for a second, but her look of appeal made him forget all other considerations. "Very well."

"Oh, thank you!" Her heartfelt look of gratitude erased any lingering doubts.

As he bade both ladies good-night, his mind was troubled. What could be on Miss Phillips's mind to ask him such a thing? Why wouldn't she go to her cousin, or to her father…or to her own pastor, Reverend Doyle? Was she in some kind of trouble?

He resolved to increase his prayers for her—and for himself—that God would grant him the wisdom to give Miss Phillips whatever she needed.

Chapter Four

Lindsay sighed in relief at the sight of Reverend Hathaway leaning against the wrought-iron fence that surrounded Portman Square. Until that moment, she hadn't realized how worried she'd been that he wouldn't be waiting for her when she left her music lesson.

He saw her immediately and straightened. But he didn't approach her, discreetly waiting across the street. She bade her teacher goodbye and tucked her drawing pad under her arm. "My maid will return the key in a little bit when I've finished my sketch." It had been the only pretext she'd been able to think of to borrow the key to the square.

As she turned from the house, she said to her maid, "Clara, please wait for me in the carriage."

The girl bobbed a curtsy. "Yes, miss."

Lindsay waited until the girl had climbed into the coach and the door was shut behind her. Then she quickly crossed the street.

"Hello, Reverend Hathaway," she said breathlessly. "Thank you for coming."

He lifted his hat in greeting and smiled. "How was your lesson?"

She was reassured by the warmth of his tone. Suddenly, the day truly felt like spring—she began to hear the birdsong and feel the fresh breeze upon her cheeks. "My lesson? Oh, it was fine." She shook her head. "I must practice more. That's what I'm always told." And suddenly, she laughed out loud for the sheer pleasure she felt. The weight of the past few weeks fell from her shoulders. Reverend Hathaway would know what she should do.

She gestured toward the large square. "Would you care to take a stroll in the park?"

"That would be very pleasant." He took the large iron key from her, unlocked the gate and held it open.

They began to walk along the hard-packed dirt path under the elm trees in the neatly laid-out square. The reason for her being there returned and her spirits fell. She said nothing for a few minutes, unsure how to begin. She had never done such a thing in all her life. But she was so confused....

She swung around to him, bringing him to abrupt stop. "I would like to ask you something. It's only a theoretical question, mind you."

He nodded, his blue eyes regarding her steadily. Why did they look even bluer out-of-doors? "Ask away. Clergymen are always having theoretical questions pitched at them."

She felt her face grow warm. Was she that transparent?

As if sensing her chagrin, his expression sobered. "What is it, Miss Phillips? What is troubling you so?"

She bit her lower lip. "If one is required to do something, to obey, but one finds the choice...distasteful, but one wants so very much to obey..."

He nodded. "Obedience can be very difficult at times."

"Oh, yes!" He *did* understand. "Have you ever felt like that? As if the Lord were asking something impossible of you, and it would cost you everything to obey?"

He was looking at her keenly now, all traces of humor erased from his features. "I think we all come to that place in our walk with Him, where He requires us to surrender all to Him."

Her spirits sank. It couldn't be. How could she bear it? "But if the choice is so...so disagreeable?"

"His grace is sufficient for thee," he answered gently.

Her shoulders slumped and she turned back to the path, resuming their walk. "I never thought my coming out would be filled with that kind of decision, as if having my own will would cause others so much displeasure, but obedience will cause me—" She wrung her hands together, unable to express her horror. "I do so want to be obedient. These last few weeks at your Bible study, I've learned so much about the Lord's word. There's so much I feel I need to learn. I don't want to be a self-willed person. You speak of the cross and dying to the old nature. But what if that old nature refuses to die?"

He walked alongside her, his hands clasped behind his back. His wooden leg didn't seem to impede him.

She discerned no limp, although the wood made a different sound than that of their shoes upon the ground.

"I've found, in the years I've been counseling the flock the Lord has brought me, that many times a person's spiritual growth is impeded by one thing alone—a thorn in the flesh, as it were, and not by a host of earthly pleasures."

"Oh, yes, that's it exactly. One thing alone!"

He glanced at her. "At least in your case, you are honest enough to admit it. Most people hide from the knowledge, and the Lord has to work on them for years before they are willing to put the item on the altar." He sighed. "In the meantime, however, they don't realize how many years have gone by, years in which they could have been growing in the knowledge of the Lord and reaching new heights."

Her spirits sank further. She didn't want that to happen to her. But the alternative! Jerome Stokes's face rose in her mind. To be betrothed to him. She shuddered.

"Come, Miss Phillips, can it be so very bad? You are a young lady born with every privilege, your whole life before you."

She turned to him, stricken. If only he knew what Papa was asking of her. "Yes," was all she could whisper. She could never speak anything ill of Papa.

They were both silent some moments, and she focused on the soft sound of their footsteps on the ground. The bark of a dog on the other side of the square and the chirp of birds barely registered with her.

She drew a deep breath. "Have you never faced that

kind of dilemma? In which…if you say no, you would be holding back from God?"

He was quiet a moment, and when she feared she had overstepped the bounds of propriety, he said, "I gave my heart and soul to the Lord as a young lad, before I was faced with many worldly temptations."

He hastened to add, "Not because I was some kind of saint, but simply out of my desperate need." He gestured with his chin downward. "After my accident, my need for God was great."

She followed his gaze, realizing he was referring to the loss of his limb. "H-how did it happen?" she finally dared ask.

"I ran out in the road after a duck." He glanced sidelong at her, his expression unreadable to her. "I was eight years old and responsible for a flock of ducks."

She held her breath. "What happened?"

He shrugged. "I didn't look before running out. A heavy wagon ran over my leg."

"Oh, my—" Her hand covered her mouth. She couldn't imagine the pain and anguish for an adult let alone a child.

"It was a miracle I survived. The wheel could just have easily run over my body. There, now, Miss Phillips, please don't be upset. It happened so long ago. Eighteen years," he murmured, as if amazed himself. "The pain and terror have long since faded."

"How…could you bear it?" she asked, her voice still faint.

"I believe I wouldn't have if not for my parents'

faith." His finely shaped mouth turned up at one corner. "And Florence's. Hers was more the bullying kind. Once I was fully healed and fitted with a wooden leg, I had to face perhaps what was harder than the physical pain I'd endured before. I had to take up my life, face the children at school, pretend I was as normal as they.

"Florence was my champion. If a boy so much as snickered behind my back or dared even breathe a nickname, she was over him, giving him the thrashing of his life."

She couldn't help laughing at the image of the spare woman fighting a big bully. "How wonderful it must have been to have a big sister," she said wistfully.

He looked at her as if he understood more than she was saying. "You have no brothers or sisters?"

She shook her head. "I always envied my friends at school who had several brothers and sisters. Tell me more of what you meant. You said your accident made you turn to God for help."

"Yes. Having Florence defend me and my parents shower their love on me wasn't enough. To be able to face every day with my head held high, I needed to know the Father's unconditional love. I needed the Lord's grace to make it through each day, knowing I was no longer a whole boy, but a—" his Adam's apple moved as he swallowed "—cripple."

"Oh, no! You're not a cripple. You are many things. A fine curate for one." Yes, that was true. His disadvantage seemed so very small in light of the whole man before her.

He smiled, but it didn't hide the bleakness in his expression. "But that's what I was in the eyes of others. In order to overcome my limitations, I had to rely on God's strength. I came to understand in a very personal way, the verse, 'My strength is made perfect in weakness.' God proved it to me time and again."

They had walked the whole perimeter of the square. Lindsay, unwilling to have their walk end so soon, said abruptly, "You were so brave to take in a... fugitive."

He blinked at the sudden change in topic. "Quinn?"

She nodded.

He shrugged. "At the time the choice seemed easy. A man came to our door on a rainy winter's night, cold, feverish, hungry. In truth, it was my sister who brought him in. I only seconded her decision."

She shivered, picturing it. "I don't know if I would have dared do such a thing."

He studied her steadily. "It sounds as if you have your own decision to make which requires bravery."

Her eyelids fluttered downward and she kicked at the dirt in her path. "I don't know if I am able to be as brave as you."

"God doesn't give us more than we are able to bear."

How she wanted to believe that!

After a few minutes, the reverend said quietly, "It would seem to me that you have already decided which is the proper course to follow."

She drew in her breath. Those were not the words she wanted to hear. Before she could respond, he continued. "I shall pray for you, that the Lord make His perfect will clearly known to you and give you perfect peace in your decision."

A masculine voice hailed them from behind. "Good day, Damien."

They both looked in surprise at the gentleman walking toward them. Lindsay immediately recognized her own pastor.

Reverend Hathaway halted and waited for the older gentleman to reach them. "Reverend Doyle."

Lindsay bit her lip, wondering what the rector would think of seeing her alone with the curate. Doyle eyed them both without smiling. He nodded to Reverend Hathaway and then to her. "Miss Phillips. How lovely to see you. What are you doing all the way in Marylebone alone?"

"Good afternoon, Reverend Doyle. I was just leaving my music lesson." She raised her chin, annoyed at how nervous she sounded, as if she had been doing something wrong.

"I wasn't aware that you were acquainted with my curate." His glance strayed to the reverend.

Her companion replied in an easy tone before Lindsay could think what to say. "Miss Phillips and her cousin came one Sunday to the chapel and I had the privilege of meeting them, thanks to your recommendation."

Instead of smiling, the rector merely nodded. "I had spoken highly of you at one time, that is true." There was unmistakable censure in his tone.

"I've been attending the reverend's Bible studies at

the parsonage with my cousin Beatrice," she added, hoping to dispel the tension she felt in the air.

The rector raised an eyebrow. "I see."

A silence fell between them. Then he asked, "I trust your father and cousin are in health?"

"Yes, they are both quite well," she answered, hoping news would not travel back to her father about this encounter.

"I am relieved. You may tell them I shall be over soon for a visit."

"Yes." Her worry grew. What would her father say? Would he forbid further Bible studies under Reverend Hathaway's tutelage?

The rector turned his attention back to the reverend. "I shall call upon you in the coming days. There is much we need to discuss."

"I am at your service," Reverend Hathaway said quietly.

"Very well." With a final glance between the two of them, the rector bowed his head and bade them farewell.

"I didn't expect to see Reverend Doyle here," she said when he had exited the square.

"He lives nearby on Cavendish Square."

"I see. He seemed displeased about something," she ventured.

"Yes, I fear so." He sighed. "For many years, he was almost like a father—a spiritual father—to me. He advised me on my studies and procured this living for me at St. George's." He turned to her. "I am not a gentleman's son, you see, but the son of a clockmaker."

Her eyes widened. "But...but you are..." She laughed

nervously. "You seem to be a gentleman." *Far more a gentleman than Jerome Stokes with all his privileges and assets,* she added silently.

"If so, it is thanks to the rector. He is the one who made it possible for me to receive a gentleman's education. He recommended me to Lord Marlborough of Portman Square who paid for my studies at Oxford."

These new facts only served to increase her admiration for the man before her. "You must have been worthy of their belief in you."

His gaze traveled over her face, almost in wonder, she would hazard. "You are remarkable, Miss Phillips."

She smiled tentatively. "Why do you say that, Reverend Hathaway?"

He shook his head slightly. "Most young ladies would not see it in that light."

"How would they see it?"

"They would see me rather as a fraud. A man dressed up like a gentleman, pretending to be something he is not."

"Oh, no!" Such an accusation angered her. "You are a man of God, whose life reflects what he preaches from the pulpit."

His cheeks deepened in color, and she hoped her words had brought pleasure and not embarrassment to him. She meant them with all her heart. A thin line appeared between his eyebrows. "Have you asked advice from the rector? He is, after all, your spiritual advisor."

She shook her head, looking down. "I don't feel I know him well enough. You see, I've been away at school some years, so I really have not seen him much." She fell silent. There was no rational way to explain that in the short time she'd known him, Reverend Hathaway was the only person whose counsel she trusted in this matter.

"Reverend Doyle is a man of great wisdom. I would advise you to talk to him."

"He must be very proud of you for helping Mr. Quinn when he was in so much trouble."

A shadow crossed his eyes, and he hesitated. "He did not approve of what my sister and I did." He hastened to add, "He was right to object. We were aiding and abetting a fugitive. We broke the law in doing so."

She felt a tremor at the gravity of his tone. "Is that why he is displeased with you?"

The reverend nodded. "I don't regret having taken Mr. Quinn into our keeping. However, I would not counsel anyone lightly to do what we did. One must be very sure what one is doing is absolutely right in God's eyes before taking such a step."

Did he think she was on the brink of making a wrong decision? Was he warning her?

She lifted her chin. "In that case, I think it was all the more brave of you to help Mr. Quinn."

The reverend's blue eyes seemed to lighten. "Thank you, Miss Phillips. Your good opinion means a lot to me."

Before she had a chance to feel the pleasure his words gave her, he continued. "Sometimes it is not easy to make the right decision. Sometimes what seems the right choice—that determined by the rules laid out—is, in fact, not the right way."

Did his words spell hope or doom for her? Was there

a way to disobey her father without losing his love and esteem? "How does one know in such a case?" she asked in a whisper, her eyes intent on his.

"By much prayer. In the end, the answer must come from here." He tapped his chest. "A person must follow his—or her—conscience, whatever the risks involved."

She nodded slowly, her gaze lifting from his slim hand back up to his face.

When the time came, would she have the courage to follow the dictates of her conscience?

Damien held up the slate toward the group of boys sitting on the floor at his feet in the cell given them to use for the lesson. "Let us review what we learned yesterday. Who can tell me what this says?"

Several arms shot up like arrows.

Damien smiled at one eager face, pale skin shining through the smudges. "Yes, Sam?"

"The Lord is my sh-shepherd!" He finished with a triumphant smile.

"Very good. Let us try another sentence." He wiped off the slate with his rag and wrote again.

As he held it up, his glance went to a dim corner of the prison cell. A group of older boys was whispering and sniggering among themselves. In a second, Jonah squatted beside them. "You'd rather end up on the gallows or the transport ship than learn yer letters, is that it?"

"Tell us about the gallows," a black-haired youth with a chipped tooth replied.

With a quick wink Damien's way, Jonah sat down

cross-legged among them. Damien continued with his lesson. He knew it was impossible to reach them all, so he appreciated Jonah's help in keeping the unruly ones occupied while he taught those who wanted to learn.

He turned back to the young pupil. "Sam?"

The underfed lad screwed up his face in preparation to read. "Th-the t-t-time of—"

Damien prompted him gently until he managed the whole sentence. When they finished the lesson, he and Jonah parceled out the food and provisions they had brought with them. Before they left, he told them a Bible story.

On their way out of Newgate, Jonah shuddered as they passed through the arched entrance. "Always glad to leave that hole."

Damien glanced at him. "I do appreciate your accompanying me. I know it's not easy to go back each time."

"It's truly a dark pit in there."

"All the more reason we must bring the light."

Jonah nodded as they made their way past the Old Bailey. "I'll never forget the day I was sentenced to be hanged." He shook his head. "To think Florence was sitting there, praying for me even then." At the corner, he asked, "You want me to hail a cab?"

"No. Let's walk."

"You certain? Florence wanted me to get her some things at Covent Garden Market."

"That's fine." Damien shook off the slight irritation he felt whenever Jonah seemed overly protective of him. He knew it was only thoughtfulness on the man's part. But by now, he'd hoped Jonah would realize Damien was capable of walking the distance of any normal man.

They sauntered down Ludgate Hill and headed west on Fleet Street, jostled by the thick throng of pedestrians. It only worsened as they approached the Strand, where they veered off at Drury Lane toward the market.

"How's the pretty Miss Phillips?"

Damien glanced sharply at Jonah. He'd told no one of his meeting with Miss Phillips the day before. "You should know as well as I, since you see her at the house as often as I do."

Jonah shrugged. "She's a fair young lady, who seems to admire you quite a bit."

Damien made his way around a large woman who stood shouting to a hansom cab driver from the curb. "If she seems to admire me, it is only because I am a clergyman."

"Is that all you think it is?"

Damien gave him a sharp look at the sly tone. The street noises grew louder as they approached the stalls and sheds occupying Covent Garden. Damien followed Jonah to a vendor's table filled with a colorful display of fruits and vegetables. Jonah poked at a pile of green cabbages. "What do you want for these sorry-looking things?"

The woman behind the table glared at him, her hefty arms akimbo. "Those be as crispy as anything you could grow yourself. A shillin' for the pound."

He grabbed up one from the top of the pyramid. "Here, weigh that one for me, be a good lass."

When he'd paid for the cabbage, they walked on.

"Oranges from Valencia!" the rough voice of a hawker called out.

"I'll take a half-dozen o' those."

"Here, let me carry them," Damien offered as they started on again.

"That's all right, I've got 'em."

Damien clamped his lips down and said no more.

"So, you're not interested in Miss Phillips as a young lady of marriageable age?"

Damien refused to be drawn. "I repeat, Miss Phillips only sees me as a clergyman."

Jonah stopped before a fish vendor's cart, and Damien stood silent while Jonah haggled over a piece of cod. As they waited for it to be cleaned and cut, he turned back to Damien, a twinkle in his dark green eyes. "Is that so?"

"She has seemed…troubled to me of late. If she can receive any counsel from the scriptures, then it is my duty to aid her in that way and no more. I am not even her proper pastor—that is Reverend Doyle's purview. I must respect his office."

Jonah mulled on that a moment, then dug in his pocket for some coins. "I beg your pardon, then. I didn't quite see it in that light. I just see you as a good-looking young gent. Don't you ever fancy yourself in need of a wife o' your own?"

Damien was momentarily saved from replying when the vendor handed Jonah his change and packet of fish. But as they resumed walking, Jonah quirked an eyebrow at him. "Well?"

Damien jabbed his walking stick into the cobbled stones. "I realized long ago my calling was to serve God, and it is a full-time occupation as you have come to observe in the time you've been residing with us." He tried not to sound as testy as he was now feeling.

Jonah remained silent, seeming to examine the other stalls they passed. Damien felt compelled to add, "The Apostle Paul put it very well. When a person is married, he becomes concerned with the needs of his spouse to the detriment of the business of the Lord."

Jonah grunted. "How is it then that most vicars and curates I see are married? Their wives seem to be their helpmates in the parish. Didn't the good book also say something about it not being good for a man to be alone?"

Damien pretended to study the display of flowers at one stall. For the first time, he regretted having taught Jonah any scripture.

Jonah fished out a coin and indicated a posy of primroses. "These blooms have nothing over the bloom in your cheeks," he told the vendor.

The pretty girl's cheeks dimpled. "Thankee, sir."

"Can you wrap them in a bit o' paper for me?" As the girl complied, Jonah murmured, "That's a good lass." He took them from her and handed her the money.

"And who's the lucky lady these are for?"

He inspected the colorful bouquet, turning it around in his large hand. "They're for a very special lady, the one who's promised to marry me."

"Ooh!"

When the girl tried to hand him the change, he said, "Keep it and buy yourself your own posy."

The girl flashed him a wide smile. "Thankee kindly, sir!"

Damien swallowed, watching the careful way Jonah placed the small bouquet atop his other purchases in his satchel. The incongruous sight of his blunt fingers handling the fragile blooms sent a curious pang through Damien. How would it feel to buy a woman flowers? He'd never know the pleasure.

Jonah's keen eyes met his at that moment. "Don't you ever fancy having a lady of your own to come home to?"

"I am content with my single state." At Jonah's raised eyebrow, he added, "You've seen my life. I'm at the beck and call of those in need anytime of the day or night."

Jonah shrugged. "That's why the Lord gives a man a helpmate."

They inched their way forward through the crowded aisle between the stalls.

"I must say I'm always amazed at the ease you have in talking to women," Damien couldn't help commenting when Jonah paused in front of a stall selling herbs and spices. The pungent aromas of cumin and cinnamon filled the air. Dried pods and seeds were heaped in large burlap sacks on the ground at their feet.

Jonah straightened from where he'd bent to examine a sack of nutmegs. "What's that you say?"

Damien wished he had kept his mouth shut.

Too late, the words seemed to register with Jonah and

his lips cracked open in a grin. "Talking to lasses is the easiest thing in the world."

Damien shook his head, unable to keep from smiling back. "I doubt you'd find many men to agree with you."

Jonah draped a brawny arm across his shoulders. "All you do is look at 'em a certain way and tell 'em they're the loveliest thing you've ever laid eyes on. Works about three-quarters o' the time."

Damien chuckled. "And the other quarter of the time?"

"Why, you just spend some blunt on 'em, and they're yours." He waved his arm. "Look around you at all the young women. I'd lay odds that any number o' them would give their spinster eyeteeth to catch a fine parson like you."

The crowded market was filled with far more women than men. Women of all ages, plump and slim, well-dressed and shabby. Damien shook his head, wondering how he'd gotten into this ridiculous conversation with his future brother-in-law.

Jonah frowned a moment, removing his arm from Damien's shoulders and adjusting the satchel he carried. "Of course, you realize, with your sister, it was different. There was nothing I could 'a done or said to win her, if the Lord hadn't o' had mercy on me."

Damien chuckled. "I think she saw what lay beneath the surface."

Jonah shook his head. "That was pretty rotten, too. No, it took God's grace to bless me the way He has with your sister's love."

Before Damien could say anything more, Jonah

gestured quickly with his hand. "See the ladies standing by the fruit vendor?"

Damien's gaze traveled to two women inspecting the fruit. One of them looked older, perhaps thirty, the other probably not more than nineteen or twenty. In their plain dark pelisses, they could have been servants out to make purchases, or young matrons doing their household shopping. "What of them?"

"What of 'em?" Jonah mimicked in mock scorn. "They're a pair of pretty lasses who'd probably lap you up like a plum pudding if you so much as looked their way."

When Damien became aware of what Jonah intended, his steps slowed, but Jonah hauled him forward by the elbow. The next thing he knew, Jonah was smiling and tipping his hat to the ladies in question. "Good day to ye, madam, miss. Have you ever seen such plump-looking grapes in all your life?"

He snatched up one of the fat black grapes and popped it into his mouth. "Sweet as honey." He addressed the older woman, but included both in his smile. "Of course, hothouse grapes don't come near to the taste of those grown outside in the warm sun and refreshing rain. When I lived in the country, I used to grow my own. Muscats, Rieslings, Gamays. You've never tasted a sweeter grape than those I harvested."

"Oh, where did you cultivate grapes?" the older one asked with a simpering smile.

"I tilled the soil on a place in Surrey."

Damien couldn't help admiring how quickly Jonah had them entranced. He looked a well-set-up gentleman in his bottle-green cutaway coat and black pantaloons, nothing like the farm laborer he used to be. Although he didn't lie, his words made the women assume he had been a landowner on some prosperous farm.

"Oh, yes, I grew apples and pears, too. I was only just telling my young friend, the parson here, that I haven't seen a fruit nor a vegetable in London yet that beats anything I grew myself."

The two women turned to notice Damien, who'd been standing slightly behind Jonah.

"Of course, he's city bred, so he doesn't know what it means to pick your own apple and feel the juice on your tongue at that first, crisp bite."

Damien thought that was a bit much, considering the orchard in his backyard, but he kept silent, allowing Jonah to have his fun.

"Would you ladies like me to hail you a cab? You've an awful lot of parcels to carry," Jonah asked.

"Oh, that would be most helpful," the older said. "We live in Cheapside. It's always hard to get a cab around here."

"Come along then, here, let me help you with those. The preacher can take yours," he said, turning to the younger lady.

As they began to move apart, the young girl suddenly looked down at Damien's legs and her eyes grew round. Without a word, she handed Damien her basket, but when they began walking, she took her place beside her companion, on the farthest side away from Damien and Jonah.

Damien slowed his steps until he was walking just

behind the group. Jonah continued chatting amiably with the older woman as if nothing had happened. Damien hoped he hadn't noticed anything.

They reached the curb and in a few moments Jonah had procured them a hack from those waiting at a stand.

As the lumbering vehicle inched away down the crowded street, Jonah muttered under his breath, "Couple o' low-class wenches. Weren't worth your time, my boy." He nudged Damien on the elbow and they crossed the street. "That girl was as sallow as whey. Plenty more where she came from!"

A block farther, Jonah hailed them a cab. The two climbed in and rode silently back toward the parsonage. Damien kept his eyes fixed out the window. Perhaps now his well-meaning friend would drop the subject of a wife for him.

Chapter Five

"Lindsay, now that you have had some weeks' acquaintance with Jerome Stokes, I want you to accept his proposal of marriage."

Lindsay stared at her father. She'd just come in from an outing with Beatrice when her father had summoned her to his library. "Papa, it's so sudden." Her voice sounded faint and her heartbeat began to thud in dread. Although she'd expected the words, hearing them spoken made her fate seem all the more dire.

"Will you deny your father the joy of knowing you are in good hands, regardless of what happens to me?"

Instinctively, Lindsay reached out and clasped her father's hands, unable to bear the thought of losing her father, too. "Oh, Papa, don't talk as if something awful is going to happen to you." His color was a bit pale, but Lindsay knew it was the lack of sunlight from all the hours he spent in his library.

"I have passed the age of five-and-forty. Many men never reach it. Few go many years beyond it."

As she listened to him in dismay, he released her hands and rose slowly from the settee. "Thankfully, I am a healthy man. I've suffered few illnesses in my life, so there is no reason to suppose you will not have me for many years yet."

He fixed his eye on her, his eyebrows drawn together. "That is not to say my time is guaranteed, my dear. Your mother would wish me to ensure that you are well provided with a good husband—"

"But, Papa," she began with a nervous laugh, "I need more time." Too long she'd avoided this conversation with her father, although he'd hinted at it since introducing her to Mr. Stokes. Was this going to be her test of faith? Obedience to her father, even if it cost her her very self-respect? Would refusing him threaten her father's health?

"And if I can live to see a few grandchildren, I shall count myself truly a blessed man."

"I'm only eighteen, Papa. It's my first season."

"Most young ladies with your beauty and fortune are married by the end of their first season."

"May I not enjoy two seasons before having to settle down?"

"Who is to say you cannot enjoy countless seasons after you are officially betrothed? You will be a young leader of fashion then with no worries of having to escape the fortune hunters or dodge the otherwise unsuitable, or of remaining on the shelf." He held her gaze coldly for a moment. "Of course, with your beauty, that fate would never befall you. But other young ladies, who wait too long, preferring to play coy, find themselves suddenly high and dry, the best picks of the season taken by their rivals—inferior in both looks and fortune—simply because they wanted to 'enjoy' their season with no thought to the future."

He patted her on the cheek. "I would not have that happen to you, my dear. Nor would your mother ever forgive me. If she were here—" he sighed "—she would guide you and give you the same counsel I am giving you, of that I am certain. Your cousin Beatrice is but a poor substitute."

"Beatrice has been very accommodating, I assure you, Papa."

"Oh, to be sure. But she is not someone who can counsel you as your own mother and father can. She has lived outside of London society too long, her means small, her vision limited."

Her father rubbed his hands together. "Yes, I believe it is now the time to announce your betrothal. In a few more weeks the season will be over. You can leave at the apex. We shall go to the country and make preparations for a sumptuous wedding in the autumn, after the hunting season, of course."

"W-would I have to be married so soon?" She waited to hear her father's next words, her breath held.

His lips thinned in the humorless smile he displayed when he was displeased with someone's argument. "You wouldn't have to, no, but I would know the reason you would wish to delay."

He had that way of waiting for her to answer. Ever since she was a little girl, and he'd tutored her in some subject from Latin to mathematics to botany, he'd explain things meticulously and then quiz her, expecting her to come to the correct conclusions as he stood over her. When she didn't know the answer, she would feel worse and worse, her mind going blank the longer he fixed his intent stare on her.

He lifted a brow. "Well?"

She bit her lip and looked down at her rigidly clasped hands. Why was she required to make a decision that seemed to be ending her life just on the brink of its beginning?

"Mr. Stokes has everything to offer a young lady of your advantages."

"Yes, Papa," she whispered.

"He has expressed his single-minded affection for you. He has pledged to me that he will do his utmost to make you happy. His fortune, coupled with yours, will ensure your comfort and protection from the fortune hunters hedging you."

"Yes, Papa." Her throat closed, and she could hardly get the two words out.

He lifted her chin with a long finger. "What say you, dearest daughter, are you ready to obey your wise father and accept his offer of matrimony? Jerome only awaits your word."

She moistened her lips and looked downward. Her eyes were brimming with tears. She tried to remember the Bible verses she had heard from Reverend Hathaway. *My grace is sufficient for thee. My strength is made perfect in weakness.* But she felt no solace. How to explain the dread that filled her heart at the thought of being betrothed to Mr. Stokes? All she could do was nod her head.

Her father's hands came up to clasp her briefly on the shoulders before he let her go. "That's my girl. I knew I could be proud of you. Your mother is smiling down at you now."

He turned away from her, his voice already businesslike with plans. "I shall inform him of your consent, and he shall ask you formally tomorrow evening at the Clarksons' dinner. I will see to it that you have a private moment with him. Wear your prettiest gown. Beatrice can help you in your selection. She has a good eye."

Lindsay stood mute, but inwardly her natural spirit began to rebel. Why couldn't she simply explain her misgivings to her father? Why was she always so intimidated around him, struggling so to please him?

She heard no more of her father's plan as she turned and headed for the door, her slippers feeling as if they contained lead in their soles, her life apparently over.

Damien looked up at the sound of a knock on his workshop door. He set down the clock he held in his hands. "Yes?"

Florence popped her head in. "Am I interrupting?"

He swung around in his chair. "Not at all. Come in. I'm mainly thinking of Sunday's sermon as I sit here tinkering."

His sister entered and pulled up a hard-back chair to the end of the worktable.

He smiled, sensing she had something on her mind. She was usually too busy to seek him out during the day.

She folded her hands in her lap. He was happy to see that since she'd become engaged to Jonah, she had begun wearing more attractive gowns. Today, she was dressed in a pretty yellow-and-cream striped dress with long sleeves. "We've set a date."

"Indeed?" At her hesitant nod, he broke into a grin. "Wonderful! I was wondering what was keeping you from going ahead."

She smoothed down her dress. "Well, we wanted to let all the gossip and rumors die down a bit…and of course, make sure there was no adverse effect to your ministry."

He waved away the consideration. "You shouldn't have let that stop you."

She immediately frowned. "Of course we should have. We weren't going to leave you to face things alone. After all, it was my doing you had Jonah here all those months."

"Well, now he's boarding with Elizabeth and Jacob, and I'm sure there's no need for him to be crowded in their cottage any longer when the two of you are planning to be wed."

"Yes, well, that is what I came to talk to you about."

He lifted an eyebrow when she paused.

"We were thinking the end of the month, on a Saturday."

He sat back. "The end of this month? That gives you

a little over three weeks. It isn't much time…I mean, I always thought a wedding entailed mounds of preparations," he added with a forced chuckle. In truth, the time suddenly seemed upon them, even though he'd known it was coming. What would he do without his sister? Except for his few years at Oxford, they'd never been apart. They not only lived under the same roof but shared the ministry.

"We don't want to do anything elaborate. It gives us just enough time to post the banns. I—we would like you to perform the ceremony. Would you do that?" Her gray eyes looked earnestly into his.

He reached across and took her hands. "Of course. I'd be hurt if you asked anyone else."

"Of course I wouldn't do that! Besides, whom else would I ask? Reverend Doyle?" She gave a bitter laugh. "He has not spoken to me since I refused the offer of his hand, and after the trouble with Jonah, we still aren't sure how deep his displeasure with you goes."

Again, he waved a hand, dismissing the topic. "Oh, don't worry about him. His pride was a bit bruised where you were concerned, and any disagreement he had with me, I'm sure it will all smooth over in a while. He just needs some time. When he sees what an upstanding citizen Jonah is, he'll come around."

She made a dismissive sound. "In any case, I wouldn't want him officiating at my wedding." She peered at him. "But is it all right with you? It isn't too soon?"

"It's perfectly all right. I will announce the banns this Sunday. And I'll make sure I have nothing else scheduled. Christenings and funerals and all other weddings shall have to wait!" He banged his fist on the table, rattling the various cogs and wheels, to punctuate the pronouncement. They both laughed.

"There's something else."

His laughter died at her abrupt change of tone. "What is it? Nothing wrong, is there?"

She looked at him a moment, and he was reminded of the way his mother used to look at him. Florence often tried to fill her place—another reason he was happy that she had finally found a husband of her own, a man to cherish and take care of her the way she had done for him and so many others. "We've found a place."

He frowned, not understanding. "A place?"

"Of our own." She looked down at her folded hands, a shy smile softening her features. "A farm."

Comprehension dawned. "Th-that's wonderful. It's what Jonah has wanted to do, isn't it?" Even as joy filled him, he realized the gap her news left in him. Somehow he never thought his sister would move out and have a home of her own.

Her gray eyes met his immediately, relief flooding them. "Yes. You know he used to farm. To own his own farm, why, it's something he never dreamed was possible for a mere laborer."

"Where is the farm?"

"Oh, not so far from here. A few miles down on the Uxbridge Road. You know this place will be developed over the next few years, so we wanted something farther west where it's still country. Jonah was talking with

Mr. Merriton the other week. He told him of a farm available." His sister hurried on, as if she were nervous.

"It sounds just the thing."

Her eyes remained on him.

"What is it, Flo?"

"It's for…sale."

He quirked an eyebrow upward. "And?"

"We had thought of leasing something." She swallowed. "But this one is for…sale." Again, she said the word as if it were difficult to articulate. "We went out to see it yesterday. Oh, Damien, it's perfect. Just the right size to farm without too much extra help. It's near enough to London to supply the markets. Jonah looked at the fields. He says the soil is fertile and well drained. There's a barn on the land and a good well…."

"So, what is the hitch?"

"It would require some capital."

He ran his fingers over the teeth on a cog lying on the worktable. "I see no problem with that. We have Father's money. Is it more than that?"

"Oh, no! But that money is for *both* of us. I couldn't take it."

"Is that your only concern?" He sat back, feeling a surge of relief. "That money is for us to use, however we choose to use it. It was from the sale of Father's business, and he and Mother would have wished for you and your future husband to have a home of your own."

"It must be divided equally between you and me."

"Florence, I don't need capital. I have this living. I'm provided with a house that's bigger than anything I need. Why shouldn't you have that money? If we didn't have it, I'd insist you share my house."

She swallowed, visibly moved. "I know you would. And I hope we can continue living a little longer under your roof, until the farmhouse is ready for us…that is, if we—" She stopped in confusion.

Once again, he squeezed her hands. "Of course you may stay with me as long as you wish. And you needn't say anything more about the purchase of this farm. I would love to have a look at it, of course. But otherwise, let's talk to Mr. Samuels at the bank, shall we?"

She seemed ready to argue some more, but he shook his head. Finally, she said, "I don't want to deprive you of what is rightfully yours."

"You won't be depriving me of anything. You see how this parish is destined to grow. Soon, I'll be a wealthy old vicar with more income than I know what to do with—except, of course, I know very well what to do with it."

"Yes, if I know you, it will all go to charity." She smiled indulgently at him.

"As anything extra you have does," he retorted.

They both laughed. As they quieted, he strove to reassure her once more. "I don't lack anything here, and since I'll never marry, my needs are few. You, on the other hand, might still have children." He smiled fondly, liking the thought of nieces and nephews. For so long, it seemed the two of them would remain single and childless.

She turned a deeper shade of pink. "I never thought

I would. If the good Lord would grant us offspring, I'd count myself a blessed woman indeed." She sobered. "It would help make up for Jonah's loss."

He nodded, thinking of his future brother-in-law's loss of wife and two young offspring before they had met him. Homeless and hungry they'd perished in the harsh winter after Jonah had been locked up in Newgate, victims of the enclosure laws, which were displacing farm laborers and bringing them to the cities with few skills. The Lord had, indeed, given Jonah a new chance.

His sister rose. "Well, we shan't decide anything until we've spoken to the banker. You never know. Don't say you'll never marry. I know the Lord has someone out there for you, too—a good, worthy girl who would make a fine wife, someone who would be your right hand in your ministerial duties and have the same heart for God."

He gave a wan smile, looking away from Florence, trying to appear as if the sentiment meant little to him…even as a picture of Miss Phillips flashed through his mind. His fingers tightened on the clock part. He must erase such foolishness from his very thoughts.

Lord Eldridge leaned toward her. "They tell me you are the toast of the season, my dear."

Lindsay smiled faintly at the heavyset gentleman on her right. He lifted his crystal goblet to her. "I can well believe it, from the look of you. Let me pay homage to your beauty before you are snapped up by one of these dandies who won't appreciate your charms like this old connoisseur." He took a long swallow of the burgundy.

When decently appropriate, Lindsay turned away from him and looked back down at her plate. Thankfully, Mr. Stokes, on her left, was momentarily engaged with the lady on his other side. All evening she'd felt hemmed in by his presence.

Her lips felt stiff from keeping a smile in place. She broke the crab-stuffed sole into pieces with the edge of her fork, but her stomach balked with each mouthful she forced herself to take.

She pressed her hands to her stomach now, hoping she wouldn't be sick before the night was through.

As the waiters removed the covers in preparation for the pâtés to follow, she glanced down the table at her father. By his jabbing forefinger and heightened color, she could tell he was in a heated debate with another member of the Royal Society. She sometimes wondered if she were a disappointment to him, not being a son who could follow his interests in mathematics and science. Perhaps if she'd been born with a more forceful character, she could debate with him as he so enjoyed…and refuse to marry the man he'd chosen for her.

Her father's glance strayed to her. He gave her a reassuring smile, which she forced herself to return. With a subtle nudge of his chin, he communicated his wish to her.

With a sinking heart, she turned in the direction he'd indicated.

Jerome Stokes swallowed a healthy draft of his ruby-colored wine and eyed her. His full lips were still stained crimson, and Lindsay couldn't tear her gaze away, even as a wave of repugnance filled her.

"The sole was excellent, was it not? Although I found the mullet a trifle dry." His tongue roamed over his teeth as if savoring the last remnants of fish.

She forced herself to look away from his mouth. As his wife, she would have to…kiss that mouth. "I didn't have any."

His hooded gaze wandered over her features. "You're looking a bit haggard. Haven't the megrim, have you?"

"I'm quite all right."

He eyed her plate as it was being removed. "You've barely touched your food."

"I…wasn't too hungry."

"As soon as dinner is over, I shall take you for a turn outside. That will put you to rights." He covered her gloved hand with his large one and pressed it.

She could only nod and turn away from him, knowing the real reason he would be taking her outside.

Although there were a dozen courses to be got through, and she ate little, she found the meal going by too quickly. It was with dread that she watched the final dishes being cleared. The glacé cherries had helped refresh her but it signaled the end of the meal.

As soon as the other ladies rose to go to the drawing room, she knew her time was short.

"Are you quite all right, dear?" Beatrice asked as they seated themselves. "You seemed quiet at dinner." She frowned, looking at her more closely. "You look awfully pale."

Lindsay smoothed down her silk gown. "Just a bit of headache."

The hostess came by and asked her to play a piece, and Lindsay almost jumped up at the chance to be doing something—anything—to forget for a few moments what the evening was for. She sat down at the pianoforte and looked over the sheet music. With shaking fingers, she finally settled on an ode of Handel's. As she began to play and sing, her breathing steadied, and for a little while she managed to put aside thoughts of what awaited her.

"That was charming. You have a lovely voice, Lindsay."

"Thank you," she murmured to the hostess as she resumed her place beside Beatrice. Another guest took up the instrument and Lindsay pretended to be listening to the music.

All too soon, the gentlemen rejoined the ladies. Her father wasted no time, strolling over to her with a purposeful step, bringing Mr. Stokes with him.

"My dear, Jerry tells me you were feeling a bit peaked at dinner. He suggests a stroll in the garden. It will be just the thing."

She rose slowly, trying to steady her breathing. "Yes, Papa."

Mr. Stokes took her by the elbow and led her to one of the doors to the garden.

She wrapped her shawl more tightly around her once they were in the chill night air.

"It is not too cold for you?"

"No, but perhaps we can soon return to the drawing room." All she wanted now was for the evening to be over. She'd been fretting about it and dreading it for so long that she'd decided it was best to simply comply with her father's wishes and make everyone happy.

"Yes, of course." They walked along the gravel pathway until they were a distance from the house. The lights spilled out of the upper level windows onto the dark garden.

"Your father has given me to understand I have found favor with you."

She moistened her lips. How could she pretend this was what she wanted? She tried to think of the pleasure she'd take in pleasing her father but her mind was numb. "Ye…yes…"

He took her hand in his. "In that case, I should like to ask for the honor of your hand in marriage."

She was silent for what seemed a long time. It was as if she stood poised at the edge of a cliff. Behind her was all that she was familiar with—her happy childhood spent in her mother's company, her girlhood friendships at her boarding school, even the amiable times recently with Beatrice. A brief flash of Reverend Hathaway—but no, she blocked out all that his image evoked. She would break down if she thought about him.

Finally, the word came out, a mere breath on the night air. "Yes."

"You have made me a most happy man." He took her chin in his hand and guided her face upward. Her first impulse was to pull back, but his face came down too quickly, his fingers locking onto her chin. His sweet cologne filled her nostrils, bringing a wave of nausea over her.

The next second, his wine-stained lips touched hers, and she recoiled. But he pressed against hers, hard, until she felt she would suffocate.

"Please," she gasped when he released her lips a fraction.

"You are so lovely," he breathed against her skin before assaulting her lips once more. His whiskers burned her cheeks. She tasted the residue of tobacco and port on his lips. She beat her hands against his chest, but he was immovable. Waves of dizziness swept over her.

Finally, it was over. She gulped in the night air.

"You will make me the happiest man," he murmured, his hooded eyes staring at her heaving chest. She turned away from him, shielding herself from his view.

But he reached out and took her elbow, forcing her gently but firmly around. "You will grow to like it, dearest Lindsay. I may call you that, may I not, now that we are to be wed? You'll grow to like it," he repeated, his voice a velvety threat.

"Is everything all right?"

Lindsay turned with a sharp intake of breath to face Reverend Hathaway.

His look and tone were so solicitous she had to fight the urge to throw herself upon his broad chest and ask for his protection. She had come to his Bible study feeling it her only place of refuge in the nightmare her life had become in a few short weeks.

She pressed her lips together, trying to maintain her

composure. "Yes, of course," she finally managed, the words coming out a choked laugh.

His blue eyes continued to regard her with concern. "I'm sorry if I seem to be overly inquisitive. I only wondered because of our talk the other day. I take it the Lord has answered your prayers to your satisfaction?"

She gripped her teacup more firmly, finding it harder to maintain her composure. Oh, how she wanted to confide her fears to him! "I—want so much to obey and yet—"

"And yet?"

At that moment, Jonah tapped his teaspoon against his cup, calling everyone's attention. "Miss Hathaway has finally settled on a date for the wedding. It's to be the last Saturday of this month and you are all invited to attend the ceremony, which our good parson here will perform."

At once, everyone began clapping and talking at once. Well-wishers crowded between her and Reverend Hathaway.

Turning away, she swallowed her anguish and told herself it was for the best. What could he do after all? He had enough worries of his own taking care of his parish. She wouldn't add to his burden.

Lindsay walked slowly to Miss Hathaway and Mr. Quinn. Mr. Quinn stood beside Miss Hathaway's chair and beamed at everyone who shook his hand. "Yes, I'm a blessed man. She's certainly marrying beneath her, but let's hope she'll succeed in bringing me up a smidgen more than she's managed already."

As the others laughed and Miss Hathaway looked

embarrassed, Lindsay extended her hand. "I wish both of you all happiness."

Miss Hathaway smiled at her, and Lindsay felt a sudden overwhelming pang of envy. What must it be like to be celebrating one's betrothal with a man one loved and trusted? For despite their differences in station, the couple clearly cared deeply for each other. She could see it at every Bible study in the way they deferred to one another and seemed to anticipate each other's needs.

"Thank you, my dear." Miss Hathaway glanced up at Mr. Quinn, and he looked at her at the same moment. Lindsay could see the silent understanding being communicated between the two, before Miss Hathaway turned back to her. "I hope you will know the same kind of joy."

Lindsay's mouth attempted a smile, but her lips felt wobbly as all she wanted to do was cry. Quickly she murmured her thanks and moved away, feeling as if her own world were ending when another's was beginning.

On the way home with Beatrice, her cousin, said "How happy Mr. Quinn and Miss Hathaway appeared. It was so nice of them to invite us to their wedding."

"Yes."

"I wonder what we should get them for a wedding gift. Miss Hathaway told me they will eventually be moving to a nice farm a few miles up the road from the chapel. Mr. Quinn is an experienced farmer, although he has never owned his own farm."

Lindsay turned to her in surprise. "They won't be living at the parsonage with Reverend Hathaway?"

"Well, it won't be for a while yet, she gave me to understand. Still, when they do leave, I wonder what the curate will do by himself? A parson needs a wife to help him with his duties."

"Does—" She cleared her throat, glad for the darkness in the carriage. "Is there anyone…?" Her voice trailed off.

"In Reverend Hathaway's life? I couldn't say. He is a very handsome man. I'm sure there are a dozen young ladies in his congregation who would be honored to be his wife."

For some reason the information did not cheer her. Of course there must be someone special. Reverend Hathaway was such a dear, kind man. The most noble man she'd ever met.

"It's a pity about his leg," Beatrice went on, "but I shouldn't think that would matter to a good Christian woman."

"Of course not."

"You seemed very quiet tonight." After a few moments, Beatrice added, "I'm surprised you didn't mention your own good news."

"What news?"

She could feel her cousin's stare in the dark. "What news, indeed! Why, your betrothal, of course."

Her eyes widened in alarm. "Oh no!"

"Why ever not, my dear? A young lady is usually very proud to announce such an event."

"I didn't feel it appropriate. Miss Hathaway seemed so happy. I didn't want to take away any of the attention from her this evening." Lindsay looked down at her lap, amazed at how one could feel such utter despair on one hand and sound so matter-of-fact on the other.

"That was thoughtful of you." Her cousin turned to peer out the window. "You are such a modest young lady. Most would be showing off her ring to all and sundry. Apropos of that, has Mr. Stokes given you a ring yet?"

"No. I told him there was no rush, that…we could pick it out together," she added hastily before her cousin could show her amazement again.

"Oh, well, that makes sense. You might as well sport something to your liking. I'm sure Mr. Stokes won't stint with jewelry. And once you are a married lady, your father will begin giving you your mother's diamonds and all the most valuable jewelry that has been in both families for generations."

Why did the thought give her no pleasure? She pictured herself, jewels draped about her neck. The imaginary weight suddenly felt like chains.

Her cousin continued talking, unaware of the turmoil in Lindsay. "Of course, someone at the Bible study has probably read about Mr. Stokes's marked attention to you in the papers. It has certainly captured the attention of the ton this season. You have made a brilliant match."

When Lindsay said nothing, her cousin asked, "Are you all right?"

"I'm just tired, I suppose."

"Yes, with so many parties you've been attending,

I'm surprised you have been so diligent in going to the Bible study. I commend you for it. I'm sure the curate does, too."

"I don't do it to be thought good."

"I assure you, my dear, that is not what I meant." She reached over and patted Lindsay's hand. "I do commend you all the same. It's not many young ladies of the ton who spend any thought on the things of the spirit. Their charitable works usually don't begin until they are gray haired like me," she added with a chuckle.

Would that be all Lindsay had to look forward to? Doing good works in her old age? Would she then enjoy a relative freedom, a freedom from her husband's unappreciated physical desire for her?

Her only hope for the future seemed to be that one day he would no longer find her attractive.

Chapter Six

"**D**early beloved, we are gathered together here in the sight of God, and in the face of this congregation, to join together this man and this woman in holy matrimony."

Lindsay sat near the front of the church with her cousin and listened to Reverend Hathaway's steady voice repeat the age-old words. Mr. Quinn and his bride stood with their backs to the congregation. There was not a seat to be had in the chapel. She felt honored the reverend and his sister had reserved these seats for them. The entire parish must have turned out for the ceremony.

The late-May day was a glorious one, warm and sunny, filled with birdsong.

"'It was ordained for the mutual society, help and comfort, that the one ought to have of the other, both in prosperity and adversity...'"

Would she ever come to feel this for Mr. Stokes? She could well imagine such sentiments between Mr. Quinn and Miss Hathaway. After all, their love had already been tested by the most supreme adversity.

Mutual society…comfort. Would Mr. Stokes ever offer her those? Whenever he was with her, all his attention seemed fixed on her physical proximity. They had no conversation between them, unless one counted his going on and on about some scientific interest he shared with her father. The two men could converse for hours while she sat silently by with her needlework in her lap.

"'Wilt thou love her, comfort her, honor, and keep her in sickness and in health; and, forsaking all others, keep thee only unto her, so long as ye both shall live?'"

Jonah Quinn turned to his bride. "I will." Lindsay caught her breath at the solemn look of devotion in his eyes.

How would it be to have a man look at one and pledge his life in such a manner? Her glance drifted to the curate. How handsome he looked in his priestly robes. The light streaming in from the stained-glass window caught on his short curls, turning them gold. His hands looked so fine as he held the prayer book before him.

How tenderly he repeated the question to his sister. How proud he must be of her on this day, how happy to be able to join her with the one who cherished her so.

She had grown to admire him more and more each time she attended his Bible study. He always made a point of asking her how she was, looking at her so searchingly with his blue eyes. How close she had been to confiding in him the last time! But they were always surrounded by so many people, and she didn't dare ask again for a private meeting.

Remembering Beatrice's words, she wondered again if there was a special person in his life. She had observed no young lady at the Bible study. She sighed as she sat in the church pew. To have a man like the reverend—a man who was so good and pure and true—look at her the way Mr. Quinn was looking at Miss Hathaway…

At that moment Mr. Quinn took his bride's hand in his and repeated the words the reverend spoke to him. "I, Jonah Michael Kendall Quinn, take thee, Florence Diane Hathaway, to be my wedded wife, to have and to hold from this day forward, for better for worse, for richer for poorer, in sickness and in health, to love and to cherish, till death us do part, according to God's holy ordinance; and thereto I plight thee my troth."

I plight thee my troth. A solemn promise of fidelity. To receive such a vow from a man one had such high regard for. Her gaze drifted back to the curate.

She brought herself up short at the direction of her thoughts. Reverend Hathaway was a man of the cloth. She had no right thinking of him in such a way. Had all her admiration for him been nothing but romantic infatuation?

Yet her thoughts persisted, even after the ceremony was over and the congregation exited the church. An outdoor reception was being held in the apple orchard to accommodate the entire gathering. Long tables laden with food and drink formed two rows between the trees.

Lindsay held a cup of cider in one hand, the other toying with the green ribbons of her new bonnet. Beatrice smiled beside her, her glance taking in the crowded yard. "They could not have had a better day for their wedding."

Lindsay held her face up to the warm sunshine. "No, indeed."

"Hello, my fine ladies. I am honored you could attend our humble wedding." Mr. Quinn approached them, his bride on his arm. Miss Hathaway—Mrs. Quinn now—looked radiant. For one whose complexion was naturally pale, today she had a positive bloom to her cheeks.

"Thank you for inviting us. We are honored you call us friends after such a short but most congenial acquaintance." Beatrice held out her hand to him and addressed them both warmly.

Mr. Quinn bowed over Lindsay's hand. "I hope you consider us friends, as well."

Lindsay blushed and smiled up at the large man. "Oh, yes! I wish you and Mrs. Quinn all happiness."

"We hope to be able to see you as joyously united as we are," Mrs. Quinn said with a firm shake of her hand.

"Th-thank you." She bit her lip.

The reverend joined them at that moment.

Mr. Quinn slapped him on the back. "Well, Damien, you yoked me at last." His twinkling green eyes looked at his new wife. "I have the feeling my new shackles will be tighter than those at Newgate."

The reverend chuckled in response. "Ah, but she has been the making of you, has she not?"

"Don't say I didn't warn you," Mrs. Quinn said to her husband.

"That you did, many a time." He bent down and planted a kiss on her cheek. "And you have indeed been the making of me."

"Now, see here, we are in company. You must be more circumspect."

"I think I may take some liberties on my wedding day." His arm came around his new wife's waist and he tightened his hold visibly. Then he turned to Beatrice. "Miss Yates, why don't you let me offer you some of the fine fare we have over here? You can fix a plate for yourself and your young cousin." With a wink in Lindsay's direction, he offered Beatrice his other arm.

"What a splendid idea." Beatrice added to Lindsay, "You don't mind being left with the reverend for a moment, do you?"

She blushed as she stole a look at the curate, remembering her thoughts about him in the church. "Not at all." When he didn't say anything, she hoped he didn't mind standing with her. He would be too nice to object.

Self-conscious all of a sudden, she watched the three-some stroll across the deep green lawn.

When she turned to the curate once again, a polite commonplace on her lips, her breath caught. His keen eyes were fixed on her. They reflected the blue sky above him. He'd removed his white surplice, but still maintained his long black cassock. The outfit warned her again of his office. She could feel the warmth stealing through her cheeks. "You must be very happy for your sister." Her voice came out embarrassingly breathless.

His glance finally left hers and followed the couple's progress. "Yes. Florence deserves a good husband and home of her own. She has been taking care of me, and our parents before that, and giving herself to this congregation so selflessly for many years. I am grateful that the Lord has blessed her with someone who will look after her now."

"Mr. Quinn seems awfully nice," she said, watching the ladies laugh heartily at something he had said. They reached one of the long trestle tables and he handed each one a plate.

"Yes, he is a good man. A man whom adversity has made all the stronger."

"The wedding was beautiful." She tried to think what more to say, wanting to prolong the conversation, but was mindful that, as host, he had many people to attend to.

His glance strayed to the sky. "The Lord provided a fine day—the finest."

"Yes. Mrs. Quinn looks beautiful in her gown. The ceremony was so romantic, just as a wedding should be. And he is so handsome. The two make a distinguished couple." She felt herself babbling but couldn't stop, she was so afraid he'd walk away.

His gaze met hers again. "I'm sure some young gentleman will have the privilege someday of awaiting you at the altar and you will enjoy just such a romantic ceremony of your own."

In those few seconds, she felt time stand still. Why couldn't it be Reverend Hathaway himself? The thought stunned her. It had been growing within her for some time, she realized, only she'd been too afraid to give words to it.

"Is something the matter?" His fine eyebrows drew together, his gaze never wavering from hers.

She swallowed past the lump that had formed in her throat. "I fear I shall never enjoy such a romantic day."

"Why ever would you say such a thing in such forlorn tones? You are a very young lady with much ahead of you. You must have all the gentlemen of the fashionable world at your feet."

A shuddering sigh escaped her. "I fear my papa has already chosen for me."

His frown deepened. "What are you saying, Miss Phillips?"

The words were harder to say than she'd anticipated. She dreaded them. It was as if while she'd kept the news back from these new friends, a sliver of hope remained.

"I…I am betrothed to…a man…." She could no longer bear to look at those pure blue eyes. "A man of my father's acquaintance." She stared down at the cup in her hands. "He is a man my father greatly esteems, but who is a…stranger to me."

"I am sorry, Miss Phillips, truly sorry," he said at last, as if the words were difficult for him to utter.

She felt tears welling up in her eyes, and dared not blink for fear they would overflow onto her cheeks. Oh, why had she blurted it out? She didn't want to ruin the day. She averted her head, holding her breath, afraid to sniffle.

A second later, his forefinger came under her chin, and very gently he turned her face upward. His face blurred and she couldn't keep from blinking. She felt two tears roll down her cheeks.

"My dear." He sounded so distressed at the sight of her tears.

She tried to muster a smile, her heart warmed by his words. "I didn't mean to s-say any…anything." She brought her hand to her face and sniffed. "Not on this happy day for you and Miss Hathaway—"

He dug into a pocket and handed her his handkerchief.

"Th-thank you." She turned her back to him a moment while she composed herself.

When she faced him once again, not quite ready to meet his eyes, she kept his handkerchief clutched in her fist.

His hand reached out to her but then he dropped it at his side. "Is there anything I can do? Anyone I can speak to?" His voice sounded unsteady to her ears.

She shook her head. "Papa has his heart set on—" she couldn't bring herself to utter the name "—on this."

"I see." Though his arms hung at his sides, his hands had formed fists, she noticed. "I shall pray for you," he said.

The words sounded so heartfelt, it was almost as if he were touching her. She was able to raise her eyes to his. "Oh, thank you, sir. Thank you." She put everything she couldn't say into those words.

"The Lord will not give you more than you can bear, I promise you, Miss Phillips." There was a tremor in his tone, as if he were willing to stake his life on the promise.

All she could do was nod, and trust in his words.

* * *

The parsonage loomed empty that evening after Jonah and Florence left for their honeymoon and the Nicholses had retired to their own cottage for the evening.

Never had Damien felt so at loose ends, so alone.

He could not get his mind off Miss Phillips.

The news of her betrothal stunned him. Married! She was too young. She was too—

His hands fisted futilely. Too—what?

No, the idea of her married to someone she didn't know, someone chosen for her by her father—

He prowled the confines of his workroom, too restless to tinker with his clocks. No, it didn't bear thinking on. He banged his fists against the window sash. It couldn't be. When had it happened? Why would her father compel his only daughter into a marriage that made her so unhappy?

Her distress had been too real. Even now the memory of her tears reawoke in him a desire to rescue her in some form or fashion. But who was he? He was nothing in her life. He had no right to do anything but mouth some platitudes about fortitude and courage.

How he'd wanted to wipe her tears away, take her in his arms and promise her she didn't have to marry anyone against her will. How he wished he could have offered her some real comfort!

Was that what she had sought him about when she'd asked for that meeting in the park? His mind went back to that day, trying to recall in detail her words, every nuance and inflection of her voice. She'd been glad to see him and troubled about doing the right thing. But he'd merely thought she had some trivial problem, perhaps a slight disagreement with her father or with a friend. What a fool he'd been. Hadn't he seen her quandary was nothing short of cataclysmic?

And all he'd been able to do for her today was promise to pray for her.

Well, at least he could make good on his word. He turned with renewed determination and knelt.

How soon was she to be married? Would she ever come to the parsonage again after her marriage? How he would miss her cheerful face and probing questions at the Bible study.

He dropped his face into his hands. This couldn't be! He must stop the train of his thoughts. He had one duty alone toward her, to pray for the Lord's will to be done in her life, for His grace to sustain her in whatever she must do.

A week later, Damien greeted Jonah and Florence on their return with more relief than he'd ever have imagined possible. Their absence had only highlighted his own solitary—permanently solitary—state. Someday soon, his sister and brother-in-law would depart for good, but he preferred to rejoice in their temporary return to the parsonage.

"You look wonderful. Honeymoons must agree with the two of you," he said, drawing apart from his embrace with Florence and turning to Jonah. The man gave him a bear hug that squeezed the air out of him.

With a final clap on the back, Jonah let him go. "I would recommend a honeymoon to any man."

Florence had never looked so beautiful, and she seemed…he searched for a word…softer, somehow. As if sensing his scrutiny, she busied herself talking with Elizabeth.

"So, lad, what have you been doing with yourself all these days on your own?"

Damien turned back to Jonah with a smile. "Keeping busy, you know. A parish never sleeps."

Jonah leaned his muscular frame against the large pine table in the kitchen and eyed Damien with a twinkle in his moss-green eyes. "The widows calling at all hours?"

He chuckled. "No, the widows were amazingly well behaved, although Mrs. Cooper did call with her daughter more than once."

Jonah gave a knowing nod. "She won't rest till she has you married off to young Charlotte."

Damien fiddled with the cutlery on the table. "Well, she'll have to remain restless as I'm not disposed to make any advances to her daughter."

"Glad to hear it. If you marry the young Cooper, you'll have her mother breathing down your neck for the next decades."

Damien shook his head with a smile.

Jonah suddenly asked, "How's Miss Phillips?"

Damien looked away from him. "I haven't seen her since your wedding."

"You haven't? You're neglecting your duties."

Damien frowned. "She is not in my parish."

"Excuse me if I misunderstood. I thought the young lady was coming to be discipled—isn't that the way you put it? Isn't that what you've been doing with me since you made my acquaintance?"

"Of course it is! But in this case it isn't as simple as that."

"Well, when one is a babe in the things of the Lord, it doesn't do to let a person go, if you take my meaning."

"I haven't 'let her go'!" He cleared his throat, attempting to compose his tone. "I have no opportunity to see her."

"Couldn't you have called on her and her cousin?"

"That would not be appropriate. Reverend Doyle is the parish priest, remember?" He didn't mention that he'd taken to perusing the society news in the paper. He'd seen various mentions of Miss Phillips attending the theater and opera. The name Stokes had frequently appeared linked with hers.

Jonah pursed his lips as if considering. "Well, perhaps we'll see her this weekend."

"See whom?" Florence rejoined them.

"Your brother here says he hasn't seen hide nor hair of either Miss Phillips or Miss Yates since we've been gone."

"Oh." She frowned at the two men. "Well, that isn't unusual. She must be a very busy young lady."

Damien drew in a deep breath and straightened away from the table. They might as well know. "Yes. She informed me at your wedding that she herself was betrothed."

They both looked at him round-eyed. "When did that happen?" Florence finally asked.

"I don't know. I believe recently." He cleared his throat. "At least I haven't read an announcement."

"Who's the lucky man?" Jonah rubbed his chin, his forehead creased.

He shrugged. "A Mr. Stokes, I believe." He colored as the two looked more closely at him. "The papers have mentioned his name a few times. She said it was someone her father had chosen for her."

Florence's head drew back. "Chosen by her father?" she asked sharply. "You mean it is not someone she has chosen for herself?"

Elizabeth and Jacob approached the table. Damien glanced around the group uneasily, reluctant to discuss Miss Phillips with so many. Yet, the elderly couple had known him all his life, and little went on in the parsonage without their knowledge.

"I believe not," he said at last. "She didn't say much to me. Only that her father had selected a gentleman of long-standing acquaintance. He must have a high regard for the gentleman if he has chosen him for his only child."

Jonah nodded. Florence seemed to be considering, her hand fiddling with the lace at her throat. Finally, she said, "It still seems awfully strange. It's only her first season, a time a young lady is supposed to enjoy having many suitors." She turned to Damien, a troubled look in her gray eyes. "Did she seem pleased about her betrothal?"

He considered how to answer. "You would have to ask her yourself."

She said no more. Damien felt badly about withholding the truth from his sister. He trusted her judgment, and perhaps she could help.

Later that afternoon, he knocked on her door.

"All unpacked?"

"Yes, at last. Jonah is settled in, as well," she added, then blushed and looked away at the reference to their new sleeping arrangements.

"I'm so happy for you, Flo."

She squeezed his hand. "Thank you."

"I wanted to ask you something."

"Yes?"

"Earlier, when you asked me about Miss Phillips."

She nodded, a question in her eyes.

"I didn't want to speak of it before the others, because it is none of my business, but she did not seem happy with the prospect of her betrothal."

Florence shook her head. "That is too bad. How can a father do something like that?"

"I wanted to ask if you could perhaps talk to her yourself. I have no way to—" He shoved a hand through his hair in frustration. "She is not of our congregation. Perhaps you, as a woman, could call on her."

"Of course, Damien. I shall call on her tomorrow."

He squeezed her arm. "Thank you, Flo. I knew I could count on you."

His sister would find out if there was cause to worry or not. She'd put things in perspective for him. Perhaps he'd been creating worries out of nothing, the combination of an overactive imagination and the fact that he hadn't seen Miss Phillips in so many days. Her distress may have grown to disproportionate dimensions in his mind. He could only hope that were the case.

The next evening, Florence sat with Damien and Jonah in the drawing room. Instead of relieving his worries, Florence's report of her visit only increased them. "I didn't like how Miss Phillips looked."

"Well, tell us, love, what did she look like?" Jonah asked.

"She looked very pale and acted nervously. I asked her how she'd been and she assured me everything was fine. She seemed determined to have me talk of my journey. She is really a dear thing, not selfish at all, as you'd expect of someone of her society."

Damien sat on the edge of his seat, willing himself to listen, knowing his sister would inform him of everything she thought important without his asking.

His sister looked from Jonah to Damien. "At first she didn't want to say anything, but I put her at ease and eventually managed to discover a few things."

The only sounds in the room were the ticking of the clock and the song of the cicadas coming through the open window. "More than just having no choice over her future husband, or even knowing him at all, she seems downright averse to him."

"Why doesn't she say something to her father?" Jonah demanded.

"She seems almost afraid of him." Florence shook her head. "She believes the fault is hers if she cannot warm to Mr. Stokes. Don't forget how young and impressionable she is."

Damien could sit still no longer. He got up and paced the room. What could he do to help Miss Phillips?

Jonah and Florence continued talking quietly. Damien came to stand before the empty grate, his fists on the mantel, his head bowed. Helpless and useless was how he felt.

"Did you hear me, Damien?"

Jonah's peremptory tone jerked his attention back to them.

"I said we need to get a look at this fellow for ourselves."

Damien turned slowly, hardly understanding his words. "I beg your pardon?"

"To satisfy ourselves that he's a gent worthy of Miss Phillips. Can you honestly live with yourself if you allow her to be shackled to some monster for the rest of her life, at the whim of her father—a man who might be so proud he can't be bothered with his daughter's well-being?"

When he realized Jonah was serious, Damien began to shake his head. "I'm sure Mr. Phillips has made a wise and careful choice."

"Ha! You've seen enough of these Mayfair coves to know how little they care about a person's feelings."

Damien stood staring at his brother-in-law, not liking the picture he conjured up. Perhaps he was right. They should know something about Miss Phillips's future husband, if only for their own peace of mind. He cleared his throat. "If I were to assure myself of this man's worth, how would I go about it?" He gave a nervous laugh. "I mean this gentleman and I inhabit different worlds. He has his clubs and I—" He made a futile gesture in the air.

Jonah leaned forward, a gleam in his eye. "That's it, we'll find out which clubs he belongs to." He smiled, warming to the idea. "It wouldn't hurt to get a look at the fellow, and what better way to find out a man's habits than see how he passes his leisure hours?"

Damien shook his head at his brother-in-law's unorthodox ideas. "You mean wait for the man outside his door until he comes out and get his measure just by looking at him?"

Jonah sat back and stretched out his muscular legs before him. The look in his eyes was indulgent. "That would serve little purpose but to look foolish. What I propose is to visit one of the gent's clubs and get a little information on the cove. Get his lay, if you ken my meaning. Find out his habits," he added at the look of puzzlement on Damien's face.

Damien glanced at Florence to see if she agreed that Jonah's ideas sounded ridiculous, but her attention was fixed on her husband.

Damien sighed in exasperation. "So, you think one can get into an exclusive St. James's club—for I am certain the man belongs only to the best—and sit ourselves down for an ale and watch him?"

Jonah chuckled and shook his head. "For someone who's roamed about some of the worst places of London, you remain an innocent, my friend. That's what I like about you." He folded his arms over his chest and smiled as if enjoying the conversation. "There are ways to obtain information." He held up a hand before Damien could offer further objections. "Perfectly legitimate ways. First, we find out which clubs he frequents. Then—" he grinned at both of them "—I can take care of this next part. It would just involve moseying on to the back of the club and getting friendly with some of the kitchen staff. All it takes is a waiter—"

Damien broke in. This had gone far enough. "Now, I'll not have anything illegal—"

"Perfectly legal. No one will be hurt, and no one the wiser. I'll just offer a little blunt to a waiter who seems disposed to talk."

Both Damien and his sister drew in their breaths. "A bribe?" she asked.

"I call it payment for some information. Bow Street Runners use this method all the time."

"What kind of information would you be seeking?" Damien asked in an even tone, liking the turn in the conversation less and less.

Jonah glanced at his fingernails on one hand. "There's no telling what you might find out about a person. Does he play for high stakes? Does he belong to any other clubs?"

Damien stood staring at him for some moments. His heart balked at invading a person's privacy in this manner. It seemed a violation. "That would be like listening to gossip, unreliable at best."

"Not necessarily." He pointed to his cuff. "I'll wager these new cuff links your sister gave me—" He glanced quickly at Florence with a smile. "Don't worry, love, this is how sure I feel about this bet." He turned back to Damien. "I'll wager these cuff links that if this gent belongs to some Mayfair club, he also belongs to some not-so-exclusive ones, where it won't be so hard for me to get in." He eyed the two of them. "Most men have habits they'd rather keep secret. They have no idea how much a servant or waiter is privy to."

Damien felt paralyzed. Fear for Miss Phillips's future warred with distaste for prying into an individual's life.

As if reading his thoughts, Jonah's words goaded him. "You have a moral obligation to get this toff's measure, see if the man is someone you could trust to treat Miss Phillips as he should."

Damien rubbed a hand across his mouth, not liking the options. He was almost ready to put an end to the notion when Florence spoke up. "I think Jonah is right."

Damien stared at his sister.

"You look shocked, Damien." She smoothed down her skirt. "But think about it. What if Miss Phillips is forced to enter into a union with a less-than-savory character? You didn't hear the fear in her voice." Her gray eyes looked troubled. "Perhaps it is only maidenly nerves. But what if it is more? Could we live with ourselves, as Jonah said, if we didn't do anything?"

Lord, what would You have me do? He bowed his head, his hands clasped behind him. Finally, he looked back at the two of them, his eyes coming to rest on Jonah. "Very well. Tell me what to do."

Chapter Seven

Damien blinked at the contrast between the downstairs tavern and the upstairs room they'd just entered. Here, brass-globed lights were placed at intervals along the tasteful wallpaper. A rich carpet muted the sound of their footsteps as they were led into the plush room.

In its center stood a long table. As they approached it, Damien saw at once that it held a roulette wheel. Men in evening clothes crowded around it, both sitting and standing.

It was already past midnight. Damien had spent the better part of the evening sitting in a hack, waiting for Jonah, who'd already scouted out the better gentleman's clubs, before directing their driver to this disreputable back-alley pub by Covent Garden.

Jonah, dressed in evening clothes, sauntered to the middle of the room as if he were accustomed to this sort of realm and chose a place to stand near the croupier. Damien noticed that there were no workmen in this room, as in the tavern below. They could as easily have been at a St. James's club.

Except for the presence of females. Not customers, but serving girls. They were all young and attractive. Damien and Jonah had not been there long when one sidled up to Damien and proffered a tray with pastries. The girl looked fresh and sweet, reminding him for an instant of Miss Phillips, with her golden curls. She had pale green eyes, however, and a very low-cut décolletage.

"No, thank you," he replied.

She batted her eyelashes at him, with a look that was at once demure and provocative. "If you change your mind, sir, I'm right here. Anything for your pleasure. Some champagne, sir?"

"No, thank you," he said, indicating his still-full tankard.

"I can take that for you, sir, if you prefer a bit o' the bubbly." She managed to sidle alongside him until her arm brushed his.

He felt a profound sadness. Where had this young girl come from? Her future held only degradation.

"Thank you," he repeated. "I shall let you know if I change my mind."

He turned to observe the play on the table, tense with the sense of the girl so close to him. She left him at last when he took no more notice of her. Moments later, he saw her directly across from him, trading banter with a portly, middle-aged gentleman. This man took one of the dainty pastries offered him and stuck it in his mouth.

His jaws still chewing, he put an arm around the girl's slim waist and brought her body flush up against his.

Damien felt sickened by the girl's laughter. At that second, she glanced boldly across at him, challenging him, as if to say if he didn't want her, there were those who did. Before she moved away from the man, he bent his head and whispered something in her ear, then took a coin from his bulging waistcoat pocket and slipped it in her décolletage. The girl giggled and swatted playfully at his hand. The man squeezed her waist closer before letting her go.

Damien tore his attention away from the tableau and sought Jonah. He'd already placed a chip on the red baize board. They had allotted themselves an amount to spend that night.

The wheel spun around as the men moved their stacks of chips onto the numbers. All talk ceased when the croupier called an end to the bets. The white ball clattered within the outer circle.

The men beside him bumped against him as they edged closer to the table, their focus on the wheel. The ball tumbled into the inner circle and finally came to a stop.

"Seven. Seven wins. Odds. Black pays." Sighs and murmurs rose around him as the winners raked in the chips.

The betting continued. Damien found his thoughts wandering as he observed the behavior of the people in the room. He prayed for them as he wondered what drove men to stake their money on little black and red slots on a wooden wheel. His heart felt heavy as he wondered about Miss Phillips's fiancé. Would she be shackled to a gambler? He'd heard about many a fortune being lost by a member of the ton addicted to the steep play at the gaming houses.

The play finally broke up with the arrival of more refreshments. A half-dozen attractive young women mingled with the gentlemen, laughing and offering them libations and food as the men rose from the gaming table.

"That's him over there, black coat and gold waistcoat," murmured Jonah, coming to stand near him.

Damien blinked, hardly catching the words, before Jonah moved off, hailing a girl and taking a generous helping of food.

Damien sought the man in question.

Jerome Stokes. The name had been branded in his mind since he'd first read it in the paper.

Damien's heart sank lower. Stokes was all that Damien was not. Tall and powerfully built, his wide shoulders were apparent through the snug fit of his black cutaway; his muscular calves mocked Damien's peg leg. A pristine cravat hugged a square jawline. Dark curls framed a wide forehead and aristocratic nose. Hooded eyes gave him the appearance of a romantic figure, and the image of Lord Byron flitted across Damien's mind.

Stokes was talking with another gentleman and hardly gave the young girl who approached a passing glance, merely taking the glass of champagne she offered him. At least the man wasn't a womanizer. The thought gave him little comfort.

After downing the champagne in a few gulps, Stokes and the other man moved to the door. As soon as it had closed behind them, Jonah was back at Damien's side. "Time to move on, my friend."

He matched his pace to Jonah's, neither too fast nor too slow. As they reentered the corridor, the other men's footsteps could be heard descending the stairs.

They made their way back down and retrieved their cloaks from a waiter just as the other men were leaving the building. Jonah slipped the young man a gold coin and said in an undertone, "A quid if you tell me where those two gents are off to. And hail us a cab while you're about it."

"Yes, sir!"

The waiter hurried after the two men. "I'll hail your coach, sirs," he called to them.

Jonah stood with his back to the door, taking his time hooking up his cloak. By the time they got outside, the other men were entering their coach, and a hack was drawing up near the curb. The young waiter stood holding the door open for them.

As they entered the foul-smelling cab, the man gave him an address. "Careful going there. It ain't the best part o' town."

"I'll take your advice to heart, thank you, my good man." Jonah gave the waiter another coin and joined Damien within.

As the carriage started to move, Damien asked, "Where are we off to this time?"

"An address near Smithfield Market."

He pictured the cattle market at this hour. "I imagine it's deserted this time of night."

Jonah patted his walking stick, equipped with a hidden dagger, on loan from a friend. "You'd be surprised."

When they arrived on the dark street, Jonah let himself down. "I'll instruct the driver to return in an hour. That should give me ample time."

Damien moved to the coach door. Jonah held up a hand. "No, you go with him. Find yourself a nice coffeehouse in a better part of town."

The sound of raucous laughter burst into the still night as the door to the tavern opened to let out a couple of staggering patrons. In the light from the doorway, Damien focused on Jonah's upturned face. "What do you mean?"

"These places aren't fit for a man like you. I'll find out what I need to and let you know what kind of cove this Stokes is."

Damien made to push his arm away. Jonah tightened his hold. "I wouldn't feel right letting you in there. And have no fear I'll do anything I wouldn't be able to tell Florence."

"It's not that. I trust you. But I must see for myself what this man is. Why he'd be at a place like this."

Jonah turned toward the pub. "There's usually only a few reasons a fellow would frequent such a place, and I don't believe he's a thief. That leaves only two options—either he's a drunkard or he's looking for a piece of skirt."

The last words made Damien feel sick inside. What kind of man was Miss Phillips betrothed to?

* * *

Damien drummed his fingers on the tabletop, his body feeling as tense as a hammer spring. He was ready to get up and head for the closed door, where he'd seen more than one man enter with a woman on his arm, sometimes two.

He'd been praying since he'd sat down, interceding for his brother-in-law that he wouldn't fall into temptation and forget the reason they were here, praying for the lost souls around him. As the hour grew late, his spirit grew heavy at the debauchery. More than one woman had approached him, but he'd murmured his refusal and turned away.

How different Miss Phillips was from the coarse women here. She was all that was good and pure. How he wished he could be in her refreshing presence and forget the degradation he was witnessing.

A fight nearly broke out in the time he sat there, as tempers grew short and gin bottles were emptied.

"Hey, more of the heavy wet here!" A burly man in a dark, fustian coat shiny with age, his shirt and neck cloth grimy, banged his glass against the scarred oak table.

A voluptuous waitress weaved her way over to him. "Lemme see yer blunt."

He threw down a coin, all the while ogling the woman as she bent over to retrieve it.

Damien nearly jumped at the heavy pressure of a hand on his shoulder. He gulped in relief at the sound of Jonah's voice. "Ready?"

Damien stood immediately.

They said no more until they were out of the tavern. The dank fog, mingled with the stench of the cattle market, was preferable to the smoky interior crammed with human flesh, and Damien inhaled deeply.

They heard the sound of wheels on the hard ground. "Ah, just in time, good man." The hackney rounded the corner and they quickly crossed the street toward it.

Hardly waiting for it to stop, Damien reached for the door handle.

When the coach was taking them away from the unsavory neighborhood, Damien leaned forward. "Well?" His brother-in-law hesitated. "You gave me your word you would not spare me," Damien said.

Jonah eyed him across the dark coach. "I'd tell you to take my word for it that this man is no fit husband for Miss Phillips and be done with it, but I want you to know exactly what kind of man he is."

With a heavy sigh, he began to speak.

Damien felt a red-hot rage grow inside him as Jonah's narrative unfolded of what he'd witnessed behind the closed door. Clearly, Stokes was no gentleman to respect a woman. If he couldn't treat a common prostitute with minimal decency, he wasn't to be trusted on any level.

They rode the rest of the way in silence. Damien's anger smoldered as Jonah's words played themselves in his mind. How could he help Miss Phillips avoid a terrible fate?

He had no standing, not even as her clergyman. If he were on a better footing with Reverend Doyle, he'd go to him now and ask his advice. But the rector had expressed only displeasure with Damien's conduct since his involvement in Jonah's life. His hands fisted, wishing to hit something. The image of Stokes's face appeared, shocking Damien with the intensity of his wish to strike it. Slowly, he unclenched his hands and eased back against the seat. He had never felt such rage against another human being—not since he'd been a helpless lad and teased for his lameness.

He was a man of the cloth, admonished to love his enemy.

But this man was set to defile an innocent woman—after defiling countless innocent women.

His hands fisted anew. He had to do something—anything—to help Miss Phillips escape this fate.

Dear God, You see what awaits her. Help her escape this fate.

Chapter Eight

A week later, nothing had changed. Lindsay had prayed long and hard, but each day simply brought her closer and closer to the inevitable day of her official betrothal ball. Finally, unable to bear it, she confided in her cousin.

Beatrice's kindly face expressed immediate concern. "Oh, my dear, I sensed a hesitation on your part, but I was so hoping you'd grow to care for Mr. Stokes. Your father seems so taken with the idea of your marriage to him. Can't you try to like him, my dear?"

They sat in Lindsay's boudoir, away from any servants and—most of all—away from her father's ears. Lindsay's hands knotted together. "I thought I could accept Papa's choice of husband for me." She looked away and struggled to form the next words. "But, I find I cannot…like Mr. Stokes, no matter how much I try. I have tried, truly, I have."

Beatrice reached out and covered her hands with one of her own. "I believe you. Indeed, I have seen it myself. You have made yourself perfectly agreeable and amenable to the gentleman." After a pause, she continued more slowly. "I find him unexceptionable myself, a man above reproach from all that I have observed. I would have been proud to have landed such a fine gentleman at your age."

Lindsay's shoulders slumped, wishing Beatrice could offer something more. How little they knew of this man, who appeared the perfect gentleman around others.

Beatrice shook her head. "Such a pity. Does your father know your feelings?"

Lindsay shook her head. "It would break his heart. I've tried to…to delay things, but he is so set upon my engagement."

"I understand. Oh, what are we to do?"

"I don't know. I had hoped…" She remembered the curate's kind words and sympathetic looks. His words *my dear* had echoed in her mind, but with each passing day of silence from him, they had faded, and with it the hope he'd ignited.

"Hoped what?" Beatrice asked softly.

"Nothing." She shook her head. "Some last-minute reprieve."

"It will be all right, you'll see. You shall grow to care for Mr. Stokes upon further acquaintance. A young bride is always skittish, I'm told." She ended with an embarrassed laugh. "It takes time to accustom yourselves to each other."

Lindsay looked away. She didn't know what she'd hoped for from her cousin, but she could see now that there would be no help from her. She couldn't blame Beatrice. Her cousin was wholly dependent on her father and couldn't very well contradict him.

Damien sat tinkering at a clockworks after dinner, his mind separated from the task, his fingers moving almost of their own volition, completing the familiar maneuvers.

Tonight Lindsay's betrothal would be announced. Her fate would be sealed. *And there is nothing I can do to stop it!*

The small spring he was holding popped from between his fingers and fell inside the enclosed clock housing.

With a stifled exclamation, he fished inside for it but couldn't reach it. Holding the clock steady in one hand, he reached for a screwdriver to aid him.

As he struggled to retrieve the tiny spring, he kept turning over and over in his mind what he could do to help Miss Phillips. The thought of her impending doom hadn't left him the entire day.

There must be *something* he could do. Anything. But what? Ever since Jonah's description, Damien had wanted more than ever to take Miss Phillips away and promise her that she would never have to marry the detestable Jerome Stokes.

It was too late, he'd kept telling himself, if the girl's father had made a binding agreement with the gentleman. There was nothing a poor curate could do to intervene. So far, Damien's prayers had seemed to fall on deaf ears. He must trust the Lord in this, he must!

"Ach!" The spring kept slipping from the tip of the screwdriver. He should give up this task tonight.

With a sense of relief he heard the chime of the front bell. He set the clock upright, his heart beginning to pound, the wild thought entering his mind that it was Miss Phillips.

Of course not! She'd be receiving her guests. He pictured a lavish party full of Mayfair's premier families. He couldn't help glancing at the mantel clock. Half-past seven. He sat, still and tense, unable to distinguish any sounds until footsteps approached his door, followed by a soft knock. "Yes?"

Betsy peered round his door. "The rector is here to see you," she whispered in an exaggerated fashion, her eyes round.

He gave a weary sigh as reality reasserted itself. "You showed him to the drawing room, I trust?"

"Oh, sir, I showed him into your study. He asked only for you, and seeing as Mr. and Mrs. Quinn are sitting upstairs—"

He nodded. "Thank you, Betsy. I should have known I could count on you."

She dipped a curtsy. "Oh, yes, sir. You can that."

Damien rose, feeling a kink in his neck from the hour hunched over the worktable, fretting about Miss Phillips. "Bring us some tea, will you?"

"Oh, right away, sir. And I'll make sure no one disturbs the two o' you."

He smiled faintly. "Very well, thank you." The whole household was aware of the delicate relationship between him and his superior since the incident with Jonah.

As Damien straightened his waistcoat and donned his coat, he felt a faint anxiety increase. He hadn't heard anything from the rector since Jonah's pardon. Doyle had made his displeasure known then, but until now, he'd not called to discuss the incident with Damien in any official capacity.

And yet, Damien couldn't muster more than slight concern over the rector's visit, his worry over Miss Phillips's fate overshadowing everything else.

Glancing at the small mirror by the doorway, Damien smoothed down his hair, knowing the rector was a very polished gentleman and would expect to be received by Damien in like manner. Taking a deep breath, he straightened, exited the shabby workshop and made his way down the corridor to the study.

The rector was standing before the marble fireplace, his hands clasped loosely behind him. Like Damien, he wore a black tailcoat and black knee breeches denoting his clerical office. He turned at the sound of the door. He wore no smile as he habitually did.

"Good evening, Damien. I trust I am not disturbing you at this hour."

Damien advanced into the room. "Not at all. You are always welcome here, whatever the hour."

The rector inclined his head to acknowledge the remark.

Damien indicated the upholstered armchair before the fireplace. "Please, have a seat. I have asked Betsy to bring us some tea."

"Thank you, but I believe I prefer to stand while I say what I have come to say."

Damien inclined his head in turn. The rector's tone was the solemn one he used when delivering an admonishing sermon.

Neither said anything for a few moments. Damien remained standing beside the other armchair.

"As you know, your conduct with the fugitive Quinn disappointed me deeply." A profound sigh issued from his chest. "Deeply."

The weight of the rector's words pulled Damien down anew. Ever since he'd had to go against Doyle's counsel, he'd felt the guilt of disobeying the one who'd guided and mentored him since he was an impressionable youth. "Yes," he replied, bowing his head. There was nothing he could say to alter what he had done or change the rector's opinion of his conduct. They both knew that Damien would not do anything differently if he had to do it over again.

With another sigh, the rector continued. "Since you were a lad, an unschooled boy laboring in his father's shop, I saw great promise in you. It was I who recommended you to your patron, Lord Marlborough, who in turn undertook to pay for your schooling."

The rector walked to the bow window overlooking the street, his slim hands still clasped behind him. "It was I who saw the makings of a cleric in you. I sensed a passion for the things of the Lord in your young bosom. I envisioned a great man of God preaching from the pulpit of one of our finest churches. This chapel was but the commencement. You could have aspired to my living one day, and who knows, even a bishopric—" He waved a pale hand in the air as he turned to regard Damien with something like contempt in his fine features.

He began his slow pace again, stopping at Damien's desk and picking up a small porcelain vase a parishioner had given him. "I have prepared a full report to the Bishop of London detailing your conduct in this unfortunate affair of Quinn's."

Despite his having expected no less, the news hit him like a physical blow. "I have absolved neither you nor Florence. Your conduct has been, suffice it to say, not that which behooves a member of the clergy of the Church of England or his sister."

The rector looked at Damien from beneath his dark eyebrows, which contrasted with his prematurely gray hair. "I have recommended disciplinary action for you."

Damien swallowed, not having expected that from the man who'd been his closest friend and advisor over the past decade of his life. He stared down at his loosely intertwined fingers. "It is no more than I deserve."

"I am glad you at least can recognize that."

Damien raised his eyes to meet the rector's once again. "I am not ashamed of my conduct, but I do recognize that I broke the law in harboring a fugitive."

The man's forehead furrowed at Damien's words. "You most certainly did." When Damien made no reply, the rector took another few seconds as if to compose himself before continuing. "It will undoubtedly take some weeks before I receive a reply from the bishop's office. Due process must be served. I am sure after reading my report the bishop will wish to make his own inquiry.

"Neither of us shall know for some time, therefore, what action will be taken." He drew himself up. "I would caution and admonish you in the meantime to lead an exemplary life. This marriage ceremony you performed for Florence and that criminal—" his thin lips curled in disdain as he spoke "—will do you no credit in this affair. I suggest you consider your conduct and that of your office very carefully in the coming weeks.

"Apropos of that, I have heard disturbing reports of late of the evangelical tinge to your sermons." His dark eyes narrowed. "I have warned you too lightly in the past, it seems, that you are a minister of the Church of England. You are not a dissenting preacher, shouting to the masses in a cornfield."

Before Damien could formulate any sort of reply, he heard the front bell ring again. Both men turned to the door at the sudden interruption. This time Damien was close enough to the front of the house to hear sounds of distress—a woman's voice. Damien took a step toward the door before stopping, his glance returning to the rector.

"You seem to have a situation you must attend to." He gave a nod of dismissal. "You may see to it. I shall await your return."

Before he could reach the door, Betsy knocked and opened it a crack without waiting for permission. She glanced at the rector, then back to Damien. "If you please, sir, can you come a moment—"

In a few steps Damien reached the door of the study. As soon as he looked toward the front entry, he stopped. Miss Phillips stood there. Relief flooded her eyes at the sight of him, and she took a few steps toward him before her pace faltered, as if unsure.

He quickly closed the door behind him and hurried to her, stopping himself before he grasped her hands. "Miss Phillips, what is it?" Wild thoughts raced through his mind. Somehow, the Lord had heard his plea and would use him to save her.

She was breathing heavily as if she'd run a distance. The hood of her dark satin cloak was thrown back. He'd never seen her look more elegant. Her hair was gathered atop her head amidst a crown of pale pink roses with a profusion of curls framing her face.

"Reverend Hathaway, please help me! I'm sorry to bother you at this time of night, but I didn't know where else to go."

This time he couldn't refrain from taking both her hands in his. "It's all right. You were right to come here."

Her eyes shone as they looked into his, and he felt he would do anything for her. "Tell me, what has happened?"

"I need your help!" Tracks of tears dampened her cheeks. Before she could say anything more, the two heard the sound of carriage wheels from the street. "He's followed me here—"

"Who?" Indignation filled him at the thought of Stokes coming after her. He would not permit that man to touch her!

Her hands squeezed his as her eyes implored him. "Please help me."

Without thinking, he put his arm around her slim frame to sustain her. "You have nothing to fear."

She jumped at the sound of a shout from the street. The next second a pounding on the door reverberated through the hallway. Damien braced himself and gave a nod to Betsy to answer it. He felt Miss Phillips trembling within his arms. "Please, he'll hurt me, he is so angry—"

"No one will hurt you as long as you are under my roof, Miss Phillips," he promised her, his tone resolute.

Miss Phillips cowered against him at the sight of the man framed in the doorway. Damien tightened his hold on her shoulder.

It was not her fiancé. The gentleman standing there was perhaps around the same age as Reverend Doyle. This man's hair was still a golden blond. His features were patrician, well formed and strong. He was dressed in evening clothes and carried an ebony walking stick with a heavy gold knob, which must have been what they'd heard banging against the door panels.

"Lindsay, you will disengage yourself from that—" the man's haughty gaze swept down the length of Damien, landing on his wooden leg "—clergyman. Return home with me this instant. Your guests await you." He never raised his voice, his tone sounding almost bored. Yet his eyes fixed on his daughter, as if by force of will alone he would compel her to obey him.

At the realization that the gentleman was her father, Damien began to remove his arm from Miss Phillips's shoulder, but she clung to him. "I cannot, Papa." Although her voice faltered at the beginning, by the end, there was a firmness so unlike her that Damien was convinced it was born of desperation.

"You cannot or *will* not?"

"I cannot."

Her father swung his cane back and forth as he surveyed the hallway. "So, this is where you have been sneaking off to."

Miss Phillips straightened. "Papa, this is Reverend Hathaway. His home is where I have been coming with Beatrice to study the Bible."

Instead of acknowledging the introduction, Mr. Phillips examined the head of his walking stick. "And has this man taught you to defy your parent and bring reproach on yourself, your family, and not least on an honorable *gentleman*—" he stressed the word, his glance flicking to Damien before returning to his daughter "—for the sake of a man who calls himself an officer of the church?"

"No, Papa, of course not." As if her outrage gave her courage, she left Damien's supporting arm and faced her father. "I came here because I had nowhere else to go. I told you, Papa, I could not—cannot—attend your ball tonight. I cannot—" her voice broke, and she looked down "—go through with a betrothal with Mr. Stokes.

I am…sorry, Papa, truly sorry to be a disappointment to you, but I cannot."

The door behind Damien clicked open, and Reverend Doyle entered the corridor. Damien turned, desperately thinking of how he could protect Miss Phillips from further censure.

"I heard a commotion—" The rector looked past Damien and, at the sight of father and daughter, he broke off. "Mr. Phillips, what is the trouble?"

"Reverend Doyle!" Relief filled Mr. Phillips's voice. "Perhaps you can shed some light on a most vexing situation I find myself in."

The rector looked from Mr. Phillips to his daughter, one dark eyebrow raised. "Miss Phillips, this is indeed a surprise. What brings you to the parsonage this evening?"

She looked like a fox ringed about with hounds as she stood mute, her gaze darting from one man to the other. Damien's heart went out to her, and he wished he could offer a ready explanation. Before he could speak, steps sounded on the stairs above Damien. "Damien, what is going on here?" Florence's footfalls were followed by Jonah's heavier tread.

"Nothing to alarm yourself about," he answered quietly, finding his wits at last. He strode to the front door and shut it firmly behind Mr. Phillips. Although their street was quiet at this time of night, they didn't need any more witnesses than they already had in the corridor. "Miss Phillips has merely come seeking my assistance, and I am happy to be of service to her in any way I can." He ended his words with a smile in her direction, striving to reassure her.

Florence slowed as she reached the bottom step. She gave a brief nod to the rector before turning to Miss Phillips and her father. "Good evening, Miss Phillips, how nice to see you this evening. I don't believe we have met your father."

"I'm sorry." Miss Phillips curtsied to Florence. "I didn't mean to call so late and without prior notice."

Florence waved aside her apology. "Nonsense, you know you may call upon us anytime. Pray come in, let me take your wrap."

Mr. Phillips replied before she had a chance to react. "That won't be necessary. My daughter is returning with me. She is due at her house for the grand ball given in her honor this evening. Even now, our guests must be wondering where their hosts are."

Florence gave him her attention. "I see." Even his sister seemed at a loss for what to do.

Reverend Doyle turned to Miss Phillips. "Come, my dear, your father is waiting." He nodded to Damien. "I think my business with you is finished for the moment. I can see myself out with the Phillipses."

"I cannot accompany you." Miss Phillips's voice sounded amazingly resolute. She returned to her place beside Damien.

Her father drew himself up. "Lindsay, I will only say this once more. You will return with me at once."

"I cannot return with you, Papa." She squared her shoulders, her expression firm despite the tears on her cheeks. "I have promised myself to Reverend Hathaway."

Chapter Nine

Lindsay clenched her fists within her skirts and fought the trembling threatening to overtake her whole body. A shocked chorus of exclamations surrounded her. No one was more surprised than she at the words she'd uttered.

Her eyes sought Reverend Hathaway's as silence descended.

Dear God, she pleaded inwardly, *please don't let him abandon me in my hour of need.* With a wave of relief, she read no censure in the reverend's blue eyes. Only by a slight drawing together of his eyebrows did he express a question, as if silently trying to communicate with her. All she could do was respond in kind. *Please help me! Please understand I must do this. I see no other way.*

"What is the meaning of this foolishness, Lindsay?"

Her father's voice shattered the silence and Lindsay lifted her chin to face him. She felt stronger already, trusting the curate would stand beside her no matter

what. "I have promised myself to Reverend Hathaway."
Doubt and fear quickly replaced her fledgling confidence at the stern look in her father's eyes, but she couldn't back down now.

With each passing hour, she'd realized she could not go through with the betrothal to Mr. Stokes. It wasn't until seeing the care in the reverend's eyes and feeling his strong arms around her that she'd realized where her hope lay.

She didn't know why she'd made such an outlandish claim. All she knew now was that it felt right to come to the reverend.

As she feared, her father turned on Reverend Hathaway. "What nonsense is this? I should have you thrashed for such impertinence."

Reverend Hathaway came to stand beside her. "It is as your daughter has said," he responded quietly.

Relief swept through her with such intensity she felt her knees would buckle. As if understanding this, Reverend Hathaway's arm came up once again to sustain her. He would not abandon her.

Her father responded with a dry bark of a laugh. "Who are you to stand in the same room with my daughter?" His look of scorn swept the length of the reverend. "Before you are so quick to steal my daughter, let me inform you, she is not of age, and as such, penniless."

"I neither desire nor expect anything that is yours."

"I will not have some maimed, fortune-hunting curate—" he spat out the words "—come between my daughter and her future husband, a *gentleman* of her own station and wealth." With a last sniff of dismissal, he turned his attention back to Lindsay. "You will return with me this instant and behave like the daughter I have brought you up to be, worthy of the name Phillips."

"I told you, Papa, I am promised to Reverend Hathaway."

"You are not in your right mind. Now, you will obey me or you will be forced to suffer the consequences." Without a word, he turned on his heel and headed to the door.

Lindsay didn't move, though fear filled her once more. Her father opened the front door and called his groom and coachman with a sharp command. When the two men entered the house, her father indicated her with a jut of his chin. "Please escort Miss Phillips to the coach."

The two men approached her, their glances shifting away, as if ashamed of what they were to do. But their footsteps were resolute.

Panic filled her. She could not go back with her father! She drew against the reverend's strong frame. But what could he do against her father and his servants?

As they reached her, she blurted out, "I have lost my virtue to Reverend Hathaway."

The phrase rang in the room, words she'd read in a gothic novel. At the moment she felt as trapped as the heroine in the dark tower at the mercy of the wicked villain. Her only hope was for the hero to rescue her.

The next moment, pandemonium broke out.

In two strides her father reached her. His enraged eyes looked into hers and a vein throbbed in his temple.

The next second he raised his arm. She flinched, cowering against the reverend.

Before her father could strike her, Reverend Hathaway stepped between them. "You will lay no hand on your daughter."

"Out of my way, you blackguard."

The curate didn't move. Afraid of what her father would do to him, Lindsay tried to come around him, but he held out his arm, rigid as steel, blocking her from her father's wrath.

"Who are you to speak to me in that tone of voice?"

"You heard your daughter. Miss Phillips has given herself to me and I intend to marry her." His normally gentle voice resonated with strength and purpose.

She clung to his forearm. She realized the enormity of what she'd accused him of, yet he had not betrayed her! The realization resonated within her, making her body limp with relief.

"Damien!" Mrs. Quinn's shocked tone echoed behind them.

"I will call the constable and have this man who wears the collar arrested for violating my daughter."

Her father wouldn't—no, no! But the set of his jaw was rigid. She had to do something.

She stepped away from the reverend's sheltering body and faced her father. "I will tell Mr. Stokes what I have told you," she said. "He will not want me if he knows I am ruined."

Her father looked down the length of his aristocratic nose at her. "Am I to understand my daughter, my only offspring—a Phillips—has given herself to a third-rate cleric?"

She quaked under the scorn of her father's eyes. Knowing there was no return from the step she was taking, she nodded her head. "Yes, Papa. We are as man and wife."

He took a step away as if the very air around her were befouled. "Then you are no longer a daughter of mine."

Inwardly, she recoiled as if he had struck her, but she stood still as if the words had not moved her.

"Damien, is this charge true?" Reverend Doyle's harsh tone broke the stillness.

Before he could respond, Mrs. Quinn stepped forward. "Of course it's not true. My brother would never—"

"I will honor Miss Phillips by marrying her."

His sister stared at her brother, her mouth agape.

"Then you may have the strumpet." Without another word, her father turned on his heel and left the house.

"You will hear from me." The rector's censorious words echoed in the stillness as he, too, let himself out of the house.

In the quiet that followed, Lindsay dared raise her eyes to the curate. Her lip trembled. "I'm sorry! I n-never meant to r-ruin you!" The tears overflowed her eyes and she could hardly get the words out. "I—I didn't k-know wh-what else to d-do!"

"That's all right, my dear." His arms came around her and she began to sob in earnest against his broad chest, the tension of the entire day draining out of her. Oh, that she never had to leave his warm embrace. "Don't cry. You are safe here," he murmured against her hair.

She was hardly aware of the retreating footsteps of the others. When she was able to raise her head, she found herself alone with Reverend Hathaway. He offered her his handkerchief, his eyes showing concern.

She turned away from him, her shoulders bowed with shame. What had she done? The words had burst from her out of fear and desperation. But now she had dragged an innocent man into her calamity. A moan of despair escaped her.

Reverend Hathaway touched her arm. "Come, my dear, why don't we go into the study?" he said gently. "It's quiet there and you can sit down. My sister is getting you some tea. You must be quite done in."

She looked into his eyes, wondering how he could be so calm. His gentle tones bespoke assurance and confidence, as if she had not just ripped apart his world.

Without a word, he led her through the nearest doorway. She hardly registered where she was although a sense of well-being enveloped her at once. The reverend guided her to an armchair. "Let me take your cloak."

She fumbled with the clasp, her fingers stiff. Seeing her clumsiness, he assisted her. "Your hands are like ice." He began to chafe them. As she looked up into his eyes, he let her hands go suddenly and stepped back a pace. He quickly undid the clasp and removed her cloak.

"Please be seated. I shall return in a thrice."

Left alone, the weight of shame descended once again upon her.

Moments later, she started at the sound of the door opening. "I didn't know what else to do. Please forgive me for involving you in my falsehood," she said, as soon as the reverend reappeared.

In a few strides he was at her side and took her hands in his again, his thumbs rubbing the tops of them. "Hush now, there's nothing to forgive." His voice was tender and the massaging motion of his warm fingers soothed her skin.

"But what are you going to do? I've ruined you." Tears filled her eyes and her voice shook.

He pressed her hands in his. "Don't distress yourself. We shall find a way out. There now," he murmured. "Tell me what happened tonight."

Staring at him, unable to understand how he could take it so calmly, she finally nodded. He rose and took the seat opposite her.

She clasped her hands in her lap, still feeling the touch of his fingers. "I don't know if you remember but tonight was the ball my father had planned for me to announce my betrothal to Mr. Stokes."

"Yes, I know." His glance shifted from hers. "I've been praying for you all these days."

Surprise and gratitude filled her that he should have thought of her. "Thank you."

"Please, go on."

She clutched his handkerchief, which she still held. "I had fully intended to comply with my father's wishes...to go through with everything. My cousin helped me dress. My father had ordered a new gown for me."

He glanced down at her. "You look beautiful tonight."

She had taken no pleasure in donning the white satin

gown with its yards of lace adorning the bodice, hem and tiny puffed sleeves. "Th-thank you," she whispered, suddenly feeling shy under his gaze. Did he think she was beautiful? Or had she lost his respect and admiration forever with her scandalous behavior?

"I had been trying—" she took a deep breath, bracing herself to go on "—all these days to speak to my father about my reluctance to go through with this betrothal. But it is so very difficult…to speak to my father once his mind is made up. His intentions are good. I know he loves me—" Her voice caught, remembering her father's repudiation of her this evening.

She had lost his love forever.

"I'm sure your father will come to understand your fears."

She dared look across at Reverend Hathaway, and once again was undone by the tender look in his eyes. "I wish you were right, but I know my father. He values rationality above all. He rarely loses his temper, but when he loses his respect for someone—" she twisted her hands together, remembering again the full brunt of her father's scorn "—he will cut them off as if they are worthless."

Reverend Hathaway shook his head and seemed about to say more but remained silent.

At that moment, the door opened and Mrs. Quinn entered the study. "Here you go, Miss Phillips, a cup of tea. That should help settle your nerves."

She hardly dared face Mrs. Quinn. What must she think of her? "Th-thank you."

Mrs. Quinn set the cup and saucer on a small table beside the chair.

"I—I'm sorr—"

Before she could finish, Mrs. Quinn put her hand over Lindsay's. "There now, none of that. We'll sort everything out in the morning." She glanced toward her brother. "Damien will know what to do."

Lindsay pressed her lips together, uncertainty filling her. How was he going to survive the dishonor?

"What you need now is to drink your tea and come up to bed. A good night's rest will help you see things more clearly in the morning."

She hadn't even thought that far ahead, to where she would spend the night. "I—I didn't think when I ran away tonight. I've brought nothing with me."

"I've laid out one of my nightgowns and a dressing gown for you." She straightened and turned to her brother again. "I shall put her in Jonah's old room, if that is all right with you."

"Of course," the reverend said. "Thank you, Florence."

"You'll find everything you need up there, Miss Phillips. We usually have spare things, since we are used to receiving unexpected guests."

Lindsay colored at the mention of "unexpected." "I apologize."

Mrs. Quinn smiled. "Hush, or you shall truly displease me." She smoothed the front of her gown. "Now, when you are ready, Damien shall escort you up to your room. If you need any assistance, I can help you. I've sent Betsy home already."

"Yes, thank you," she murmured, embarrassed again. She didn't have her maid with her but would certainly not want to bother Mrs. Quinn. "I shall be fine by myself, I assure you."

"Well, if you change your mind, don't hesitate to tell Damien. He can summon me. I shall bid you both good night then."

When they were alone once again, the reverend said, "Pray continue with what you were telling me."

"Won't your sister wonder…shouldn't I explain to her, as well?"

"It's all right. I shall fill her in with whatever I feel she needs to know in the morning. Please, don't worry. As she said, we are used to receiving all kinds of people here." He smiled slightly. "Don't forget, it was my sister who brought home a fugitive from the law."

She couldn't help a smile, but quickly sobered as she considered his comparison of her to a former criminal and fugitive. Whose crime was worse, she wondered?

As if sensing her distress, he said gently, "Here, drink your tea before it gets cold. It'll do you good."

"Yes." She turned her attention to the cup, trying to still the trembling in her hands as she lifted it. "I can hardly think."

"You were telling me how difficult you found it to express your…aversion to Mr. Stokes."

She nodded. "Papa had his heart set on this betrothal. I tried to like Mr. Stokes, truly I did. But the more I was with him, the greater my…" How could she describe what the man made her feel?

"That's quite all right. I understand. You needn't go any further."

"Thank you," she whispered. They sat in silence a few moments. Lindsay ventured to take a small sip of tea. After a moment, she felt herself able to continue. "He frightened me. The way he always looked at me." *The way he took every opportunity to touch me,* she thought, too ashamed to say it to the reverend. Instead she shuddered. "It made me feel…dirty."

"Yes, quite." The words were clipped, and his jaw set as if what she'd said displeased him.

She flushed, realizing how unseemly her conversation was. "I'm sorry. I shouldn't be speaking this way."

"No, it's quite all right. You did right to come to me this evening. You shall not be forced into a wedding you are not willing to enter into. I can promise you that."

When she'd finished her tea, he stood. "Come, you must be exhausted. I'll take you up to your room." He lit a candle for her from the hall table and handed it to her.

"Thank you." She followed him up the dim staircase. For a second her heart ached at the sound and sight of his wooden leg as he ascended. If he'd been born in her sphere, how he would have shone at tonight's ball, dressed in evening clothes. What a dashing figure he would have cut! If he had been her intended, how she would have looked forward to tonight's announcement and celebration of her upcoming nuptials. She wouldn't have cared if he had a wooden leg.

Instead, she'd forced him into a declaration. Oh, what had she brought upon him?

He stopped outside a door at the far end of the corridor and turned to her with a smile. "Good night, Miss Phillips. Please don't worry about anything. We'll talk in the morning. But, please, there is no hurry. Sleep as late as you'd like."

"Thank you. I don't know what I would have done if you hadn't—" Her voice broke.

He lifted a hand as if to comfort her, but then dropped it. "There now, none of that. You did the right thing. Sleep well. May the Lord grant you a peaceful rest tonight."

She bit her lip, her heart too full to say anything more. With a nod of her head, she turned and entered her room.

Damien stood outside Miss Phillips's door a moment. What an astounding turn of events. He could hardly fathom it.

One fact kept leaping out at him. *The Lord heard my prayer.* Not in any way he could have imagined, but that mattered little. The important thing was that Miss Phillips was no longer in danger of marrying the dissolute Stokes. Relief and joy flooded him.

He hardly dared think of the rest. Even now the thought that he and Miss Phillips would wed was so inconceivable he could not yet grasp it.

After a largely sleepless night, turning everything over in his mind, he was up at first light. As soon as he sat down with a cup of tea in the kitchen, both Florence and Jonah entered the room. "You are down early."

Florence gave him a slight smile. "Could any of us

be expected to sleep much last night?" She looked around her. "Miss Phillips has not yet arisen?"

He shook his head. "I told her to stay upstairs as long as she liked this morning when I bade her good night."

"That's good. It will give us a chance to talk."

They remained quiet as they served themselves. As soon as they had said the blessing, Florence looked up. "Miss Phillips didn't say anything last night about why she should make such a terrible accusation against you?"

His brother-in-law was looking at him with sympathy in his green eyes. "Poor thing looked done in last night," he said, pouring some cream over his porridge. "I'd be surprised if she could string together a decent sentence."

Damien sighed. "Yes, she was quite overwrought."

Florence looked from one man to the other. "But to make such outrageous accusations! I would never have credited it of her. She has always behaved with decorum." She shook her head. "What is to be done now? If only Reverend Doyle had not witnessed it all, we might have salvaged the situation. There is no telling what he will do. Apropos, why was he here last night?"

Damien braced himself. He hadn't decided how much to share with Florence, but he knew she'd have to be told everything eventually. "He came to inform me of the report he has sent to the bishop."

Florence's teacup stopped halfway to her mouth. "What has he said?"

"He has recommended disciplinary action for my part in Jonah's escape."

"Insufferable jackanapes!" Jonah looked at Damien sheepishly. "I didn't mean for you to have to pay for my actions."

"Of course you didn't. Don't worry, the bishop is going to look at the entire matter, including the prince's pardon of you. I can't imagine he will want to censure me in light of that."

Florence pursed her lips. "Except for the fact that after Miss Phillips's conduct last night, Reverend Doyle now has plenty to fault you with."

Damien could find nothing to say.

"Do you think the girl's father really meant what he said about cutting her off?" Jonah asked.

Damien picked up a fork and toyed with it. "She is his only child. I can hardly imagine he'd repudiate her forever, especially if she came to him and confessed she'd made up the whole story." He looked from one to another. The moment of truth had arrived. "However, I don't believe she will want to do that, not in the immediate future, nor would I advise her to."

Florence drew her breath in sharply. "Why ever not?"

"Because it would mean she would be forced to wed the man her father has chosen for her. I believe Miss Phillips said what she did last night because it was the only way of escape she could see."

"Even if it means your ruin?" He knew his sister's angry tone only expressed her frustration.

"You are not wholly aware of the kind of man Mr. Stokes is, so I can understand your feelings." He glanced at Jonah. "I believe when you hear what Jonah has to tell you about him, you will agree that anything is preferable to her marrying him."

Jonah nodded grimly. "The man is a wolf in sheep's clothing, no doubt about it, my dear. If the girl weds him, she'll be ruined herself. I shall fill you in after breakfast."

Florence's lips tightened and she looked down at her plate. "How could her father have chosen such a man for his only daughter?"

Jonah threw down his napkin. "Because the knave belongs to all the right clubs, travels in Mr. Phillips's circles and probably toadies up to him. Don't forget, Miss Phillips is worth quite a penny. As is this Stokes. You know how these gentry coves are, they want to keep their wealth together." He shrugged, then grinned at Damien. "'Course, she's a pauper now. That doesn't mean anything to you though, does it, Parson?"

Damien shook his head slowly, amazed as always by his brother-in-law's discernment. It was as if Jonah had already guessed the course Damien had decided upon.

Florence shook her head at him. "You, Jonah, are a hopeless romantic. What is to be done when rumors of this come to the congregation and there is talk about things Damien is wholly innocent of?" When her husband said nothing but continued to regard Damien with a speculative look in his eye, Florence turned to him. "If I can talk no sense into either of you, what is left to do? Calmly accept your ruin? After all the years of sacrifice to see you where you are today?"

Damien looked down at the bowl of porridge he'd hardly touched, marshaling his thoughts. The first hurdle would be presenting his decision to his sister. He needed her on his side. Folding his hands together on the edge of the tablecloth and clearing his throat, he looked across at her. "The first thing to be done is to marry Miss Phillips as soon as possible." At the look of disbelief in her gray eyes, he continued quickly. "I will try to obtain a special license directly from the archbishop this morning. Obviously, after last night, the rector would be unwilling to perform the ceremony, but I believe I can ask a colleague of mine who lives in—"

"Damien, you can't be serious—"

"Why shouldn't the lad be serious?" Jonah cut in. "You've been telling me all along he should wed. Well, now's the perfect opportunity."

She turned upon her husband. "You cannot encourage Damien in this madness! Goodness, Jonah, don't you understand the magnitude of what that girl has done to him with her careless words last evening?" She turned back to Damien before Jonah had a chance to respond. "Even if you did marry her, it will not erase the accusations. People will believe you actually stole a young maiden's virtue!" She shook her head, as if too distraught to utter another word.

"I understand what you are saying, Flo, and I agree. However, after careful thought and much prayer, I have concluded that for the immediate future, there is no recourse but to marry Miss Phillips. Her father will not take her back unless she agrees to wed Mr. Stokes.

And that is clearly out of the question. In the meantime, she has nowhere to go. She has no one but her cousin, who is completely beholden to her father. Even if she had family to turn to now, she is ruined. No, she must marry."

He held up his hand when he saw Florence about to speak. "Before you say anything, hear me out." He looked down at his place setting, the next part more difficult to say than the previous. "When I say I will marry Miss Phillips at the soonest possible date, I mean I will marry her in name only."

A profound silence greeted his words. When he ventured to look up, he saw them both looking at him, dumbfounded. He cleared his throat, fighting embarrassment. "I will give Miss Phillips my name and protection, but I shall not touch her." He felt his neck flush with color. "I cannot believe her father will cut her off forever. Someday when they are reconciled, I want to be able to release Miss Phillips from any connection to me so that she may return to her father in the same condition in which she came to us. When she is of age, free to marry someone of her own choosing, and of her own station, she will be able to return to her world and enjoy that which is rightfully hers."

Florence continued staring at him. Finally, drawing in a long breath, she said, "Regardless of how much you selflessly sacrifice for her sake, her name will still be ruined."

He bowed his head a fraction. "That may be true, but in time, memories will fade. Miss Phillips will be a wealthy young lady, with all the attributes of beauty and breeding you have seen for yourself. I am certain there will be a gentleman who will appreciate her for what she truly is and love her the way she deserves. I do not want to deprive her of that opportunity."

"Might you not be that man?"

He regarded his brother-in-law for long seconds. Finally, he said, "No. My life would be no life for her. It would not be fair to require someone of her station and upbringing to share in my calling."

All was quiet for a moment.

"And if she loves you, lad?" Jonah's soft voice broke the stillness.

Was that sympathy or pity in his brother-in-law's eyes? Did it matter? No. He'd had long moments of dreaming about winning Miss Phillips's love last night and had discarded such flights of fancy as hopeless wishes to be relegated to the deepest recesses of his heart, to be witnessed only by himself and God.

"She is young and impressionable. If she came to me last night, it was because she was desperate and had no one else to turn to. Perhaps my role as Bible teacher has won her confidence. But I will not take advantage of that. Someday she will want to return to the world she belongs to."

Jonah said nothing more, sitting back in his chair with a sigh.

"And what are we to tell Reverend Doyle? What will he say when he hears of your hasty marriage?" said Florence quietly.

"Mayhap he'll be pleased because Miss Phillips is a lady," Jonah said with a shrug.

"But not one he has chosen," she immediately countered. "And one who has been disowned by her own father, a powerful man in his congregation." She sighed. "It will only need that he bring this to the attention of the Bishop of London."

Damien acknowledged what she was saying. He'd thought it all through last night. "I'm willing to pay the price."

She raised a skeptical brow. "For her?"

He could not answer directly. How to tell Florence that he would do anything Miss Phillips asked of him? That his heart had swelled with pride last night when she'd come to him, when she'd thought of *him* as her knight in shining armor? That she came to him penniless and he could offer her every material good he had. "It's the right thing to do. The *only* thing to do."

Florence looked at him a moment. Then, reaching for her husband's hand, she addressed Damien. "Very well, you know we stand behind you in whatever way you choose."

Jonah's large hand wrapped around his wife's and he nodded. "That you know, lad. Come what may, we'll be behind you."

Damien's throat tightened up and he barely managed a whispered thank-you.

The next interview was perhaps equally difficult. He'd spent the rest of the morning in his workshop, tinkering with a French ormolu clock that needed cleaning. But his ear had been attuned to the slightest sound as he listened for Miss Phillips to come down.

Around ten o'clock he heard his sister leave for the market. Through the back window, he observed Jonah making his way to the fields with Jacob. Betsy and Elizabeth came out a few moments later and began hanging out laundry. The day was clear but with a brisk breeze that whipped at the wet garments as they were pinned to the long lines. He could almost smell the fresh scent of windblown linens.

He turned back to the clock escapement and carefully placed a drop of oil on a gear tooth. With a rag, he rubbed it over the rest of the teeth.

The chimes of another clock on the shelf across the room had just rung eleven when he heard footsteps on the stairs. He set down his rag and made his way to the corridor.

Miss Phillips stood hesitating at the foot of the stairs. At the sight of him, she started, her hand going to her throat, as if she hadn't expected to see him there. "Good morning."

He smiled. She looked well rested though still pale. He recognized her gown as one of Florence's. The flowers were gone from her hair and it was dressed simply, but she looked as beautiful as the finest porcelain figurine. "Good morning. I trust you slept well."

"Yes. I'm sorry, I seem to have overslept. Has everyone breakfasted? I couldn't get to sleep right away."

"I understand. We all had a bit of difficulty sleeping.

Come, why don't you breakfast now? I believe my sister has gone out, but I'll tell Mrs. Nichols to fetch you some fresh tea. Would you care for some porridge or bread and butter?"

"Anything would be fine."

When he'd shown her to the dining room and given Elizabeth instructions, he smiled at Miss Phillips. "Just fetch me from the workshop when you've breakfasted." He gripped the back of a chair and looked down at the table. "I think we should talk."

"Yes," she said in a low tone.

Once again, he waited in his workshop, this time more nervous than before. He gave up any attempt at work, his fingers incapable of grasping the minuscule screws and springs.

Hardly a quarter of an hour had passed when he heard a soft knock on the door. "Come in."

"You wished to see me."

He rose and ushered her in. "Yes, I thought it might help if we talk a little about—" he could feel his cheeks redden "—what we plan to do."

"Of course." She entered hesitantly, her eyes widening at the sight of all the clocks. Her glance came back to him, puzzled. "I didn't know...you are a clockmaker?"

"Mainly a repairer of clocks these days, when I have a few moments to spare. My father was a clockmaker," he explained.

She nodded. "I remember."

He stood, very aware of his wooden leg in the small

space. "We can sit in the drawing room upstairs or in my study if you prefer."

"No, this is fine." She looked around for a place to sit, and he hurried to bring the only other chair over to the table.

She sat down primly, her slim hands folded on her lap. "What an interesting collection of clocks." She studied the parts of one that he had laid out on his worktable.

He smiled ruefully. "Studying their inner workings seems to help me puzzle out things I'm facing as curate."

She moistened her lips. "I see."

When she said nothing more, he turned away from the clock pieces and gave her his full attention. Suddenly, his palms felt sweaty and his collar too tight. Would she think him completely mad to suggest what he was going to suggest? But what other course was there? He cleared his throat. "I gave a lot of thought to your situation last night."

Her stricken eyes met his. "I'm sorry for all the trouble I've caused you. I've been thinking. I shall go back to my father this morning and confess the truth—"

"No!" When she blinked at his sharp tone, he attempted to continue more calmly. "What I mean is…I don't think that's the best course for you to follow."

She twisted her hands together on her lap, clearly distraught. "What I did to you was unforgivable. My only excuse is that I was not thinking clearly. I can only hope what was said last night will go no further and that I can somehow make amends." Her voice choked and he reached out a hand to her.

"No more apologies. Please believe that I understand why you did what you did last night." He cleared his throat, trying to keep from reaching out and comforting her the way he wished. "What I wanted to discuss with you is what I believe is the, ahem, best solution for the present."

She sat quietly, waiting for him to continue. He felt his face flush. Fixing his gaze on a small clock spring lying on the table, he said, "I believe we should marry as soon as possible."

He glanced at her. Instead of laughing at him, a look of relief seemed to pass over her features. "Yes."

He let out an inaudible breath he didn't realize he'd been holding. The worst was over. He could face anything else.

He hurried on. "We won't really be married, I mean in the, ah, conventional sense." Again, his neck felt too thick for his collar and his cheeks were hot.

She blinked. "Not really married? I don't understand."

He coughed. "I mean we shall be married. I shall apply for a special license, so we needn't wait for the banns to be posted or hold the ceremony in our own parish. But," he said, and swallowed, unable to look at her, "we shan't be sharing a bedroom."

When she said nothing, he stole a glance at her. She frowned in puzzlement. "But all married people have separate bedrooms."

He realized in that moment how innocent she was. "Yes, er, that may be true of the families in your social sphere. But most married couples share a bed. What I mean to say is that, unlike what you told your father last evening, your virtue will remain intact while you remain under my protection. We will not…uh…be joined in the way God intended when he brought man and woman together in holy matrimony. There will be no children in our union." He hurried on, wanting to get this subject over with as quickly as possible. "You will have your own room here at the parsonage and I wouldn't expect you to do what a curate's wife is expected to do. I mean in an official capacity, although the parishioners will, of course, believe we are truly married."

"I see." She was no longer looking at him. "When I told Papa…when I involved you in this—my situation—I was ready to accept the consequences of my words. I'm willing to become your wife…fully."

His heart leaped—she could be his in every way he'd dreamed. Then it tumbled back down to grim reality. She didn't realize what she would be giving up. "I…thank you. Your words mean a lot to me." On an impulse he reached across to her and tenderly touched a lock of her hair. She looked up at him then and he read longing and fear. He smiled sadly. "But I am not willing to take advantage of your trust."

At the question in her eyes, he attempted to explain. "You are very young. You have your life ahead of you." She began to shake her head and he stopped her with a motion of his hand. "You came to me out of desperation. I am here to help you in any way I can as your brother in our Lord Jesus Christ. I agree to be espoused to you in name only, to shelter and protect you as long

as you need until such a time as you choose—or can—
return to your own home."

At the renewed shaking of her head, he leaned back
in his chair. "I know you don't believe it now, but someday your father will realize what he has done. He will
want you back."

"No."

The word came out stark and uncompromising. He
continued, making his voice more resolute than he felt.
"You are his only offspring, his only daughter. He will
not have you throw your life away on being a mere
curate's wife. He will come to his senses and offer you
your home once again."

"He may view it as throwing away my life, but I do not."

"Your father has behaved precipitously. I'm certain
in time he will seek a reconciliation. When that happens,
I want to be able to say to him truthfully that you can
return to your world as pure and untouched as on the
evening you sought refuge here. By having this
marriage annulled you can resume your old life, and
someday—" he pressed his lips together and looked
away, finding the next words difficult "—marry a man
of your own choosing."

It seemed as if she wanted to interrupt him but then she
stopped, and he plowed on. "Someone you can love, and
who will be the kind of man who is worthy of your love."

She bit her lower lip, a sheen appearing on her eyes,
and his heart constricted, appalled that he would make
her cry. Before he could know what to do, she rose and
walked to the window.

"You don't know my father if you think he will seek a reconciliation." Her voice sounded calm, and Damien wondered if he had imagined the tears.

"He is very hurt and angry right now, I'll allow. At the very least, pride will prevent him from coming to you. But given time, perhaps a few years, when you are of age, I am sure the two of you will want to mend this breach."

She touched the lacy undercurtain. "Do you really think so?" Her tone sounded skeptical.

"Yes, by God's grace." He strove to infuse his words with encouragement. "When that happens, I will not have you yoked in an unequal union that may have long since grown burdensome to you, which you only entered into out of desperation because you had no other recourse."

Again she bit her lip, her fingers clutching the lace curtain, but she said nothing.

Unable to stop himself, he stood and went to her. He reached out a hand, wanting to touch her, but stopped short, making a fist instead. "What is it? Have I said something to displease you?"

"No," she whispered, dropping the curtain and half turning from him. "It's nothing. You are too good to me. Let us…hope you are right and that my father will be more forgiving in a few years."

"You'll see. He will accept you back in your own home. You will have reached your majority and will be free to choose a husband of your own—"

Her large brown eyes turned to him, this time the sheen unmistakable. "Please, say no more, I beg of you."

How he wanted to take her in his arms. But he had no right. As he struggled with himself, she walked past him.

Startled, he stepped back.

She paused at the door. "If that is all, please excuse me."

He nodded his head. "Of course."

She bobbed a quick curtsy. "I will do whatever you think best. I await your further instructions."

Damien stared after the door, its quiet echo like a death knell in the cluttered workroom. Although it had cost him more than she could ever know to speak the words he had, he was not the only one in turmoil. Despite his best efforts to assist Miss Phillips, he could see that he had wounded her—deeply.

Chapter Ten

"Dearly beloved, we are gathered together here in the sight of God…"

Lindsay had just heard those words at the marriage of the Quinns. And now, they were being spoken for her and Reverend Hathaway—Damien, she corrected herself. She still blushed remembering when he'd first asked her to call him by his given name, only a few days before the wedding. Everything had happened so quickly, she could scarcely believe she now stood at the altar with him. Her greatest fear had been that somehow her father would stop the wedding.

She inhaled deeply, only now beginning to believe she would well and truly be Mrs. Damien Hathaway. She snuck a peek at her soon-to-be husband's profile through her thin veil. He was staring straight ahead at the young curate performing the ceremony.

Damien had introduced her to his former classmate and friend, but Lindsay couldn't remember the clergyman's name. So many times in the rush of the morning she had felt giddy with nerves. But Florence's firm presence and Beatrice's tender counsel had carried her through and now she stood, ready to repeat the solemn vows of love, honor and fidelity to the man standing so seriously beside her.

There hadn't even been time to have a proper wedding dress made. Dear Beatrice and her personal maid had contrived to smuggle out many of Lindsay's gowns from home—her father had not permitted her to retrieve anything herself from her house. Lindsay had gone once to her home, only to find the butler she'd known since childhood not permitting her entry.

That had hurt more than her father's anger and disdain the night of her flight. This was evidence of the cold rancor her father now harbored. She knew nothing would move him, despite what Damien had told her.

Today, she wore her best gown, thanks to Beatrice— an ivory muslin. Beatrice had purchased matching silk ribbons to replace the blue ones that had decorated it before. On her head, she wore a crown of white silk rosebuds atop the lacy veil Beatrice had fashioned for her.

She glanced to her future husband again. He looked as serene as always. Unlike her, he seemed to be listening closely to the solemn words being uttered on the state of holy matrimony. Lindsay could not seem to focus on anything that morning. All her thoughts came back to one: was she ruining Reverend Hathaway's life? She'd asked herself the question so many times in the darkness when sleep refused to come that it had become a refrain with no answer. He had been nothing but attentive and kind in the days following her terrible lie to her father, but always she detected a curtain across Damien's blue eyes. There were things he was not showing her. Was he trying to protect her, or merely shielding her in his unselfish way from the upheaval she was causing in his life?

His sister had made it plain that Lindsay had done an unforgivable thing. Not in direct words. She'd welcomed Lindsay into the parsonage and congratulated her on the upcoming nuptials. But in the days leading up to the hasty marriage, Florence had attempted to show her the different tasks the mistress of the parsonage carried out. The more she showed her, the more ignorant Lindsay felt. Florence had not been able to repress several deep sighs as she toured her through the account books, the herbal garden, the stillroom, where all her medicinal distillations were kept.

"What do they teach young ladies of the ton?" she'd muttered one evening when Lindsay had not been able to darn a sock in the heaping basket.

"I've only learned fine embroidery at Miss Pinkard's Academy," she answered quietly.

Florence pressed her lips together in that way that showed more clearly than any words her disapproval.

But she would have been able to endure all this and more—including the funny looks of the parishioners after Damien had introduced her formally on Sunday last and announced their impending nuptials—if her marriage were a real marriage.

Ever since Damien had spelled out so clearly the parameters of their marriage to her, despair had lodged around her heart and wouldn't budge. If she had felt fear and agony before, thinking she must marry Mr. Stokes, how much more desolate Damien's gently spoken words about an annulment had made her.

She was about to speak age-old words that joined her to him and he to her, and yet he was to be no husband to her. How she'd wanted to tell him the day would never come when she'd want to turn her back on him and return to her old life. How could she, when she loved him?

But how could she ever say that when clearly he didn't love her and was only marrying her as a means to help her? It was pity that motivated him. Pride prevented her from throwing herself at him. Once again shame flooded her as she recalled how she'd left him no choice that night with her awful lies. He'd never reproached her, yet every kind word and gesture reproached her a hundredfold.

"Into this holy estate these two persons present come now to be joined…"

The words smote her, making a mockery of the union she would enjoy with the man standing beside her, and she felt anew the conviction that she had done something dreadful.

"If any man can show just cause why they may not lawfully join together, let him now speak, or else hereafter forever hold his peace." Lindsay tensed, still expecting her father to appear at the rear of the small church and denounce their wedding.

But the only sounds in the old stone building were a few rustlings of the people standing directly behind her—the church clerk and Jonah and Florence, their two witnesses.

It had been a harrowing week, as Damien and Jonah had gone back and forth to her father's house and then to the offices of his solicitors, trying to obtain her father's permission. Damien had finally even had to hire his own solicitor before her father had at last consented.

She felt doubly ashamed, as they'd had to continue the charade of her loss of virtue. She knew from Florence that there was the awful question of disciplinary action toward Damien from the church for his supposed conduct toward her. But he'd reassured her that everything was going to be all right, and she'd preferred to accept his words than to go back and confess the truth to her father.

"Ye will answer at the dreadful day of judgment when the secrets of all hearts shall be disclosed, that if either of you know any impediment, ye do now confess it."

Once again the clergyman's words struck fear and dread into her heart for the awful lie she was perpetuating.

But nothing happened, and she continued to stand in her ivory muslin beside Damien and the other witnesses. The minister turned to Damien and began, "Wilt thou have this woman to be thy wedded wife, to live together after God's ordinance in the holy estate of matrimony? Wilt thou love her, comfort her, honor and keep her in sickness and in health; and forsaking all others, keep thee only unto her, so long as ye both shall live?"

Damien turned his eyes on her. As he said the words "I will," she had the sense he was truly pledging his troth to her. That all those things the curate had stated—forsaking all others, keeping himself only unto her—he was actually promising to do for her.

Before she could read anything more in his beautiful blue eyes, the minister turned to her and began listing the same vows. She tried to concentrate on the words, but could not take her gaze off Damien.

"Wilt thou have this man to be thy wedded husband, to live together…"

She swallowed then, lifting her chin a notch, her eyes never wavering from Damien's, and repeated, "I will." Once again, she felt a tangible connection between the two of them, as if they were the only people present and God Himself were witnessing their vows.

"Who giveth this woman to be married to this man?"

Her father did not step out to take her hand, but Jonah, who had offered to give her away, came to stand on her other side and took her right hand in his large one. She could have wept when he gave her a quick wink and squeezed her hand. He'd been nothing but kindness to her in the past few days, seeming to guess her every fear and guilt, and reassuring her that she was doing the right thing.

The minister took her hand from Jonah's and offered it to Damien. He took it in his right hand. His slim fingers enfolded her hand and she drew strength from them.

"I, Damien Ashton Hathaway, take thee Lindsay Catherine Phillips, to be my wedded wife, to have and to hold from this day forward, for better for worse, for richer for poorer, in sickness and in health, to love and to cherish, till death us do part, according to God's holy ordinance; and thereto I plight thee my troth."

They let go of each other's hands, and then, as she'd been instructed earlier, she took Damien's hand in hers and repeated the same words. "I, Lindsay Catherine Phillips, take thee Damien Ashton Hathaway, to be my wedded husband, to have and to hold…"

Jonah handed Damien the ring. Lindsay held out her left hand. He slipped the slim gold band he'd told her had been his mother's around her finger and then his fingers rested atop her hand. "With this ring, I thee wed, and with all my worldly goods I thee endow: in the name of the Father, the Son and of the Holy Ghost. Amen."

Then everyone was bowing their heads and repeating the Lord's Prayer. Once again, the curate was joining their right hands together and saying, "Those whom God hath joined together let no man put asunder."

She felt a profound sense of relief that no one could come between them now. A shudder of horror went through her as she contemplated how close she had come to having the same pronouncement uttered over her and Mr. Stokes.

"You may kiss the bride."

The minister's words startled her. Before she knew it, Damien lifted her veil. The next second his face was drawing close to hers, and then his lips touched hers softly, almost hesitantly. She felt the earth rock beneath her. Before she could react, before she could reach up and put her arms around his neck the way she longed to, he retreated.

She still felt the imprint of his warm lips against hers as he turned to face the minister again.

The minister pronounced a blessing over them, and then it was over. Jonah offered her his hand and a wide smile. "Congratulations, dear girl. You've tied the knot with my good and true friend Damien." Then he gave Damien a hearty embrace and Florence gave Lindsay a quick peck on the cheek and murmured her congratulations, as well.

They didn't linger at the altar but went to sign the registry. Her hand shook slightly as she signed her maiden name for the last time. All the while she relived Damien's kiss. She turned to him in wonder as he took her arm lightly and guided her down the steps into the morning sunshine.

They were well and truly married. The thing she'd most feared—that somehow her father would prevent it— had not happened. She glanced quickly up at the puffy white clouds against the blue sky and promised God to behave from now on. She would never tell such a lie again, as long as she lived. If only she could remain Damien's wife. She would be a good wife, proving indispensable to him, so he would never want to return her to her father.

Damien helped her into the coach they had hired for the trip back to the parsonage. The Quinns rode with them. Once they were all seated, all her fears and guilt returned.

Only the crunch of the wheels on the dirt road and the clatter of the horses' hooves broke the stillness.

Lindsay didn't know what to say or do, her naturally friendly personality subdued in the face of Florence's serious countenance.

"Are you all right?"

She turned with relief at Damien's low tone and gave him a tentative smile. "Yes, thank you."

"Beautiful morning." Jonah's tone was jovial.

"It is indeed," replied Damien.

Lindsay moistened her lips. Was she expected to contribute to the conversation? But what could she say that would be welcome?

"A perfect day for your wedding." Jonah grinned at them both, and Lindsay offered a smile.

"Yes. We were certainly blessed," Damien said.

"We've been having a spate of fine weather. The plowing is coming along nicely."

"I'm sorry you missed working on your new farm today."

Jonah frowned at him. "And miss your wedding? I'd as lief be shut up in Newgate!" he said with another wink at Lindsay. She couldn't help smiling back but was quickly cowed by Florence's frown at her husband.

"How can you say such a thing?"

"I can come out and help you with the plowing on Monday," Damien offered. Lindsay stared at him, surprised at his offer. A clergyman plowing in the fields? But Jonah's acquiescence surprised her even more.

"We can make a day of it, if the weather holds. If you bring Miss Phillips—beg pardon—Mrs. Hathaway with you, she and Florence can spend the day together."

"Excuse me," Florence responded immediately, "if you wish Damien's wife to be able to take the reins of the parsonage, I still have much to go over with her about its daily management."

Jonah smiled at his wife, unfazed. "Very well, you continue on with your task." His green eyes twinkled at Lindsay. "If she's half the taskmaster she was with me, you'll be ready to take over the entire parish in a fortnight."

Florence sniffed and looked out the window.

Damien turned to Lindsay, concern in his eyes. "You needn't do anything more than you wish. I didn't marry you to take on all the duties of a clergyman's wife, I assure you."

"That's all right," she said immediately, then an awkward silence ensued once again as she thought about the reason he had married her.

As if sensing the awkwardness, Jonah spoke up. "I promised Jacob we'd finish up your fields this coming week."

"As soon as you finish your own," Damien told him. "I'll assist Jacob, as well."

After a few moments of more silence, Jonah slapped his knees. "Yes, it was a fine service."

Suddenly, the coach leaned to one side as a wheel fell into a rut in the road. Jonah put a steadying hand on his wife's arm. "Easy there, love." Lindsay felt a pang at the note of tenderness in his voice and the look that passed between the two as she murmured her thanks.

When they'd regained an even pace, Jonah addressed

Damien again. "Have you invited the minister to the wedding breakfast?"

"I did, but he excused himself. It's a bit far for him to come. Only Jacob and Elizabeth—and Betsy—will be there." Damien glanced at her. "And your cousin, of course."

Dear Beatrice. Her only ally. None of her schoolgirl friends had responded to her invitations.

She still found it strange that the only other wedding guests were to be servants. Never in her life, no matter that she'd known her father's servants since childhood, would she have shared social events with a servant.

After a few more attempts at friendly conversation, Jonah lapsed into silence and the party rode the rest of the way without exchanging a word.

Lindsay spent the intervening time reliving Damien's kiss and thinking that this day had changed her life forever.

She couldn't help comparing her wedding day with the one she'd witnessed a scant few weeks ago. Even though Damien had announced his impending marriage to his congregation, eliciting shocked murmurs, he had not specifically invited anyone to the nuptials. Whereas the entire congregation had seemed to be present at the Quinns' wedding ceremony, no one had come to theirs. Undoubtedly few would care to travel to the village outside London, Lindsay told herself.

Just as she was beginning to feel sick from the coach's swaying, due to her empty stomach and tense nerves, they finally arrived back at the parsonage.

Damien helped her down from the old coach, then went to pay the driver as Lindsay waited for the others to descend. She didn't even feel she could precede them into the house, no matter how many times Florence had told her she was now mistress of the parsonage.

She breathed a sigh of relief when she saw the other coach, carrying Mr. and Mrs. Nichols, their daughter and Beatrice, arrive. Lindsay hurried over to receive her cousin.

"You looked so beautiful, my dear," her cousin said as soon as she'd been helped down by Mr. Nichols. "I couldn't help shedding a tear. It was a beautiful wedding."

Lindsay felt a lump grow in her throat and couldn't speak. The two women looked at each other and Beatrice squeezed her hand as if she understood all that was going through Lindsay's mind.

"Come along, everyone, refreshment awaits," Jonah's friendly voice boomed out.

They entered the dining room on the ground floor. Lindsay stood with her cousin, unsure where to be seated. Until today, Florence had sat at the foot of the table as mistress of the house.

Lindsay didn't have long to wait. As soon as Florence entered from a quick inspection of the kitchen, she approached Lindsay. "Please take your proper place," she said, indicating with a nod of her head.

Lindsay walked toward the end of the table, feeling with every step that she was unworthy of the place of honor. Damien joined her almost at once and held the chair out for her, giving her a smile.

Lindsay listened to the conversation around her and nibbled on the selection on her plate: fresh bread and farm butter; cold meats and slices of cheese and stewed fruits. She joined in the toast for their future. Beatrice and Jonah kept up most of the conversation, with Damien and his sister joining in occasionally.

Lindsay was the outsider. What would she do when Beatrice left? She sighed, praying for the strength to carry out the charade she'd begun.

After lunch, Beatrice bade them farewell.

"You don't have to leave so soon, do you?" Lindsay asked at once.

"Yes, my dear. I have a long way to go and must start my journey immediately."

"Go? Where are you going?"

"Your father has requested I return to my home."

"Oh, no!" Another thing Lindsay was responsible for.

Damien had been listening to their conversation and he approached. "You are welcome to make your home with us, Cousin Beatrice."

Beatrice turned to him with a warm smile. "Thank you, dear boy. You don't know how your kind invitation warms me. But I am returning to my sister's home. I was residing with her before Lindsay's father summoned me to help in her coming out. My sister depends on me for help with her numerous family." She turned back to Lindsay. "I shall be fine, although I shall miss you dreadfully. You have been like a daughter to me in these short months."

Lindsay felt herself tearing up again. "I hope you can visit us."

"Yes," Damien said immediately. "You are welcome here anytime."

Amidst more promises, Beatrice made her departure. Outside, Lindsay hugged her tightly, feeling as if her last lifeline was leaving.

"There, there, dear girl, I know I leave you in good hands." Beatrice eased away from her and took her hands. "Although this union began in a somewhat unorthodox fashion, I feel in my heart everything will work out fine."

Lindsay pressed her lips together. "I…I'm frightened."

"Everything new is frightening. If you need any help, don't hesitate to go to Reverend Hathaway. He looks to be a good, compassionate man. I know he'd do anything to help you adjust."

Lindsay looked down. She could not burden Damien with more than she'd given him already. How would she ever live up to the woman he deserved? "Pray for me," she said to her cousin.

Beatrice gave her hands a final pat. "I will, my dear, be assured of that. Now, go on in to that handsome young husband of yours and let me be on my way."

"Write to me," Lindsay said as her cousin leaned out the carriage window.

"I will. And I want to hear all about the doings here at the parsonage."

Lindsay waved until the carriage disappeared in the dust of the road. When would she ever see a familiar face again? She turned and looked southward toward Hyde Park. Mayfair and the world she had known since birth were closed to her now. The reception her friends had shown her to news of her wedding made that clear.

She slowly pivoted and faced the parsonage door. A new life awaited her. A world she'd forced herself into by way of deception. Would God ever forgive her for it and bless it?

When she reentered the parsonage, it was so quiet she wanted to run back outside to the sunshine and sound of birdsong and carriage traffic. But she squared her shoulders and made her way down the corridor. No one was left in the dining room and all signs of the breakfast had been cleared away. She heard voices coming from behind the kitchen door. But she wanted to find Damien first. She needed to be reassured by his kindly face. She ascended the stairs and looked in the drawing room but it was empty. Back downstairs, she faced both his study and his workroom, but both doors were shut and she didn't have the courage to knock. What would she say? Finally, with a sigh, she entered the kitchen.

Florence, Mrs. Nichols and Betsy turned to look at her. They were drying the dishes and putting away the remaining food. "I w-wanted to see if you needed my help."

"Thank you, my dear, but I wouldn't have you doing any chores today. It's your wedding day." Florence shooed her out the door when Lindsay hesitated, wanting to tell her she had nowhere to go and nothing else to do.

Back in the silent corridor, she decided to take a walk. Yes, the fresh air might do her good. She went toward the coatrack to fetch her spencer and parasol.

After an hour of exploring the back orchards and fields beyond, she returned, tired but feeling better for the walk. A quick search of the open rooms showed no one. Finally, with another sigh, she headed for her room. She would take a nap. Perhaps Damien would be about when she woke up.

Lindsay woke with a start, her room dim, feeling disoriented. She put a hand to her disheveled locks, trying to place herself. The next second she looked down at her hand on the coverlet. The thin gold band glinted up at her. She was a married woman.

After a few moments, thinking about all the events of the morning, she rose. She made her way to her dressing table and sat down. Her cheeks were rosy from sleep, her hair cascading down her shoulders, her eyes large and frightened. Slowly, she took out the remaining pins from her hair and brushed it. After coiling it back round again and arranging the locks about her face, she straightened her dress and rose.

Once again, the house presented a daunting silence. This time, not even sounds from the kitchen could be heard. Finally, she settled down in the drawing room with a novel from the pile Beatrice had left her from the lending library.

It seemed ages later—she'd finally been able to settle her thoughts on the story after plowing through the first few chapters with little understanding—that the door opened and she looked up startled. A deep feeling of relief engulfed her when she saw Damien standing in the doorway.

He looked surprised. "Hello. I didn't know you were here."

Had he wanted the room to himself? "Yes. I—I've been here some time now."

"Oh. I didn't know if you were awake. Florence told me you had gone up for a nap."

She felt herself blushing. "Yes. Just for a little while, when I didn't see you—anyone—around. I...I went out for a walk earlier."

He approached her chair in the bow window overlooking Hyde Park. "You went for a walk on your own?"

"Yes. Is that all right? I didn't want to disturb you."

"It's quite all right, and you needn't have feared disturbing me. I was just tinkering with tomorrow's sermon." He seemed to blush, as well. "I went for a walk too, so you see, we could have walked together."

She felt her own cheeks redden and she looked down at her book.

"What are you reading?"

"Oh, just a book Beatrice left me...to while away the time."

"I'm sorry if you were bored."

"Oh, no, that is, your sister insisted I could do nothing to help today, so I—" She splayed her fingers in a shrug. "I felt a little at loose ends is all. Where is everyone, anyway?"

His eyes didn't meet hers. "Jonah and Florence have left."

"Left?" Her voice rose in surprise.

"Yes. Jonah decided to move into their new farmhouse. It took me quite by surprise as well, since I didn't expect them to move until next week or the following." He began fiddling with his watch chain as if nervous. "But Jonah decided this afternoon—at least that's when he told me—that he and Flo would go there temporarily. But Florence will be back tomorrow morning. She wants to continue helping you settle in." He coughed, his discomfort apparent. "You don't mind, do you? You needn't do anything you don't wish to. My sister just wants to be helpful, but she can be a little direct at times. If she makes you feel uncomfortable, just say the word, and I'll talk to her."

"Oh, no!" She almost reached out to grab his arm in alarm. "No, please don't," she said more calmly. "I appreciate all the time and patience she is taking with me." She smoothed down her skirt over her knees, feeling exceedingly awkward now that she was actually alone with him. It was the first time since the night she'd come to him, and since that awful interview with him the next morning. Her eyes widened in sudden concern. "They haven't moved out because of me, have they?"

"No, of course not," he hastened, but then his eyes slid away from her again. "I mean, Jonah's notion of a newly married couple needing some time alone together probably had something to do with it. Please don't take it amiss—he meant no harm by it. We both tried to dissuade him, my sister and I, but he can be a stubborn fellow sometimes."

"I see." Dear Jonah, trying to help out. She dared not

look at Damien now. So, both he and his sister had not wanted her to be left alone with him. The thought lowered her spirits even more. Of course her wedding was a sham. She had done nothing but incommode poor Damien.

She'd taken vows today, which were unwanted.

His voice interrupted her. "Are you hungry?"

Her gaze flew up to him. "What? Oh, I…don't know." It had been hours since the little she'd eaten.

"I had just been looking for you to see if you cared for some supper. Mrs. Nichols laid some out before she left. There's tea if you'd care for a cup."

She stood immediately. "Oh, I didn't mean to keep you waiting."

His hand came up to touch her arm. "You didn't. I had just now come to look for you, and I'm sorry I kept you by yourself so long."

She swallowed, looking at his hand, feeling its light touch, longing to be held by him, to be reassured that all was truly going to work out. But instead, he let her arm go and continued talking, unaware of her thoughts. "We usually eat a light supper, as you've seen. I had nothing planned for this evening. I shall probably just sit here and read. If you'd like, we can pray together and read the scriptures afterward."

"Yes, I should like that very much," she said softly, the beginnings of a smile forming on her lips. Maybe, if nothing else, she could still turn to him as to the man of God who had so drawn her since the first day she'd heard him preach.

He returned her smile.

* * *

Damien unfolded his napkin, feeling decidedly uncomfortable in the large dining room. Lindsay—he felt unworthy to be calling her by her Christian name—was at the far end of the table. The arrangement had never bothered him with Florence, but now he felt it would be awkward enough to carry on a conversation without feeling he'd have to raise his voice. Her tone was often so soft he had to strain to catch her few words.

He bowed his head and began his accustomed blessing. He barely heard her "amen" echoing his own when he finished. No, this wouldn't do. He cleared his throat. "Would you like to—that is, when we're alone together at table, would you prefer to sit closer? I don't mean to rob you of your rightful place..."

Relief showed on her face. "I would much prefer to sit closer." She began to rise as she spoke and carried her plate to the place at his right.

When she was settled beside him, he passed her a plate of cold chicken. "Mrs. Nichols is a fine cook, as you've been able to see since you came here." Then he remembered where Lindsay came from. "Though I'm sure she cannot rival your father's cook."

"Mrs. Nichols is indeed a fine cook," she said immediately. "Papa has a French chef, but I find Mrs. Nichols's cooking both savory and wholesome. It reminds me of being at Chillingsworth. Our country seat," she replied to his raised eyebrow.

"Of course. Did you spend much time there as a child?" How much he didn't know of her. How would she possibly adjust to life in a small parsonage after the life she'd known? His spirits fell as her face lightened, looking happier than it had all day.

"Oh, yes! Before I went off to school, I spent much more time there with Mama than in London. It was a lovely place, up in Derbyshire. I could roam about the grounds much more freely than here in London. Of course, I haven't spent that much time at our house in Mayfair. I was away at Miss Pinkard's most of the year."

"Tell me more about your time in the country." He listened as he took an occasional bite of food, more entranced by her words than the food before him. For the first time since coming to the parsonage, she was showing some animation. Had the presence of the others, particularly Florence, constrained her natural enthusiasm so much? He felt suddenly glad Jonah had insisted they leave for the evening.

His sister meant well, but she couldn't help showing her disapproval and worry over his decision to carry through with the marriage.

It was done now. He'd promised to love and cherish Lindsay until death parted them. He intended to honor that vow, even after Lindsay returned someday to her father's house.

By the time supper was over, they had regained the companionableness of those times she'd sat in his Bible study. They retired to the drawing room and opened their Bibles, reading a passage together and discussing it. She had marvelous insight for one who hadn't read the scriptures much before.

Betsy brought a tray of tea up later in the evening. "You may leave it," he told her.

Lindsay poured the tea. As she handed him his cup with a smile, suddenly Damien couldn't believe it was his wife doing the honors in his drawing room. He felt a wave of gratitude wash over him. Even if she were never his true wife—and she wouldn't be, he repeated to himself—he was more thankful than he could ever say to have her sitting across from him, taking on the role.

"Thank you," he said.

"How early will you be going over to the chapel tomorrow morning?"

It would be her first official Sunday with them. "I generally go over about half an hour before the service. You needn't go over so early. Florence usually sees to everything the evening before—that the flowers are at the altar and the communion elements in place—but she will probably arrive early tomorrow morning."

"That's quite all right. I can go with her and see what needs to be done." She looked down at her cup. Her tawny eyelashes brushed her translucent skin. "I want to be able to do everything a curate's wife is expected to do. I should visit the members of your congregation, shouldn't I…and act as your hostess here when you have gatherings…and I don't know…play the organ?" She looked up, concern shadowing her large brown eyes.

"I don't play the organ, but I do play the pianoforte."

He laughed. "It's very nice of you to want to do everything possible, and there will be some duties, as that of hostess, that I would appreciate your help with, but

I won't overburden you with chores. You can continue your life—the one you are more accustomed to—as much as you'd like. I don't want you to be overwhelmed by this new role."

"It would be no burden for me, I assure you."

He cleared his throat, not wanting to curb her enthusiasm or good intentions, but understanding better than she what the job entailed. "Being a curate or curate's wife involves never-ending tasks that few people see or acknowledge. Florence and I have been doing this for many years and have become accustomed to the demands of the life." Seeing her expression, he said, "I don't mean to discourage you. I want you to feel free to do as much or as little as you feel inclined to do. I just want you to break into it slowly until you see how much you truly care to take on. I shall never reproach you for anything you do or don't choose to do."

He didn't feel he had her full agreement but didn't know how else to make her understand how quickly she could be weighed down by the obligations of the office if she tried to do everything at once.

As they drank their tea, he felt the camaraderie they'd achieved was broken. The night stretched ahead of them, like a specter hovering in their midst. Before the wedding, Lindsay had retired to her room when Florence and Jonah went up. Now, it was just the two of them.

Finally Damien, unsure what to do, picked up his book, a treatise on Hebrews, and began to read. When he looked up, he saw that Lindsay had also picked up the novel she'd been reading earlier.

The only sounds were the ticking of the clock and the turning of a page. He was acutely conscious of Lindsay's every move. He knew the second she closed her book. A few seconds later, she rose, laid the book on an end table and approached his chair. "Would you care for another cup of tea?"

"Yes, I think I will." Her slim hand held the china pot over the cup he held out. "Thank you," he said as she retreated.

The clatter of a saucer on the tray signaled she was putting her cup down. "I think I shall go up now."

He raised his eyes to meet hers. The moment of truth had arrived. He rose but kept his place in his book with his finger. "I think I shall remain here a little longer."

She merely nodded although she looked at him a few seconds longer without saying anything. "Very well, then. I...I shall bid you good night."

"It must have been a tiring day for you."

"No—yes. I suppose a little." Still, she remained standing there without moving. He could feel his heart begin to thud, unsure what to do, willing himself to remain where he was, as if this was the way newlyweds were supposed to behave.

The pulse thudding in his ears drowned out everything else when she began to walk toward him. What was she going to do?

She stood about a foot from him, as if expecting something, but still he stood, unable to look away from her, not knowing what she wanted. He remembered the sweet feel of her lips against his those few seconds at the end of their wedding ceremony, a memory he'd shut from his mind. But now, it clamored for recognition. His gaze fell to her mouth and suddenly he ached to take her in his arms and feel her lips again.

The next second she took another step toward him, so close she was almost touching him. She rose on her tiptoes, touching him lightly on the shoulders to retain her balance. Her face neared his and he thought she was going to kiss him on the lips, but then she moved her head. He smelled the sweet scent of her as her lips brushed his cheek.

And then she was standing once more away from him. "Good night, Damien. Thank you again for everything."

He could only nod dumbly, too shaken by the feel of her against him, the flowery scent of her so close to him.

He didn't move until he heard the sound of the door close after her and then he fell back on his chair, the book in his hand forgotten.

The full impact of his situation hit him. He was now a married man. He had a young, beautiful wife upstairs. In another world, she'd be waiting for him, and he would be eager to share this first night with her. His head fell in his hands as despair seized him. He could not give in to this pretty, storybook fantasy. How was he going to survive living under the same roof with her? Knowing she was only a door or two away from him? Every instinct, every fiber of his body commanded him to run after her and take her to himself.

His eyes fell on the wooden leg stretched out before him and his spirits sank even further. She would soon see the awful mistake she'd made—or been forced into by her circumstances—and would come to despise him or, worse, be sickened every time she looked at his wooden leg.

He must preserve her chastity if he ever hoped to return her to her father. He must!

He picked up his worn Bible and flipped to the book of Job, to a familiar passage. His hands shook as he turned to the page. His eyes roamed down the passage until alighting upon the scripture he sought.

I made a covenant with mine eyes; why then should I think upon a maid? He clenched his hand into a fist, repeating the words, making them a promise to himself. He would not harbor impure thoughts toward Lindsay. She was under his protection. He would honor his own vow of chastity to her.

Chapter Eleven

Lindsay walked slowly up the stairs to her room. The full fatigue of the day descended on her like a weight. Why did she only feel it now? Was it because of the dismissal she'd just received from her new husband?

She knew nothing of the ways of a man and woman. All she'd known, apart from her father's anatomy textbooks, was gleaned from her novel reading. She passed Damien's bedroom door and felt her face grow hot at the sudden longing in her to go and lie upon his bed so he'd find her when he retired.

As she entered her solitary room, she felt a wave of desolation wash over her. She set down her candle, hardly necessary in the twilight, and went to stand in front of her mirror. Did Damien not like her in that way? Was she not attractive to him?

With a sigh, she turned away from her mirror and began her nightly struggle to get undressed. She was without her personal maid and her clothes were fancier than the simple schoolgirl outfits allowed at the academy, where the girls helped one another undress.

In her nightgown, she sat down to brush out her hair. Her strokes slowed, once again thinking of her new husband. How bold she'd felt, her heart hammering in her chest, when she'd gone to kiss him good-night. He had not responded, neither pushing her away nor drawing her closer. Had she done the right thing? She'd had to thank him…. She held her silver-backed brush in her hand, staring unseeing at her reflection, remembering only the feel of his cheek against her lips, the soft scent both soapy and masculine, its texture smooth and rough at the same time, like a fine emery board. So different from her own, she thought as she brought her fingertips to her cheek.

With a deep sigh, she resumed brushing her hair. Tomorrow, she would begin her new life in earnest. She would face the entire congregation as Mrs. Damien Hathaway for the first time. She would be charming and friendly and win their approval as their curate's wife.

She would "study to show herself approved" as the word said, meekly learning everything Florence had to teach her. She would make herself indispensible to Damien so he would never want to send her back to her father—never.

By the time the receiving line had thinned out, Lindsay didn't know if she could keep her smile fixed in place. Although Damien stood by her side at the entrance to the small church, and his congregation greeted him cordially enough, many eyed her with less than friendly looks. She detected curiosity and judgment and some outright coldness, but few had greeted her with genuine friendliness.

"Good morning, Mr. and Mrs. Hayward," Damien said to the last couple. "So nice to see you this morning. May I present my wife, Lindsay Hathaway?"

The middle-aged couple inclined their heads to her before turning back to Damien and engaging him in conversation for a few moments.

When the last parishioner had left, Damien said to her with a smile, "How are you doing after your first Sunday?"

She returned his smile, determined by neither look nor gesture to indicate that anyone had made her feel less than welcome. "Fine."

"Let me have a word with the church warden a moment. If you'd like to walk back with Florence, please do so. Or, if you'd care to wait for me, I shall be only a moment."

She quickly looked around for her sister-in-law. Thankfully, she was already outside with her husband. "I'll wait for you, if that's all right."

He merely nodded and reentered the sanctuary.

Lindsay breathed deeply, feeling her first and perhaps most difficult test, that of facing Damien's congregation, was behind her. Of course people would eye her suspiciously. Florence had warned her that they had been taken completely by surprise at Damien's announcement of his impending marriage.

"They'll think Damien has behaved less than honorably toward you. A hasty marriage is little better than an elopement at Gretna Green," Florence had said with a shake of her head.

It disturbed Lindsay greatly that they could suspect anything untoward of Damien, but she could say nothing. It was all her fault, and anything she said would only make things worse. She could only hope time faded the details of their marriage.

Damien rejoined her with a smile and offered his arm. He no longer wore the ankle-length cassock and surplice but breeches and tailcoat. "Shall we return to the parsonage?"

She smiled in answer and placed her hand in the crook of his arm. He led her around the churchyard to the rear and across a field. The day was overcast but warm and she felt her spirits lift. "I enjoyed the message."

"Did you? I'm glad." He sounded genuinely pleased. "You didn't think it too complex?"

"No, not at all." They discussed it some until arriving at the back entrance of the parsonage.

Florence was in the kitchen when they entered. Delicious aromas wafted over from the range. "Ah, there you are. If you care to take off your wraps, Mrs. Hathaway, I will show you what needs to be done here."

"Yes, of course." She always felt disapproval in Florence's tone. She unbuttoned her spencer and Damien helped her off with it.

"I'll hang it up in the front entry if you'd like."

"Yes, thank you." She handed him her bonnet, as well. "Let me fetch my apron," she told her sister-in-law. She'd never in her life worked in a kitchen before and still found it hard to adjust to the notion that a lady should do so.

After washing up in the scullery, she did as Florence instructed her, making sure everything in the dining room was laid out properly. Betsy bobbed a curtsy to her in passing. "I'll just bring in the dishes, ma'am."

"Yes, of course."

Dinner proceeded smoothly, mainly due to the presence of Jonah. He kept Lindsay smiling, even laughing, with his running commentary on the food, the morning's service, anything and everything. His shrewd green eyes didn't seem to miss anything.

"I say, Florence, why this formality between you and Mrs. Hathaway? You're sisters now. Shouldn't you be calling each other by your Christian names?"

Lindsay felt herself blush as she looked over at Damien's sister. She still didn't feel quite right in having taken her sister-in-law's place at the table.

Florence turned to her husband across the table. "I shall be glad to, if Mrs. Hathaway gives me leave."

"You mean you're waiting for her permission?" Jonah raised his eyebrows in mock surprise to Lindsay. "Well, then, what do you say, Mrs. Hathaway? Do your new brother and sister have leave to call you Lindsay?"

"Of course you do. I didn't realize you were waiting for my permission." Again, she felt as if she'd been in the wrong.

"Thank you, Lindsay," Jonah said immediately. "I am Jonah, as you are probably aware of. A notorious name it is, to be sure."

She laughed. "Notoriety? Perhaps we have a little of that in common."

Jonah joined in her laughter although she noticed the other two did not. Her laughter died on her lips. How could she laugh at having ruined Damien's reputation?

"I'm having a tea this afternoon for some of the ladies at church to get to know you…Lindsay." Florence paused a fraction before uttering her name. "I hope you don't mind my taking the liberty. It's to introduce you before I depart."

"Of course not, thank you, Florence." Why did she feel so awkward addressing her by her first name? She was surely not that much older than Lindsay and certainly much younger than Beatrice, whom she hadn't had any trouble calling by her first name. "That was very thoughtful of you."

"Wonderful idea, Flo," Damien said in an enthusiastic tone before looking at Lindsay with a slight lift of his eyebrow as if to ask her approval. She gave a barely perceptible nod and smile to reassure him that everything was fine, though her appetite had suddenly left her.

The afternoon began well enough. A dozen ladies at least, of all ages, began arriving by mid-afternoon. Both Damien and Jonah had disappeared, leaving the "ladies to their devices," as Jonah had put it before donning his coat and hat and exiting with Damien.

Now, Lindsay sat with her hands clasped in her lap as Florence introduced each lady.

"Thank you for coming," she said with a smile to a

lady and her daughter, who appeared about Lindsay's age. Lindsay gave her an encouraging smile, but the girl and her mother seemed to look right through Lindsay, holding themselves very straight as if by their proximity to Lindsay they might contract something undesirable.

"Florence, how are we to do without you?" the older woman said, turning away from Lindsay.

The young lady was a pretty brunette named Charlotte Cooper. "Would you care to have a seat?" Lindsay asked her.

The girl looked down her nose at the chair Lindsay indicated. Finally, when Lindsay thought she'd flounce away, she sat, her body slightly turned away from Lindsay.

The other ladies were talking together in little groups of twos and threes about the room. Florence had decided to oversee the pouring of the tea so that Lindsay would be free to converse with her guests. Now she sat with her hands knotted together, wishing she had the tea service to occupy herself with—and hide behind.

"Have you lived here all your life?" Lindsay asked Miss Cooper. She was dressed quite fashionably for the small parish, which boasted more farmers than ladies of quality.

"All my life," she said with a sniff, not deigning to turn around when she spoke. "I've known Reverend Hathaway since he came here. That was six years ago. He'd just taken orders."

"I see." Why was she telling her this? It made her sound as if she had some special relationship to Damien.

"How long have *you* known Reverend Hathaway?" Her amber gaze eyed Lindsay as she flung the question at her.

"I, uh, not as long as you," she said with a little nervous laugh.

"Mama and I—indeed, the entire congregation—were shocked when he announced he was to be married. We had no idea—no inkling—he even planned on such a step." She sniffed again, jutting her pert nose in the air. "It is not something to be entered into lightly by a clergyman. A congregation has a right to meet their curate's future wife. What if she doesn't suit? Why, we all thought he would choose from among his own congregation."

Lindsay had a sudden understanding. Had Miss Cooper wished to marry Damien? She looked more closely at the young lady. Her lavender sprigged muslin and matching color spencer were very fetching against her dark curls. "I shall try my best to be a good curate's wife."

Miss Cooper scrunched up her nose. "I don't believe anything you do will erase the taint of a rushed marriage. Why weren't you married by Reverend Doyle here at the chapel? He is Reverend Hathaway's superior and has always been involved in all the happenings at the parish."

Lindsay swallowed, unsure how to answer. "We…that is…the rector was unavailable on such short notice."

Miss Cooper suddenly stood. "If you will excuse me, Mrs. Hathaway, I find I cannot sit here any longer. I came to satisfy myself about the disturbing particulars of this marriage, but you have said nothing to put my fears to rest."

Before Lindsay could form a reply, Miss Cooper turned on her heel, her skirts swirling around her ankles, and walked swiftly away. Several ladies looked at her, a silence descending on the room. Lindsay felt her face grow warm.

Miss Cooper went to stand beside another young lady, and the two put their heads together, whispering. Lindsay swallowed, her gaze traveling slowly around the room. The coldness emanating from the women lashed her like a stiff north wind.

Florence rose. Like a queen, she swept from behind her tea table and brought a cup to Lindsay herself. "Here you go, my dear."

With shaking hands Lindsay took it from her. Its rattle was the only sound in the room.

Florence turned to the ladies. "I hope you all welcome Lindsay to this parish and make her feel at home. She is Reverend Hathaway's wife and needs all our support and encouragement. She is very young, just out of school. I'm sure she will make my brother a fine wife and a superior addition to this parish." Her stern eye roved over the gathering. "For my sake and Reverend Hathaway's, please take the time to get acquainted with her."

A ripple of murmurs went around the room. Lindsay stared into the cinnamon hue of her tea.

"Welcome to our parish, Mrs. Hathaway," a soft voice said above her. She raised her head to find an older woman she'd been introduced to earlier standing before her with a smile.

"Th-thank you," she whispered, trying to smile.

"I am Mrs. Moore." She waved a hand. "I don't expect you to remember that until we've had a chance to get better acquainted. May I?" She indicated the seat vacated by Miss Cooper.

"Of course."

She settled her ample form on the seat. "I've known Damien Hathaway since he was a young tyke, and I've prayed for many years for a nice young woman for him to wed." She smiled complacently. "It's wonderful to see my prayers answered at last."

"I hope I can be a good wife to him."

"I'm sure you shall, my dear." Her gaze swept the room. "It isn't easy to face so many new people at once."

The older lady stayed at her side for the remainder of the tea, engaging her in pleasant conversation revolving around the parish. Only one or two other ladies joined her at intervals. The rest remained conversing among themselves or with Florence.

Finally, it was over, and Lindsay excused herself as soon as possible to go to her room. Her nerves felt strung out, and all she wanted to do was shut herself away somewhere.

Had rumors of her accusations against Damien reached his congregation? Was she to be ostracized because of her hasty marriage? She buried her face in her pillow, feeling ashamed once more over her conduct. Would she ever be able to erase it?

The weeks that followed improved little for her. Although grateful for how Florence had stood up for her at that first tea, Lindsay soon found her sister-in-law's opinion hadn't changed much in private. Several times, she'd heard Florence suck in her breath in impatience at Lindsay's inability to carry out a task she was showing her. Keeping the household accounts was the worst. It seemed every penny spent—from the Nicholses' salary to what a length of ribbon cost—was noted in the ledger. Lindsay's pages were all smudged and crossed through with mistakes she'd made. Florence kept reminding her to enter in any expenses she'd made, and Lindsay kept forgetting.

"A curate's income is not great, and it is imperative you know where every penny goes, so that you may see where to economize if you are short at the end of the quarter."

"Yes, Florence," she replied in her meekest tone, thinking of the pretty bonnet she'd spied in the shop window on her last outing. She supposed it was out of the question to even think of purchasing it. Perhaps even purchasing the ribbons to dress up her old bonnet was beyond their means.

She'd never seen so many sheets, stockings, shirts and other linens that needed mending. Gone was the pleasure of embroidering pretty colored flowers and leaf borders at the edge of a handkerchief or cuff. Black or white thread was all she needed these days.

The one or two times she'd asked Damien if she could accompany him on his rounds had ended in gentle refusals. It was either too dangerous or too dirty. She was only able to accompany Florence on her visits to women in the immediate vicinity, and most of those visits were excruciatingly tedious since she had to sit mute in the face of the women's continued hostility to her.

When not mending, many afternoons were spent singing and painting. There was no pianoforte to practice on, but at least she could sing. If there was enough sunlight coming through the western window she would sit at her easel and paint her still life watercolors. This afternoon she'd picked a posy of anemones and poppies, and put them in a pretty old vase of blue and white china.

She hardly saw Damien until suppertime and the few hours at dinner when Jonah and Florence would accompany them. Rarely, though, did she see him alone. She wondered if she had displeased him in something, but he was always polite and solicitous, asking about her day. No, it was more likely he was regretting having been forced to marry her.

She sighed. How different from how she'd imagined life would be at the parsonage with him. Close conversations and Bible studies together, helping him in his work…raising his children. This last thought brought a warmth to her cheeks and a deeper sadness at the realization of what would never be.

She shook aside her melancholy and dipped her brush into the red paint, dabbing it onto her canvas.

When the sun descended behind an oak tree, she knew it was time to stop. She sighed again and sat back, staring a moment at the picture. "Pretty pictures," as Florence had said one day in a dry tone.

She set her brush in the glass of water and wiped her fingers on a rag. Maybe a cup of tea would help. Glancing at the mantel clock, she saw it would be a couple of hours yet before Damien returned. She knew he was at the orphanage at Marylebone this afternoon and he usually didn't come home until just before supper on those days.

She made her way to the kitchen. Hearing Jonah's low tone, she paused, not wanting to interrupt his conversation with his wife.

"You say the bishop has written to him?"

"Yes," came Florence's voice, worry evident in the one syllable. "Damien didn't even want to tell me. The bishop wants to review Damien's conduct over the last few months, including giving you refuge here at the parsonage and his recent wedding."

Lindsay's heart began to pound and she found she couldn't move from the doorway.

"That hasty marriage in no way helps his position now. In fact, it weakens it desperately. He might have been able to defend himself in his earlier conduct since the prince regent himself issued you a pardon. But to marry quite suddenly, and to have to disclose that the bride's father has cut her off—"

Lindsay's fist went up to her mouth as if to silence her very breathing.

"Oh, why did she have to embroil him in this scheme? I can understand her wanting to defy her father, but to latch onto our poor Damien…"

"There, there, love," Jonah said. "I think she's the best thing to happen to Damien. 'Tis unfortunate her father was so opposed to the marriage and so set on the one with that loathsome gent."

"I've tried my best to prepare her for her life here, but I think she's as ill prepared as the day she came to us. The women still haven't warmed to her. I think too many were disappointed at Damien's sudden marriage. It was almost as a repudiation of all the fine young women in our own congregation. Like a slap in the face to their mothers." Florence sighed.

"Now, now, just give Lindsay a little time. How can the churchwomen not warm to her? She's such a sweet young thing."

"I don't know. Sometimes, I think that's almost a drawback. If only she were a little more forceful, a little stronger to face all that she must face."

Jonah chuckled. "Are you certain that's what Damien needs?"

"What do you mean?" came Florence's sharp tone.

"Maybe it's time Damien had someone to look after, someone that needs to lean on him for a bit."

"Oh, Jonah, if he needs anyone right now, it will be someone who can weather the coming times. What will the bishop say? Damien told me in no uncertain terms that we were not to say anything to Lindsay. Oh, what has she brought on poor Damien!"

Lindsay heard no more. She imagined from the murmurings that Jonah had taken his wife in his arms.

She wrapped her own arms around herself, wishing she had someone to run to and seek comfort from. When she heard further movement in the kitchen, she backed away, fearful of being discovered.

She forgot her tea and hurried up to her room, sick

with worry. Would Damien be dismissed? Would he lose everything? And why hadn't he told her anything?

"How was your time at the orphanage?"

Damien looked up from his plate and tried to muster a smile for his pretty wife. *Wife.* He still felt a sense of amazement every time he uttered the term, even in his mind. How could this beautiful, ethereal creature be bound to him in the eyes of the world, in the eyes of the Church, the law?

"Very good," he replied. He hesitated to go into any detail for he knew she wanted to accompany him to the orphanage. Thus far, he'd put her off with vague excuses, insisting he didn't want to overtax her with all her new responsibilities at the parsonage.

But every time he glimpsed the disappointment in her eager face and watched the light slowly fade from her eyes, he felt afresh the constant struggle to keep his distance from her, for her own good.

Every day he had to fight to stay away from her when all he wanted to do was see her every moment. And every night he had to stay put in his study to keep from running after her when she ascended to her room.

"Were the boys well behaved?" she asked.

"Yes. Jonah is always adept at keeping the unruly ones under control." He looked down at his plate, his mind going back to the correspondence he'd received from the Bishop of London. Despite his assurances to Florence, he was troubled by the communication. He'd thought his involvement in his brother-in-law's escape from the law would have been dismissed when Jonah had received his royal pardon.

"Do you have any plans for tomorrow?"

He looked up again, startled, and realized he had been silent for some minutes. "I need to work in the study a bit. I'm preparing some written documents."

"Your sermon?"

He looked away from her, his cheeks flushing. "Yes, and other things." The last thing he wanted to do was worry Lindsay. "What about you?" he asked, needing to get the focus off himself. "Do you have anything special planned? How are you coming along with the women of the congregation?"

"Fine." Though she smiled, her tone held no enthusiasm.

He gazed down at her plate. She had eaten little, causing Damien to worry afresh. Was she regretting her rash decision to marry him?

Damien set down his fork and knife, his own food unfinished. "If you'll excuse me, I believe I shall go into the study." He needed to satisfy the bishop. Above all, he mustn't let any breath of trouble come near Lindsay. She'd already suffered enough at her father's hands.

She looked at him a moment, then looked back down at her plate. "Will you be long?"

"I, uh—" He paused. How he longed to drop all his responsibilities and take her in his arms. How he longed to tell her his worries and fears. Instead, he rose and tucked in his chair. "I believe it will take me some hours. Please don't wait up for me."

It was a pity Jonah and Florence's farm was so far from town. Things had been easier—in many ways—while they were still here in the evenings. Now that they were gone, it was difficult for Damien to resist the temptation of knocking on Lindsay's door when he retired each evening. There was usually light visible from the crack beneath her door, light which beckoned him…but which he'd force himself to hurry by on his way to his lonely room beyond.

Lindsay spent the next morning arranging flowers at the church altar. As she set the final pink moss rose in place, she turned at the sound of footsteps. Perhaps the warden had returned to lock up behind her.

She drew in her breath at the sight of Mrs. Cooper coming up the center aisle.

Lindsay left the flowers and went to meet the woman.

"Good morning, Mrs. Cooper. How lovely to see you."

The woman looked down her nose at her. "You will not get away with your wicked behavior."

Lindsay fell back. "What do you mean?"

The lady eyed her up and down. "You know perfectly well what I mean. I have discovered your father was against your match and has since disowned you. You went against his wishes and moved into the parsonage without the benefit of holy matrimony!"

"I was there at the invitation of Reverend Hathaway and his sister!" Lindsay panicked, knowing she must do all in her means to protect Damien. "He did not stay at the parsonage but moved to the Nicholses' cottage until our wedding."

"A marriage not even sanctioned by your own father! It is as disgraceful as an elopement. How can you stand over us? You are little better than a disgraced woman."

Lindsay had no words to defend herself. If only Mrs. Cooper knew how innocent she was of these accusations. Her husband hadn't even touched her!

But she stood silent until Mrs. Cooper, with a final "You shan't get away with this!" turned and marched back down the aisle.

Lindsay sat down on the stone steps to the altar, her head in her hands. What was she to do? She couldn't stay here. Damien's life would only get worse and worse. Florence's words came back to her, bringing tears to her eyes. Damien had been up till past midnight in his study. Were those "written documents" he'd had to prepare some kind of defense of his conduct for the Bishop?

If Mrs. Cooper began to spread vicious rumors among the congregation—would they reach the ears of the bishop? What then?

How long she sat there, she didn't know, but finally she rose, resolved. Entering the kitchen, she nodded to Mrs. Nichols. "I shall be going out today."

The older woman smiled. "Would you like Betsy to accompany you?"

"No, that's all right. I shall hail a hack. I—I'm going to visit some friends. I shall probably be out all day. Don't expect me for dinner."

Mrs. Nichols frowned. "Very well, madam. Take care, now."

"Yes."

Lindsay went up to her room and changed her dress. She put a few things into a small bag, having no idea where she'd go but knowing she couldn't stay here any longer. Perhaps she'd be able to stay with a school friend until getting word to Beatrice. Would Beatrice be able to offer her shelter?

She left by the front door so Mrs. Nichols would not see the bag she carried.

Damien looked for Lindsay when he came out of his study for dinner. When she didn't appear at the table and he noticed no place was set for her, he asked Betsy.

"Oh, Mum said Mrs. Hathaway went out today."

"Thank you." That was strange. She hadn't mentioned anything at breakfast. Perhaps something had come up.

He popped into the kitchen to ask for the particulars.

Mrs. Nichols turned from the range. "She only said she was visiting friends."

"Oh." He felt both relief at knowing her whereabouts and disappointment that she'd said nothing to him about it. He drummed his fingers on the tabletop. "She didn't say whom?"

"No, sir. Just that she'd be out most of the day and not to expect her back for dinner."

Could something have come up—an emergency?

"Would you like me to send Jacob out to look for her?"

He tried to smile. "No, that's all right. I'm sure she'll be fine. She probably went to Mayfair."

"I'm sure she did. I'll let you know when she returns, if she comes through here."

"Thank you. I'd appreciate that."

He hurried through his dinner, missing Lindsay's presence. She always took an interest in his activities. Already she had learned the name of every church member.

After his solitary meal, he sat at his desk to work on his sermon.

As the case clock in the hall chimed four, he pushed back his chair. His response to the bishop's inquiries was almost completed, but he'd hardly written a word of his sermon. He eyed his list of other duties. There were a few parishioners he must visit. But first, he'd see if Lindsay had returned.

He frowned when Elizabeth told him she hadn't. "'Tis a bit odd. But it's early yet."

He walked over to the kitchen window as if he might at that moment catch Lindsay opening the gate and walking down the garden path. But there was no one, making the scene look lonely and empty. "Any idea where she might have gone?"

"None at all, sir. She hasn't been out much except with Florence. Such a nice, quiet girl, not gadding about like so many society ladies. And now that Florence is gone, the dear girl has hardly been out at all."

The words pierced him. In his own efforts to preserve his distance, had he kept her shut in, never considering how she must be feeling in her new surroundings, away from all she held dear?

He donned his hat and took up his walking stick. "I'm

sure she will be back any moment. Tell her I've just gone to call on a few parishioners and will return shortly." Surely when he returned, Lindsay would be home.

Chapter Twelve

As soon as he entered the kitchen and saw the expectant look on Mrs. Nichols's face, his heart sank. "She hasn't shown up?"

"No, sir. I was sure she'd come walking in with you. Betsy's been looking out the door every quarter hour and been up to Mrs. Hathaway's room half a dozen times, just to make sure we didn't miss her coming in the front. I'll send her up now again."

"No, that's all right. I'll go up myself." He turned away from their worried faces and hurried up the stairs. He didn't realize he'd been holding his breath until he opened her door and saw the room empty.

His shoulders slumped. Where was she? Quickly, he turned to the other rooms, hoping against hope to see her in one of them. He checked the drawing room. But her easel stood off to the side, her paints put away, the settee vacant.

On the way back downstairs, he stopped once again

in her room, lingering a moment in her doorway. As he approached her dressing table, he smelled the scent of her eau de toilette. His eyes searched for the bottle but it wasn't on the mahogany tabletop. That's when he noticed how bare it was. There was no comb or hairbrush. He turned to scan the rest of the surface areas more closely. Her Bible was nowhere to be seen. His heart began to thud as he realized the implications.

Perhaps she'd left her Bible in the drawing room. He opened the cupboard to look at her gowns. Were any missing? He'd have no way of telling, even though she didn't have many. He suddenly felt a stab of conscience, thinking how many gowns she must have been forced to leave behind when she'd left her home.

He turned back to the room, his brow creased. Where had she gone? He hurried to check the drawing room again. His hands shook as he picked up books from the table surfaces. There was no sign of her Bible. She wouldn't have taken her Bible on a visit to a schoolgirl friend, would she?

One of her novels fell from his hands.

What had caused her to leave without even a note for him? She must be staying at a friend's, but why not let him know?

Fear stabbed his gut. And hurt. Why would Lindsay leave him without a word? Had she run away? The ugly thought that he'd refused to acknowledge could no longer be denied.

Had Florence said something to her? He dismissed the thought. She wouldn't have seen Florence today.

Yesterday? He felt tempted to ride out to the farmhouse and see if they might know something, but he discarded the idea, thinking Lindsay would probably return by the time he went there and back.

By evening he was frantic. Something was wrong. He could feel it in his heart.

He peered out the window. *Lord, where is she?* A young lady out on the streets of London wasn't safe. Why didn't they keep a carriage so he could at least know she had adequate transportation about the city?

He went to find Jacob and Elizabeth, no longer attempting to hide his worry. "I'm going out to look for her."

Jacob and Elizabeth stared at him then slowly nodded, relief on their faces. Damien grabbed his hat and stick again, this time deciding to take a hack. As he turned to walk down the path, Jacob came up behind him.

"I'll go with you, son. Two will be better than one. Any idea where her acquaintances live?"

"Not a clue. I just thought I'd ride to Mayfair and walk around the squares in hopes of seeing her."

They spent the next few hours doing just that, but to no avail. The streets gradually cleared of pedestrian traffic, the lamplighters lit the lamps and the watch stationed themselves in their booths.

He couldn't imagine Lindsay alone, even in the finer quarters. He even stopped by her former house. It was an enormous house on Grosvenor Square. A carriage drove up to the entrance. Damien watched from across the street, debating whether to present himself.

An elegant couple descended from the coach and made their way to the entrance. A liveried servant opened the door for them. Sounds of music came from within.

Jacob nudged him. "You know the place?"

"It's Lindsay's home."

Jacob merely nodded. After a moment, he said, "If you'd like, I'll ring at the service entrance and ask if anyone's seen her."

He considered, then shook his head. "I doubt they'd tell you. It looks like her father is entertaining. I don't think she would be here in that case." Her father's life certainly seemed to have gone on without his daughter. As far as Damien knew, Mr. Phillips had made no overtures to Lindsay since her marriage.

"I'm sure she's returned to the parsonage, Damien."

"Yes, I'm certain of it myself."

They hailed another hack and rode back in silence. When they returned Betsy hurried out. "Is she with you?"

"She's not here?" Jacob asked at the same time. Instead of entering the parsonage, Damien turned down the street. Jacob immediately asked, "Where are you going?"

Damien rubbed a hand wearily across his face.

"I don't know."

"I'll come with you," Jacob offered.

"No. Stay here. I'll just be walking in the vicinity. If she should return—"

"I'll look for you immediately."

"Thank you."

"Be careful, Damien. The streets aren't safe at night."

* * *

The cool evening air stung his eyes. Where was she? Was she cold? Hurt? Banishing images of her lying beaten and robbed in some alley, Damien strode down the front walk and onto Edgware Road. How he wished Jonah were with him.

There was no one and nothing on the wide road. Only a few lights twinkled from the row of houses farther down. He made his way toward Hyde Park Corner and the toll gate there.

He looked down Oxford Street where some coach traffic still traveled. Turning the opposite way, he headed down Uxbridge Road where everything was dark. A thousand terrible thoughts crowded into his mind of all the possibilities that could befall a young woman out alone on the streets at night.

Dear God, Show me where she is. Let her be safe inside somewhere. He didn't even know what friends she might have. How remiss he'd been, not finding out more of her world. He'd been so busy avoiding her that he'd neglected even the most basic attentions.

Jabbing his walking stick into the road, he started off, drawn to the chapel. He needed the Lord's direction.

He passed the fashionable new stucco houses along St. George's Row and entered into the silent church-yard. Approaching the heavy studded doors, he took the key from his pocket, unlocked one and eased it open. The dark sanctuary greeted him. He always felt an immediate sense of peace when he entered the empty building.

He walked down the center aisle, giving God thanks for His comfort and grace. He wished he'd brought a lantern. No matter, his eyes would soon adjust and he didn't need light to pray.

He reached the altar. Before kneeling down, he turned and scanned the area before him, thinking how different the church was when there was no one there. He squinted at a shadowy bundle on the front pew. Hesitating only an instant, he walked toward it.

It was a person. How had someone gotten into the church? His heart pounding wildly, he bent down. The next second a cloud shifted, allowing a glimmer of moonlight to shine through the stained-glass window. He almost collapsed in relief at the sight of Lindsay's golden locks.

He touched her lightly. "Lindsay?"

"Wha—?" Her disoriented voice signaled her waking. Her eyes widened with alarm. He immediately tightened his hold on her arm, afraid she'd fall off the pew as she began to sit up.

"Where am I? Damien!"

"Easy there. You're all right." Relief poured through him so he could hardly speak. He sat beside her, putting his arm around her, trying to refrain from clutching her to himself. Gratitude at having found her unharmed was the only thought in his mind.

The next second she collapsed against his chest, her voice breaking. "I'm sorry, Damien! I'm so sorry!"

His alarm rekindled and he tightened his hold on her. "Are you hurt?" He tried to move her away from him to see, but her hands clutched harder at his coat and she shook her head against him.

She began sobbing in earnest. He didn't know what to do. With his free hand he groped for his handkerchief and tried to give it to her. She took it from him but her crying didn't stop. All he could do was shelter her in his arms. Her shoulders shuddered and he rubbed his hands over her back, murmuring soothing words. What had happened to her? Who had upset her so? He could ask nothing until she was calmer.

When her tears finally dwindled into a few sniffles, he dared say, "None of us knew where you were. Mrs. Nichols said you'd gone to visit a friend, but no one knew where. When you didn't come back by dinner, and then supper, we grew concerned." He coughed, suddenly embarrassed to admit how worried he'd been.

She drew away from him just enough to look up into his face. The scant moonlight illuminated her tear-streaked cheeks. How he wanted to bring his hands up to cup them…bring his lips to hers to kiss away all trace of tears. Her words put a stop to his thoughts. "I…I'm sorry. I didn't think anyone would notice my absence."

"Not notice your absence?" He stared at her through the gloom. "How could you think that?"

She sniffled, looking down, saying nothing.

Realization dawned on him. "Did you think I'd care so little I wouldn't notice you'd gone? I thought you'd—" he swallowed "—run away."

"I did," came her small voice, and he felt stabbed afresh. She quickly added. "Not from *you*." A deep sigh shuddered through her. "But from what I…I've done to you. I've caused you so much harm."

"Nonsense. You've done nothing to be sorry about. Get that silly notion from your pretty head."

At her stubborn silence, he tightened his hold on her. "You've caused me nothing I can't face. It is I who should be sorry. I've been treating you abominably."

"No, you've been so patient with me."

"I've left you alone, not thinking how strange and new this life must be for you. Please forgive me."

"It's just I've felt so useless at the parsonage. And I've brought such calamity upon you. I'm so ashamed." Her voice sounded wobbly again.

The admittance of how he'd failed her convicted him afresh and he drew her against him. "None of that. You've brought nothing of the kind to me." Nothing but joy—bittersweet joy—but joy all the same. "Why do you say such things?" He felt the softness of her hair against his lips, the slimness of her back under his hand and wished…for more.

"I overheard about the bishop. You're to be censured because of me. Because of the lies I told. The ladies of the congregation despise me and I deserve it. I've ruined your life."

"No, you haven't. Who has been treating you so ill? You must tell me, and I shall deal with them."

She shook her head against his chest. "Oh, no!"

He smoothed his hand down her back, trying to reassure her but feeling helpless to ease her pain. "If anyone has treated you unkindly, it is probably because they are jealous of you—your beauty, your fine manners, all that is noble and good in you."

"I'm s-sorry I'm crying so much. I d-don't know why it is. I must be homesick." She gazed up as if horrified she'd said something wrong. "Not for all I left behind, but for knowing who and what I am. Nothing I do here is right."

"I'm sorry for not noticing how unhappy you've been." How could he tell her he'd stayed away from her deliberately? And in doing so, he'd made it worse for her. Instead of loving her, he'd proved himself a selfish individual, caring only about protecting himself. "Let me make it up to you."

She drew away from him and reluctantly he released her. "You know what I'd like best?"

He stared at her in the dark, wondering what she would say. "Whatever it is, I'll do everything in my power to give it to you."

"Oh, will you?" He read hope and anticipation in her tone.

"Yes." Anything to bring joy to her face again.

"I should dearly love to be more involved in your work. Not here at the parsonage," she added quickly. "I mean, when you go about your rounds—teaching at the orphanage, the kinds of things you and Florence are involved with at Newgate, at the workhouse…" Her voice dwindled away in doubt as he remained silent.

His heart fell in dismay at her request. If there was anything he wanted, it was to shield her from the sordid world he entered so often in his call as minister. "I…"

He stopped, trying to find a way to dissuade her without further discouraging her.

"Oh, please don't refuse me this! It's what I should like more than anything in the world!"

He sighed. "It's dangerous work, often filthy. I wouldn't want you to expose yourself when there's no need. There's ample for you to do with serving the congregation here as a hostess—"

Before he'd finished speaking, she'd turned away from him, her shoulders slumped.

He tried to think of a way to distract her. "Perhaps tomorrow, if the weather is as nice as it has been, we could go out for a drive or—" he had a burst of inspiration "—a picnic somewhere out in the countryside." He remembered something he'd heard a parishioner talk about. "Perhaps a boat ride."

"Yes, that sounds lovely." There was no enthusiasm in her tone. "But only if it doesn't take you away from your duties."

"It's quite all right. Perhaps getting away will inspire ideas for the sermon I'm struggling with right now."

"Maybe I can help you." Her tone brightened a bit.

"Yes, perhaps you can," he said in relief. "Come, let's get you back home. Everyone has been frantic."

She rose when he did, his arm still around her. "I'm so sorry I worried them. I didn't mean to cause anyone concern. I must apologize to Mrs. Nichols."

"That's all right. I'm just so glad you came here." He frowned. "Why were you here? How did you get in?"

She glanced around the darkened church and shivered. His fingers tightened around her shoulder as if to warm her. "I should get you back. You'll be chilled in here," he said.

"No! I mean…not yet."

He nodded, wondering what she dreaded so much.

"I came here when I got tired of walking." A smile lifted the edges of her lips. "I'd been walking all day. I didn't know where else to go. I finally came back here. The door was open and old Mr. Henderson was working in the back. I slipped inside and hid until he left. I just…needed a quiet place to sit and think."

"I shall have a key made for you. I often come here to think and pray. I was going to do that now, as a matter of fact."

She looked into his eyes once more. "But it's so late."

"I needed the Lord's guidance to find you. Jacob and I looked everywhere we knew. I kept telling myself you must be spending the night with a school friend, but when you sent no note, I couldn't help imagining the worst."

He took her lightly by the elbow and led her out of the church, turning to lock it after them. As they walked around the back toward the parsonage, she said again, "I do so wish you would let me come on one of your visits to the orphanage."

Her tone sounded so wistful he couldn't refuse. Perhaps if she went once, she'd be discouraged by the sight of so much need and would leave the work to him. A visit to the orphanage wasn't as dangerous as one to the workhouse or prison. "Very well. Perhaps the day after tomorrow, you could accompany me."

She stopped and turned to him, bringing her hands together. "Oh, truly! That would be wonderful!"

He couldn't help the warmth filling his heart at her enthusiasm. Would that he could make her feel so joyous every day!

The next day Lindsay stood at the edge of the large pond in Marylebone Park as Damien negotiated the rental of the boat. She still could scarcely believe he'd taken the whole day just for her.

After paying, he climbed aboard the rowboat from the small dock. She tensed as the boat rocked under him. Would he maintain his balance? Her arm reached out, but she dropped it almost immediately, remembering his dislike of being treated like a cripple.

He turned to her with a smile, a hand held out.

She placed one hand in his tentatively and lifted her skirts with the other. She stepped off the low dock onto the boat and stood a moment as the boat rocked under their feet again.

"All set, sir?" The owner of the boats for hire handed him the rope.

"Yes."

Lindsay settled upon the small seat at the stern, then watched as Damien sat facing her on the one thwart in the boat, closer to the bow. He took up the oars where they rested in the oarlocks and pushed away from the dock.

She sighed happily as the boat pulled away from shore. If only she could leave all the unpleasantness of the parish behind as quickly. She lifted her face to the warm sun. The day was perfect.

"Enjoying yourself?" Damien asked. She opened her eyes and met his with a smile.

"Oh, yes! Thank you for bringing me here today." She looked around at the vast parkland beyond the pond where a few sheep were grazing. "I've never been up this way before, though it really isn't so far from Mayfair."

The large pond was in the center of Marylebone Park. Away in the distance a forested slope was dark green against the blue sky. Puffy white clouds floated above her.

"Yes. I thought you might enjoy it. I haven't been here in an age. My sister and I used to come here often, growing up rather nearby." His arms pulled against the oars. "Soon it might be closed off if the regent has his summer palace built here. Construction of some of the villas has already begun."

When they'd first arrived, they'd passed the beginning of the terrace houses at the southern edge of the park. "I imagine it will be quite elegant when it's completed."

"Yes. But it's a pity ordinary citizens will no longer have access to it. Already the tenant farmers' leases haven't been renewed."

"Where will they go?"

He shook his head. "Who knows? Either they must find other farms to lease or move to find employment in the city."

She'd never thought of things like that. Her life had always been ordered for her. She gazed fondly at Damien. He had such a heart for the least important individual.

The small boat reached the middle of the pond. Large willow trees trailed their feathery branches into the dark water at its edges. An occasional swan or pair of ducks glided past them.

She fiddled with the tasseled end of her parasol. "It's not too much for you?"

He raised his eyes to hers, a slight frown of incomprehension bringing his brows together. "What?"

She gestured. "Rowing."

"No, it's all right. It involves my arms, not my legs." The words were spoken with an abruptness she'd never heard from him before. Her cheeks colored and she didn't know where to look. Unfortunately, her focus couldn't help shifting to his lower legs, the one, a long and shapely calf in its black stocking, the other a polished brown wooden stick.

What had she done? She bit her lip, removing her gaze and fixing it once more on the horizon. The beginnings of the city were visible through the trees at the southern end, and the muted sounds of construction came to them.

"I'm sorry," he said softly.

Her eyes flickered to his and she was caught by the intentness of the blue irises. "For what?"

"I didn't mean to snap at you."

"Oh, you didn't. I'm sorry for thinking you couldn't handle the boat. Please forgive me."

His lips curved upward and she remembered the feel of them on hers. How she yearned to reach toward him. But she'd probably rock the boat until it turned over. She couldn't help smiling at the image of them both in the water. It would feel good on this hot day.

"What are you smiling about?"

"Oh! Nothing." She couldn't help laughing at the sheer wonder of being out on the water alone with Damien and having him smiling at her as if no one else existed for him at the moment. "I just had a funny thought of us tipping the boat over and going for a swim."

His smile widened into a grin. "A swim would be a lovely thing on a day like today."

She wondered if he could swim with his wooden leg. His smile faded as if he read the direction of her thoughts. She quickly looked away again.

They rowed for a while longer in silence.

"When Mama was alive, I'd often go on outings like this with her at our country house. But since she died, and I've been away to school, life has been so different." She took her eyes off the scenery and looked at him. "Tell me about your parents."

"My parents were always so proud of me, although unwarranted, I assure you. I could do no wrong in their eyes, and perhaps because of that, I always wanted to do my best for their sake. I knew how hard they worked so I could go to school." He shook his head in amusement. "Even though I know if I'd ended up following in Father's footsteps as a simple clockmaker, he'd have been just as proud."

"He sounds like a fine man."

Damien nodded thoughtfully. "He was."

She smiled at the obvious admiration he had for his

father. Then she sobered. She'd admired her father, perhaps too much, and had disappointed him beyond words. "My papa was always trying to teach me things when I was younger and still at home—things that interested him, like mathematics and scientific method—but he finally gave up, saying I was too stupid."

"No!"

She blinked at the vehemence in his tone.

"I meant that you're not stupid at all."

She warmed at the praise. "Oh, he didn't say it in a mean-spirited way, only as an observation. He has that way about him. He never raises his voice to me—at least not until the night I came to you." She dipped her hand in the dark water. "He would just say things to me in the same way he'd remark about an experiment he was conducting. He told me I'd do better to stick with my watercolors and music."

"Both of which you do admirably."

She raised startled eyes to him. "I didn't think you'd noticed."

His eyes shifted away as if she'd caught him at something. "I've heard you singing and seen your pictures on the easel. I'm sorry we have no pianoforte for you to practice on."

"That's all right."

His gaze rested on her once again. "I'm sure in his own way, your father has always been very proud of you."

"Perhaps. He admires my…beauty. Like one of the butterflies in his collection. I often felt like a great big blue one he captured in Africa when I was a child. It's quite stunning." She blushed as she realized how she sounded. "I don't mean I'm stunning, but my father admired it so much, he had it put away beneath a glass case.

"I remember thinking what a pity it was pinned down until my father told me not to worry. It couldn't feel anything anymore. It was all dried up inside."

"Well, you were half-right."

She tilted her head at him, puzzled by what he meant. He was looking at her so warmly, she felt herself blush. She opened the fan she had looped around her wrist and began to fan herself.

"Is it too hot for you out in the sun?"

"No, I'm enjoying myself immensely."

He maneuvered the boat down a stream that emptied into the pond at the northern end. Here, more willows and large elm and oak trees offered shade. He rowed upstream until they came to an abandoned farm field. "Shall we have our picnic?"

"Yes, it's perfect, there under the tree." She closed her parasol and pointed with it to a chestnut tree not far from the stream.

He rowed close to the edge, then stood and pulled the boat with the oar until it bumped against the bank. He stepped out of the boat, taking a half jump through the reeds, and secured the rope around a stump. Then he held out a hand to her. "Here, let me help you. The edge is a bit muddy."

She clutched her parasol in one hand and waited to see what he would do. He grasped her about the waist and lifted her as if she weighed nothing at all. She clutched at his shoulder with her free hand. "Oh!" She said, then quickly added, "Don't hurt yourself."

"One thing about a wooden leg, it doesn't matter if it gets muddy."

She gasped, her gaze flying to his. But his eyes only twinkled back at her and suddenly they were both laughing. He set her down on the grassy bank, and her hand brushed the length of his arm before letting go of him.

He stepped away from her, his eyes not meeting hers, and busied himself with their picnic hamper and blanket.

"Let me take something."

"It's all right. I have everything. Come, you pick out a spot."

She led them to an area under the chestnut tree where the grass still grew, and the shade was speckled with sunshine that shone between the large leaves.

"Perfect." His voice expressed approval.

They set about spreading the blanket out and she knelt down and began unpacking the basket. "Mrs. Nichols outdid herself. Did she think we were going to be gone for a week?" She laid out rolls stuffed with sliced sausage meat and spread with mustard, cold pieces of chicken, blocks of cheese, hard-boiled eggs. "Oh, strawberries!"

Damien chuckled. "She believes one's digestion is directly related to one's state of happiness."

"Yes, I can see that."

Damien removed his hat and said a blessing.

As she fixed her plate, she asked, "Do you ever think about it much—having a wooden leg?" She held her breath, hoping he wouldn't take offense. He sat now with his good leg bent, the other stretched out.

He seemed startled for a moment but then replied thoughtfully. "Hardly anymore. It was difficult in college, not being able to play at sports, but since taking up the curacy, I've come in contact with so many less fortunate souls, whose condition in life is so much more severe than mine, that I'm thankful every day for all the Lord has blessed me with."

She smiled, thinking of her own well-being at that moment. "He has blessed us, hasn't He?"

He returned her smile and she felt the happiness grow within her so she thought she'd burst with it. "I can't wait to accompany you to the orphanage."

His smile faded. "Don't expect well-behaved children. They're a rough lot by and large. They've had to be to survive."

"Tell me about them," she said softly.

And he did, and she listened, feeling she could for hours, feasting her eyes on him.

A little bird had landed on the grass close to them and Damien threw it a crumb. Soon, there were half a dozen sparrows hopping on the grass, picking up the crumbs as soon as they fell.

The two of them sat very still and Lindsay watched, fascinated, as a couple of the birds drew nearer and nearer until they were almost within touching distance of his hand. She never tired of watching his hands. They were so expressive, his fingers long and slim.

"I used to be quite good at this as a boy," he said

quietly. "I'd play out in the woods and fields all day in the summer."

His patience was rewarded. Finally, the boldest of the little sparrows picked the crumb from the center of his palm, where it lay open on the ground.

His eyes met hers and he smiled, sitting back and brushing off his hands. "Jesus tells us we are of more value than many sparrows."

She nodded, thinking of her father's stuffed bird collection. How very different Damien's interest in these birds was from her father's in the dead species he collected and displayed.

All at once she experienced a yearning to get beyond her husband's reserve and know the Damien he hid from the world. The yearning was so deep it left her breathless. Would he ever let her get beyond the man who was always gentle and good-tempered, caring for even the least in the Kingdom of God?

How she longed to be the one who helped him with whatever weakness, pain or fear he might experience. But would he always try to protect her from the more serious sides of his work, and keep her sheltered like the butterfly in her father's glass case?

Chapter Thirteen

Damien looked up from the lesson he was giving to the group of twenty boys. At the far end of the sparsely furnished orphanage room, Lindsay sat on a low stool, a ring of young boys around her on the floor, their small, young faces rapt as she read to them from a storybook. A toddler of two sat on her knee, two of his fingers stuffed into his mouth.

Warmed by the sight, Damien turned his attention back to the older pupils, who ranged in age from five to fifteen. "Alfred, please read this sentence to me and fill in the verb."

The twelve-year-old boy with the lanky, pale hair and sad gray eyes squinted at the words on the chalkboard. "Y-yester-day wh-en I c-came home late, my m-mother—" The boy paused and scrunched up his face further at the blank chalk line in the sentence.

The silence stretched out and the boy was no nearer

the answer. Damien's glance roamed over the other boys. "Anyone care to answer?"

Two arms shot up. He chose the younger boy.

"Had already laid supper on the table," the boy finished proudly.

Damien turned back to the first boy. "Do you see why the missing word should be 'had'?"

Alfred pushed out his lower lip, still puzzling it out. "'Cause it was suppertime?"

The other boys roared with laughter, causing Lindsay to look up. Damien reassured her with a smile. "Yes, that is so. But the boy is late for supper and his mother has not waited for him. Thus, he must use the auxiliary verb 'had' to show that supper is already on the table. Do you see that?"

"Alfred's too slow to see anything," a large fourteen-year-old said from the rear row of desks.

Damien eyed him. "Since you are so much quicker than he is, Joel, why don't you do the figures for me in your mathematics text when the rest of us go outside to play in the yard?"

The boy slammed his book on the desk as the others laughed.

"All right, next exercise." Damien turned to the black-board. "Michael, can you read the sentence, please?"

"When I arrived at school, the bell…"

Later, in the large stone courtyard of the orphanage, the boys chased after a ball while the younger ones clung to Lindsay's skirts. Damien heard her tinkling laughter as she held two by the hand and instructed the others to form a circle.

He watched her as he kept half an eye on the older boys. He had never expected things to go so well. Since yesterday's picnic, he'd been living in a sort of cloud. He caught himself every few minutes remembering something, from the way Lindsay had looked sitting across from him to the feel of her slim waist when he'd lifted her out of the boat. For a few hours, he had almost believed they were courting and had a future together. He shook aside the notion as he did each time it formed in his mind. He must never forget he was only her protector for a time. As soon as her father showed any signs of softening, Damien would let her go.

Even this morning, he'd hesitated when introducing Lindsay as his wife to the boys. The more the world knew of her as Mrs. Hathaway, the more difficult it would be for her to return to her father. But she'd been so happy to come and looked at him so appealingly that he couldn't deny her request. He grinned, remembering the boys' reaction. At first the oldest ones had whistled and told her how pretty she was, but her response had been so ladylike, they'd soon been shamed into behaving like gentlemen.

"Reverend Hathaway, catch!" His attention swung back to the game, and he reached up just in time to catch the ball.

After the recess, they spent a few hours in the girls' half of the orphanage, giving reading and arithmetic lessons. Lindsay had brought some of her drawing materials and enthralled a group with a lesson.

In the late afternoon, they left the austere building at the eastern edge of Marylebone. Damien glanced up and down the street seeing no hacks available. Usually, he walked the few miles home, but with the day advancing and Lindsay with him, he didn't think it advisable.

"We shall probably have to head down to Oxford Street to find a coach," he said in an apologetic tone.

"I don't mind walking."

She was always willing to do anything he proposed, never complaining. He marveled at her spirit. "We shall need some new storybooks soon. The children love to be read to," she said.

"Perhaps some of the women in the parish would be willing to donate a few of their children's old books."

"Perhaps."

He glanced over at her. "Are any of the ladies thawing yet?"

She didn't look at him. "Mrs. Moore is a dear. She has tried to enlist some of the other ladies, but it seems as if every week, there is some new rumor about me. It's almost as if someone is making mischief, but then I tell myself I am imagining things." She shook her head. "In time, they should become accustomed to me."

They said no more for a bit. He wished he knew how to help her, but the more he tried to stand by Lindsay, making it clear to the congregation that she was his wife, the less it seemed to help. He wished he knew who the mischief maker was, if in fact one existed at all.

"Your drawing lesson was a marvelous idea—" His sentence was cut short by a dirty-looking young man who jumped out of an alley and stood in front of them, brandishing a cudgel.

"Who've we got 'ere?" he drawled, planting his feet apart and slapping the stout weapon against his dirty palm.

A group of youths emerged behind him. Damien took hold of Lindsay's arm, his eyes scanning the group. They were obviously a gang, one of the many that inhabited the neighborhood around the workhouse and orphanage.

Damien gauged their intent. The oldest, a heavyset youth as tall as Damien, looked about eighteen years of age. The youngest, a dirty urchin, appeared a sturdy twelve. In all, there were five of them.

Damien attempted to walk forward, keeping his tone steady. "Kindly let us pass."

The leader took a step directly in front of Damien and lifted his cudgel to his chest, effectively blocking Damien's way. He turned to the others, mimicking Damien's accent. "'Kindly let us pass.' D'ye hear, lads, we've got a toff."

The next instant the youths circled around them. Damien drew Lindsay near and gripped his walking stick.

"And look at 'is lady. Wot a fine-looking dame she is." The youngest one flicked one of Lindsay's curls and she flinched.

Damien shielded her with his body, feeling a sudden rage rise within him. "Leave the lady alone." His voice shook with anger but he feared that he wouldn't be able to defend her.

Raucous laughter greeted his words. "Jealous, are you?

What if I touch 'er like this?" The leader shoved Damien aside and rubbed the back of his hand against her cheek.

"Please!" she implored him.

Damien saw red. With a feral sound, he lunged at the young man, tackling him and pinning him to the ground.

The next moment someone wrested him off the gang leader and held his arms pinioned behind him. "Run, Lindsay!" he yelled before another youth punched him in the gut and he doubled over, the wind knocked out of him.

The leader righted himself and swung his cudgel at Damien. "Why, you—"

Lindsay screamed. Damien felt the blow like a sledgehammer to his arm and he fell to the ground. Lindsay rushed to him, kneeling beside him. "Are you all right? Damien! Say something."

Pain shot through this arm. Gritting his teeth, he attempted to push himself up.

"Wot's the cripple going to do?" The leader swung his cudgel in front of Damien's face before kicking him in the gut. Damien doubled over on the ground at the impact.

Lindsay scrambled to her feet. "How dare you attack a parson! You cowards!"

"Lindsay, don't," he tried to say through the haze of pain flooding him. He had to stand. He had to protect her.

While their attention was on Lindsay, he managed to get to his knees.

"You—you overgrown knaves!" Lindsay shouted at them, grabbing Damien's walking stick and swinging it at them. This caused them to jump back. They formed a circle around her and began to jeer.

He had to get their attention off of her. His gut screaming in protest, he pushed himself to his feet. "Leave the lady alone."

Deliberately, he shoved at the leader. "Only a coward attacks a lady."

The young man turned to Damien. "Look, fellas, the cripple's stood up. Let's have some fun. Grab his lady."

The largest youth grabbed Lindsay and held her by the waist. She began to scream and struggle. Damien rushed to her, but the gang leader grabbed him from behind and held him fast.

He fought against his hold but the other man was stronger. "Hold still or we'll hurt the lady."

The fight went out of Damien. Fear clawed at him as he looked at Lindsay's terrified face.

The youngest boy grabbed the walking stick from Lindsay and began to mock him, stooping over and wobbling on his legs, one hand in front of him as if begging. "Alms for the one-legged man, alms for the lame!" The taunts began in earnest.

Praying that their attention would remain on him and off Lindsay, Damien stood quietly.

But Lindsay kicked her captor on the shins and he let out a yelp. "We've got a wildcat here!"

"Leave the lady alone," Damien said again quietly, eyeing the boy. "Have your sport with me, but let her go."

"Did you 'ear that, lads?" jeered the leader, tightening his hold. "The parson says we can 'ave our sport with 'im. Wot are we waiting for?" At that, they all turned on him.

Damien prepared for the beating that was to come. Anything would be preferable to having any one of them lay his filthy hands on Lindsay. He prayed she'd make a run for it.

His walking stick was stabbed into his middle. Damien flinched, causing them all to laugh. He clenched his stomach, praying that he wouldn't disgrace himself before Lindsay.

"Leave him alone. He is a man of God, you black-guards!" Lindsay screamed with fury.

He shook his head at Lindsay in warning.

"A 'man o' God'?" came the mocking tones. With more zeal, they tugged at his coat and pulled his watch chain until it came loose. "Oh, this'll fetch us a pretty penny," the youngest boy cried, holding up his watch. The leader grabbed it from him and stuffed it in his pocket. "Search for his handkerchief."

"Here's his pocketbook." Another gang member took his leather wallet and shook it open. The younger ones went scrambling for the few coins that fell out of it. They looked at Damien in disgust. "Hardly more'n a few coppers." Damien knew to carry little money when he went about his rounds in this neighborhood. "Where's the rest of yer blunt?"

"I don't have any."

He received a blow to his cheek that knocked his head back. He worked his jaw, hoping it hadn't been dislocated.

"If you 'aven't any more blunt, we'll see wot else you've got o' value."

The younger boy laughed. "Wot about his wooden leg?"

All eyes focused on his leg. One of them kicked at it. "Nice piece of polished oak, I'll wager. It'll fetch us a few quid."

Damien braced himself. Rough hands tugged at the leather strap holding it in place. He would have fallen if his arms hadn't been gripped from behind.

The youth waved his wooden peg leg in the air with a triumphant shout. "Look at this. I can knock someone over the 'ead wiv this stick!"

The next second, the boy jerked to a stop at the clatter of horse hooves and carriage wheels down the street. "Away, men, away!" the gang leader shouted.

In a flash, they scattered down the alley. Damien fell to the ground. With a cry, Lindsay came to him, but he was already struggling to stand.

She took him by the arm and helped him up. "Are you all right?"

"I'm fine," he assured her, looking at her closely. Black fingerprints smudged her cheeks and her hair had come loose from her struggle. Futile anger rose again at the manhandling she'd endured. And he'd been able to do nothing to prevent it. "Did they hurt you?"

She shook her head almost impatiently. "No, but what they did to you! Oh, I could murder them!" She touched his jaw with her fingertips. "It's swelling." With a half sob, she dug into her pocket for a handkerchief.

"They even stole your handkerchief," she said as she wiped the dirt from his face.

"Thank the good Lord for sending help." He looked at the approaching coach.

Without a word, Lindsay draped his arm across her shoulder to support him. Her slim form was surprisingly strong. "Are you sure they didn't hurt you?"

"I've been through worse." Now that the immediate danger was past, Damien found it hard to look at Lindsay. The humiliation of the encounter and his present condition came to the fore.

As the coach drew near, she waved at it. "Stop! Please stop! We've been robbed."

With a jingle of harness, the horses drew to a stop, a cloud of dust billowing around them. A groom swung down from the footboard in the rear.

"A gang has set upon us and robbed my husband," Lindsay cried out breathlessly as the man hurried to them.

The groom's eyes widened at the sight of Damien. "Are you all right, sir?" His glance flickered from his face to his leg, and Damien felt the strain of staying upright on one leg.

"If you could be so good as to take us back to my parish on Edgware Road," he managed, his body feeling pummeled and bruised.

The groom gave another bow. "If you will excuse me a moment, sir, I will arrange it." He returned to the coach and conferred at the carriage window with the man within. In a few moments he was back.

He handed Damien a card. "My employer offers you

use of his carriage to wherever you and your wife need to be conveyed."

Lindsay took the card before Damien could reach out his arm, which had begun to throb abominably. She held it out for him to read. *Mr. Robert Bellamy* was engraved in a fine script with a Mayfair address. "Thank you. We should be most grateful," she answered for Damien.

The man coughed and held out his hand. "Would you like me to assist you?" he asked in a hesitant voice.

"They beat my husband terribly and stole his wooden leg," Lindsay replied before Damien could say anything.

He felt the flush stain his cheeks.

The groom *tsked-tsked.* "Terrible things that happen on our streets these days. In broad daylight, too."

Damien hopped to the coach door, the young groom supporting him on one side, Lindsay hovering on the other. By the time they reached the coach, the pain was nearly overwhelming. Damien fought to remain conscious.

A distinguished-looking gentleman leaned out of the door and grasped his arms to help him up. Damien swallowed a groan at the pressure on his swollen arm. "My goodness, what happened? What did they do to you? Are you hurt, sir?"

"I'm all right," he managed, falling onto the seat. He turned to the groom and gave him the address of the parsonage.

"Very good, sir. I'll convey it to the coachman."

Damien leaned back against the swabs, angry at himself, feeling as helpless as a beached seal. "I'm very grateful for your help, sir," he said to the coach's owner.

Then he turned to assist Lindsay, but the groom handed her up into the coach.

She sat down beside Damien. With a quick nod to the owner, she turned to face Damien. "Are you all right?" she whispered, taking his hand.

He nodded, unable to say more due to his humiliation as much as the pain.

As the coach began to move, they both turned to the gentleman seated opposite. Mr. Bellamy looked to be in his sixties with gray hair worn in the older style of a queue. His clothes, too, were in the past fashion of knee breeches. His pale, well-tended hands rested upon a walking stick as he studied Damien. "You are a clergyman?"

"Yes, sir." He introduced himself and Lindsay, the rumble of the coach jarring every sore muscle in his body.

"You were set upon, my man tells me."

"Yes, by a gang of young men."

"Shameful to set upon a clergyman!" he said with a decisive shake of his head. His sharp eyes focused on Damien's leg. "And a cripple. What is the city coming to?"

Lindsay squeezed his hand as if she understood his mortification at the ugly term. "There is a lot of delinquency," he said quietly. "With little gainful employment and much less schooling, the youths prey on those who have more than they do."

"They need to be transported, I say." Mr. Bellamy thumped his walking stick against the floor.

As they neared home, Damien's spirits continued to plummet. Thankfully, Lindsay carried most of the conversation with the old gentleman, turning frequently to

Damien to ask him if he was all right. He merely smiled and nodded his head.

All the while, he relived the pain and humiliation of the encounter. His worst fears had come true. He could not protect Lindsay. What would have happened to her if the coach had not arrived in time? What kind of man couldn't protect his own wife?

When they arrived at the parsonage, Lindsay called for Jacob.

"Please fetch a doctor. Hurry!"

After his shock at the sight of Damien, Jacob hurried forward. "Of course, madam. Let me help him in first."

She stood aside but Damien was already at the coach door, clutching at its sides though he looked as pale as death. "It's all right, Jacob," he said. "It's only a few bruises. A doctor won't be necessary."

Jacob helped him descend, then he and the groom sustained Damien between them up the walk.

Lindsay bit her lip, imagining the pain he must be in. It was awful to see him have to hobble up the walk one-legged. Tears smarted her eyes in renewed anger at those who had brought this about.

She turned at the sound of someone clearing his throat.

"Oh, I beg your pardon," she told the elderly gentle-man as she held out her hand. "You have been ever so kind. I cannot thank you enough for all your help. The Lord sent you at just the right moment to rescue us! I shudder to think what would have happened."

He patted her hand. "It's quite all right, my dear lady. You run along to that fine husband of yours." He sighed sadly. "What a pity about his leg. Such a worthy-looking gentleman."

Lindsay hid her impatience at the man's continued references to Damien's disability and lifted her chin. "Yes, he is a most worthy man." How brave Damien had shown himself and how proud she was to be able to call him her husband.

Bidding Mr. Bellamy a last farewell, she hurried up the path. "Mrs. Nichols, has the doctor been fetched?"

"Yes, Betsy has run for the apothecary. Jacob is tending him now."

She breathed her first sigh of relief. "Thank you, Mrs. Nichols." Her voice broke.

The housekeeper put her arm around her. "There, there, madam. Our Damien will be all right. Now, come, I've given him a strong cup of tea. You look as if you could use one, too."

She smiled tearfully at the older woman. "Oh, thank you. It was such a fright."

"I can imagine. Why don't you come with me and tell me what happened."

"Just as soon as I look in on Damien." She stopped as they were about to enter the house. "What's he going to do…about…?" Lindsay paused, embarrassed at having to say anything about Damien's leg.

But Mrs. Nichols seemed to guess. "Oh, don't worry, madam. He has a spare one." She pursed her lips. "He'll have to get a second one made, though, I suppose. But he'll be all right for a few days, as long as no other calamity strikes." With a shake of her head, she patted Lindsay's hand and bustled away to the kitchen.

Lindsay hurried to find where Jacob had taken Damien. She found them in the study. Damien was holding a cold compress to his cheek. He smiled when he saw her.

She breathed a sigh of relief. "How are you feeling?"

"A little the worse for wear," he said wryly.

Jacob excused himself and left them alone. Damien reached out a hand for her and she clasped it eagerly, grateful that they were both safe and sound. "Are you sure you're all right? None of them hurt you?" he asked her.

She marveled that all his concern seemed to be for her. "Oh, no. But I was so angry at them." She took in a shuddering breath, remembering how much she'd wanted to scratch their eyes out for what they were doing to Damien. They could have simply robbed him and left him. Instead, they'd had to humiliate him. She'd hated them in that moment. How she'd wished she'd been a man so she could have run after them and give them their due. "How can there be such cruelty in the world?"

"There are many reasons. Suffice it to say it's a fallen world."

She shook her head, not ready to accept such a simple explanation. "They were bullies. And the youngest. He was just a boy! They shouldn't be so hardened."

He rested his head against the chair back. "You don't

know what their life has been like up to now, what it is like to know no kindness from the day you are born."

She was silent. How she wished she could reach over and brush the hair off Damien's forehead, but she didn't dare. Instead she said softly, "You were so fearless."

He looked away from her, letting her hand go, his expression sobering. "No, I was very much afraid for you." After a moment he added. "I wasn't very good at protecting you today."

She placed her hand on his arm. "I was so thankful you were there with me. No one could have been braver."

He shook his head. "Don't give me too much credit. I was angry at them for the way they grabbed you. I wanted to beat them up, like any man would, for daring to touch you. But I couldn't do a thing."

"Don't say that. There was nothing you could do, nothing any man could have done!" She could see that her words weren't reaching him, but she desperately wanted to make him feel better. His jaw was beginning to show a bruise. She remembered his arm had sustained a terrible blow and must be paining him greatly. As she relived the event, she suddenly had a realization which made him all the more dear to her. "You let them make sport of you to protect me, didn't you?"

He was silent a moment. "There wasn't much I could do otherwise. I was quite outnumbered. Besides, I'm a cripple." There was no denying the self-derision in the quietly spoken words.

"You are not! I'm sure you could have bested that

insolent young man who was the leader of them if you hadn't been outnumbered."

"I'm sorry you had to be caught in the middle."

"I'm not," she answered stoutly. "I'm glad I was able to see what you risk each day when you go on your rounds to help others."

He rubbed a hand across his eyes. "This was what I had feared might happen one day if you accompanied me on my rounds outside the immediate vicinity of the chapel."

"Oh, please don't make me stay in because of this!"

He said nothing.

"I want so much to help you in your work," she said, leaning forward. "Even today, I'm sure your behavior touched some of these young men—perhaps the youngest. I'm sure they won't soon forget you."

He finally met her gaze but she could discern no agreement. "I'm sure I did nothing to draw them to God's saving grace. I behaved like any 'toff' they meet. I became angry and tried to defend what was mine. I showed them nothing of the love of the Savior, for I was too enraged by their treatment of you."

The words that should have thrilled her gave her a strange sadness. He was disappointed in himself but she didn't understand why. He had behaved bravely and she was proud of him. But his eyes remained haunted and she felt he had withdrawn to a place where she couldn't reach him.

They were torturing Damien, beating him with his wooden leg and that awful cudgel. Damien shielded his face with his arms, but the cudgel left him bloody and bruised.

Lindsay awakened, heart pounding, perspiration dampening her forehead. The stillness around her finally made her realize it had been nothing but a horrible dream. A nightmare. Slowly, her heartbeat returned to normal, but her fear remained. The afternoon's incident came to vivid relief in the pitch dark room. She pictured Damien pinioned by those awful youths, allowing himself to be attacked in order to protect her.

A wind whistled outside, causing her to slide down further beneath her covers.

What if someone broke into the house? It happened frequently in London. There was no one in the house except her and Damien. Jacob and his family lived in a cottage at the rear of the grounds. They wouldn't know a thing. He and his wife were too old to be able to defend them anyway.

The longer Lindsay thought on these things, the greater her fear grew. She glanced toward her door. Damien was only two rooms down. How she longed to go to him. He'd reassure her.

But she couldn't do that. He needed his sleep. Although the apothecary had ascertained that there were no broken bones, he'd told Damien to rest a few days.

But as the minutes ticked on, Lindsay's desire to be near Damien increased. The remnant of her dream whispered around her. She heard the echo of the ruffians' jeers and saw their cruel kicks in her mind's eye.

Finally, her heartbeat pounding in her ears, she eased

the bedcovers away from her and groped for her dressing gown. She slid out of bed, her bare feet touching the soft carpet. It took all her courage to leave her bed but the thought of another human face—the kind, friendly face of the one she trusted most—beckoned her forward.

She reached the door, her dressing gown still clutched in her hands, and opened it, staring down the corridor. It was very dark—she couldn't even see the window at the far end. Swallowing, she stepped into the hallway and eased her door closed.

She walked barefoot down the corridor. Never had it seemed so far. She passed Florence's old room. Finally, she stopped outside Damien's door. She heard no sounds from within and had a moment of panic, thinking herself alone in the house. She gripped the doorknob and turned it. It made a rattling sound and she feared she would wake him. Wasn't that what she was going to do anyhow? She felt guilty once again. Maybe she could just slide in beside him and not awaken him. As soon as it was light, she'd leave.

She'd come too far to turn back. She would not face her lonely room again. She needed human warmth and companionship. No one would hurt her if Damien was beside her. All she needed was to touch his face, to assure herself it had only been a dream, that he was all right.

She walked slowly across the room, unfamiliar with its layout and fearing she'd bump into something in the dark. She headed toward its center, knowing his bed must be there.

Stifling a cry, she hit her knee against the edge. Feeling along the side of it with her outstretched arms, she made her way towards its head.

Suddenly, she heard a rustle of bedclothes. "Who's there?" His voice sounded calm, as it usually did, but a trifle fuzzy with sleep. She breathed a sigh of relief at its familiar timbre.

"It—it's only I—Lindsay."

"Lindsay?" Wonder turned to alarm. Another rustle of bedclothes indicated he'd sat up. "What is it? Is something the matter?"

"Yes. I mean, no. I'm all right. It's just…" She swallowed, embarrassed now. He'd think she was a baby. She remembered her father's cold tones whenever she'd say something he considered immature for her age.

"What is it?" His voice had softened.

"I had a nightmare."

She heard him take a deep breath. "I'm sorry. It's understandable. It was a harrowing experience for you. Perhaps if I prayed for you—"

"May…may I stay here tonight?" Her voice sounded shaky. Would he be horrified by her request? She held her breath, biting her underlip. *Please,* she prayed, *don't let him send me back to my room.*

Chapter Fourteen

Damien was silent so long, she was sure he was going to refuse.

"Please," she whispered. "I'm scared."

She heard him sigh. "All right." The bedclothes rustled some more as if he were shifting. She tiptoed forward and inched her way onto the soft feather mattress. The space felt warm and cozy. Before she could cover herself up properly, he was doing it for her, bringing the blankets up to her chin and tucking her in as if she were a child. She turned to him gratefully. "Thank you. I hope I don't disturb you while you sleep."

"It's all right." His voice was a soft breath above her. The next thing she knew he put his arm around her and she was able to snuggle up against him, being careful of his bruised side.

"I'm not hurting you, am I?"

"No, it's fine."

He felt warm and solid. She brought her hand up to

his chest and felt his steady heartbeat. Oh, how right it felt! She closed her eyes and smiled in the dark.

"Tell me about the dream."

She took a deep breath, not wanting to recall the horror of it. "We were surrounded by that gang of boys again," she began, then stopped, not wanting to describe how brutally they were beating him. "Their faces were awful. They were so cruel." She shuddered and hid her face against his chest, reassured by its broad strength and the smell of his cotton nightshirt.

His hand squeezed her shoulder. "Don't think of it. It was only a dream. The Lord saved us and sent us help."

His soft voice soothed her until she could forget the dream and think only of the warm, firm presence beside her. She grew drowsy and soon drifted off, wondering if now she would truly be his wife....

Damien held himself rigid until he heard Lindsay's soft, even breathing, telling him she had fallen asleep. The shock this afternoon amidst the gang of boys was nothing compared to awakening from a deep sleep to find Lindsay in his room. His defenses had been down. He would have helped her back to her room, but the real fear in her voice had undone him and he couldn't deny her request.

He'd vowed to keep her pure. And now here she lay curled up against him, so close she could feel his heart-beat and he could feel the steady rhythm of her breathing.

Suddenly, he felt angry tears of frustration well up in his eyes as he became conscious of his leg, picturing his ugly scarred stump as he lay in his bed. The afternoon's attack played itself in his mind in all its humiliating detail.

What this afternoon had shown him was how little he resembled the man of God he had believed himself to be. Since he was a young boy and had found solace for his crippled condition in the Lord, he had tried his best to emulate Him.

Turn the other cheek; pray for those who despitefully use you; bless those who curse you. These had been the words he'd lived by. Since his ordination as a minister, he'd lived a clean, humble life, trying to win those lost souls in the street by showing them love. And this afternoon, all he'd felt was blind rage and hatred toward those who had dared to touch the woman he loved.

The woman I love. This afternoon had also taught him how deep his love for this young woman brought into his care had become. Knowing she was asleep now, he dared stroke her hair. It felt like silk. She nestled in the crook of his arm. Her nightcap rubbed his chin and the end of her long braid fell over his hand. She smelled good, like a spring breeze blowing in from the outdoors mixed with the wholesome starch of freshly ironed clothes.

But he would never be able to sleep with her body pressed against his. He prayed for control. *Please God, don't let me take advantage of her innocence. Give me strength. Please help me!*

Finally, when her breathing deepened, he dared ease

his arm from beneath her, grimacing in pain as he shifted on his back, trying not to disturb Lindsay. Before he moved farther from her, he leaned down and kissed her tenderly on her cheek. She smelled so sweet. His fingers curled into fists as he fought for control.

Finally, with a strength of will he didn't think he possessed, he moved to the far edge of his bed and turned away from her, dreading the long night ahead of him.

His clock ticked on, marking the seconds, then minutes. The night stretched out before him interminably.

His thoughts returned to the attack that afternoon. If anything had proved how unfit he was to take care of her, it was that. Not that a whole man wouldn't have been hard-pressed to defend himself and a lady against those burly young men and boys.

But another man would not have been walking there with his wife. He'd carry a knife sheathed in his walking stick, or keep his own carriage. He couldn't be robbed of a leg and left helpless on the ground, unable to walk, much less fight.

Damien's life was another, he reminded himself. His call was to minister to those that needed to hear the gospel most, and many times they were not the souls sitting in the pews on Sunday, but those on the highways and byways, in the orphanages, workhouses and prisons, places he couldn't—shouldn't—have taken Lindsay, no matter how much she wanted to accompany him. He vowed he would never put her at risk like that again—especially since he was so powerless in the face of danger.

* * *

Damien opened his eyes to find sunlight filling his room. It must be mid-morning at least. He brought a hand up to his temple, wondering why he'd overslept.

Lindsay! Immediately, he looked at the place beside him on the bed and breathed a sigh of relief to find it empty, although the pillow's indentation and the drawn-back covers told him Lindsay's appearance in his room last night had been no dream.

He reached over and touched the pillow. A single strand of golden hair gleamed against the white linen. He picked it up and rubbed it between his fingertips. It felt like silk. He turned to the small table by his bed and opened his Bible, laying the hair within its pages.

Sometime in the night he must have finally fallen asleep. He yawned now, still feeling tired. He must rise—he had several visits to make as well as his sermon to prepare. He pulled off the bedcovers and stared for a moment at his legs, the outline of the whole one under his nightshirt and the empty space below the knee of the other one. It filled him with disgust as he remembered the boys' ridicule the day before.

Just as he was about to get up, he heard a knock on the door. "Yes?" he said, unable to hide the alarm in his voice.

Lindsay peeked around the doorway. Quickly, he pulled the bedclothes back over himself to hide his stump, and sat against the pillows, his heart thudding in sudden panic. "Lindsay."

Her smile seemed brighter than the sunshine itself. She also appeared as fresh as butter in her frock and apron, a clean cap on her golden hair. She carried a tray in her hands. "Good morning. I was hoping you'd be awake. I brought you some breakfast."

He gripped his bedclothes in his hands, the impulse to stand and help her strong. But he knew it was impossible until he strapped on his leg.

She brought the tray to his side of the bed and he reached out to take it from her, in the hopes that she'd move away.

"You didn't have to do that," he murmured. Was this arrangement to be one humiliation after another?

"I know, but I just wanted to thank you for taking pity on me with my childish fears." She perched on the edge of the bed, her eyelashes fluttering downwards.

He settled the tray on his lap, shifting in the process so he wouldn't touch her. "Your fears weren't childish. You had a terrifying experience yesterday." He looked down at the tray, remembering so many frightening incidents from his childhood.

"Were you scared yesterday?"

"I was terrified for you." He sighed, rubbing his temple. "I should have been better able to protect you."

Her eyes flashed. "Oh, no! You did wonderfully. No one could have overpowered so many attackers! Please don't feel badly. I couldn't bear it."

He couldn't help smiling at her obvious distress for his sake.

"So, if I feel frightened again, I may come to you?"

He swallowed. What did she mean exactly? Before he could formulate a reply, she continued, "I mean, may I come to you at night? That's when things appear scariest."

Her eyes were so guileless he didn't have the heart to refuse her. "Of course."

"I didn't rob you of sleep?"

He cleared his throat, fiddling with the edge of the rolled-up napkin on the tray. "No."

"I'm glad. I was afraid when you didn't appear at breakfast that you might have overslept because of me. I know sometimes one has trouble falling asleep again when one is woken up in the middle of the night."

Unable to tell her truthfully how long he'd lain awake, he fixed his gaze back on the tray. Everything looked appetizing. A blue ware plate held a thick slice of fried ham and a sunny egg. Triangles of toast stood on a rack, a small crock of butter and a crystal dish of jam beside it.

If only he could enjoy it, but his stomach was tied up in knots with her sitting there, looking so beautiful. He pulled off his nightcap and ran his fingers through his hair, attempting to bring some order to it. He hadn't even had a chance to wash his face and couldn't very well rise now. He cringed just thinking of hobbling one-legged in front of her to the washstand.

She got up and smoothed the coverlet where she'd sat, her hand grazing his thigh. "Please, have your breakfast before it gets cold." She stood close to him, right at the edge of the bed. How sweet she smelled, like roses. "Here, let me pour you a cup of coffee. I brought a cup for myself, if you don't mind. I thought it would be a little like our picnic the other day." He could hear the smile in her voice though he dared not look up. "Here we have no worry about ants, although I must be careful not to spill anything." As she spoke, her hand came into view and she picked up the round little pot with its painted flowers and poured them each a cup.

He swallowed, wondering how he was ever going to manage to eat anything. She set the pot down, and her hand came up to his face. She brushed back a lock of his hair that had fallen over his forehead. He couldn't tear his gaze from hers.

Her brown eyes held only warmth. "Come, don't you like anything I brought you? I thought it would be a treat from your usual porridge."

"Yes, how thoughtful of you." His fingers gripped the edges of the tray. Finally, as she moved away, he managed to bow his head and say grace. She perched on the other half of the bed. He picked up his mug and brought it to his lips.

"Don't let your food get cold."

He unfolded his napkin and began to cut into his ham and eggs as she spoke about what had transpired in the household below this morning. "Mrs. Nichols let me fry the ham and eggs myself. Did they turn out all right?" She looked worried until he nodded his head, trying to smile with his mouth full. She returned his smile and he felt warmed by the relief in her face.

Truthfully, it seemed so natural to have her sitting there…like a wife. His attention fell to her hands as she held her cup on her knee. He couldn't see her left hand from where he sat, but he knew she wore the thin gold band he'd given her on their wedding day. He realized that she wore no other jewelry. He narrowed his eyes, looking more closely at the rest of her. When he'd first known her, she was always fashionably dressed. Never ostentatious, but always with some little thing, a pair of dangling gold earrings, or a fragile necklace at her throat, sometimes a brooch fixed to a velvet collar or pinned to her garment.

She moved suddenly, turning her body toward him, and he caught sight of the thin gold band. His heart swelled with a sudden, uncontrollable pride. The wedding band was a mark of his right to her. It announced to the world that she was his. He glanced down at the matching band on his finger. Just as he was hers.

How true the latter statement. He was hers until the day he died, whether she ever knew it or not. But the band on her finger also mocked him. It represented so much, so much that he would never enjoy. Its bright clean shine taunted him now. *A husband in name only.*

His eyes rose to find her regarding him strangely. "I'm sorry," he said with a slight shake of his head, feeling his cheeks redden. "What did you say?"

"I just asked you to pass the coffeepot."

He did as she asked and poured some into the cup she held out to him, hearing the sound of the hot liquid spilling into it above the sound of his thudding heart.

"Thank you," she murmured. "The sugar, please?"

"Of course." How stupid of him. He held out the bowl to her. She took it from him, her fingers brushing his. Did they linger? He held the sugar steady by sheer dint of will.

Sham of a husband. His mind mocked the pretty, cozy scene. All a sham. She in her pretty mobcap, her golden curls tucked behind her delicate ears. He pressed his lips together, unable to picture how he was to endure the coming day…weeks….

When he'd finished eating, she came around to his side of the bed again and bent to take his tray.

"Leave it. I'll take it down."

"Nonsense." She began to lift it.

He held up a hand. "Don't, or you'll make me feel like an invalid."

She looked up at him, stricken, and immediately let the tray go. "I didn't mean…" She backed away from him. "Excuse me." Without another look back, she hurried from the room.

In the stillness after the echo of the closing door, Damien's head dropped back onto his pillows, his eyes shutting for an instant. He felt worse than he had yesterday when he'd lain helpless in the street.

Slowly, he laid the tray aside and got up from the bed, half hopped over to a chair and sat down to strap his peg leg on, his movements slow and ponderous.

Once again, recriminations heaped themselves upon him. He'd saddled a pretty young lady to a cripple and he saw no way out now. Her father had made no overtures. More and more people were coming to know them as a true married couple.

When he finally finished washing and dressing, he

made his way downstairs in search of Lindsay to apologize for his careless remark.

Knock, knock, knock went his wooden leg against the staircase. The sound disgusted him as never before, even when he'd been a young lad and had first had to accustom himself to its detestable sound.

He reached the bottom of the stairs and began his search. The drawing room was empty and his heartbeat sped up. What if she'd left again? No! The thought hit him harder than the kick to his gut one of those youths had given him yesterday. *Please,* he prayed, *let her be here to accept my apology.*

Suddenly, the thought of losing her was more than he could bear. How could he ever give her up when the time came?

That night Lindsay paced in her bedroom after she'd donned her nightgown. What was she going to do? Or rather, *where* was she going to spend the night?

The day had passed uneventfully. Damien had apologized for his remark, saying he'd been overly sensitive since the day before. She'd assured him it didn't matter, swearing to herself she wouldn't make him feel like an invalid or cripple or less than a man, ever again.

But she'd still sensed that same wall of reserve around him, which she'd hoped would be breached after their night together. She stopped in front of her mirror and stared at herself. Her hair cascaded down past her shoulders after brushing it out. Her white gown, modest with its frilly collar and long puffy sleeves ending in wide swathes of lace covering half her hands, made her look like a schoolgirl.

Would Damien reject her if she went to his room again tonight? The fear of the previous day's attack had largely passed, so it was not a question of being scared of staying in her own room by herself. No. It was a question of loneliness.

Dreadful loneliness engulfed her. She didn't want to be without him tonight.

Damien had said she could come back…if she was scared, she reminded herself.

She had to find out. She had to risk his rejection because she couldn't go on this way, being his wife in name only. She pulled her hairbrush one last time through her hair and set it down. She took her hair up in her hands then let it go slowly. She wouldn't braid it tonight but leave it loose.

Taking a deep breath, she marched to her door, her heart beginning to pound until its thud drowned out all other sounds.

Damien had not yet retired for the evening. As usual, she'd bidden him good-night, leaving him reading in the drawing room. Tonight, she would wait for him in his room. When he discovered her in his bed, would he ask her to leave?

Every evening Damien forced himself to sit in the drawing room until Lindsay rose to retire. He steeled his features to betray nothing but friendly solicitude when she finally set aside her book for the night, and pretended an interest in his own book that he was far from feeling.

Even after she left, it took him some time to focus his attention back on his work. This evening the words kept swimming before his eyes as his thoughts returned again and again to the previous night and Lindsay's warm presence in his bed. A longing for her fought with relief that he'd survived it. Her virtue remained intact.

Finally, well after he knew she would have fallen asleep, he rose and closed his book. After winding the clock and checking the locks, he took his candle and climbed slowly upstairs.

As he entered his room, he glanced briefly at the closed curtains around his bed, puzzled. Mrs. Nichols or Betsy usually didn't come up to his room in the evening.

He thought no more about it but went about his nightly preparations for bed. The last thing he did was sit on the chair and repeat what he had done that morning in reverse, unstrapping the thick leather band and removing the wooden leg. Then he blew out his candle and pushed aside his bed curtain.

He had settled himself on his back in the dark, his mind beginning a prayer, when he heard soft, steady breathing at his side. His body tensed, every muscle rigid in stunned disbelief.

With utmost care, he turned on his side and reached out. His fingers came in contact with silky curls. He swallowed, not daring to move. He hazarded a whisper. "Lindsay?"

"Damien?" came the sleepy reply.

Before he could decide what to do, she turned to him and curled against him. "You finally came up."

He blew out a breath, trying desperately to hold himself in check. "Why aren't in your own room?"

"Because I belong here," she answered after a few seconds, her voice becoming more alert.

"I don't think this is a good idea."

"Why not?"

He paused. "Because you're a woman and I'm a man."

"You are my husband and I am your wife."

He sighed heavily. "I took an oath in which I promised to protect you. That included returning you to your father someday."

Long seconds passed. Finally, she moved away. When he glanced her way, her back was to him.

Slowly, he eased as far away from her as he could.

Despair overwhelmed him. This was too much for him to bear. How was he going to make it through the night without touching her?

Give me strength, he began to pray.

The long night hours stretched before him.

Lindsay awoke to complete darkness. She became aware of being wrapped in someone's embrace from behind. Then she remembered her gamble.

"Damien?" she whispered.

He didn't answer, but continued to hold her, nuzzling the back of her neck. Was he awake?

Was she finally to know what it meant to be his wife?

Slowly, she turned to him, afraid of halting his caresses. She began to return his kisses, praying that all barriers between them would fall that night.

Suddenly he separated his lips from hers. "Lindsay?" came his hoarse whisper. Before she had a chance to answer, he was pushing away from her. "Oh, no, I'm sorry." His whisper couldn't mask the horror in his tone.

She couldn't let him stop now. In desperation, she clung to him, wrapping her arms about his neck and kissing his cheeks, his jaw, pressing her body to his. *Kiss me back. Kiss me back, please, Damien,* she begged silently. When he remained unmoving, she pulled back a fraction. "It's all right, Damien," she whispered, "I'm your wife."

She would not let this night be over without becoming his wife in truth.

And then he was kissing her as if he couldn't get enough, his hands digging into her hair, his body responding to hers.

Damien awoke to full sunshine. Someone must have pushed aside his bed curtains.

He felt sated, like someone who has indulged in every delectable morsel available to man. Then he remembered. Full awareness came in a flash. He glanced at the empty place beside him, the covers folded back, an indentation still visible on the pillow.

It had not been a dream. As memory flooded back, he realized it had started as a dream but had ended in flesh-and-blood reality. He turned into her pillow, burying his face in it, breathing in the lingering scent of her, reexperiencing the delights of the flesh.

His wife. *Dear Lord, what have I done?* He'd done

the unpardonable, what he'd vowed to himself and God not to. *Forgive me.* How could he ever return her to her father, to her rightful world?

He tried to piece together a full recollection of the evening. He had started out lying as far away from Lindsay as possible, but sometime in the night he awoke and, finding her in his arms, exchanged with her kisses and caresses more ardent than he'd ever imagined possible. His body stirred at the memory. Disgusted with himself, he sat up, his head dropping into his hands. What was he to do? He was a vile, despicable man. He'd ruined the woman he loved.

He couldn't undo what he'd done.

Feeling the weight of guilt and responsibility like double millstones, he slowly got out of bed. Somehow he must face her. Face her and what? Apologize? Get down on his knees and ask for her forgiveness? To what purpose? He could never give her back what he'd stolen from her. Now he could never return her to her father, her home, her world.

Even as these thoughts raged within him, he remembered Lindsay's behavior. She had come to him. She had clung to him, practically begging him to love her. He rubbed a hand over his face, remembering her sweet touch, her impassioned kisses.

Why must he return her to her father? Wasn't she happier here with him?

No! Soon, she would be worn down by the life of a poor minister's wife. A poor, *crippled* minister's wife.

He strapped on his wooden leg angrily and went

through his morning ablutions feeling like a man condemned to bear the burden of guilt for the rest of his days. He hated the reflection that stared back at him in the glass as he shaved and washed.

He didn't see Lindsay until he entered his study after a quick and tasteless breakfast. She was writing at his desk, a place she was not usually to be found. Had she been waiting for him?

He cleared his throat softly and she laid aside her quill and turned to look at him immediately with a smile. "There you are, lie-a-bed."

He could feel himself coloring at the teasing endearment. She rose and came to him as he stood like a stone in the doorway. His heart smote him at the trust he read in her eyes. She held her hands out and he grasped them automatically. "Good morning," she said.

He swallowed painfully. "Good morning."

"Your hands are cold." Hers felt warm and soft as they squeezed his. She tilted her head up expectantly. Hardly thinking what he was doing, he leaned his face down. His lips met hers and he was lost, all the sweet sensations and memories rushing through him once again.

Her arms came up and wrapped themselves around his neck. He couldn't help bringing his own to her waist. Her lips were so soft; they parted beneath his.

No! This couldn't—it *mustn't*—be!

Another part of his mind demanded satisfaction, lulling him with the thought that this was only a kiss.

She could be with child after last night. The thought

slammed into him, the enormity of the consequences staring at him in the full light of day.

His child.

Gently, he put her away from him. His eyes fell to her slim waistline as he felt a sudden burst of fierce, male pride. The next second, he looked down at his wooden leg.

"Now I'm really your wife." Her voice was laced with warmth.

The words denounced him. She didn't realize what she was saying, how she was condemning herself to a future that would make her unhappy. He tried to smile but felt the condemnation choking him.

Her fine eyebrows drew together when he remained silent.

She was so beautiful the thought of giving her up was like a physical blow. He grasped her hand, telling himself he would make it up to her. He'd be stronger from now on and not give in to the temptation standing before him.

"I never meant to...to do what I did last night. I'm sorry." He let her hand go and turned away, jabbing his own hand in his hair.

She was silent some seconds, so he had no idea of her reaction and didn't have the courage to turn around.

"I'm not."

Her stout tone compelled him to face her. Her chin was tilted up, her shoulders straight. Her eyes didn't waver from his, though her color remained high. Never had she looked more stunning.

How could he drag her down further when she was behaving so nobly, so charitably toward him?

"You are too generous," he said softly. When she made as if to say something, he continued, knowing he must say it before he turned coward again. "We—I mustn't let it happen again."

He saw the shock in her eyes turn to pain but he plowed on, knowing how much greater her hurt would be if he gave in to his flesh. "I vowed I would return you to your father intact. I have broken that vow and I will have to deal with that for the rest of my life. But I won't further ruin your life." When she shook her head and took a step toward him, he held up a hand and she stopped abruptly.

"There might be children."

She gasped and her hand went to her abdomen. He felt such a rush of longing for her that he had to clench his hands to keep from grabbing her up in his arms. "Please don't come to my room again," he said before turning on his heel and quitting the room.

It was for her good, he told himself. For the good of her future. There was no other way.

Chapter Fifteen

Lindsay stared down at the green grass turning beneath her feet. What should have been a glorious early-summer day was a pit of misery. The warm sunshine mocked her. She'd left her morning tasks, saying nothing to Betsy's inquiry, and walked out to the garden, through the orchard, unsure where to go. She'd ended up at the beginnings of a field, and dropped into an old swing hanging from a massive oak tree.

The rope twisted above her head as she pivoted aimlessly.

She should be weeding the garden or helping Mrs. Nichols and Betsy in the kitchen, or poring over the account books at the neat little desk she'd inherited from Florence. Everything had been left up-to-date and orderly by her sister-in-law before she'd departed to her new life.

Instead, Lindsay felt no inclination to do anything but mope.

A week had gone by since the night she'd shared

Damien's bed. How happy she'd been the next morning, thinking that at last they were a real married couple. But his rejection the next morning had hurt her as nothing before.

Since then he'd been polite as usual but more aloof than ever.

What compounded her misery was the fact that Damien hadn't taken her along on his visits to the needy. The only time she'd accompanied him to the orphanage he'd hired a hack and had it wait for them. She knew it cost him more than he was able to spare, so she'd made up some excuse not to go the next time.

But she missed the children horribly and felt as useless as ever. At least Jacob had agreed to show her some things about gardening and allowed her to spade one corner of the large kitchen garden for herself.

She could feel the tears welling up in her eyes as she contemplated her life at the parsonage. Useless. That's what she was. She'd thought she'd be able to win Damien. Instead, she seemed to have caused him more pain. He didn't want her.

"Hallo, what's my favorite sister-in-law doing all the way out here?"

She started at the sound of Jonah's greeting. She looked up to see him marching through the orchard toward her.

Hurriedly, she wiped at her damp cheeks. She must look a fright in her morning gown and apron. "Hello," she called out, averting her eyes. "I didn't expect you today. Is Florence with you?"

He planted himself in front of her with a broad smile. "That she is. I left her to visit with Damien a bit while I came out to fetch you." He studied her keenly. "Now, what's ailing my pretty young sister on such a beautiful day?"

She looked down again, half turning from him as she wiped the corner of one eye. "Nothing. I just have something in my eye."

"Hmm." He didn't sound convinced. To her surprise, he suddenly squatted down and looked up at her. She couldn't hide her face from him. She bit her lip, not knowing what to say.

"Come, what is it, lass, that's bothering you? Is it Damien?"

She remained mute, though she could feel her cheeks warm.

"He's a young lad, inexperienced with the ladies. Mayhap he hasn't known the right thing to do or say to his young bride. But I know he cares for you."

"Oh, he's very good to me. No one could be better."

"But?"

She couldn't help the fresh tears that welled up in her eyes and she tried to hide her face behind her hands. "He d-doesn't love me or w-want me. I forced myself u-upon him. I'm so ashamed!"

Jonah gently pried one hand away from her face and held it, waiting patiently until she stopped crying.

As she dabbed at her face with her handkerchief, she fixed her attention on the grass at her feet, too embarrassed with her confession to look at her new brother-in-law, a man who'd always been nice to her but was still practically a stranger.

"Are you sharing his bed, lass?"

Her eyes flew to his, astounded by the frank question.

"Forgive me if I offended you, Lindsay, I'm a plain-speaking man. You can tell me to shut up or to mind my own business, but you look so forlorn, nothing like a young lady recently wed should look." He gazed at her so earnestly that her embarrassment died. She felt she could trust him with her shameful secret.

She knotted her hands in her apron and shook her head. "Only once," she whispered.

"And?"

Her glance slipped away from his, finding it difficult to confess the rest. "He seemed so sorry afterward and said it mustn't happen again. I don't know why it's so wrong."

Jonah's calloused hand squeezed hers. "It's not, dear child. You go back to him. He'll not turn you away, or my name's not Jonah Quinn."

She shook her head, but he repeated, "You just go to him, lassie."

She stared at him. Could he possibly be right? Would she dare?

He stood and reached out his hand. "Now, let's go on back to the parsonage. Florence will wonder what's keeping me. She wanted to see you especially."

As he helped her up, he said, "She's been worried about you, how you're getting along. She'd have come sooner, but I stopped her, wanting to give you and Damien some time to yourselves." He glanced sidelong at her as they walked back through the orchard to the house. "How are the church ladies treating you?"

She sighed. "About the same. They act as if I've stolen their curate from them."

He chuckled. "I'm sure they think that. It's jealousy, that's all. They're used to having the young man all to themselves and along comes a beautiful young lady and steals his heart right out from under them. I'm sure there's more than one disappointed young miss."

She shook her head, hardly believing his assessment. "I could bear it all much better, I think, if I knew Damien loved me."

"Don't you doubt it. And remember what I told you. You go to him. The good Lord will take care of the rest."

He made it sound so easy. But what if Damien turned her away? She couldn't bear it.

As if reading her thoughts, Jonah winked. "Don't give up. Now, Florence has some good news to share— that is, *we* have some news."

She shaded her eyes, unable to resist his smile. "Oh, goodness, what is it?"

He chuckled, picking up his pace. "She'll never forgive me if I let it out before she's had a chance to."

Her heart lifted and she quickened her step to keep up with Jonah.

Florence beamed at Lindsay and Damien. "We're expecting a child sometime midwinter."

Lindsay's breath caught. Was she imagining it, or did her sister-in-law's face have a glow to it? Florence's eyes met hers and Lindsay read a hesitancy, as if she were waiting for Lindsay to react.

Lindsay took a step forward and suddenly the two women were embracing. "That's wonderful news." Her words caught, and she teared up. "I'm so happy for both of you."

When they released each other, Florence was also wiping her eyes. "Ever since I found out, it seems I've been weepy about everything. Not like myself at all."

Jonah put his arm around his wife. "I always need to have a clean handkerchief at the ready."

Florence laughed then turned to her brother. Damien leaned over and kissed her cheek. "God be praised."

"I never thought I might be blessed with motherhood, but—" her glance met her husband's, and Lindsay felt a stab of envy at the clear love and joy between the two of them "—the Lord is so gracious. He has blessed me with the finest of husbands, and now has looked with favor upon us to bless us with a family of our own."

Damien held out his hand to his brother-in-law but Jonah stepped forward and grabbed him up in a bear hug. When he turned to her with a wide smile and held out his hand, she felt his joy touch her. As his large hand enfolded hers, she could not begrudge them their happiness. She'd heard how he'd lost his two children and his first wife. "I wish you both all joy."

"Thank you, lass. No one could be happier than I at this moment."

Lindsay had to partake of their evident satisfaction

during their visit. The baby wasn't due until early in the new year but they already spoke of their plans for a nursery.

Later, when the two men went downstairs to take a walk through the orchard and fields, Lindsay sat alone with Florence. After talking of church matters for a while, Lindsay ventured to ask her, "What is it like to be expecting?" She remembered Damien's words to her, *you could be with child.* A part of her hoped and prayed it was so.

"I haven't been stricken by any of the unpleasant things one hears so much from women—nausea, not being able to hold down any food—but I do notice a sensitivity. I seem to be crying about everything, even when I'm happy about something. I never used to cry before." She sighed and shook her head.

Lindsay took a deep breath and forced out her next question. "What is the...first sign?"

Florence eyed her sharply but said nothing. "Loss of one's monthly flux is the first sure sign. But one usually waits for another cycle to be sure."

Florence cleared her throat, her hands clasped in her lap. "Now, tell me, how it is going at the orphanage?"

Lindsay swallowed her disappointment at her sister-in-law's obvious reluctance to go further into the subject. Did she know of Damien's vow not to touch his wife? Would she disapprove of what had happened?

She remembered Jonah's words. *Go to him...he'll not turn you away.*

A part of her quaked at such a bold suggestion.

Another realized that she was willing to risk all to be with her husband, body and soul.

* * *

That night, she sat up in her own bed, afraid she'd fall asleep before Damien came up. She was as tense as one of his clock springs. Would he make her leave? Would he spurn her? She sat there for at least an hour before she heard him in the corridor. Her insides trembled as she listened to the opening and closing of his bedroom door and her mind whirled.

Would he love her as his wife once more? Damien had been as tender and as passionate as she could have dreamed. Never would she regret what had happened between them. She thought of the change in Florence. She seemed softer than before. Would Lindsay be blessed in the same way, with a child as proof of the beautiful union between Damien and herself?

Finally, when she was sure he must have fallen asleep, Lindsay crept barefoot to Damien's room. She stood outside his door, hardly daring to breathe. Surely his candle had been snuffed by now.

She opened the door, her hand gripping the knob. Good, the room was dark, the curtains drawn. Could he hear the beating of her heart? She wasn't sure if she preferred he be asleep already or still awake.

Clutching the front of her dressing gown, she eased the door closed, then tiptoed across the room. Standing before the heavy bed curtains, she listened a moment, then, taking a deep breath, she drew them apart.

As she climbed into bed, he made a fast movement as if sitting up. "Lindsay?"

Quickly, she got under the covers. "Yes, 'tis I."

She turned to face him, knowing the moment of truth had come. It had been so easy, listening to Jonah. Now, her pulse hammered against her eardrums and her stomach roiled in fear. What if Damien didn't want her?

But Damien said nothing.

What was she going to do? She reached out to him but her hand landed on the empty bedding. Peering into the shadows, she saw his form. With a sinking heart, she realized he'd moved all the way to the other side. Jonah's encouragement propelling her, she scooted over until she bumped against Damien's arm. She dared rest her fingertips upon it. To her dismay it felt rigid under his sleeve.

"Lindsay, don't."

She drew her hand away immediately, feeling as if she'd been reprimanded like a child.

Jonah had been wrong.

She couldn't go back to her room. She'd never be able to face Damien again. Even as she thought about what to do, her lower lip began to tremble.

She wouldn't cry! But a sob escaped her and she hastened back to her own edge of the bed.

"Lindsay?"

She didn't answer, too busy trying to muffle her sobs.

She felt him ease closer to her. "Lindsay, what's the matter?"

"N-nothing." She sniffed.

"Please don't cry." He sounded genuinely anguished.

"I—I'm not." She wiped the tears on her cheeks.

He touched her shoulder and the dam broke. She began to sob in earnest.

"Please don't cry, Lindsay. It's best this way. I never meant for this to happen."

"I'm sorry, Damien, I never meant to be a…burden to you. I'll leave you—"

Somehow she was facing him and his arms were wrapped around her. She knew she'd have to leave, but for now, it felt so good to be held against his warm chest. "I'm sorry," she kept repeating, and he kept shushing her, comforting her, as his hand stroked her back.

"I—I didn't intend to disturb you," she sobbed against his chest. "I know you don't want me."

"Not want you?" His voice showed amazement. "How could I not want you?" He drew away from her enough to peer into her face. "You're the most wonderful, the most beautiful, the most perfect woman a man could ever have for a wife. Of course I want you."

"You do?" Now it was her turn to stare at him in amazement.

"Of course I do." His voice slowed. "But that doesn't mean we should."

Hope flared within her. He did want her! "Why shouldn't we? You are my husband. I am your wife. You want me. I—I want you." There, she'd said it aloud, bold as brass, admitted what she'd not even dared admit to herself.

Silence answered her, broken only by the thud of his heart beneath her palm. She could make out nothing of his features in the dark. As if by instinct, she reached out with her hand and touched his lips. She heard his intake of breath. Then, instead of drawing away, she felt the soft pressure of his warm lips against her fingertips.

She needed no more encouragement. A strange sort of exultation coursed through her and she closed the gap between them. She touched her lips to his, allowing him no time to push her away…not tonight… not ever…

The next morning when she came down to the dining room, Damien was already there. He looked up as soon as she entered, and they stared at each other a second. A tentative smile came to his lips, which she returned immediately. "Good morning, my dear," he said when she drew close to his chair.

Her smile broadened and she leaned down and kissed him on the mouth, even though Betsy hovered at the other end of the table.

"Good morning. I seem to be the sleepyhead today," she replied. As she straightened, she noticed his heightened color. She glanced toward Betsy. Was he embarrassed?

"Good morning, Betsy," she said brightly, going to her place at the table.

Betsy smiled. "Good morning, ma'am. Sleep well, did you?"

Lindsay unfolded her napkin, looking down, her face warm. "Yes, very well." She had slept quite soundly.

As Betsy poured some hot chocolate into her cup, Lindsay glanced at Damien, who was looking at her. He quickly looked back at the paper. How handsome he was. Her heart swelled to think what a wonderful husband she had. Her hand stole to her abdomen. And maybe, by God's grace, she would be with child soon.

Perhaps then Damien would forget about returning her to her father and her former life.

You are summoned to appear before the Bishop of London on the 21st of August, 1812, at three o'clock…

Damien stared down at the paper in his hands, foreboding weighing his spirit. The supervisor and spiritual head of the entire parish wanted to see him. Reverend Doyle had not warned him of this meeting, but surely it was a direct result of the complaint the rector had lodged against Damien.

He tapped the edge of the thick paper against his chin, pondering. Glancing out his study window, he observed Lindsay walking through the garden in a pretty frock and wide straw hat. As beautiful as the colorful array around her, she wandered among the beds, clipping flowers into a basket she held on her arm.

He pulled his gaze away, despising himself anew for his lack of willpower where his bride was concerned. *Bride.* The word condemned him as his unrestrained behavior had condemned her. Even though they'd been married now for over two months, he still thought of her as a bride. In that time, despite his vow, he had proved himself weak where Lindsay was concerned. He no longer tried to figure out the future, no longer dared even think of it. His days were filled with ministry work, his nights with the joys of marital bliss.

The missive in his hand crumpled and he realized he'd crushed it in his fist.

He looked at it now, a stark reminder of his failings. Perhaps the future he so feared was rearing itself up at last.

He would just have to wait until the appointed day. With a sigh, he turned back to the sermon he'd been working on. The scripture he'd jotted down jumped out at him. *Yet if any man suffer as a Christian, let him not be ashamed; but let him glorify God on this behalf.*

If he was called on to suffer because of his role as a brother to Jonah, he must be prepared to see it through. With renewed inspiration, he began to write, his heart lifting as the words began to flow and he pictured the sufferings Jesus had had to endure for the sake of all humanity.

A short while later, his study door opened and Lindsay came in with a vase full of flowers. "I brought you some lilies and delphinium and, let's see," she said, and eyed the large bouquet. "A few daisies, foxglove and roses." She set it on a corner of his desk.

Damien couldn't help smiling at her. She always brought brightness to his life. "Thank you," he finally remembered to say.

Instead of moving away from his desk, she leaned over it and continued arranging the flowers. She was so close her skirt, with its tiny rows of embroidered green leaves, brushed his knee. The light muslin dress was as airy as the flower petals, revealing the contours of her slim figure. Her arms were bare, her hair mussed as if she'd just flung off her bonnet. He clutched the edge of his desk to keep from grabbing her and pulling her into his lap.

She stood back and eyed the flower arrangement. "There. That should sweeten your study."

You are all the sweetness I need. He stopped himself from saying half the things he'd like to say to her. He'd never even told her he loved her—dared not tell her in his desperate effort to keep her heart free of him, knowing all the while that the tightest cords had already been forged by his own weakness.

What would happen when she got tired of her life at the parsonage and wanted to return to her proper station in life?

Lindsay's smile faded. "Damien, why are you frowning so?"

He shook his head and attempted a light tone. No need to spoil the companionable moment with his troubles. "It's nothing." He inhaled deeply. "The flowers smell lovely."

She pondered him, a somber look in her large brown eyes.

"What is it?" he said.

"You have had such an air of sadness about you ever since we became man and wife." She removed a daisy from the vase and twirled it between her fingers. "Is it because of me?"

"Of course not!"

"Then what is it? Is it wrong of a husband and wife to pleasure each other?"

They'd never spoken so directly of their…relations. He hardly dared look at her. As he harnessed his thoughts, he pretended to straighten the papers on his desk.

"Is it because of your leg?"

Involuntarily, his fingers began kneading his kneecap. "Let us say this stump is symbolic of so many things," he said in a low tone, feeling her gaze on the missing limb.

"What do you mean?"

She was waiting for an answer, and she deserved to know why he held back from her. Too restless now to sit still, he stood and walked a few steps away from her. "I mean, yes, my leg, or lack thereof—" he gave an abrupt laugh "—kept me from seeking a wife early on in my life. Later it only helped remind me of the reasons for remaining unmarried."

"Why ever should having lost part of your leg keep you from having a wife?"

He swung around to her, running a hand through his hair. How difficult it was to express things that had been part of him for so long, but which he'd never confessed to another living soul. "I'm a man devoted to God's work. I'm single-minded in my focus. There are perhaps other clergymen to whom the church is merely a comfortable living. They make admirable husbands."

He spread out his hands. "For me, it's my life. It would be unfair of me to ask a woman to follow me. It is monstrous of me to ask it of a gently bred young lady—an heiress—like yourself."

She jutted out her pretty lower lip. "And what if I *wanted* to share that life with you, Damien? What if it fills me to see souls being helped? You've hardly let me accompany you to your ministries outside the chapel—"

"A whole man could protect you," he interrupted

angrily. "A cripple is not only an object of ridicule, but can scarcely protect himself."

Before he'd finished speaking, she was standing close to him. "The Lord protects you each time you leave this house and go out to minister to the poor. He protected us both that day. Why do you doubt He'll continue protecting us?"

He rubbed a hand over his face, unable to answer her but knowing she didn't understand the dangers fully. As the seconds dragged out, he couldn't help reaching to take a ringlet of her hair between his fingertips, smiling sadly. "You are very noble and kind, and I know you are very brave in wanting to share in my life. I never meant to know you as a husband when I agreed to marry you. I fully meant to return you to your father and your old life." He swallowed. "Each time we know each other as man and wife, I feel I'm digging a hole deeper for you, a hole you'll never be able to climb out of. And it's all my fault."

She shook her head vigorously. "I never want to go back to my father's house, to my old life."

"You may say that now, but you are very young." He returned to his desk. "You don't realize how grueling this path of mine is. I can never forgive myself for robbing you of the life you were meant to enjoy...nor can I afford to become double-minded in my work, fretting every time I think of how I ruined your life, when all I meant was to protect you from your father's wrath."

She touched his elbow. "How can I ever convince you you haven't ruined my life but made it complete?"

He looked down at her and felt himself go weak in

the knees. What love and trust he saw written in her eyes. However, that only deepened his guilt. "I have robbed you of your rightful future. You have become my wife through my own fleshly weakness without having a chance to discover what your future truly held."

Her hand tightened on his arm, and his gaze dropped to her just-parted lips. He bent his head and gently kissed them. "You are my temptress and I have no idea how this will end." His eyes fell on the letter from the bishop and he felt a further weight.

She put her arms around him. "Don't sound so sad. You make me feel I have wronged you."

"No, absolutely not. It is I who have wronged you."

He stepped back reluctantly. How easily he could have continued kissing her right here in his study.

She turned to his desk as if she, too, had to get her thoughts under control. When she noticed his papers, she touched the bishop's letter. "What is this? It looks very formal."

"It's from the Bishop of London. He wants me to call upon him."

She turned to look at him. "Is it about hiding Jonah here this past spring?"

He nodded, then shrugged, trying to make light of it. "Most likely it is."

She frowned, still studying the paper. "I thought that had all blown over by now."

"The wheels in the church move slowly and it has probably taken the bishop this long to assemble all the facts in the case."

She turned worried eyes to him. "You can't still be held responsible for that, can you? Not when the prince regent himself issued Jonah a pardon."

He smiled, making his voice as reassuring as possible. "I'm sure you're right. In any case, I shall soon discover what the reason is."

"Will he—the bishop—also question you about your hasty marriage?" Her gaze was directed back at the letter and her tone sounded offhand.

Damien hesitated, not fooled by her tone. "I believe my written statement will have more than adequately answered any questions he might have regarding my conduct. I don't anticipate any more questions in that area."

She nodded and said nothing more, but the memory of her false accusations hung between them and Damien wondered if they would come back to haunt them at this late date.

Chapter Sixteen

The closed room of the bishop's quarters was stifling on this August day. Damien looked from Reverend Doyle to the elderly Bishop of London. He felt as if the two men had discussed him at length already.

"Your conduct of late has been questionable at best," the white-haired bishop said from his chair behind his desk. "Reprehensible at worst."

Damien looked down at his clasped hands, then back to the bishop. "If I could know the charges, Dr. Randolph."

The bishop glanced down at the thick document in front of him. "You aided and abetted a criminal in his escape from the law."

Damien leaned forward. "Sir, in the report I submitted to you, I explained the unusual circumstances surrounding Jonah Quinn, a man innocent of the charges he had been sentenced for."

The bishop glared at him. "Reverend Doyle has described to me thoroughly how you took upon yourself the initiative in a way that cannot be condoned in a man of the cloth who is under the authority of others. You knowingly and willingly deceived your superior."

Damien clenched his hands, frustrated in his desire to make the bishop understand. "I know I was wrong to keep this from Reverend Doyle." He glanced at Doyle, but read no hint of yielding in his stony countenance. "But a man's life was at stake."

"A criminal of the lowest order," Doyle put in.

Damien stifled a sigh of impatience at his mentor and friend of so many years. Why couldn't Doyle understand? Why wasn't he interceding on Damien's behalf?

They debated at length but it was clear the bishop did not accept Damien's defense. Rector Doyle had too thoroughly laid his own version of events before the bishop.

"If that is little enough," the bishop continued, "you compromised a young lady—the daughter of a prominent gentleman—and were forced to marry in haste. Scandalous behavior for a member of the clergy of the Church of England."

"Sir, I can assure you, there is nothing in my conduct—"

The man shot him a stern look from under his gray eyebrows. "Do you deny that the young lady accused you of compromising her virtue?"

Damien fell silent at the question. In the stillness of the office, the bishop's words rang a death knell for any hopes he had for this interview. Clearly Reverend Doyle had informed the bishop in the worst possible way what he'd witnessed the night Lindsay had come to the parsonage. Damien's deepest fears were coming to pass.

He felt his collar tight around his neck. Clearing his throat, he attempted an answer. "It's true that our betrothal was a bit sudden."

The bishop tapped the document with his forefinger. "This report states that your wife was betrothed to be married to a gentleman of good standing, a man chosen by her father, and that she broke that engagement and accused you of compromising her virtue." His bottle-brush eyebrows seemed to twitch at Damien.

Damien wiped the perspiration beginning to sheen his upper lip. He glanced at Reverend Doyle, but found him staring straight ahead. "Miss Phillips—that is, Mrs. Hathaway—my wife came to me, asking for my help. Her father was forcing her into a betrothal against her wishes."

"Is that reason to compromise a young lady of virtue?" The question was delivered in a cold, uncompromising tone.

"No, sir."

"Did you or did you not behave dishonorably with Miss Phillips outside the sanctity of holy matrimony?"

The seconds ticked away. If he denied the charge, he would be calling Lindsay a liar and compromise her reputation. He felt caught between damnation on one side for lying and damnation on the other for accepting a charge he was not guilty of.

"Well? Answer me, Reverend Hathaway."

He swallowed. "Yes, sir," he whispered, his eyes shifting down to his lap. His fate was sealed.

"Speak up, man!"

He raised his eyes slowly until he was once more staring into the remorseless eyes of his accuser. "Yes, sir."

The bishop thumped his fist on the documents. "Despicable! For one of our clergy to behave so abominably, and on the heels of the Quinn affair." He spoke to the vicar now as if Damien were no longer present. "We cannot condone such behavior in the church. You were right to bring such a report to my attention."

Damien looked at Doyle, the words hardly registering. The rector ignored Damien, replying to the bishop in the soothing tones Damien was familiar with.

Damien sat staring at the rector. Why would the man who had nurtured Damien's dream of becoming a pastor since he was a boy now destroy him? Of course he had to report such misconduct to the bishop. But what astounded Damien was that Doyle himself had believed Lindsay's accusation. It was almost laughable. Any other friend would have doubted and come to him to demand the true story. But not Doyle. He had immediately carried the tale to the bishop, as if only waiting for the opportunity to denounce Damien.

He remembered King David's words, "mine own familiar friend, in whom I trusted, which did eat of my bread, hath lifted up his heel against me."

"His conduct has been of great concern to me for many months," Doyle droned on. "A decided evangelical strain to his sermons…teaching those in the workhouse to read…poor example to those in his congregation…" The list of his crimes and misdemeanors mounted. When had Doyle prepared such a compilation of grievances?

Damien's focus rested on the black onyx ring on the rector's long, pale index finger. There had been a breach in their friendship ever since Doyle had discovered that Damien and Florence had hidden Jonah. But the cooling of their relationship had actually begun earlier. Damien thought back. It hit him. Ever since Florence had turned down Doyle's offer of marriage and then accepted Jonah's instead! Could the man who had almost single-handedly defined Christianity for Damien prove to be so spiteful and small-minded?

A disappointment so profound settled upon Damien that he no longer heard the discussion going on around him. The church he had served so faithfully all his life was condemning him for behaving out of love and a desire to serve others.

It was with a start that he realized the bishop was addressing him. "You have disgraced the sacred office you were given. You are a reproach to the orders you took." The bishop folded his hands before him. "There is no course open for you but to resign your curacy."

Damien waited for the pronouncement to shake him to the core. Instead he felt numb. He bowed his head. "As you wish."

Doyle rose, and Damien followed his example.

The two said nothing to each other until they stood outside the bishop's chapel on Aldersgate Street.

Damien turned to his superior. "Tell me, sir, do you

really believe I compromised Miss Phillips's virtue before I married her?"

Doyle's nostrils seemed pinched in disdain. "I have no reason to suppose otherwise. I heard the young lady accuse you myself."

"She was not accusing me. She was begging her father not to force her into a marriage which was abhorrent to her."

"Are you saying she lied?"

Damien looked down at the pavement, unwilling to say so. Then hardening his jaw, he faced the rector again, feeling only contempt for a man he'd respected and looked up to for so long. "I'm saying, in all the years you've known me, do you think I would be capable of such a thing?"

The two men eyed each other steadily. "Frankly, your behavior has become increasingly worrisome to me for months. Since your part in Quinn's evasion from the law, nothing you do would shock me."

"I see." There was nothing more to be said. "I will remove myself from the parsonage as quickly as possible."

The older man merely gave a curt nod of his head. "I will begin a search for your replacement immediately."

Damien cleared his throat, hating to have to ask this man anything more, but knowing he couldn't leave without saying goodbye to his flock. "Will you permit me to address my congregation a final time?"

The man was silent a moment as if weighing the benefits and disadvantages. "You may announce to your congregation your departure at this Sunday's sermon."

"Thank you, sir," he said, his voice not quite steady.

He headed swiftly down the street, not sure where he was going. All he knew was he wanted to be away from the man he'd called friend for so many years.

Receiving no answer to her knock on Damien's study door, Lindsay opened it and peered in. His desk looked as neat as he'd left it several hours ago. She turned away, unsure where to look next.

She bit her lip, her concern growing. It was nearly suppertime. Where could he be? Surely his meeting was over. She'd been praying for him off and on all day. Although he'd reassured her it was nothing extraordinary, she couldn't help feeling a sense of disquiet.

In the few months they'd shared their lives, she'd learned one thing about her husband. He rarely confided in her. He spent many hours in prayer or studying God's word, closeted in his study or sitting on a stile far out in the fields, but whenever she tried to draw him out about his deepest thoughts, he made light of things.

Surely, he couldn't always feel even-keeled and content about all situations. His frank words about their marriage earlier in the month had been a rare revelation. Even though they had pained her, his words had also encouraged her. Perhaps Damien was beginning to trust her love for him enough to share his apprehensions with her.

She wandered down to the front of the house and checked the coatrack again. His hat and walking stick were still missing. Finally, able to stand it no longer, she grabbed her parasol and left the house, uncertain where to look, mindful that she would miss him if she left, but tired of being on the watch for him.

She had so wanted to share her own news with him.

She'd been wanting to for a few days—nay, weeks— but had kept waiting, first to be more sure, and then, to wait for just the right moment. She couldn't help touching her abdomen lightly, thinking about the new life growing within her.

She'd just missed her second cycle. Surely, she must be carrying Damien's child! The thought filled her with such joy, she didn't know how she could contain it another minute. She'd never been good at keeping something to herself. Always, at school, she'd shared her secrets with her friends.

Now, she had no one. No one except the Lord. She glanced up at the pale blue sky before continuing through the kitchen garden and making her way toward the rear of the chapel. Perhaps Damien was there.

Since meeting Damien, her relationship to God had grown deeper. Damien had taught her how to seek God's counsel first. For weeks now, ever since she'd missed her first cycle, she'd been rejoicing in secret with the Lord, as each day brought more certainty that He had blessed her womb with a child. A child formed from her love for Damien, an affirmation that she'd been forgiven for her false accusation against her beloved.

She entered the dim chapel. Disappointment filled her when it appeared empty. As soon as she entered into the sanctuary and looked toward the altar, she stopped. Damien was there, kneeling. The colorful late-afternoon sun through the stained-glass windows fell across his back. An air of stillness enveloped him and made her pause.

She so wanted to talk to him, but he seemed deep in prayer. Would he be angry with her for interrupting him now? He was never angry with her. Removed at times, but never angry.

Lord, she prayed, invoking one of her ongoing prayers, *show me how to break down Damien's wall of reserve and sadness. I've done all I know to do.* Taking a deep breath, she made her way down the aisle.

He must have heard her as she grew closer, for he looked over his shoulder. When he saw it was she, he slowly rose to his feet.

"Were you looking for me?" he asked when she reached him.

She nodded, reassured by his calm tone. "You were gone so long. I didn't know where you might go after your meeting, so I thought I'd look here."

He smiled slightly. "I'm sorry I didn't let you know I was back." His gaze shifted from her and he sighed.

She reached out and touched him lightly on the arm. "Did everything go all right?"

He didn't answer. Instead he motioned to the pews. "Would you like to sit down?"

"Very well."

He waited for her to sit before taking his place beside her. "It's peaceful in here, is it not?" he said.

She glanced at him, unable to read his mood. He seemed almost too calm. "Yes."

"I've always enjoyed being here when there's no

one else. Not that I don't enjoy morning and evening prayer services."

His pensive gaze fixed on the altar. "This has been my church for so many years," he said finally. "It's been the only pulpit I've known."

Something in his tone gave her a queer feeling in her stomach.

"Maybe someday you'll have a bigger pulpit."

He smiled slightly but didn't look at her.

"What's wrong?" she whispered.

"I have resigned my curacy."

She almost smiled. Was he making a jest? Surely she hadn't heard properly. When he turned to her at last, the look in his eyes was bleak and she began to feel dread. Never had she seen him look this way. He was the one who was tranquil in every storm.

"Damien, what happened this afternoon?"

"The bishop asked for my resignation." He leaned his elbows on his knees and kneaded his forehead with his fingers.

"Why would he do such a thing?" she asked in a whisper.

"Actually he had a whole document describing my shortcomings."

"How can that be? Your congregation loves you." Her voice rose in outrage.

"Not all of them, apparently." Was that a tinge of cynicism in his tone? It was so unlike him, she could only stare.

With a sigh he sat back in the pew. "The main accusation is my aiding Jonah when he was a fugitive," he said at last, no longer looking at her.

"But that was ages ago! And didn't the prince himself pardon Jonah? I don't understand."

"It seems the bishop considers my role in hiding Jonah a bad example for the congregation." He spoke slowly as if he had difficulty putting his thoughts together. "He spoke also of my sermons of late and their evangelical bent."

She shook her head, still in a muddle. Was she too ignorant of church affairs to understand? Finally she stood, too angry to sit still. "It's not right. You are the finest, most godly man I know. How can they just dismiss you?"

He smiled slightly. "Thank you for your kind words, but I'm not nearly as admirable as you think." His fingers were digging into his kneecap, a gesture she'd come to recognize as the only thing that signaled any agitation in him. She quickly sat beside him again and covered his hand with her own.

"You *are* the most godly man I know! Don't let anything the bishop says make you doubt yourself. Your sermons are uplifting and—" she searched for the right word "—convicting at the same time. I've never had sermons which made me want to do better the way yours do. Your sermons challenge me to look into God's word. How can the bishop think you are a bad influence on your congregation? It's monstrous!" He said nothing. "Isn't there someone you can appeal to?"

He shook his head. "No, he has sole jurisdiction over

those in his parish. Besides, the rector is in full agreement with him. He is my supervisor, who is most familiar with all that I do. If he disapproves of my work, well," he said, and gave a slight shrug of his shoulders, "there is nothing more to be said. I am nothing but a lowly curate."

She turned away, unable to comprehend it. She glanced up at the altar. *Dear God, is this some kind of nightmare? Why is this happening to the dearest, most saintly man there is?*

All thoughts of sharing her own secret evaporated, her joy crushed. As she watched Damien's profile, a weight, darker than any she'd ever known, settled over her heart. Damien felt so guilty about her, responsible for her fate. Once he knew she carried their child, a being which bonded her to him for the rest of their lives, how would he react?

Lindsay wiped the perspiration from her brow and straightened. Her back and shoulders ached from all the cleaning and packing, but she couldn't allow herself more than a few minutes respite. There was simply too much to be done.

Kneeling on the floor in front of a box, she surveyed the emptiness of the room that used to be their cozy drawing room. Carpets were rolled up. Sheets covered all the furniture. Books were packed away along with vases and a few other decorative items that didn't belong to the parsonage.

She eased up off the floor. Every day now she felt

nausea that only went away momentarily when she ate a little something. Thankfully, she didn't feel sick enough that anyone would notice, but she had to force herself to go about her tasks.

It was a mercy everyone's attention was on Florence and her condition. She now seemed to be full of energy, and Lindsay was hard-pressed not to appear a laggard.

Lindsay walked over to an upturned crate and poured herself a glass of barley water from a pitcher. Most of the furniture would remain in the parsonage, as it belonged to the church. Damien had found them some rooms to rent in a house not too far away in Marylebone. It was a pity they would be farther than ever from Florence and Jonah, too distant to see them on a daily basis.

"Anything more to take down?"

Jonah's cheerful voice startled her. She turned to him, making an effort to smile. "Yes, those three over there are ready."

He went to the crates she indicated and proceeded to nail them up. Jonah and Florence were carting most of their things to the farmhouse, since they'd be able to fit very little into their new lodgings.

She still had hardly had a chance to adjust to the notion of Damien not being the curate of St. George's. In less than a week, they'd had to pack and vacate the parsonage.

"You look a mite pale," Jonah said. "Why don't you go down and Elizabeth will fix you a cup of tea and a bit of food?"

"I'm all right. There's still so much to be done before tomorrow."

"Florence and I will stay until everything's finished."

"Don't let Florence overdo."

Jonah chuckled as he went to the next crate. "She thinks she has the capacity of a half-dozen women right now. Don't you worry, I'll make her lie down soon."

Damien came in then. He nodded to Jonah, then came to her. His blue eyes peered closely at her a few seconds and she strove to appear normal. Many times, she'd wanted to blurt out her news but she held back. Though he hadn't expressed any regret at losing his curacy, he'd grown more quiet and thoughtful. That alone showed her the hurt he must be suffering.

The betrayal of his oldest friend and mentor, Reverend Doyle, was the worst part. It made her question her role in her husband's life more relentlessly. If he weren't burdened with her, might not he be better off now?

"How is everything?" he asked with a look around the room.

She injected cheerfulness into her voice. "We are almost finished."

He smiled. "Good. I'll make another run with Jonah to our new place with the last boxes."

"Will we be ready to move in by this evening?"

"Yes." A shuttered expression appeared on his face. "I've told the rector I would turn in our key to the church warden on Sunday."

She nodded, not knowing what else to say. For her, this had been home for only a short time. For Damien, it had been several years.

She longed to reassure him that she would strive with

all her ability to make his new home as agreeable as his last, no matter how few material possessions they had. But for the moment, it seemed better to remain silent.

On Sunday morning he preached his last sermon. Lindsay was shocked to see that half the church was absent. Had so many parishioners turned against Damien?

She surveyed those sitting in the pews. Mr. and Mrs. Cooper were not present, nor was their daughter, Charlotte. They'd been the most determinedly cool toward Lindsay since her marriage to Damien.

There was Mrs. Moore. Lindsay felt a surge of relief at the older lady's smile and returned it. Mrs. Oliver also nodded at her as their glances met. How nice of her friend to come and show her support.

When Damien began to read the morning prayers, Lindsay settled back, always enjoying the way he read the scriptures.

When it was time for the sermon, he walked slowly into the pulpit, looking regal in his white surplice and green stole. Her heart went out to him in that moment as he stood alone. The words of Christ came to her about counting the cost. Was this part of the cost Damien must pay for following his Savior? To be willing to stand when the world judged him?

She sat straighter, her hands folded in her lap, hoping to show by her demeanor how proud she was of her husband. As if he felt her encouragement, his gaze met hers. She smiled and gave him a small nod, and a light seemed to shine in his eyes.

He cleared his throat, looking out at the church. "Dear brothers and sisters, today, I come to you with a heavy heart. You see, it is to be the last time I address you, beloved congregation. I want to thank you for the years of patient endurance as you received a green preacher, fresh from his studies at Oxford, and bore with me as the Lord worked in my life to be able to feed you His word…."

By the time he finished his message, Lindsay couldn't keep the tears from running down her cheeks. What was he to do now? He was a born preacher. She couldn't imagine that the Lord had something else for him to do. As she peeked at the faces nearest her, she saw she was not the only one affected.

After the service, she waited for Damien to change out of his vestments. A couple she knew only slightly approached her. She smiled, expecting expressions of sympathy as some of the other parishioners had offered, but they didn't return her smile.

"I hope you're satisfied with yourself now."

"I beg your pardon?"

"You tricked our poor reverend into marrying you. Now, he's in disgrace with the church and has lost his curacy. How can you live with yourself?"

She was too shocked to do anything but stare mutely.

"Reverend Hathaway is such a good man. There's not an evil bone in his body. It's a tragedy that he succumbed to the lures of an unscrupulous young lady when there were so many worthy young women in his own congregation."

"What are you talking about? Reverend Hathaway was dismissed because of helping Jonah Quinn hide here." Her voice died away at the look of contempt in their eyes.

"Is that what he told you?" the husband said. "You'd best examine your own conscience, my lady. When a woman lays a trap for a man, accusing him of stealing her virtue..."

Fear and doubt strangled her. Was she the reason Damien had had to resign? He had said nothing! She turned away, clutching the back of a pew. And here she'd believed she'd come to know him. How foolishly naive she'd been.

Before she could do anything, Damien entered from the vestry. "There you are. Shall we greet the remaining parishioners?"

His tone was light. How could he treat her this thoughtfully when she was the cause of his disaster? Silently, she followed him to the entry of the chapel, her mind awhirl. They remained standing there quite a long while replying to well-wishers. Damien had already spoken to many privately over the past few days, but now everyone felt the sadness of leave-taking.

"You must let us know if you have a church again," one man said.

"I will, thank you." Damien bowed his head politely and turned to another parishioner.

Mrs. Moore shook his hand. "I feel in my heart this is not the end of the road for you, young man, but only the beginning."

"Thank you, dear lady."

With some final farewells, they left the church. They were silent walking back to the parsonage. Lindsay glanced several times at Damien, wanting to question him immediately but hesitant to confront him when he must be devastated.

She was feeling none too well herself, and when they arrived at the parsonage, she excused herself after removing her bonnet.

"Are you all right?" His tone, as always, expressed immediate concern. She wanted to weep. He was always sensitive to her needs, when all she'd done was bring ruin to him.

"Just a bit tired is all."

"I'll have Mrs. Nichols send you up some lunch if you'd like."

"That's all right. I…I'm not feeling too hungry." She would probably lose anything she put in her stomach right now.

"Well, at least a cup of tea and some biscuits." He paused. "I know it was a difficult morning for you."

She stared into his eyes. Would he never confide the truth to her? "More so for you."

"The Lord is gracious."

She turned away from him slowly, wanting to weep from sadness and remorse.

Damien stood at the foot of the front stairs listening to Lindsay's slow tread until it faded. He hoped this move wasn't too much for her. She was looking decidedly pale, and her appetite hadn't been good in the few rushed meals they'd been able to share.

Hopefully, she'd be able to settle down once they were in their new rooms. A wave of despair swept over him at the thought of the two dingy rooms they would now call home. It was in a seedy neighborhood at the edge of Marylebone, too close to where they'd been attacked.

He'd debated with himself a dozen times about approaching her father to confide the situation to him and ask him to take his daughter back.

But the knowledge of how he'd stolen her virtue stopped him. How could she return home now?

He saw no answer. With a sigh, he headed for his study, a room bare of all but the original furniture. It mocked him. He'd never been anything but a pilgrim within the walls of this parsonage he'd called home.

It wasn't until late that evening that Lindsay finally found herself alone with Damien in their new home. All week, Jonah and Florence had been with them, finally helping them to unpack and put their few belongings in order. The rooms were furnished, although the tables and chairs had clearly seen better days. Florence had said that between the two of them they'd quickly sew some new curtains and spruce the place up.

Lindsay could hardly bear the solicitude. She wanted to cry out that she didn't deserve any of it.

Now, in the silence of the small parlor, her anguish grew. It was clear Damien would tell her nothing. She rose and said to him, "I think I shall retire."

Damien looked up from the Bible. "You must be tired."
She simply nodded. "Good night."

In the twilight shadows of the cramped room she undressed and lay down on the lumpy bed, staring up at
the stained canopy, dry-eyed. What was she to do? She
had ruined Damien's life, and now likely carried his
child in her womb. Her hand rested atop her abdomen,
as it did of late. The thought of a growing life within
brought both joy and fear.

If only she could share this news with Damien.
Would he be pleased or would it only add to his worries?
She turned on her side, allowing herself to dream of a
life with Damien and their child…their children. She
dreamed of hearing him preach from the pulpit, and of
teaching their children the right way to go. She pictured
her role next to him, bringing the gospel to the needy.
Were all those dreams turned to ashes now?

What did this new neighborhood hold for them? It
was not far from where they had been attacked by the
gang of boys. As she usually did when she thought of
that afternoon, she began praying for them. As she
prayed, the image came to her of Damien preaching to
them. Did the Lord want him to minister to those in this
neighborhood?

Puzzled, she continued praying. Gradually, she
grew drowsy, barely aware when Damien finally entered the room.

The memory of the price he was paying for her lie
came back to her. She stiffened in the bed, not wanting
him to be aware that she was still awake. He undressed

in the dark as he always did. He never allowed her to see him when he'd removed the peg. But she'd shown him that she loved every part of him, if not with words, then with her touch. In the darkness, she'd caressed the leg, though he'd shied away at first. No part of him disgusted or frightened her.

When he climbed into bed beside her, he stayed to his side, as was his habit. Every night it was she who curled up beside him. But this night she, too, kept to her side.

The following day she rose early, the day promising to be hot, and began to familiarize herself with her new cooking facilities. In spite of her meager kitchen, she managed to start a fire and set a kettle to boil. Then she hung another pot over the fireplace with water and oats.

They would be able to do very little cooking here, and buying cooked food would be expensive. Thankfully, Florence and Jonah had left them with an ample supply of things from their farm.

"Good morning."

She turned to greet Damien.

"You're up early," he said when he approached her and bent to kiss her cheek.

"Yes."

"Are you feeling better today?"

"Yes." Until she put something in her stomach, the nausea would not subside.

"Here, let me stir that for you."

"You shouldn't have to cook."

But he took the wooden spoon from her hand. Feeling too queasy to argue, she straightened and went to sit in an armchair. In the morning light, its upholstery revealed many more stains than it had the evening before. She sighed, thinking perhaps Florence would help her sew some slipcovers. *If* she could afford to buy the material. Perhaps some Holland cloth wouldn't be too dear. She had no idea how much money Damien had available. She'd never discussed finances with him. He'd given her a monthly household amount and never questioned how she spent it.

"You're very quiet."

She started and looked up. "What are you going to do now?"

He stared into the pot as he stirred. "I've been thinking about that very thing all these days. And now the reality confronts me. I need to find work to do."

She was unable to picture him as anything but a clergyman. The thought she had last night about ministering to their new neighborhood returned to her now.

"I will go to the different clockmakers and offer my services."

She drew in a sharp breath. How could he go back to being a simple clockmaker?

"Do…do you have any money at all?" she finally ventured.

"I have a small sum. Florence and I were left some money from our parents, but I gave most of it to her when she married for the purchase of their farm." He gave a short laugh. "I didn't think I'd need much besides what I earned from the curacy. Naturally, she and Jonah want me to have anything back they can spare." He looked at her, as if asking for her understanding. "I said no, of course. I know they'll need it until the farm begins to pay for itself, as I have no doubt it will. Jonah is very knowledgeable. But," he said, "you must forgive me for not consulting with you first. You have as much a say over our goods as anyone. This affects you, as well."

"You did right." She tried to put a bright face on things. "This is all we need. As long as we can afford these rooms."

He gave a small nod, as if he wanted to say more.

"Let me get some bowls," she said, when he remained silent.

As they sat across from each other at the small round table covered with one of their nice clean linen cloths from the parsonage, she asked, "Will you not be able to do any ministry?"

"I have no authority from the church."

"What about your work at the orphanage and workhouse? What about the prison? You cannot just leave it. Who will take your place?"

He rubbed a hand across his forehead as if the questions pained him. "I don't know."

"Will Reverend Doyle appoint someone else?"

"I don't know," he repeated, although this time more slowly. "He did not initiate these ministries. Florence and I did."

"Will Florence continue?"

"As much as she can from where she lives. And after

the birth of the baby…" He shrugged and looked down at his bowl.

"You cannot just leave these people. They need you."

He looked at her and she read turmoil in his blue eyes.

She chewed the corner of her lip, wondering if she should say what had been on her mind. "Why don't we continue to minister to them? I know we have little to offer now, but we must believe the Lord will continue to provide." As the words tumbled out of her, her enthusiasm grew. "You can preach to them on Sunday. Does anyone ever preach to them on Sunday?"

He said nothing, but seemed deep in thought as they ate.

She finished her breakfast, feeling a little better when she'd eaten her porridge.

When he prepared to leave, he asked her, "Will you be all right here by yourself?"

She nodded, although the prospect of being shut up within these dingy rooms depressed her. "I shall be fine. I think Elizabeth is stopping by later."

"That's good." With a final look at her, he bent down and kissed her softly on the cheek. How she wanted to turn her head just a fraction and meet his lips. But she no longer felt worthy to call herself his wife. She'd brought him to this state.

In the silence of his departure, she turned to tidy up, fighting the desolation that threatened just beneath the surface.

Chapter Seventeen

It was late afternoon before Damien returned. He felt bone-weary, hot, thirsty and discouraged. But at least he had some good news to bring home.

Home. He stopped short at the word, his hand on the knob. A pair of rooms he'd only spent one night in. More humble than any he'd ever lived in. Yet, it was home.

And he knew why.

Lindsay's sweet face appeared in his mind, her dark eyes shining with pride as they had when she'd managed to lay out a simple supper last night and prepare breakfast this morning.

Lindsay made it home. Wherever he lived now would be home because of her presence. The despair that had been weighing him down all day lifted a fraction as he pushed open the door.

The sitting room was empty, though everything was neat and tidy. The small round table had a clean cloth,

A Bride of Honor

and tea things were laid out. He stopped on the threshold, noting the small vase of daisies upon it.

Closing the door softly behind him he entered the room and gazed slowly around it. He noted other touches here and there, a paisley shawl draped over the stained couch, a row of the few books he'd brought with him set out on a shelf, the grate before the fireplace scrubbed clean and a fire burning in it with a kettle on the hob.

"Lindsay?" No answer. He walked across the room and into the bedroom beyond it. He stopped short, seeing her lying on the bed, dressed, her arm curled under her head. She usually didn't sleep in the daytime but lately she had been looking drawn. Undoubtedly the stress of moving.

He crossed noiselessly to the bed and stood observing her. Her golden hair spilled over her shoulder, where it had come loose from its pins. One lock lay against her cheek, and he couldn't help leaning down and brushing it away. He had missed feeling her body curled up against his last night.

The touch was enough to awaken her. Her dark eyes stared up at him with gradual recognition. What started out as a smile quickly turned to a look of worry and she began to rise. He pushed her back gently with a hand and sat down on the edge of the bed. "You needn't get up."

"Wh-when did you return?" She sounded disoriented.

"Just now." He kept his hand on her shoulder. Suddenly, he found himself leaning down and touching her lips with his, forgetting everything else. He needed to feel her warmth, her sustaining presence. He deepened the kiss without intending to, his resolve to protect her from himself momentarily forgotten. Her arms wrapped around him. With what sounded like a small sob, she began kissing him back fervently.

Before he knew it, he had forgotten everything else and sought only his wife's presence.

The shadows were lengthening and they were forced to light the candles when they finally sat down to supper.

It was the first time they'd ever made love in the daylight. He'd always avoided having to force her to see his leg. But she'd been so tender and loving that he'd actually begun believing she didn't see the ugly, deformed limb that he did.

"There, it's hot," she said, turning from the fire with the kettle to pour some water into the teapot.

She looked delightfully rosy, dressed only in a silk dressing gown, her hair knotted loosely at the base of her neck, tendrils falling around her face.

He bowed his head over their supper of bread and butter and some sliced meat. When he looked up, he realized he was famished. He'd eaten no dinner at noon, preferring to continue seeking work than coming home with nothing good to report.

He dug into the simple fare with relish. With his hunger satisfied, he sat back and took the teacup in his hand. "I found some work at a clockmaker's not too far from here. It will keep me occupied a few hours a day, leaving me enough time to visit the orphanage and workhouse, if the wardens there still wish me to come."

He cleared his throat. "I shall have to tell them I no longer come as a clergyman."

"Is that necessary?"

He blinked in surprise. "To do otherwise would be to deceive them, don't you think?"

She nodded slowly, seeming to mull over what appeared quite clear to him. "I was thinking that whatever the rector or bishop do to you, you still remain a man of God."

At his raised eyebrows, she continued. "God has called you to preach the gospel. I can't see you doing anything else. If someone tries to tell you you can no longer do that, whom are you to listen to? You have done nothing wrong. Your conscience is clear." She looked down at her plate. "I'm the one who lied. You have not exposed my lie out of a desire to protect me."

How had she guessed? He had tried so hard not to reveal it to anyone.

Her large brown eyes looked into his now. "Why didn't you tell me that was the true reason you were dismissed?"

He swallowed, wanting desperately to be able to reassure her he did not hold her responsible. "There was no point. You were not the only reason. I told you, the bishop had an entire catalog of errors." He gave a bitter laugh. "If anyone was to blame it was my own rector. It was Doyle who supplied the bishop with all the information."

Before she could argue further, he reached over and covered her hand with his. "Whatever the reason for my being defrocked, I have no wish to do anything differently. You were—and *are*—my wife." In spirit and in truth now, he realized. There was no going back. No chivalrous route to restore her to her former life, no matter how much more attractive that life appeared now.

Instead of filling her with happiness, his words seemed to bring more sadness. With dismay he watched tears fill her luminous brown eyes. "I'm sorry, Damien. I'm so terribly sorry for all I've caused you."

"Oh, Lindsay, don't cry. The Lord has a plan for me, you will see."

That seemed to restore her. With a sniff, she straightened. "I regret the circumstances that brought you to this pass, but I believe you should continue to preach…with a clear conscience."

She seemed so sure. "But I have no pulpit any longer."

"You have a ready audience at the workhouse, at the prison, at the orphanage." She looked toward the window and waved her hand. "Indeed, you have an entire city waiting to hear the gospel. Remember those boys in the street."

He could hardly forget them.

"I haven't been able to get them out of my thoughts," she continued. "Each time I think of them, I pray for their souls. When can such souls ever hear the gospel? They will never enter into a church."

The more he listened to her, the more he marveled at the words coming out of her mouth. Was God using this very young woman who had lived a sheltered life to speak to him about his path?

He shook his head. He mustn't allow himself to grasp at straws without truly knowing if they came from God. He noticed her plate. "You've hardly touched your food. Aren't you hungry?"

She seemed surprised at his attention. "I suppose not." She picked up a piece of bread and bit into it.

Her dressing gown was open at the throat, revealing her pale skin. His breath caught, remembering its silken softness. "You've lost weight. You must have a care." He tried to inject a note of cheer into his voice. "I don't want you to weaken on me. If you want to be part of this ministry…" He paused, the words having come out unplanned.

But at the look of anticipation in her eyes, he couldn't dispel the sense that she was truly his companion and partner in ministry…in life.

She leaned toward him. "Oh, I do so want to be part of your work. I already feel part of it."

When he still didn't say anything, she continued, her voice pleading, "May I come with you this Sunday when you preach?"

He leaned back and rubbed his face. "I don't know if I will preach."

She smiled. "You will. You cannot do otherwise."

Long after Lindsay slept, Damien rose from the bed and lit a lamp at the table where they'd eaten supper. He spent that evening reading the word and on his knees in prayer.

Finally, as the first tinges were lighting the sky, he

sat back staring at the Bible open before him. "To the one we are the savor of death unto death; and to the other the savor of life unto life."

God had given him the gift of preaching to take the word of life to a dying world.

"For we are not as many, which corrupt the word of God: but as of sincerity, but as of God, in the sight of God speak we in Christ." He knew in his heart that he hadn't corrupted God's word. His words had been sincere and his message was Christ.

His eye fell to the beginning of the next chapter. "…need we, as some others, epistles of commendation to you…Ye are our epistles written in our hearts, known and read of all men…"

Lindsay's words came back to him. Did he need the bishop's or the rector's commendation? The souls he'd ministered to at the workhouse and orphanage had come to Christ through his preaching. They'd been forgotten by the rector, by the church. Did he have a right to forsake them now?

Dear Lord, You've given me a desire to preach and minister to the least of them in this great city. I've been stripped of my pulpit, my credentials. He fingered the pages of the Bible open before him. What credentials did he need? Those given to him by men, or those given to him by the Lord Himself?

His heart began to beat as the message was birthed in him, a message of hope inspired by his own recent hardships. With steady fingers, he took up pen and paper, words rushing through his mind.

* * *

Lindsay longed to sit down, but there was no seating at the northeast corner of Hyde Park, only dusty earth and grassy lawn on which to stand. The September sun beat down on her face despite her bonnet. She adjusted her posture, kneading her lower back with one hand.

Even though she loved to hear Damien's preaching, this Sunday morning, she felt distinctly off. She didn't know quite what was wrong with her. She was almost positive she was with child. She'd heard from Florence that a woman had a series of minor complaints including the fatigue and general malaise that she'd been feeling for some weeks.

Damien was closing his sermon, and she knew it wouldn't be long before they could leave. Although, from their experience last week, she knew people gathered around him afterward to talk with him for as long as he remained.

She surveyed the crowd in front of her, feeling her heart swell. The number of bystanders had doubled from last week. There must have been at least fifty people. Word of her husband's inspirational, moving sermons was apparently spreading.

Sudden pain surged through her lower abdomen. She grimaced, her pleasure in the crowd forgotten. This couldn't be right. Frantic, she tried to get Damien's attention, but a crowd surrounded him.

"Mrs. Hathaway!"

She turned with an effort and almost sagged with relief at the sight of Mrs. Moore.

"I thought it was you there." The elderly woman approached her with a smile and took her hand, then peered at her. "Why, whatever is the matter, dear? You don't look yourself."

"Pl-please can you get Reverend Hathaway? I'm not feeling well." She gasped at another onslaught of pain.

"Certainly, dear. Steady there. I shall be back in a thrice." She patted her hand and bustled away.

In a moment, Damien was at her side. "What is it? You look pale."

"Please—" She tried to speak through the pain. "Can we go home?"

"Of course."

As he looked about him, Mrs. Moore spoke up. "It's a good thing I brought my carriage. Come, it's right here at the curb. I can convey you both home."

A look of relief washed over his face. "Thank you, Mrs. Moore. You don't know how much I appreciate it."

"Say nothing more. Come along."

Lindsay took one small step. Pain seared her middle so hard that she staggered.

"Lindsay!" Without another word, Damien lifted her in his arms.

A footman held open the carriage door. As Damien began to ascend the steps, Lindsay felt a discharge. "Oh, please, no!" she cried, her hands gripping her abdomen.

"What is it? Tell me!" Damien's voice was frantic as he laid her down on the seat. He bent over her and wiped her brow with his handkerchief. "What is it, love? You are in great pain?"

"Help me!" she gasped between each wave of pain. What was going on in her body? "Something's wrong, Damien." She grasped his hand. "Please don't let anything be wrong!"

Mrs. Moore settled across from her as the coach began to move. "There, there, dear, we'll soon have you home." She turned to Damien. "She's bleeding," Mrs. Moore said quietly. "Is she with child?"

Damien gaped at the older lady, his mind going from incomprehension to shock to horror in those few seconds. Could it be? He looked down at Lindsay, whose head rested in his lap.

Her eyes were closed, her complexion deadly pale as if all the blood were rushing out of her. His glance fell lower and terror filled him at the red staining her light gown. *Dear God, don't take her. Please don't let her die. Please, don't let me lose her.*

Lindsay's hold on him tightened. "Please, Damien, don't let anything happen. Don't let anything be wrong." A fresh onslaught of pain seemed to course through her lower body. "Help me, Lord, please don't take my baby from me!" she cried, her arms holding her abdomen as if to protect it.

Tears pricked his eyes. Dear God, he prayed, a baby! How long had she known? Why hadn't she told him?

But all thoughts were forgotten as she turned pleading eyes to him. "Help me, Damien! Please, help me!"

"Yes, love. Anything, I'll do anything," he murmured, holding her and stroking her hair.

"Good, we are almost there," Mrs. Moore said. "I shall have my coachman summon a midwife. There's a woman our family has used for many years. She is to be trusted."

"We can summon a physician, anything—"

"Don't trouble yourself, Reverend. This woman is more experienced than most physicians. She has rarely lost a child."

By the time the coach stopped, Lindsay's consciousness was ebbing. Damien lifted her down, afraid with each movement she would lose more blood.

"D-Damien?" Lindsay sounded so weak.

"I'm here, love. Hold on."

He climbed up the dark stairs, praying he wouldn't stumble and drop his precious charge.

Finally, he was able to lay her gently on the bed.

Mrs. Moore hovered behind him. "Is there anyone else you'd like to summon—a female relative?"

Damien tried to focus on her words. "Yes, my sister." Florence would know what to do. Lindsay clutched his hand and he didn't dare move from her side.

Mrs. Moore left the room, returning with an oilcloth. "Here, help me lay this beneath her. It will have to do for now."

He helped roll Lindsay to one side as the older lady spread out the cloth. Lindsay doubled over with pain and he nearly cried out as if her agony were his own. What he wouldn't give to be the one to suffer in her place.

"We'd best undress her, remove any stays, and make her as comfortable as we can."

He untied his wife's bonnet and began unbuttoning her pelisse. Mrs. Moore's more competent fingers untied her sash and undid the long row of buttons down the back of her dress. "Do you have a nightgown for her?"

Nodding, he turned to the cupboard. When he came back to the bed, Mrs. Moore had managed to removed Lindsay's dress and was undoing her stays. He swallowed at the sight of so much blood. A baby forming inside his wife, and now taking her life's blood. Why hadn't been he more observant? Wiser? Of course she must be with child! And now she might lose her life because of him.

He handed Mrs. Moore the nightgown. Lindsay's body looked chalky white and his heart clenched in fear. *Dear God, please, please don't take her from me. I'll do anything, pay any price.*

"Damien, I'm scared."

Jolted from his prayer by her whisper, he passed a hand over her sweating brow. "I'm here, love. It's going to be all right."

He helped Mrs. Moore put the nightgown over Lindsay's head and guide her arms through the sleeves. The movement of her body brought a whimper, a sound that tore through Damien.

Mrs. Moore leaned toward her. "There now, dear, lie quietly. The midwife will be here soon." She helped her back down against the pillows.

Damien remained at Lindsay's side, his hand clutching one of hers. He felt lost, as if the earth had shifted beneath his feet and he knew neither what was up nor down, backward or forward. Her hand was ice-cold and he chafed it absently, his eyes horrified at the sight of blood already soaking through the light blanket that covered her.

He almost fell to his knees at the thought that he was losing his young wife, but a gasp of pain from her made him forget all else but her distress. He leaned closer. "It's all right. I'm here. Nothing will hurt you," he crooned to her.

By the time the midwife arrived, he was desperate with worry. "Thank goodness you're here. Can you please help my wife? She has lost so much blood."

With a brief nod to him, she set down her bag and went to the bed, pulling away the blanket. After a cursory examination, she covered Lindsay once again and turned to Damien. "How long was she with child?"

The calmly spoken words were like a hammer blow. There was no other possibility left now. "I don't know. She hadn't said anything to me."

She gave a clipped nod, but before she could say anything more, Lindsay cried out again. "My baby, help the baby!" Her hand pressed his convulsively.

"Mr. Hathaway, I'm afraid you must leave the room."

How could he possibly leave her? "Can't I stay?" he asked the woman.

"It's not seemly, sir, for a man to be in the birthing room." Seeing the determination in his eyes, her voice softened. "It will only distress you to see her like this. Don't worry, we shall take good care of your wife."

The elderly Mrs. Moore came up to him. "There, there, Reverend, trust us to take care of dear Mrs. Hathaway. My coachman has gone to fetch Florence. She can help us."

Florence. "Thank you, that was most thoughtful of you."

She patted his hand. "We'll let you know as soon as it's over."

As soon as it's over. The words, instead of comforting him, sounded ominous. He looked down at Lindsay. She lay unconscious. Fear ate at him.

Mrs. Moore touched his arm. "It's best if she not know what is going on."

"It's the amount of blood she's lost. She'll come 'round again when it's over," the midwife stated calmly.

Reluctantly, Damien let his wife's cold hand go. "I'll be in the next room. Please, call me if there's anything—"

"You may be assured of it, sir."

He nodded and made his way to the door. There he turned and looked at Lindsay, still as if death had already claimed her soul, leaving her body a pale shell.

"Pray for her."

He started at Mrs. Moore's serious tone.

"Yes, of course."

Quietly, he let himself out of the room and went into the small sitting room, which they had only vacated that morning. How long ago that seemed. Lindsay had been happy, preparing breakfast, then tidying everything up afterward while he meditated on his sermon.

Damien alternated between kneeling and pacing in the small room. How could he not have known Lindsay was with child? Why hadn't she told him? Shoving a hand through his hair, he stopped at the window and looked down at the street through the filmy lace curtain. A wagon piled with kegs stopped behind a small flock of sheep. The driver yelled and waved his whip at the youth who was herding the flock.

They were so intent on their tasks with no idea that a few floors above them a young woman's life was draining from her.

No! He wouldn't think that.

He sank down to his knees before the grimy window, bowed his head into his hands and began to pray over again. *Please don't take her from me,* he begged, though he felt no worthiness to be her husband. Even though he knew it was not the way to pray, he began bargaining with God. *I'll do right by her. I'll return her to her father. I'll bring about a reconciliation with him. Only, please, dear Lord, don't take her.* His chest heaved with sobs; he lowered his head to the floor, feeling helpless to save his beloved young wife. *Take the babe if You must, but don't take her from me. Please.*

He didn't know how much time had passed when he was shaken by the shoulder. "Damien, what's happened? Mrs. Moore's coachman told us to come quickly, that the young lady was ill. What has happened to Lindsay?"

Grateful for his sister's presence, Damien rose to his

feet, feeling stiff and numb. He nodded to Jonah who stood behind Florence, looking worried.

"She's in trouble, Flo." His voice broke and he had to struggle a few seconds before he could continue. "She was…with child and she's losing it."

Her gray eyes held understanding and sorrow. "Oh, dear, no! How did it happen?"

Remembering Florence's own condition, which now was becoming visible, he guided her to the sofa. If only he'd known Lindsay was also with child! How much more careful he would have been of her health. He remembered all her work moving, how tired she'd been recently, how pale. The images smote him.

Quietly, he recounted to Florence and Jonah what had happened. Florence kept shaking her head and clucking softly. "Poor child."

"How long have you known, lad?" Jonah spoke for the first time, his keen eyes upon Damien.

Damien felt himself flushing with shame. "I didn't."

Florence gasped. Even Jonah looked amazed.

"She said nothing to me. I was too stupid—" he turned away, once again on the verge of breaking down "—too ignorant to notice. I should have noticed." He clenched his hands.

Jonah pressed his shoulder. "Don't fret yourself. We all know what you've gone through in the last month."

"That's no excuse."

"You're a young man, not expected to know about a woman's things."

"I've been to enough sickbeds to know something of

the way of women," he said grimly. So many poor women he'd assisted in their last minutes of life, dying from childbirth or the fever that afflicted so many afterward, and he'd been callously unaware of his own wife's condition. He shook his head. "I don't understand why she didn't tell me."

"I'm sure she didn't want to worry you, what with losing the curacy," Jonah said.

Damien stared at his brother-in-law, who seemed so much more discerning than he. He nodded slowly. "Undoubtedly that was it."

Florence put her arm around him. "Don't feel so badly. Lindsay is young. Perhaps she didn't realize it fully herself until just recently. Let me go to her."

Florence left, and Damien and Jonah sat silent. A while later, Jonah got up to tend the fire and make tea. They heard very little from the other chamber. Why wasn't Lindsay crying out? Was she already gone?

Damien sat with his head in his hands, hardly able to pray any more except to beg for God's mercy.

Finally, the door to the room opened. The midwife emerged, a bundle of soiled sheets in her arms. Damien went right to her. She did not keep him waiting.

"Your wife is alive."

He sagged with a relief so profound he would have collapsed but for Jonah's strong arm around him.

"She is not wholly out of the woods. The next few days will be critical. She lost quantities of blood." The woman paused, looking at him gently. "She lost the baby."

Damien turned away from her and the others, his

eyes filling with tears. He had asked the Lord to take anything but Lindsay. The sorrow at the child he would never know suddenly overwhelmed him.

The next second, Florence's arms were around him. "I'm sorry, Damien, so terribly sorry." They held each other tightly. He felt an aching hollow inside.

He drew away from his sister and faced the midwife again. "How is my wife?"

"Quite exhausted. She is sleeping quietly now." She gave him a keen look. "Many women who lose a child, especially those who are young, take it hard. You'll have to be patient with her."

"Yes, of course."

After that, Florence took charge, seeing to the dirty linens and setting out a cup of tea for the midwife.

He had no idea when the woman left, and too late, he realized he hadn't even paid her. But Florence told him it had been taken care of. Mrs. Moore pressed his arm at some point and made her farewells, telling him she'd send her coachman around to drop off some food over the next few days and asked him to let her know if he or Lindsay needed anything. Damien had only strength enough left to mumble his thanks.

And finally, he and Florence were alone. After sending Jonah home to look after the farm, she'd insisted on staying overnight to tend Lindsay.

"I don't want you to wear yourself out," he told his sister. "I should have been more careful of Lindsay."

"You don't know that. She is a healthy girl, and a body can do a lot. One never knows why these things happen."

Damien only nodded, too worried about Lindsay's life to think beyond the moment. In the past month, he'd been stripped of everything he held dear. Everything but Lindsay.

He would do all in his power to cherish her and help her recover.

Chapter Eighteen

Lindsay opened her eyes. Daylight assaulted them, forcing her to squint. She lifted a hand to shade her eyes and gasped with pain. Her hand fell back to the bed, too weak to do more.

Someone moved beside her. "You're awake."

She glanced up to see Damien leaning over her. Why was she in bed, and he bending over her?

She remembered.

Reaching up, she sought his hand. His immediately enfolded hers.

"The baby—" she began, her lips already trembling, tears welling up in her eyes.

He bent down and smoothed her forehead with his other hand. "It's all right. Don't try to talk. Preserve your strength."

She tried to sit up but stopped at the pain. "Tell me. Please."

He knelt at the side of the bed, not letting her hand go. "I'm sorry, dearest. The midwife did all she knew."

His face began to swim before her as his words sank in. Her mouth trembled violently. She clutched his hand to her cheek. "Please, tell me my baby is all right!" The words were difficult to speak, her throat parched, but nothing else mattered. *My baby! My baby! Lord, please, no!*

Damien continued murmuring soothing words as she cried, still clutching his hand. When at last she felt spent, he gently wiped her face with a handkerchief. "Let me get you something to drink."

She lay breathless, too weak to speak or cry or even hold Damien's hand any longer. She heard water being poured, but she was too weary to open her eyes.

"Here, drink a little of this." He put his hand beneath her head and eased it up. Obediently, she took a few sips. He wiped her mouth dry and eased her back against the pillows.

She closed her eyes once more, beginning to feel a blessed lethargy invade her. "Tell me what happened."

He drew up a chair and once again took her hand, which rested listlessly in his. She had no strength to do more. "You were in pain and bleeding." He cleared his throat softly. "I didn't realize you were with child. Please forgive me."

For the first time, she noticed the unsteadiness in his voice. She opened her eyes and read the suffering in his. "I'm s-sorry. I was going to tell you," she said, each word coming out with effort. "In the chapel that afternoon. But

that's when you told me you had to resign your curacy."
She sniffled. "I just couldn't…burden you then."

His hand pressed hers softly. "That would have been
no burden."

At his gentle words, she began to cry.

"Oh, Lindsay, I should have realized. I'm a brute, an
ignorant brute. I was so caught up in my problems, I
didn't notice anything different."

She tried to shake her head against the pillow. "It's
not your fault. I'm the one who's to blame…." Once
again she began to cry. She'd staked everything on this
baby. If only she could give Damien a baby, he'd love
her. But she'd lost it. God had judged her.

She'd deceived her father and ruined Damien's good
name, and now she must pay the price.

Too weary to fight the cloud of despair, she closed
her eyes, allowing depression to engulf her.

When she opened her eyes again, the knowledge of
her loss hit her at once. How she wished she could fall
back asleep. But she was fully awake, conscious of everything that had happened. Why hadn't she told
someone sooner? Maybe if she'd had some advice,
she'd have known how to better care for the tiny life
growing within her.

Had she overexerted herself? Had all the lifting and
carrying of their belongings from the parsonage hurt the
baby? Why then was Florence's baby still intact?

Tears filled her eyes again and she curled up on her
side, wanting to hide from everything and everyone.
She didn't want to see Florence with her maternal glow

and increasing waistline, evidence of a life flourishing within her.

But the door clicked open and Florence entered with a large bouquet of autumn flowers in a vase. "Good morning, Lindsay. Jonah picked these for you from the farm. He is anxious about you and hopes you are up to company soon."

Lindsay said nothing but turned her gaze from her sister-in-law. Florence set the vase on a table where Lindsay could see it. Then she went to the drapes and pushed them open. Lindsay couldn't help glancing at her when she turned around and approached the bed. Her stomach was round and visible now, like a soft bulge under her gown. Lindsay looked away.

Florence's hand touched her forehead. "Good, you don't feel feverish. The midwife said we must watch for that in the coming days. Would you like some tea, or a little gruel?"

Lindsay shook her head.

"You must put something in your stomach. You've lost a vast amount of blood and must be feeling very weak."

"Please," she whispered, "I want nothing."

Florence poured a glass of water. "Here, at least have a sip of this before I go."

Lindsay allowed Florence to lift her head as Damien had done and took a sip before shaking her head.

The next time someone came in she was relieved to see it was not Florence but Damien. "Florence says you don't want to eat anything. I've come to beseech you to take a little something."

His look was tender and kind, and it made her want to cry again. She pressed her lips together, determined not to shed any more tears for what was never to be.

"Let me bring you a little broth. Please, Lindsay?"

She didn't have the heart to refuse him, he who'd been so good to her, and to whom she'd brought such misfortune. She merely nodded.

He smiled. "I shall be back immediately."

A few moments later he came in holding a tray, as if it had already been prepared and was waiting outside the door. He set it down at the end of the bed and came to her. "Let me help you." He placed a pillow behind her, then helped her sit up. She winced in pain.

"I'm sorry. I'm probably manhandling you like a clumsy oaf."

"Not at all," she assured him, despite the pain. What did it matter what her body endured now anyway?

He set the tray down on her knees. Then he tied a napkin around her neck and took a chair beside her, lifting a spoon. "Would you like me to help you?"

She nodded, too weary to speak.

He brought a spoonful up to her mouth. The meat broth warmed her. But after three spoonfuls she thought again of her loss. Her throat constricted and she could swallow nothing more. She pushed his hand away weakly.

"Come, love, just a few more. You need to get your strength back."

Her breath stilled at the word on his lips. *Love.* Had he really called her that? She seemed to remember he'd called her that before. Did he truly love her? Tears filled her eyes again. She didn't deserve his love. "What is it, Lindsay? Please don't cry."

She turned her face away. "I'm just tired."

He waited quietly until she was calm again, then urged her. "Come, just a few more spoonfuls."

She allowed him to bring the spoon back up to her mouth. It was easier than trying to argue, and she felt too tired to do anything more. When the soup was finished, Damien patted her mouth and removed the napkin. "Perhaps you'll be up to a cup of tea and some biscuits a little later."

She tried to smile but felt it a poor effort. He removed the tray and helped her lie down again, smoothing the coverlet over her and adjusting her pillow beneath her. "Is there anything more you'd like?"

She shook her head. Why was he being so good to her? She'd done nothing but harm him since the day they'd met—a day Lindsay was now sure he'd rue for the rest of his life.

Several weeks later, Damien saw Florence and Jonah at Newgate when they were there to minister to the inmates.

"I'm sorry I have not had a chance to come in some weeks." He rubbed his face and looked away. "I've been quite busy." That didn't begin to describe his mental and physical exhaustion.

"You look tired. How is your ministry?" Florence asked.

He met her gaze and smiled. "The Lord has given me

more souls than I can possibly minister to." His smile faded. "I rejoice in that, but I fret thinking I cannot possibly reach them all, nor help them with what they need. There is *so* much need." He smiled ruefully. "Well, I don't have to tell you that."

She nodded. "Of course not. Praise the Lord that He multiplied your ministry. I'm sorry I haven't been able to help more."

"You have your own ministries and your work on the farm now. Besides, soon you will have a baby to care for, too." Bittersweet joy filled him at the knowledge of the coming event. His own pain had faded to an ache in the recesses of his mind, but he knew it was not so for Lindsay.

As if reading his mind, Florence asked, "Is Lindsay not able to accompany you at all? It has been enough weeks for a full recovery, has it not?"

"Not quite, but she is coming along fine, according to the midwife's last visit."

"Is Lindsay quite all right?"

"Physically, the midwife said she is well."

"Did she say anything about being able to bear more children?"

He nodded slowly. "She didn't think there should be any problem. Of course, she can't be wholly certain. Only time will tell." He looked down, thinking how far away that possibility seemed. He had not dared touch Lindsay since the tragedy, remaining on the couch he had used during her convalescence. And she had not asked him to rejoin her in their bed.

"How is she otherwise?" Jonah asked.

Damien hesitated, unwilling to say anything negative about his wife.

"Lindsay seemed very quiet the last time I saw her," Florence said.

Damien nodded. "I don't know what to do. She gets up and dresses herself and prepares breakfast. She never complains, but she shows no interest in anything around her."

"Perhaps if you involved her once more in your work."

He gave a short laugh, raking a hand through his hair. "I've tried. She thanks me politely and invents some excuse for why she can't go out with me. I didn't press her at first. I wanted to make sure she was feeling recovered, but the midwife assured me there is no reason she cannot go out. In fact she recommended something to keep her busy."

He sighed. "It's as if something died inside her along with the baby, and I can't bring it to life again."

"Oh, Damien." Florence shook her head sadly. "It just takes time. You must be patient." Her own hand rested atop her growing belly. "I don't come as often as I'd like. I feel it pains her to see my condition."

He nodded, unable to deny the fact. "I appreciate that. Though I miss seeing you both every day the way we used to."

Jonah clapped him on the shoulder. "There now, lad, don't trouble yourself about us. Lindsay's grief will pass and we'll get together again as before. Someday you two will have another babe and she'll forget all about this time of sorrow."

He nodded, not wanting to express his deeper

concern that the rift between Lindsay and himself was greater than he feared. Did she blame him for the loss, he asked himself when he lay awake at night on the narrow sofa in the sitting room? He certainly blamed himself for not having been more discerning of her condition. What kind of pastor was he when he couldn't even see the condition of his own wife?

After parting from Florence and Jonah, Damien returned home. Lindsay was in the kitchen washing some dishes. He took up a tea cloth and began to dry the cups and saucers.

"I can do that," she said at once.

"It's all right. I like helping you."

She said nothing more.

"Are you tired?"

She shook her head.

"Would you like to lie down?"

"I'm fine."

As soon as she was finished, she returned to their sitting room and sat down with a basket of mending.

"It's a pleasant day outside, not too cold. Would you like to go for a walk before it gets too dark? The fresh air would do you good."

"No, thank you. I think I'll just stay in."

He sighed and fell silent, wishing he knew what to do. "There was a good crowd on Sunday."

"That's nice."

"I've been thinking of starting a Bible study here one evening a week."

She stopped her work and looked at him.

"Would you mind that very much?"

After a few seconds, she replied, "Of course not." But there was no enthusiasm in her voice the way there would have been in the past.

"You wouldn't have to do anything. I can take care of serving tea." He coughed. "But I'd like it if you were here with me."

"I'm sure they wouldn't care about me." Her head was bent over her work again, the lamplight golden on her hair.

He was going to argue but thought better of it. Perhaps she'd relent when the time came.

His new ministry was beginning to bear fruit. Every time he was tempted to ask Lindsay for help, when he saw her sad countenance, the words died on his lips. Sometimes he wondered if the loss of her child had made her realize her mistake in marrying him. Perhaps she'd fixed all her hopes on her child, and the loss only reflected another failure. After all, their material loss was due to his failing. What kind of husband and provider was he?

Perhaps at last she was ready to return to her father. The only irony was that now it was too late to annul their marriage. It had been well and truly consummated, child and all.

Damien sighed. Annulment or not, he would have to find some way to get Lindsay back to her father. It was the only way to salvage an otherwise dreadful situation.

Lindsay opened the door of her lodgings and tensed.

Florence stood in the corridor, a hesitant look on her face. "Hello, Lindsay, may I come in?"

Lindsay's glance fell downward. Pain lodged about her heart at the sight of her sister-in-law's growing belly. She quickly looked back up. Florence's face radiated well-being, her normally pale cheeks full and rosy.

"Yes, of course. How are you, Florence?" She opened the door wider and allowed her sister-in-law access.

Florence smiled. "I was on my way to the orphanage and thought I'd stop by to see how you were. I brought some fresh eggs from the farm." She held out a wire basket lined with a cloth inside.

Lindsay took it from her and stood awkwardly. She couldn't even remember the last time she'd seen Florence. "Thank you." She motioned to a chair. "Please, have a seat. Did Jonah not come with you?"

"No, he's at the farm. He sends you his best regards and hopes to accompany me the next time."

Lindsay offered her sister-in-law tea, but she declined. When they were both seated, an uneasy silence fell. Lindsay smoothed down her skirt, not knowing how to proceed. Her skills at making polite conversation seemed to have left her. Before she had a chance to hunt around for a topic—or to brace herself to ask Florence how her confinement was proceeding—Florence herself cleared her throat. "Damien tells me you haven't been out."

Lindsay made a vague motion with her hand. "The weather…"

Her sister-in-law sat regarding her until Lindsay felt uncomfortable. Finally, she said, "Is it wise to spend so much time sitting alone?"

Lindsay looked down at her hands. "I have nowhere I wish to go."

"I'm sorry, my dear. I know it must be difficult."

Lindsay's eye's flashed. "You know?" She gazed pointedly at her middle. "You know what it's like to lose the infant you had pinned all your hope upon? To lose the greatest gift you will ever give to your husband?" She stood, unable to bear it anymore. "To know you will never be able to hold that infant in your arms and suckle it?" Her voice broke, and she turned away angrily, a fist to her mouth.

Florence was immediately at her side, but Lindsay turned her back on her.

"I'm sorry, Lindsay. I know I'm the last person you want to see right now. I never thought I would be blessed with a child. Who was I, an ugly old maid? But the Lord had mercy on me, the way He did on Hannah in the Bible and so many other barren women." She touched Lindsay on the arm and Lindsay could no longer suppress a sob. "The Lord will bless you, too, Lindsay. He will, my dear, I *know* it."

Lindsay bit down hard, willing herself not to give in to tears. But her shoulders began to shake. Florence put an arm around her and led her to the settee. "There, let it out. It's good to cry." A smile tinged her sister-in-law's next words. "Jonah taught me that. I, too, tried for too many years to hold everything in." Her hand rubbed Lindsay's back and shoulders. "Have a good cry. Grieve for your wee babe."

When Lindsay felt spent, Florence gave her a handkerchief and gently pushed her curls off her forehead. "You know, Damien is very concerned about you."

"I have caused him nothing but grief," she said in a hollow tone.

"Nonsense." Lindsay almost smiled at the sound of Florence's more customary brisk tone. "There are plenty of ways you can begin to help him if you choose."

Lindsay looked up at her, hope beginning to awaken in her breast.

"You could begin by helping Damien in his labors. Don't you see how his ministry is growing? He needs help. He was thrown out of his pulpit and the Lord has blessed him with a ministry without walls. There are souls out there, needy souls who have nothing and nowhere to go, and he is pouring himself out for them. He is visiting the needy and the orphans as our Lord commands us. And then he comes home to what? To witness your tragic countenance. He will drop of sheer exhaustion if he receives no aid."

"But he has always kept me from helping him." She smiled sadly. "I know it was to protect me, but I wanted to be included."

Florence squeezed her shoulder. "Well, now is your opportunity, I would say. Prove to him you are made of sterner stuff than he has given you credit for. Be his right hand."

Lindsay's heart began to beat in anticipation. "I'm afraid I've caused him nothing but trouble—"

"Get that nonsense out of your head! He needs you. But he will never force you to do anything. He feels badly enough over your loss." Her voice softened. "It's his loss, too."

Lindsay covered her mouth. How selfish she had been, not considering Damien's grief.

"Now, now, it's time to gird yourself up. Wash your face and I'll fix you a cup of tea. You'll want to look your best when Damien comes home."

The next morning as Damien sat by the window at his morning devotions, he heard a knock on the door. Lindsay was still in the bedroom, so he rose and went to answer.

A girl of about thirteen or fourteen stood in the doorway, a boy behind her, craning his head around. They both looked ill kempt and dirty, and were breathing heavily as if they'd run up the stairs. The boy was staring at his peg leg. Before Damien could greet them, the girl said, "Please, can you come quick? There's a woman needs you. She's dying."

"Of course. Where have you come from?"

She named the street, a poor neighborhood Damien had been ministering to often of late. "I'll come immediately." As he turned to get his coat, he asked, "Does she need anything?"

The girl shook her head. "She's too far gone for anything this side o' heaven."

Just as Damien was on the point of leaving, Lindsay emerged from the other room. "I thought I heard someone—" She broke off at the sight of the children. She looked at Damien in his coat, a question in her eyes.

"I must go out a moment. A sick woman—"

Before he could finish, she went to him. "Would you like me to come with you?"

He heard the hesitancy in her voice and realized how much the words had cost her. His arms ached to hold her. He wished he could erase all her hurt. "Yes, I should like that very much," he said softly.

"All right."

A feeling of relief flooded him, making him realize only then how much he'd been wishing for this moment. He touched her arm. "That's my girl. Let me get your cloak. It's chilly outside."

On their way down the stairs, Lindsay asked the girl about the sick woman.

"It's a woman what lives in the room next to ours. Mum has done what she could, little eno'. The woman's always ailin'. There's a babe, too."

At the word *babe,* Damien turned quickly to Lindsay. She looked pale but that was her normal color nowadays. "Is the infant sick, as well?" she asked.

They reached the street and followed hurriedly after the children. "Dunno," the girl panted. Every time the boy turned around to see if they were still following, Damien noticed the boy's sharp eyes kept going to his leg. He looked faintly familiar, probably from his many visits to the neighborhood.

They walked several blocks past the Middlesex Hospital after which the streets became narrower, the smells more disagreeable. Damien held Lindsay close to him, the memory of the attack still vivid. His glance darted about the crooked alleys, not liking the look of the many loitering individuals.

Thankfully, it was fully light and many people and vehicles were upon the road. The children stopped at a narrow brick building sandwiched between two others. Several windows were boarded up, the stoop broken down.

The girl turned to them, hesitation on her face, as if afraid they would leave before reaching their destination. "It's up two flights."

"Lead the way." Damien helped Lindsay over the holes in the wooden steps. They paused a moment in the dark and smelly passage.

"Ain't you coming?" the boy's voice floated down to them from halfway up the stairs.

"Yes, I'm just getting my bearings." With a silent prayer, Damien followed the sound of their footsteps, hoping they'd make it up the stairs without twisting an ankle or worse.

They heard the sound of a child crying before they reached the door. The girl and boy had already entered, leaving the door ajar. A few other, younger children lingered in the hallway. One of them, a slovenly girl, her fingers in her mouth, stared at Lindsay as they passed.

Filth was everywhere—unwashed clothes in heaps, refuse piled in corners. Lindsay gasped at the stench of rotting food and human waste. Damien held her arm, guiding her past the women lounged about the room. One old crone looked at Damien. "You the parson? Hope you're not too late," she cackled, showing a mouth devoid of most teeth except two sticking out at opposite ends of her gums.

"Where is she?" he asked in a low tone.

She waved him toward a dark corner of the room, where a group of women crowded. The sound of crying had stopped and when they reached the corner, they saw a child sitting at the foot of the narrow cot where the dying woman lay. The child looked around two years old. She sucked placidly on her thumb, her other hand clutching a dirty-looking rag.

Damien glanced at the other end of the bed. A woman—a pale, emaciated shadow of a woman—lay against dirty sheets, her lank blond hair spread across the pillow. Damien went to her, the other women making way silently for him.

The woman's lips were chapped. "Is there any water you can give her?" he asked the nearest person, a thin, middle-aged woman.

"She don't want nothing no more. Too far gone."

At the low sound of their voices, the woman's eyes fluttered open. They looked sunken in her wan face. Damien took the limp hand lying against the blanket.

"You..." she rasped.

"Yes, I'm here." He turned to the women, his eyes seeking Lindsay. She stood beside him. Reassured that she was all right, he addressed one of the women. "Please, get me some water." He fumbled for his own handkerchief, the only clean thing in the room, and handed it to her. "Soak this and bring it to me, please."

Eyeing it speculatively, the woman took it. He turned

his attention back to the woman on the bed. She had closed her eyes, but at the press of his hand, she opened them again and struggled to say something. Damien leaned closer to her.

"I need…"

Someone nudged him from behind. He turned and saw with relief the other woman had returned with his handkerchief. "Bless you." He took the wet cloth and pressed it gently against the woman's lips. She sucked weakly for a few seconds, then lay back exhausted.

She opened her eyes again. "Please…"

"Yes, what would you like me to do?"

"Pray…for me."

He squeezed her hand. "Certainly." Immediately, he closed his eyes and began to pray.

When he said "Amen," she opened her eyes again. "Thank you, dear sir." She took a few labored breaths then attempted to speak again. "My…baby…"

He looked at the child who still sat quietly. One of the women standing by the bed nodded. "That's 'ers. Don't know what'll become of 'er."

"Take care of my baby," she gasped, her eyes beseeching him.

He eyed the women forming a circle around the bed, but each one averted her eyes. Finally, the one who'd handed him his handkerchief shrugged. "No one can take 'er. We've enough children of our own we can barely feed."

Damien looked at the child again. Her trusting blue eyes met his. Despite her tangled hair and dirty face, she was lovely. He turned to Lindsay. She was staring at the child.

The room was silent for a moment, and then one of the women jerked her head at Lindsay.

"What about you, miss? Can't you take 'er?"

Damien's heart froze in his chest.

Chapter Nineteen

Lindsay started as if she'd been shouted at. Her eyes turned to Damien, and he read stark, raw fear in their brown depths. He took hold of her hand and squeezed.

"She's a sweet little thing," another woman added. "Never gave her mum no trouble. Look at 'er, sittin' so quiet like. Nuff to break your 'eart."

"Don't you want 'er?" the girl who had come to fetch them asked shyly. She stood at the foot of the bed with the boy, probably her brother, still beside her.

In an effort to protect Lindsay, Damien spoke. "The orphanage—" He stopped at the look of indignation on the faces around him. He understood perfectly. It was the last place he'd want to send a child, especially a two-year-old.

"As good as killin' 'er if you send 'er there!" an older woman spit.

Lindsay pushed her way toward the child, almost as if she were propelled. The women made way for her. When she reached the girl, she hesitated. At that moment, the child looked at her and held out her dirty little rag. "Da—"

Lindsay reached out her hand and touched it. "That's very pretty, my dear."

A woman beside her said, "'Er name's Abigail."

"That was my mother's name," Damien said quietly.

Lindsay's eyes met his.

"You'll take care of 'er, won't…you?" the dying woman whispered in a halting voice.

Lindsay reached the woman's side and clasped her hand. It felt dry but tightened on hers with surprising strength. Tears welled up in Lindsay's eyes. "Please—" The woman's blue eyes implored her.

How could she accept this child? The pain of her own loss was too recent. *Lord, don't ask me to lay my heart open to this poor babe. I can't.* Even as she said the words silently, she found herself nodding her head. The woman immediately released the pressure on her hand and smiled wanly.

Damien leaned over the woman and said, "You'll get well again and take care of her yourself."

A look of fear displaced her smile. "I shan't. She'll be all alone."

Lindsay squeezed her hand. "No, she won't. She won't be alone, I promise you. I'll take care of her myself."

Immediately, the woman lay quiet again. What had she done? Lindsay looked back at the child, who was now looking at her mother. She'd given her word to take Abigail's mother's place. Her lip trembled at the enormity of her promise.

Only vaguely did she hear Damien recite the Twenty-third Psalm and then the Lord's Prayer. The woman's lips followed his silently in the last one. Lindsay closed her eyes, allowing the words to minister to her, as well.

Afterward, the woman's agitation grew again. "I done so many bad things…"

"God forgives you. You have a savior in His son, Jesus," Damien said, smoothing the hair from her forehead. "You needn't fear. Trust in Jesus who has paid the price for your sin. He will receive you."

The hour grew late. Lindsay had no idea what time it was or how much time had passed. The girl began to cry again. Prying her hand carefully from the dying woman's, Lindsay reached for the child. As she brought her up in her arms, the small body cuddled against hers, warming her in the chilly room.

Lindsay stroked her soft hair, feeling the tangles. Finally, the child fell asleep, her thumb in her mouth, her rag pressed to her chin.

It was dark outside when the woman passed away. Damien bowed his head and said a final prayer, thanking the Father for having received her. Finally, he covered the woman's face with the sheet.

"I'll make arrangements with the undertaker for her burial," he told one of the women. "Is there anyone who should be notified?"

Several of the women shook their heads. "She'd no one."

Damien approached Lindsay. "Let me carry the child. You must be tired."

Lindsay felt strangely unwilling to relinquish Abigail. But her arms ached with holding her, and finally she allowed Damien to take her.

"Are you all right?" he asked.

She nodded. "Just a little stiff." Her eyes didn't leave the child. "Will she be warm enough?" Giving him no chance to answer, Lindsay turned to the women and asked for a blanket. Someone found a filthy one. It would have to do for now. Abby stirred against Damien and he glanced down, a look of tenderness in his eyes.

One had died and one had lived. Why had her unborn baby had to die? Her heart ached with the question. The tears began to fill her eyes until Abby's face blurred. She didn't want to be drawn to this child who was another's. But then she remembered the child's helplessness. Abby was all alone in the world.

No. She had Lindsay and Damien.

The cold, hard knot inside her began to give way. The questions she'd not dared ask herself all these weeks as she'd buried her feelings came tumbling out even as the tears spilled over her lids and fell down her cheeks. *Why couldn't I have my own baby to love? The fruit of Damien's and my love?*

"Lindsay?" Damien's voice was filled with concern. "Perhaps I can find someone from St. George's who will be able to take her."

"No!" She swallowed, surprised at the vehemence in her tone. "I mean, we—I can take care of her."

His eyes searched hers. "Are you sure?" he asked softly.

"I know nothing of toddlers, but…" Her voice trailed off.

"I know little, either. Perhaps together we can offer her a home."

Lindsay looked at him, at the hope in his eyes, and she remembered Florence's words. Perhaps, he, too, needed this child to love.

The little girl sighed in her sleep. The tiny sound drew Lindsay's attention. Each time she looked at Abigail, she felt her own loss afresh. Yet other emotions filled her. She'd promised a dying woman to care for her babe.

A sense of awe overcame her. Perhaps by fulfilling this promise, the awful void she'd lived with since the loss of her baby would begin to fill. She glanced at Damien again. Perhaps they could begin to be a family after all, just in a different manner from the one she'd seen in her dreams.

Lindsay patted Abby's hair dry before the fire. She'd just given the girl her bath and prepared her for bed. A few weeks had gone by since the evening they'd brought the orphan home and since then, she'd blossomed.

"Mama." The girl twisted around and held the comb up. "Comb."

Lindsay breathed in the sweet clean smell of her. "That's right, dear. Mama's going to comb your hair." She adjusted Abby on her lap and set down the towel. "Mama's going to make your hair very pretty. She'll put a bright bow in your hair once she has combed it."

Abby sat happily on Lindsay's lap in a pretty little

nightgown Florence had given her. Lindsay slid the comb through the child's damp golden locks. *Dear God, I thank You for bringing Abigail into my life.* She now understood the meaning of bittersweet. The pain of her own loss was still with her, but she could never regret the joy the new child gave her each day.

As she gently worked the comb through a tangle, she heard a knock on the door. Who could it be? Damien was the only person she expected and he wouldn't knock. "Just a moment," she called out.

Setting Abby on a rug well away from the hearth, she smoothed her skirts and made her way to the door.

Her landlady stood there with her usual sour expression. Not bothering with a greeting, she jerked her head toward the stairs. "There's a gent's carriage below and a footman asking for you."

Lindsay's eyes widened.

"He seemed in a hurry."

Lindsay glanced at Abby. "Could you watch the child a moment?"

The woman took a step back. "I'm a busy woman."

"Very well. Can you send him up here?"

Wordlessly, the woman turned away.

Lindsay frowned. No one of her former life had visited her since she'd married Damien, and she could think of no one else who drove a fancy carriage. Perhaps a former parishioner of Damien's.

A few minutes later, another sharp rap sounded on the door.

"Tom!" She recognized one of the grooms from her

father's house. "What are you doing here? How did you know where to find me?"

The man bowed politely. "Your father's secretary sent me to fetch you."

Her pulse quickened. "Me?" Had her father finally had a change of heart?

"Mr. Phillips is ill."

She clutched the door frame. "Ill?"

"Yes, miss—madam."

Fear filled her. "How serious is it?"

"Quite grave, madam. You'd best come. He's calling for you."

What was she to do? She glanced from Abby to the groom. She couldn't just leave. But her father needed her.

For the first months of her marriage she'd dreamed of a visit from her father. But to be summoned to his bedside to find him gravely ill—she'd never wanted their reunion to be like that.

"Mama." She turned quickly to see Abigail coming toward her. Lindsay scooped her up in her arms and brought her back to the doorway. The groom's eyes widened. "Your—?" His face reddened.

"She's an orphan who recently lost her mother. We're bringing her up," she said with a smile.

"Yes, madam."

He waited and she realized her dilemma. "I can't leave her. I must wait for my husband to return."

The footman pursed his lips and shook his head. "I don't know if you should wait. Your father is very sick."

Her breath caught. She must go to him.

"I shall have to take the child with me," she said finally. "Perhaps one of the servants can look after her while I see Father."

He nodded, looking relieved.

"But I must take some things for her."

"I can wait for you."

"All right. Come in and have a seat."

It only took her a few minutes to gather a few things for Abigail. She glanced at her own dresses hanging on their hooks, wondering if she would have to stay, or if she should just go to her father's first and return here if she needed anything. But then she remembered her full cupboards in her old room. If her father had not rid himself of everything of hers when he'd disowned her, she would have more than enough there. In the time she'd lived with Damien, she'd learned to live with so much less and be much happier.

She wished she could see him before she left. Instead, she had to be satisfied with penning him a hurried note.

With a longing look around the shabby room she'd shared with Damien for the past few months, she closed the door behind her and followed Tom down the stairs, Abby in her arms.

Damien climbed wearily up the narrow stairs to his rooms. The day had been arduously long, between ministering to the inmates at Newgate and visiting some of the poorer quarters by the hospital.

"Your wife's gone," the harsh voice of his landlady

called up the stairwell. He turned in the dark passage and looked down where she stood with her neck craned up to him.

"I beg your pardon?"

"You 'eard me. Up an' left. Took the babe with 'er."

Her meaning was beginning to penetrate. "Mrs. Hathaway went out?"

"That's right. Up and left with a fancy man in livery. Left in a toff's carriage, the likes o' which we 'aven't seen in this neighborhood in my lifetime." Without another word, she entered her own rooms and slammed the door.

Damien stood immobile, the echo of her closing door ringing in the passageway. Without giving himself a chance to puzzle things out, he turned and hurried upstairs, although he was unable to stop from thinking of the time Lindsay had run away. He shook his head to dispel the thought.

When he opened the door and felt the chilly room, his glance went immediately to the empty grate. His heart began to thud at the unnatural stillness.

He set down the satchel and walking stick he carried and slowly entered the room. Pushing aside the wave of apprehension, he called out in a normal tone, "Lindsay?"

Silence answered him. He looked in the bedroom. No one. Not even Abby's things disturbed the neat arrangement of the bed. He frowned. Despite Lindsay's efforts, having a baby in their cramped midst always meant a certain amount of disorder.

Slowly he backed out of the room. He searched the

parlor for any sign of what had happened. Almost immediately he saw a paper on their small dining table. He picked up the folded sheet with "Damien" written on it in Lindsay's handwriting. Foreboding chilled his soul like ice. With shaking fingers, he opened it.

Dearest Damien,

I write this in haste. Father is gravely ill and a carriage has been sent to fetch me. I was hoping to see you but couldn't wait. Don't worry about Abigail. She is with me. She will be well cared for if I have to remain for any length of time. I will try to return as soon as possible.

Do not be concerned about me. I trust Father has kept my things in my old room if I should need a change of clothes.

God bless you, and please pray for Papa.

Yours,

Lindsay

Damien reread the message. Her father was "gravely ill." Damien felt a start of concern for the man he'd met but once. Of course Lindsay had to go to her father. Perhaps now she would be at last reconciled with him.

This is what Damien had hoped for, had prayed for. He should go to her.

Feeling a sudden urgency, he picked up his hat and stick again and hurried back out.

The ride from his neighborhood to Grosvenor Square

was like traveling from darkness to light. Dingy, boarded-up buildings and narrow, muddy streets gave way to light-colored limestone facades and neatly paved streets.

He paid the driver and walked up the steps to the massive front door. It was only the second time he'd faced the house Lindsay had grown up in.

He lifted the knocker and let it drop.

A few moments later, when he'd given up hope that anyone would answer the door, it opened to reveal a tall butler with an impassive face. His glance fell to Damien's wooden leg.

Damien resisted the urge to step back. "I'm here to see—" he hesitated at the word in face of the man's braided uniform and forbidding stare "—my wife. Mrs. Lindsay Hathaway."

Without a word, the man stepped aside. After waiting a second, Damien stepped across the threshold into the shadowy interior.

The door closed with a soft bang and the butler left him.

As he stood there, he looked around the entryway. He'd rarely been in the finer homes of Mayfair. This one was grander than most he'd seen. Marble statues sat on pedestals. A majestic staircase curved toward him at the rear, darkness visible through a window at the landing. A crystal chandelier hung suspended from the high ceiling.

He stepped toward a tall case clock set along one wall, examining the timepiece with the eye of a professional. It was a fine piece of workmanship.

Before he could study it further, he heard rapid footsteps on the staircase. He turned to see Lindsay hurrying toward him. His heartbeat picked up at the sight of his wife, and he realized then how worried he'd been that he wouldn't see her.

"Damien!" she said, reaching him and holding out her hands. "You came. You saw my note."

He nodded, clutching her hands in his, wanting to enfold her in his arms. But the imposing entryway, the oil paintings, the statues surrounding them stopped him.

Reluctantly, he let her hands go. "How is your father?"

Her pretty eyes clouded and he read real worry in them. "He's quite feverish. Please pray for him."

"Of course I will. Was he glad to see you?"

She nodded. "Yes, it was as if I'd never left him." She smiled, letting out a long breath of relief. "He has forgiven me for leaving him. I know it shouldn't matter, but I'm glad."

"Certainly it matters." He tried to smile and be glad for her, even though he felt the tentacles of her old life reaching out to pull her away from him. "How long will you be here?"

"I don't know. He lapses in and out of consciousness." She bit her lip and her eyes filled with tears. "I'm so afraid he might not wake up." She searched his face, as if for reassurance. "What if he departs without acknowledging you as my husband?"

"He hasn't done so?" The news shouldn't have surprised him, yet it fell like a blow.

"He behaves as if I haven't married. I can't contradict him in his present condition."

"Of course you can't. How is Abigail?" he asked, anxious about the little girl and eager to get off the topic of her father.

Lindsay smiled. "She's wonderful. The staff have taken to her as if she were their little pet. We are looking for a full-time nurse for her, in order to give me more time to be at Father's bedside."

"Yes, I see." A full-time nurse. It made Lindsay's stay at her father's sound more permanent.

"But come," Lindsay said, taking his hand in hers and pulling him toward the stairs. "Let us go into the parlor. I shall ring for tea...."

By the time he left the Phillips mansion, Damien was full of gloom. It was the first time he'd seen Lindsay as mistress of the type of home she should have been presiding over.

He walked all the way back to the farthest edge of Marylebone. His gloom deepened as the neighborhoods changed back from well lit and spacious to dark and narrow.

By the time he returned to his cold flat, he knew his prayers had finally been answered. Lindsay had been returned to her rightful world.

No matter the reason she'd been called away or the fact that she promised to return quickly. Deep down, he knew she would never return. Her father would never let her go again.

Damien had always known this day would come. He'd planned to bring it about himself, in fact. Annulment, hadn't that been his original intent? And now that it was here, completely unprovoked by him, he found his world shifted beneath his feet.

The reality of a life without Lindsay hit him so hard he doubled over. How could he survive? He stared at the fireless grate, seeing in its blackened interior the desolation of his life.

He bowed his head, his fingers digging into his skull, trying to stem the tide of hopelessness threatening to drown him.

Damien awoke early according to his habit. The rooms seemed deathly silent. Since Lindsay's miscarriage, he had been sleeping in the sitting room on the couch. Last night he had slept in their bed, needing to be near her somehow. He'd buried his face in her pillow, breathing in the scent of her.

And he'd been dreaming of her. He lay perfectly still, trying to recapture the dream. He'd been holding her, and she'd been smiling at him. Remembering her departure brought despair so heavy he couldn't face the day before him.

If only he could slip back into sleep. His limbs felt like lead. He couldn't even utter his usual prayers.

Dear God, why did You bring her into my life? Why let me grow accustomed to her presence when it was not to be?

His fist ground into the pillow in frustration. How he wanted to go to her! Maybe she needed him. No! She had everything she needed there. He must give her up.

Yet the thought of not seeing her that day—or in the

coming days—took away an interest in anything or anyone else. He knew he had things he must do, people he'd promised to see, but he couldn't think of any of them. He just didn't care.

A harsh laugh erupted from his lips. He'd thought he could give Lindsay up on his own. He'd planned to restore her to her father someday? What kind of fool's paradise had he been living in? Each day he'd dug himself deeper, binding himself more securely to her. Seeing her smiling face, listening to her soft voice, watching her keep the account books or make a simple breakfast in their fireplacc... She'd proved herself a willing and indispensable helpmate in both a comfortable parsonage as well as the most dismal London slum. His head sank back onto the pillow. How was he going to make it without her? And why would he want to?

A week later, Lindsay descended the last step of the wide staircase and willed a different answer to her question than the one she'd received each day during her stay. "Any post for me?" she asked her father's footman.

"No, madam. There was nothing."

"Very well. Thank you." Lindsay's tone revealed nothing of the worry and urgency growing in her. She'd not been able to step outside the house while Papa's life had been in danger. But two nights before, the fever had finally broken. She felt a gratitude beyond measure for God's grace.

But why had she heard nothing from Damien since

his visit? She could understand if he had been too busy to stop in, although that also hurt. But to not write? What could be wrong? She must overcome her pride and write to Florence. The thought brought a sense of shame. What would his sister think to know her brother had not communicated with his wife? She must be aware of it. Was she relieved Damien was now well and truly rid of his unsuitable wife? The proof of it was she had heard nothing from Florence, either.

Lindsay turned and headed back up the stairs. Even though she'd received nothing from her husband, she had sent him daily missives during the days of vigil over her father, keeping him posted of her father's condition and Abby's new words and skills.

Before reentering her father's bedroom, Lindsay paused and took out the only letter she'd had from Damien, the day after he'd visited her. She unfolded the creased sheet of paper. She could recite it by heart now, but it helped to see his writing and hold the paper he had held in his hands.

Dearest Lindsay,
Thank you for communicating your whereabouts to me. You can be sure that I shall pray for your father, and for your well-being, of course. Please do not overtire yourself or concern yourself about me. The Lord shall sustain me. Give Abigail a hug and kiss from me.
    You have all my well wishes,
    Yours,
    Damien

With a sigh she refolded the letter and held it against her breast a moment before putting it away in her pocket. She pushed open the door and put a cheerful expression on her face. Indeed, she was grateful with all her heart that the Lord had spared her father's life. And as soon as she could, maybe even today, she'd order the carriage and go to Damien.

"Is that you, Lindsay?" Her father's voice was still weak but he was alert.

"Yes, I am here, Papa." She approached the heavily draped bed.

"Where were you?" he asked, his hand fumbling on the counterpane.

She took it in hers.

"Just peeking into the nursery to see Abigail and checking on the post."

He ignored her mention of mail and said instead, "It's been a long time since that room was used."

She smiled as she took her seat. "Yes. It's nice to see her enjoying all the things I loved as a child."

He coughed and she poured him some water. "Perhaps I shall soon be well enough to climb the stairs," he managed.

"Don't hurry it. You have been gravely sick. You must regain your strength."

He nodded and shifted his head against his pillow. "No news?"

She blinked at the question. "News?"

He made a motion with his hand against the counterpane. "Yes, from where you were living."

She looked down at the bedcover with a small shake of her head.

"I've summoned my solicitor."

Her eyes lifted, startled. "Your solicitor?"

He looked at her steadily. "Yes. When you broke your betrothal, I was quite angry with you, as you well know."

"Papa, that is in the past now."

"I changed my will, as I said I would."

"Yes, Papa, I know," she answered quietly.

"I wasn't going to have some…some fortune hunting, depraved cleric—" His voice rasped, and his face turned a mottled red.

"Papa, please, calm yourself. There was never any danger of Damien taking what was yours. He was not— nor is—interested in what is yours."

Her father's hands knotted in the bedclothes. "Despicable, cowardly, immoral—" Another coughing spasm hit him.

"Papa! You mustn't speak so." She tried to lift his head to ease his coughing.

When he had calmed, she said quietly, "Damien is my husband."

He glared at her. "He is not your husband. We shall have that taken care of as soon as permissible."

She stared in dismay at the venom in his tone. "What are you saying, Papa?"

"Before I fell ill, I had everything researched by our solicitor." His breath came in short gasps. "Granted it won't be easy, but there are ways to terminate your *marriage.*" He shuddered at the word as if he could hardly bear to have it on his tongue.

"Papa, we mustn't talk of this now." She tried to smooth his coverlet.

He brushed aside her hands. "You cannot…stay married to a man who has disgraced you." He shook his head and gulped in some air. "And now lost his living as a curate. The man is a discredit to his profession."

"Papa! He lost the curacy because of me—because he stood by me and refused to expose my lie!"

"If he lost his living it was from his scandalous conduct."

"No, Papa. Damien would never do anything like that. The fact is he never stole my virtue."

Her father finally seemed to hear what she was saying. "What are you talking about? I heard you with my own ears."

She looked down a moment, hating to relive that night of her shameful conduct. "I lied to you." She raised her eyes, pleading with him to understand. "I know it was despicable of me, but I was so desperate not to marry Mr. Stokes."

Her father stared at her, his hands falling limp on the coverlet. "You lied to me? Why, Lindsay, why?"

She cringed at the look of disbelief in his eyes. "I'm sorry, Papa. I was so scared to tell you how much I disliked your friend. I didn't plan to lie to you. I ran away that night, only knowing I couldn't marry Mr. Stokes." She reached out a hand to her father. "I did not mean to disgrace you. Please believe that. Damien did nothing wrong. He merely stood by me when I came to him. He did not expose my lie, even though it meant disgrace to him. He has lost everything because of me. No one could have behaved more honorably than he."

"He would have saved us all a lot of trouble if he had spoken up that night." As the notion grew, her father's ire returned. "I'm sure he saw an opportunity for himself and seized on it. He is a blackguard and a scoundrel! No, I will not permit you to remain married to him. We will find grounds for an annulment. Fraud. Breach of contract. He is not the man he made you believe he was, nor has he lived up to the man you believed you married."

"Papa, please don't say such things. You'll harm yourself." Lindsay gently pushed him back against his pillows, alarmed by his heightened color and shaking hands. He was so angry, Lindsay wasn't even sure he could hear her any longer.

"Lindsay," her father said in a quiet rage, "you will kill me if you stay married to him!"

Chapter Twenty

The week passed with excruciating slowness for Damien. Each day he fought against his desire to go see Lindsay. Finally, he could stand it no more. He returned to Mayfair.

The same butler opened the door, but before Damien could say anything, he spoke. "I have been given orders not to admit you."

Damien stared at him in disbelief, hardly comprehending the words. "Orders by whom?"

The man looked down his nose at him. "Orders from the master himself."

"Please send a message to my wife to tell her I am here."

"She is with her father and not to be interrupted."

Without a word, Damien turned away from him and descended the steps, not knowing which way to turn or what to do. If he wrote to her, would she get his message? Why hadn't he written before?

Did she think he'd abandoned her?

In the days following, Damien went through the motions of preaching and ministering, keeping himself under rigid control, not allowing himself to think beyond the present moment. Any breach in the dam would let loose a torrent he knew he wouldn't be able to shore up. Thankfully, he didn't see Florence or Jonah for some days as Florence was in the final months of her confinement and keeping close to home.

When he next saw Jonah at Newgate, he told his brother-in-law before he had a chance to ask about Lindsay, "Her father was deathly ill. She had to return home to nurse him." He hurried on before his voice betrayed him. "He had no one else."

Jonah's eyes scrutinized him. "You've been by yourself since when?"

"Over a week now."

"Why didn't you tell us? You could have come to stay at the farm."

He shook his head. "I'm closer to my ministry here in town."

Jonah put a hand on his arm. "Anything you need, you know you've only to ask."

He nodded, turning away. Thankfully, Jonah assumed it was a temporary absence.

"How is her father? What have you heard?"

"He is recovering slowly now."

He felt Jonah had more questions, but was grateful when he didn't voice them.

Later, he trudged wearily back to his rooms. He stopped short at the sight of the boy who'd come with the older girl that day to summon him to Abigail's mother's bedside. Memory of that day awakened painful memories.

The boy met his gaze. Something about him bothered Damien, but he couldn't pinpoint what. He stopped in front of him when the boy continued looking at him. "Does someone need me?"

The boy looked down at his feet and kicked at the dirt, shaking his head. Damien noticed his cracked shoes. When he said nothing, Damien asked gently, "Is there something I can do for you?"

"I...uh..." He rubbed his nose and shuffled his feet more.

"What is it, son?"

At the word *son,* the boy gave a startled glance upward. Before Damien had a chance to decipher it, words tumbled from the boy. "I'm sorry for what we did to you that day. We shouldn't've acted that way. It was mean and cruel taking your leg from you and leavin' you like that."

Comprehension dawned on him. "You were part of the gang who attacked my wife and me?"

The boy sniffed, refusing to look up, and nodded. "I'm sorry. Felt bad about it ever since, but I was afraid to speak out. Afraid the others would laugh at me and worse."

Damien nodded in understanding. "Yes, I'm sure you would have had to pay a stiff price for disobedience." After a moment, he said, "Are you still part of that band?"

He shook his head. "I run away every time I see 'em, but I'm afraid they might catch me."

Damien reached out a hand and pressed his shoulder. "I understand. You know there's one who can protect you and defend you."

The boy stared at him. "You came to help that woman the other day. You didn't care how poor she was. I never see no parson come into our neighborhood. You treated her like she was someone."

"She was someone. A child of God."

"Can…you pray for me? I don't want them to catch me."

"Sure, son. Why don't you come upstairs with me? Maybe I can find you a bite to eat."

About an hour later the boy left. Damien gave thanks to God for that soul and prayed for the wisdom to continue helping the boy, Peter. He sighed, feeling too tired to do anything more than sit in front of the fire.

He didn't realize he'd dozed off until a sharp knock jolted him awake. "Just a moment," he called out, confused for a moment, wondering if Peter had returned. Rising too quickly, he almost lost his balance.

He rubbed his hands over his face, trying to awaken fully. When he opened the door, he stared at the stranger before him. A middle-aged man, a gentleman, dressed in sober dark garments, removed his tall beaver hat. "Reverend Hathaway?"

"*Mr.* Hathaway."

The man handed him a calling card. "Mr. Goldsmith of Goldsmith, Quimby and Dean."

Damien frowned. "Yes? What can I do for you?"

"May I come in?"

"Yes, of course. Forgive me." His wits were still fuzzy from sleep.

When the door had shut behind the gentleman, Damien indicated a chair by the fire. "Please have a seat."

"Thank you. Mr. Phillips is my client. He sent me to see you."

Lindsay's father. What could it mean? He could only picture the man lying ill although Lindsay's last letter had indicated he had pulled through the crisis. But what would he be doing dealing with his solicitor so soon after his illness?

When the two were seated, Damien asked, "How is Mr. Phillips?"

"Much better. Steadily on the mend. He has a strong constitution." The man coughed discreetly. "The presence of his daughter, of course, aids him in his convalescence."

"Yes, of course," Damien said.

"Mr. Phillips had his daughter's...er...precipitous and somewhat unorthodox marriage much on his mind—" he cleared his throat "—even before his illness."

Damien said nothing. There was no response to such a statement.

"Indeed," the solicitor went on when Damien didn't speak, "for months he has been in consultation with me about the possibilities of an annulment."

Annulment. The word reverberated in the room. "How—" Damien cleared the hoarseness from his throat. "How is that possible?"

The man crossed his legs. "It is not an easy procedure by any means, but not as impossible as it might seem. Given the most recent information Mr. Phillips has received, we now believe the way has been made clear for said procedure."

Damien shook his head to clear it. "Recent information?"

"Yes, from Miss Phill—that is, Mrs. Hathaway herself."

Lindsay had given him some information about their marriage? He could only stare at the man, more and more puzzled.

"Pertaining to the fraudulent claims made by Miss Phillips concerning your…er…conduct prior to the matrimony."

Damien straightened, his mind beginning to focus on the man's meaning. "You mean the fact that Mrs. Hathaway claimed to lose her virtue?"

"Precisely." The man's eyes took on a sharpness. "*Claimed* being the word in question here. For the fact, Reverend Hathaway, is that Miss Phillips had *not* lost her virtue, is that not so?"

Damien felt as if he'd been put on the witness stand. Why should this man treat him so, when he had no reason to hide the fact from him? "That is correct. Miss Phillips was chaste when she came to me, and remained so while under my protection."

The lawyer leaned forward, beginning to show some animation as if they were now coming to the heart of the matter. "Mr. Phillips will be happy to know you are prepared to acknowledge this fact."

"Why should I not?"

"Because it is key to an annulment."

A chunk of ash fell onto the grate in the silence. "How does this affect our present marriage?" Did Lindsay's father know his daughter was no longer untouched? That she'd even carried Damien's child?

"I do not know if you are aware of the contingencies for an annulment, but among them is fraud."

Fraud? The word sent a rush of foreboding through him.

"Mrs. Hathaway was underage when she made the fraudulent claim respecting her loss of virtue. Therefore, her father consented to a marriage between the two of you. I believe it can be effectively argued that fraud was involved to obtain her father's consent. If we can prove this, it should pave the way for an annulment between Miss Phillips and yourself."

Damien listened with growing disbelief at the conversation. Hardly able to formulate the words, he managed to ask, "Is this what Miss—Mrs. Hathaway has requested?"

The lawyer fiddled with his watch chain, not meeting Damien's gaze. "This is how I have been instructed to proceed by my client Mr. Phillips. It is my understanding that Miss Phillips is not opposing her father's wishes."

Damien's shoulders slumped. He had not heard from Lindsay in a couple of days. Had she finally realized she belonged with her father?

He should be glad. She would be free.

"Reverend Hathaway, are you all right?"

He forced himself to sit up and face the lawyer. "Yes, quite." He struggled to order his thoughts. "If you have the legal grounds to proceed with the annulment, why come to see me?"

"I came here to inform you of the circumstances as they stand now and to ascertain whether you will cooperate with our motion to annul this marriage, or whether you will be opposed."

He could still oppose the move?

For a moment, time stood still for him. When he'd married Lindsay, he'd planned on returning her to her father. Now, he had a chance to keep her bound to him. But he'd never wanted that for her.

The secret hopes he'd nourished that Lindsay would return to him rose up to mock him. Hadn't he listened to the lawyer? She'd realized that an annulment was for the best. Instead of feeling relief, he felt only a hollow ache that all hope was gone.

"I have been instructed to offer you full reinstatement to the church, full restitution of your name—" the man coughed once again "—and a sizeable sum of money as indemnification for all you have suffered since that unfortunate day."

"Unfortunate for whom?" The words were said so quietly he didn't think the solicitor would catch them.

"Why, for you." He looked around the squalid surroundings. "You have suffered much since the day of your matrimony. Miss Phillips and her father wish nothing more than to see you fully reinstated to your former position."

Damien stood and turned away from the man, unable to endure listening to him anymore.

The man rose behind him. "If you wish more time to consider this proposition, you may have a few more days. But let me warn you, the longer you delay, the more detrimental to Miss Phillips's name."

Damien swung around to face him. "You may tell your client that I need no more time. He may proceed with the annulment. I shall not oppose it." He held up his hand. "But I want to make it clear I will accept no payment from Mr. Phillips, nor anything else from him."

The man's eyes rounded. "But, sir, your name, your reputation—"

Damien made his way to the door and held it open. "None of that is his concern. Now, good day to you, Mr.—er—"

"Goldsmith."

"Mr. Goldsmith."

The man bowed and stepped over the threshold, turning back to Damien. "I have taken the liberty to leave my card on the table if you should wish to contact me. Otherwise—"

Damien heard no more. The click of the door latch ushered in silence once more.

Lindsay had told her father of her false claim. Why would she tell him that unless she was seeking a way out of her marriage?

She would at last have her freedom. An annulment was not as terrible as a divorce. An annulment meant she had a chance to rebuild her life, perhaps to remarry some day.

Slowly, he turned back to the room. He would do as Lindsay and her father wished. It was what he had wanted all along. The Lord had answered his prayer. Lindsay would have her freedom, her former life restored to her.

Why then did he feel so dead inside?

Abigail reached out her pudgy hand for the floppy rag doll Mr. Phillips held up. "Say 'dolly.'"

"Do-lly."

"That's right, dolly."

Lindsay hugged the girl about her waist as they sat on her father's bed, glad to see him better today. She'd been so afraid of his state a few days before that she had not dared bring up the subject of her marriage again. Instead she'd written to Damien, telling him that her father was on the mend. "That's a good girl. That's your new dolly Grandfather has given you."

Mr. Phillips handed her the doll.

"Dolly," the girl repeated, gazing at the new toy in her hands.

"She's a beautiful child," Lindsay's father said as he lay back on his pillows.

Lindsay rested her chin against the child's silky hair and looked across at her father. "She is, isn't she?"

"She can stay with you as long as you like."

She blinked at her father. "Of course."

"Do you want to make her your ward officially?"

She pursed her lips. "I hadn't thought that far ahead, but, yes, I do," she said, nodding her head more emphatically as the idea grew.

"Otherwise some member of her family—or someone who claims to be—might show up someday and try to take her away from you."

She squeezed the child closer to herself. "Oh, no!"

"People will do anything if they smell money."

She laughed, relieved. "In that case, I have no worries, since I've no money of my own."

Her father smiled indulgently. "All I have will be yours one day."

"You disinherited me, or don't you remember?"

He waved a pale hand. "That is over. I've already instructed Mr. Goldsmith to change my will back."

She was touched. "You didn't have to do that, Father."

He frowned, uncomprehending. "But you're back. Of course I had to."

She cleared her throat softly. "Does that mean you forgive me?"

"You acted foolishly and hastily. You have compromised your own future, but I believe there is still a remedy."

Lindsay stiffened. "Papa, I told you, no annulment is possible."

"On the contrary, my dear. After some consultations with Mr. Goldsmith, we may have a solution."

She strove for a calm tone, unwilling to alarm Abby. "What are you saying?"

"You gave us the key we needed," her father continued. "Fraud. You lied to me about your supposed loss of virtue to that cleric. My consent was based on false information. Mr. Goldsmith says we have a very good case for an annulment. Hathaway will not oppose the move to annul and will cooperate."

Lindsay stood, careful not to jar Abby, and stared at her father. "What are you talking about, Papa? I am married to Damien, whether you like it or not. No annulment is possible."

"An annulment is not only possible, but it is the only solution as I see it to reinstating you to your rightful position here at home."

Lindsay set Abby down on the bed where the child continued to play with her new doll. "Papa, I have no intention of remaining here. As soon as you are well enough I am returning to Damien. That is my rightful place. I've made no secret of that."

He made a face of disgust. "That won't be possible in any case. The curate has given his full consent."

She stared. Damien consented to an annulment? Her greatest fear had come to pass. "How do you know this?"

"Mr. Goldsmith went to see him yesterday."

She should have gone to Damien herself! Why had she let her father's weak condition prevent her? "What did Damien say?"

"Why, what I supposed he would when offered a sizeable amount of money and restitution to the church."

Lindsay felt so faint she was forced to retake her seat. Her father had offered Damien money? A bribe? How despicable!

Her father smiled thinly. "So, you see, that cleric is not the saint you make him out to be. He is as weak as most men."

"You're lying. Damien would never accept money from you." But Damien had not replied to her letters.

"Wouldn't he? Not even to help the poor rabble he preaches to?"

Her conviction weakened. No, it couldn't be true.

"Lindsay, I know it is difficult to accept, but think, my dear, how much better an annulment will be. You have suffered nothing but hardship saddled to that curate. You will be reinstated to your former position in society if you remain here, and your daughter will have every advantage."

Lindsay forced her breath to calm, knowing she was fighting for her marriage, for her very survival. "Forgive me, Papa. I do not mean to upset you, but your talk of annulment has shaken me."

"Then let us speak of it no more. Mr. Goldsmith will take care of everything. He can also arrange Abigail's future while he is about it. Let your mind be easy."

Despite her father's delicate condition, she had to put a stop to this line of thinking. Once again, her father was making decisions for her as if he owned her, body and soul. He had put her off once, but she would not allow him to control her any further. She would not consent to losing Damien without a fight. For the first time in her life, she had something worth fighting for.

"Papa, I must make one thing clear. Mr. Goldsmith will arrange nothing for me. If you must disinherit me, so be it, but I intend to return to Damien. He needs me. I need him. My life is with him now."

Her father heaved a sigh. "You were never head-strong before you met that cursed clergyman. He has taught you nothing but rebellion and defiance. He's dragged you into poverty and degradation."

"Damien has taught me none of those things! He has taught me to be a true follower of Jesus. I'm the one who brought him to the poverty he now suffers." Her throat suddenly closed up, thinking of Damien alone and deprived as he must be now. "I must go to him." She suddenly felt a sense of urgency. She had to see him and get to the truth!

A sense of panic filling her, she bent down and grabbed up Abby from the bed. "Come, darling, we must go visit your Papa."

"Lindsay, I forbid you to go to that man!"

Balancing Abby on her hip, she looked at her father. Her heart quailed at the sight of him still looking so frail. The two stared at each other. "I love him, Papa, and he needs me."

Finally, he broke the connection and shook his head. "What happened to the daughter who looked up to her father and respected his wisdom?"

"I grew up, Papa. Don't forget, you taught me to think and analyze. Damien has taught me—" she swallowed, her gaze going to Abby "—how to love."

"And if he doesn't want you?"

She remembered her father's words and fear filled her. "You said he agreed to an annulment?"

"Oh, yes. At least he understands, as I, that it is best for you."

Did Damien truly want to be free of her? *It is best for you.* Her father's words echoed in her mind.

Clarity abruptly pierced her. Damien was trying to give her back her old life. Dear, foolish, noble man! Why hadn't she understood that? All those months living with him, seeing his sadness over believing he had taken something away from her. He'd never understood that he'd given her so much more than she'd ever had. He had been a true example of Christ-like love to her. Strength clothed in humility.

She moved toward the door. "Papa, I must go. I'm sorry."

"No!"

"Papa, don't be upset. I love him and he needs me."

Without waiting to hear more protests, she exited her father's bedroom, deaf to his protests. "We're going for a short ride, my dear," she murmured against Abby's ear.

With fingers that shook, she prepared Abby for the chilly December day. She threw a few things into a satchel, intending to stay at her home, with Damien, if she could help it. *Dear God, show Damien that we belong together as a family.*

When Lindsay arrived at the run-down lodging house, never had a home looked better. The landlady was exiting as Lindsay entered the building.

"Back, are ye?"

"Of course I am. This is my home." With a flourish of her cloak, Lindsay sailed past her and on up the stairs.

Her confidence shriveled to nothing by the time she arrived at their door. It was deathly silent up here. Would Damien be home? Uttering a prayer, she took hold of the knob and turned. She sagged in relief to find it unbolted.

The first thing she experienced was the cold in the room. No cheerful fire burned in the grate. The sight that greeted her wrung her heart. Damien sat hunched over the small table, a lone candle lighting the gloom of the early evening, his attention fixed on a dismantled clock.

Before she could take a step, Abby made a noise.

Damien immediately looked up and froze.

"I'm back," she said softly.

He rose so quickly, his chair toppled backward. After he'd righted it, he advanced, shoving unruly locks from his forehead with his hand. "Lindsay—! Wh-what are you doing here? I thought—" he stopped and she detected the flush on his cheeks.

She took a step into the room and shut the door quietly behind her. "You thought what?" She stared at him, trembling inside lest he reject her.

He swallowed, his eyes never leaving her face. "Your father…he-how does he fare?" he stuttered.

"He is on the mend. Quite out of the woods. I told him it was time for me to come *home*." She stressed the word deliberately, watching his reaction.

"He didn't—uh—speak to you?"

"About what?" She would not make it easy for him to disavow their wedding vows.

At that moment, Abby squirmed to get down. She stared up at Damien and suddenly smiled, holding out her rag doll. "Dolly?"

His glance fell to her and he crouched down. "Hello, there, poppet, what do have there?"

His smile wrung her heart and Lindsay yearned to

throw herself on him. She held back and watched the interplay between him and Abby.

"Dolly."

"Yes, I see you have a doll. How pretty she is. What is her name?"

She looked at him puzzled. "Dolly."

"Yes, of course. Dolly." When the child took a step toward him, he put a hand on her hair and caressed it. "It's nice to see you again. I've missed you."

"Is it nice to see me, too?" Lindsay asked him, the words unplanned.

His eyes met hers immediately and he swallowed. Suddenly, he stood. "You're trembling." He looked around the room, as if noticing the temperature. "I'm sorry, I don't have a fire made up. Come, sit down, and I'll get it going and get you something hot to drink." Before she could say anything, he took her to the settee, then knelt down and began arranging the kindling.

By then Abby was tired, so Lindsay busied herself spreading a blanket on the couch. The child lay with the doll held close. "Why don't you have a fire?"

He paused a second in his work. "I find it best to only light one a day, to save fuel."

Her heart broke for his deprivations. All the time she was at her father's, living in the lap of luxury...

When the kindling began crackling in the grate, he brushed off his hands and checked the water in the kettle.

Lindsay glanced at Abigail, and seeing she was asleep, stood and approached the hearth.

Damien took a step back.

"The cup of tea will be ready in a moment."

"I don't care about the tea."

"Yes, well…then please, Lindsay, have a seat." He pulled out one of the chairs at their small, round dining table though he remained standing. How many meals hadn't she prepared and shared with him here? Before she'd get teary-eyed she took the seat offered.

She clasped her hands on the tabletop in front of her. "I missed you, Damien. Did you miss me at all? Why didn't you answer any of my letters?"

He stopped in his act of spooning out the tea leaves. Slowly, his gaze connected with hers. "I wanted you to have your freedom."

"I am married to you."

"Didn't your father—" He cleared his throat. "Didn't your father tell you about the possibility of an annulment?"

She could read the struggle in his eyes.

"I missed you, too." The words came out a hoarse whisper as he stood looking down at her, the tea forgotten.

"Then why didn't you write to me?"

"I want you to have your freedom," he repeated.

"I belong here, to you."

He rubbed a hand over his jaw. "I—your father, I mean, his solicitor made it sound that you agreed to an annulment."

She stood, unable to bear any more. "What nonsense. I told my father no annulment was possible. I am married to you for better or worse."

"You were forced into it."

"Because I wanted to be. I have loved you from the first day I met you."

"Oh, Lindsay—"

At the emotion in his tone, she needed no more encouragement. She took a step toward him and suddenly, she was in his arms, pressed so tightly she could hardly breathe. It was as much as she could have wished. She wanted to laugh and cry at once. "Why didn't you answer my letters? Not even a word—"

She was cut off by his lips against hers. Nothing else mattered at that moment but his kiss, his mouth seeking hers hungrily.

"God forgive me," he finally managed when they broke apart. "I tried so hard to give you up. I don't know if I can again."

She laughed, her arms tightening about his neck. "You don't have to. I'm here to stay."

He tried to release her, but she clung to him. "You can't stay here." He raked a hand through his hair, emitting a frustrated laugh. "Look at this place. I don't even have enough coal to burn."

"I brought twenty pounds with me," she said, her eyes twinkling. "We can live on that for now."

His blue eyes looked tenderly into hers. "I am not the right husband for you."

She stared back at him steadily. "You are if you love me."

The atmosphere grew very still. "It is because I care for you with all my heart and soul that I want something better for you than I can give you."

"If you love me, you'll have the courage to tell me, the way your actions have shown me ever since I've known you."

He looked down, avoiding her eyes. The seconds ticked by. Finally, he sighed, his chest pressing against hers in a shuddering intake of air. "I cannot lie to you, dearest Lindsay," he finished in a whisper, his eyes once more looking into hers. "When I spoke those wedding vows, I spoke only truth."

"Then nothing can separate us," she said, bringing her face up to his again.

His kiss was slow and gentle this time, as if the two of them were sealing a pact. There was no turning back, no matter what the future held.

When they sat across from each other at the table again, he said quietly, "I will do all I can to provide for us, but I warn you, it's not an easy life. It's not what your father wishes for you, nor I."

She smiled indulgently. "Perhaps we can move in with Florence and Jonah for the time being. Or maybe with Elizabeth and Jacob?"

"I'm sure either would take us in, but it's not the answer. I must find a more lucrative way to make a living."

She reached out and covered his hand with hers. "You will not leave the ministry. God will provide. You shall see."

He nodded, clearly wanting to debate the issue further. But she pressed his hand. "Trust in the Lord you showed to me, and you will see what great things He has in store for us."

His eyes looked into hers. "He brought you into my life, and for that alone, I will be forever thankful." His glance fell on Abby, who had murmured in her sleep. "And now he has given us a family. I trust in His provision."

Lindsay smiled, satisfied. God would take care of their future. She knew that now, without a doubt. After all, He had given her Damien. That was all the proof she needed.

Epilogue

One year later

Lindsay patted Alistair Jonah Hathaway on the back after his feeding. He was a good baby, and she was thankful for the plentiful supply of milk she had for him. Already he had gained a few pounds since his birth a fortnight ago and was looking rosy and cuddly.

"There," she murmured, hearing him burp against the towel draped over her shoulder. "Now, sleep well and let Mama listen to Papa preach. That's a good boy."

She settled her son into the wicker cradle at her feet and turned to face the church from where she sat in the chancel.

The sanctuary was filled to capacity. Little wonder, since it was the inauguration of the new building. The congregation held several members of the ton, including the Bishop of London, but the vast majority were laborers, shop owners, servant girls and even some less savory individuals.

Young Peter gave a small wave from where he sat in a pew. His sister jabbed him in the ribs.

"A good crowd today, isn't it?"

Lindsay turned to Florence at her side and nodded with a smile. Beside her sat Jonah with their baby daughter, several months older than Alistair, asleep on his shoulder.

On Lindsay's other side sat her father with Abigail on his lap. After Lindsay had returned to Damien, she had continued visiting her father daily. At first, he'd refused to see her until she agreed to an annulment, but when she remained firm, he finally relented.

"I always thought you were your mother's girl," he'd told her one day during his convalescence. "Sweet tempered and soft." He smiled at her for the first time since she had defied him. "You have proved to be not so easily malleable. I am happy to see you have something of me in you."

She returned his smile uncertainly, unsure where he was headed. "What do you mean?"

"You are stronger than I ever gave you credit for. Not afraid to stand up for your convictions."

She stooped to help Abby right a pile of blocks she had toppled. "I stand up for those I love."

He nodded, then paused as if the next words cost him

some difficulty. "I hope there is room for your father in that love."

"Oh, Papa." She dropped the wooden block and reached out her hand to him. "I've always loved you and always shall." She lowered her voice. "If you'll give yourself the chance to know Damien, you will see what a fine man he is. A man to be proud of as your son-in-law."

He said nothing, just pursed his lips and nodded.

She was, therefore, stunned when a few days after her visit to him, his solicitor had called on them and told them her father owned a building in their neighborhood which he wanted them to occupy. If they agreed to renovate it and use it for the ministry, he would furnish all the costs. Shortly thereafter, Damien received an official summons from the Bishop of London.

"It seems the charges against you concerning immoral conduct were unfounded," the bishop had said, much to Damien's surprise.

Damien was reinstated into the church. When told of a new living, he had not accepted immediately. Instead, he had consulted with Lindsay, and after much prayer, he had told the bishop he would accept a curacy only if he could begin a new church in their neighborhood. To their surprise the bishop had agreed.

Her father had made a sizeable donation to begin the building of the church right next to their home.

Today was the first Sunday service in the new church. "Let us give thanks to the Lord." Damien stood in the new pulpit and lifted his voice. It carried the length of the sanctuary, strong and sure. Lindsay rose along with the rest of the congregation as the choir began a hymn of praise.

Her husband's eyes met hers from the pulpit and she smiled. Yes, they had much to give thanks for.

* * * * *

QUESTIONS FOR DISCUSSION

1. Damien is the last man a person would qualify as vain. He has accustomed himself to his disability, so he hardly ever thinks of it anymore. Why does meeting Lindsay for the first time throw him off balance?

2. Lindsay is a young lady of the fashionable world. What draws Lindsay to Damien when she first meets him? How is he different from her father?

3. Damien Hathaway and Lindsay's father are opposites in both their personalities and outlooks. How do Damien's humility and unassuming way begin to undermine her father's more autocratic, know-it-all manner toward his daughter?

4. Damien has grown into a man who is concerned about the least in God's kingdom. How does this sensitivity attune him more than most to Lindsay's situation regarding her father's choice of a husband for her?

5. Damien was used to having his older sister defend him when he was younger. Why does his brother-in-law, Jonah Quinn, think it is good for Damien to have a woman who needs looking after?

6. Lindsay reveals very little of her fears and aversion to her fiancé until the very night her betrothal is to

be announced. Sometimes when we are afraid of someone or something, we hide our true feelings until a dam bursts inside, and the resulting outburst is more harmful than if we had expressed our misgivings early on. What might have been the result if Lindsay had spoken to her father sooner?

7. The night Lindsay comes to Damien and declares he will marry her, he immediately backs up all her claims. Why is Damien so quick to accept and even welcome something that will ultimately ruin him?

8. When Lindsay first meets Damien, she gives him the impression of someone very young and naive. But when adversity strikes, she shows him she is made of sterner stuff. How does this draw them closer together and prove to Damien that she is the wife for him?

9. Why is Damien so determined to maintain his marriage to Lindsay as one in name only?

10. Is it a reasonable assumption on Damien's part that Lindsay will want to return to her own world someday, and that her father will seek a reconciliation?

11. What are some of the problems Lindsay runs into trying to be Damien's wife? Why doesn't she confide in Damien?

12. Lindsay wants desperately to be part of Damien's street ministry, but Damien is reluctant to expose her to the dangers. When they are mugged and his fears prove true, he undergoes a humiliating defeat at the hands of the gang. How does Lindsay view her husband through this ordeal?

13. Damien is forced to resign his curacy because of the scandal surrounding his marriage. How does Lindsay prove to be his greatest ally and motivator during this time of trial?

14. When Lindsay finds out the real reason Damien has been dismissed, she feels guilt that she has brought ruin on him. When she suffers a miscarriage, she feels she is being punished. How is this kind of guilt destructive and unwarranted?

15. In the midst of Lindsay's guilt over bringing Damien to this state, he finally begins to accept their marriage and view their rented rooms as home. It is Lindsay who convinces him he is still a preacher even if he has been defrocked by his congregation. Why is it important that he come to this place of viewing himself as a man of God, and not of a denomination?

HEARTWARMING INSPIRATIONAL ROMANCE

Experience stories
centered on love and faith
with a variety of romances
just for you,
with 10 books every month!

Love Inspired®:
Enjoy four contemporary,
heartwarming romances every month.

Love Inspired® Historical:
Travel to a different time with two powerful
and engaging stories of romance, adventure
and faith every month.

Love Inspired® Suspense:
Enjoy four contemporary tales of intrigue
and romance every month.